Echoes of the Dead

Anthology

The Indie Author's Advocate Collection

Echoes of the Dead

The Indie Author's
Advocate Collection

Contents

Boy on the Bike
Travis VanHoose

Dead and Dating
Anya Bayne

Spectral Hunger
Aja Lace

A Ghost from the Past
Pepper Anne

Living My Best Afterlife
Janet Lee Smith

Whispers on the Wind
Daphne Moore

THE WINCHESTER HOUSE
MAYA BLACK

Boy on the Bike

Travis VanHoose

Boy
on the
Bike

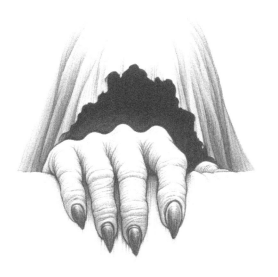

Travis VanHoose

Boy on the Bike

Now that Emmett Perry was a father, he was delighted with the neighborhood he elected to call home. He had purchased his first house six years ago, and in the first year, he hadn't had a child to call his own. That all changed after a one-night stand resulted in the creation of his perfect son, Nathan. Though Emmett and the child's mother were unable to establish a healthy romantic relationship, they had a fantastic friendship and excelled at co-parenting, so much so that most of Emmett's drinking buddies were both impressed and openly jealous.

"I don't get it, man; you don't even pay fucking child support, and you still get to see your kid." Bobby Franks was *two-shades to the wind*, downing his fifth Jack and Coke of the night. He was one of Emmett's most jealous friends. He had four children with four different women and jumped at every opportunity to complain about how much he paid in child support.

"When you don't treat every woman you date like shit, there are all types of benefits," Emmett shot back at his friend.

It was true Emmett didn't pay child support. When he and his son's mother, Renea, decided to give co-parenting a shot, they had agreed to split all expenses surrounding Nathan. Renea was a strong-willed and independent woman. She had another eight-year-old child when she got pregnant with Emmett's son. She refused to go after the child's father for child support. She believed that too many women took advantage of the system and knew that claiming assistance would result in having to interact with her other child's father, whom she despised.

From the moment Nathan was born, the child was showered with love from his parents, and he was all the better for it. Nathan was such a loving and caring child. When around either of his parents, the look in his eyes showed you exactly how happy he was.

Emmett got an excellent deal when he purchased his house in Enigma Springs, Ohio. He had been living in a crummy apartment, which was all he could afford working as a bartender. But a hundred-thousand dollar inheritance allowed him to acquire a house and to start working on his drinking problem, which he knew was getting the best of him.

Randomly driving around the general area he hoped to find a house in, he saw a little old man hammering a homemade FOR SALE BY OWNER sign into the lawn of a decent-looking brick home. The man had to have been in his seventies. He wore a button-up, long-sleeved shirt covered in old jeans and overalls.

Country to the core, Emmett thought to himself as he pulled up before the house and started a conversation with the man.

Emmett learned that the house at 217 Cauley Place had been empty for over a year. The old man's daughter, who owned the house, had unexpectedly passed away from a rare blood disease. She had died sitting in her favorite chair in the living room with a fresh glass of sun tea still in her hand when she was found.

After his daughter's death, a lengthy legal process began to claim the deed to the home. During that time, the old man, who introduced himself as Jerry, had spent nearly every waking day working on remodeling the house. He and his wife planned to sell their home and their daughter's and move to Florida. They were longing for a quiet life after retirement.

"Too many strange things happen in this damn town," Jerry

whispered to Emmett. "It's time for us to part ways and seek out greener pastures."

Emmett laughed, but he knew the man's words to be true. Enigma Springs was unlike other towns. It was a special place with a dark history riddled with bloodshed and horrifying legends. Still, he called it home.

Jerry gave Emmett a tour of the house, and he was immediately impressed with all the hard work the old man had done on the interior. All the wood floors had been refurbished, the walls were freshly painted, and the kitchen cabinets had recently been replaced. New tiling and appliances had also been added to the kitchen.

There were three small bedrooms on the first floor, a bathroom, and a living room that opened into the kitchen with the small makings of a dining room. The basement was unfinished but clean, and Emmett saw no sign of water damage or mold.

Jerry was asking ninety-eight thousand for the house, but Emmett could tell the old man would most likely come down on the price if he pushed hard enough. Jerry told him they had just sold their own house and had to be out in a month, so Emmett knew he had some *wiggle room*. He also had an offer in mind he didn't think the old man would refuse.

"Think we can come down on the price if I hand you a cashier's check in the morning?" Emmett watched Jerry's eyes light up.

In the end, Emmett offered Jerry eighty-eight thousand in cash. They could bypass legal fees with lawyers and realtors, execute a Quick Deed, and call it a day. There would be no closing costs, and both men would walk away all the better for it.

Jerry said he'd have to talk to his wife about it, but Emmett knew the answer would be *yes*.

He had been right, as Jerry had phoned him a little over an hour later to say he'd accept the offer.

A week later, Emmett moved into the house along with one of his drinking buddies, Gareth Longe. Gareth worked as a bouncer at Bert's Brewery, the same bar Emmett bartended at. Like Emmett, he was just shy of forty. But their looks couldn't have been any different.

Gareth was six inches taller than Emmett and had broad shoulders with muscular arms covered in tattoos. His legs were huge, and he had the beginnings of a beer gut, even though he worked out six days a week. He was a fighter at heart, which served him well as a bouncer.

Even when a fight wasn't brewing, he'd *stir one up* so he could lay hands on someone. It annoyed Emmett to no end, but he had a soft spot for the guy who had lost both his parents and his fiancé within a week of one another. All three had been in separate car accidents when they met their end.

Another thing Emmett liked about Gareth is that he wasn't needy. Even though they lived under the same roof, they didn't spend much time together. They had lives outside the house and were content to chill in their rooms and didn't need to speak daily. They were both loners, so the living situation was perfect. They were great friends but didn't constantly need to remind one another of that fact.

A month after moving into 217 Cauley Place, the distance between the two men grew, though neither acknowledged it. Emmett had decided to quit the bar business. He needed to get away from the *bar scene*. He knew it would be a struggle, but he was committed to it for the sake of his son.

Drinking and blow were the two main things Emmett and Gareth had in common, and now that Emmett had removed himself from the central place they partied, they didn't see one another that much.

Emmett's idea was to quit hard liquor cold turkey and avoid all drugs apart from a bit of marijuana here and there. Hard liquor and cocaine were his central vices, and he knew if he didn't cut them out immediately, he'd end up being a sad *barfly* for the rest of his life. He also knew he could save a shit ton of money by drinking a few beers at home as opposed to at the bar, where they were double-priced and required a tip. He had a slight gambling addiction and would play pull-tabs or make bets in pool or darts, which he rarely won.

Once he quit his job, he and Gareth didn't see much of one another except for passing in the house or the rare occasion Gareth decided to spend a night at home rather than chasing tail at the bar.

The first Friday Emmett was alone in the house was his most challenging. He craved social interaction and had to fight every impulse he had to start his transformation the following day instead of right then. By six in the evening, he was squirming on the couch, unable to focus on the TV show he was watching. He needed to get up and move around. He decided to walk to a gas station down the street to grab a case of beer. He chose not to drive, thinking that the walk would help rid himself of some of his nervous energy.

I'm going stir-crazy, and it's only been one fucking night. Emmett shook his head in disgust. He couldn't believe he had allowed his addiction and lifestyle to get him to this point. He repeatedly reminded himself that he was doing it for little Nathan. He wanted to be a good father that his son would be proud of.

Walking through the neighborhood, Emmett smiled ear to ear. Many of his neighbors sat on their porches, having drinks or spending time with one another. They each raised a hand and waved as Emmett passed by. Others played with their kids on their lawns, trying to wear them out before bedtime.

A group of teenage boys rode their skateboards up and down a concrete slope at the end of the street. They cussed up a storm and tried to act older than they were.

God, I feel old. Emmett laughed as he watched the boys *dicking around*. He missed those carefree times from his youth when he felt invincible and had his whole life ahead of him.

It was a nice night out, not too hot, with a light breeze.

When Emmett returned to his house with a fresh case of cold ones, he decided to sit on his front porch and enjoy the fresh air. The walls inside the house seemed to be closing in on him, and he thought the fresh air would help him relax. He placed the case in the refrigerator, pulled out two beers, and went to the front porch, where two chairs and a small glass table waited. He put the beers on the table, pulled his cigarettes and lighter from his pocket, and set them alongside the bottles. He then pulled out his cell phone, opened his favorite music app, and pulled up a '90s Alternative playlist. He pushed PLAY, set the phone aside, lit a cigarette, and cracked open a beer. He downed half the bottle in a single gulp, looked out over his porch railing, and surveyed the neighborhood.

You're going to be happy here, Emmett thought. *Everything will fall into place, and you'll finally be at peace.*

It was nearly ten at night, and Emmett had a good buzz. He wasn't as *shitfaced* as usual at that hour, but he had only been drinking beer and not liquor. He decided that to get a good night's sleep, he'd need to increase his buzz. He had some weed in his room, which he retrieved and brought to the porch along with his orange glass bowl. He packed the bowl, sparked the weed, and took a couple of deep hits. He chased the smoke back with another chug of beer.

Something caught his attention from his line of vision to the right. He exhaled another cloud of smoke and looked to the corner, where he saw a young kid riding a bike. The kid stopped at the stop sign on the corner, turned the bike around, and sped back in the opposite direction. A coldness ran through Emmett's bones.

It was Emmett's first sighting of the boy on the bike, but it wouldn't be the last. The boy on the bike was about to impact Emmett's life significantly. An impact that would stick with him for the rest of his days.

Emmett had been out of work for three days and struggled to keep busy. The days were the easiest. His child's mother worked the day shift and would drop their son, Nathan, off at eight in the morning. Emmett would get to spend the next nine hours with his son. Nathan was five and full of life. Emmett would spend the day playing with his son inside and outside if the weather permitted. Just being around Nathan filled Emmett with strength. He knew he could get his sobriety under control every time he heard Nathan laugh or saw a smile cross his face.

Renea would usually pick Nathan up a little after five unless Emmett needed to run errands, in which case he would meet Renea in the parking lot of her place of employment to hand Nathan off. This was always the worst part of the day. The part where he had to say goodbye to his son. Some days, Nathan would cry and throw a fit, breaking Emmett's heart. On those days, he wished he and Renea could have worked things out.

Emmett's problem was how to occupy his time once Nathan was gone for the day. Most of Emmett's friends were people he had met at the bar. He wasn't strong enough to go out and hang with his friends in that type of setting. At least not yet. He still longed for the burning sensation he got when he sipped on whiskey or Tequila. He also longed for the social aspect of sitting around and bullshitting with other bar patrons. But he knew he had to stay strong. The longer he did it, the easier it would be. He truly believed that.

Acquiring a job in the evening was something Emmett was also working on. He knew he couldn't rely on his inheritance long-term and needed to figure out what he wanted to do now that he wasn't bartending. His only passion was writing, but he didn't think he could honestly make a career out of that. He planned to get a *mind-numbing* night job to occupy his time when he didn't have Nathan. He believed he could genuinely lay off the bottle if he did that.

Everyone handles addiction in their own way, at their own pace. This is something Emmett believed with his whole heart. Most of his old drinking buddies didn't understand why he thought he had a problem. They didn't understand because he was still drinking beer at home. They'd ask why he couldn't at least come out and have a beer with them, even if he wasn't going to indulge in shots. Emmett would try to explain that that was the problem. He would not stop taking shots if he went to the bar and got a good beer buzz.

Emmett was sure that if he spoke to a specialist, they would tell him he would never be able to obtain sobriety unless he completely cut out drinking altogether. He understood this method of thinking, but he truly believed with his whole heart that it wouldn't work for him. He felt that after drinking beer in the evenings, after five, he would slowly curve and control his addiction. He'd give it a month or two, and if he still deemed it a problem, he'd consider joining AA or an outpatient rehab.

If Emmett had gotten a night job the moment he began his self-treatment, he would never have seen the boy on the bike. He would have never experienced all the terrifying things that were about to unravel in his life.

Each day, after Nathan returned home with his mother, Emmett would grab a case of beer and sit on his front porch, listen to music, browse the Internet, and engage in friendly chatter with his neighbors with whom he was slowly making connections. He also began to work on his lawn like an obsessive. Anything to keep his mind busy without thinking about drinking, drugs, or gambling. It was a struggle, but he was managing himself well.

Directly across the street lived a nice man, Levi, who had custody of his two teenage sons. They were both well-behaved and spent most of their time indoors playing video games. Levi was in his mid-forties and was recently engaged to a sweet woman who had moved in with him. Levi had introduced himself on the third day he saw Emmett smoking a cigarette and drinking a beer on his porch.

"I see you're a Miller guy," Levi came walking across the street with a beer in one hand and a cigarette in the other. "I'm Levi."

Emmett stood and shook the man's hand when he arrived at his porch. "Nice to meet you, Levi. I'm Emmett."

"How are you liking the neighborhood so far?"

"It's not too bad, lots of kids around, seems safe."

"Yeah, we never have any problems around here, nothing like Lake Shore Drive." Levi laughed.

Lake Shore Drive was a very troubled street in Enigma Springs, Ohio. There were rumors of murder, rampant domestic violence, and cannibalism. A few months before moving into his home on Cauley Place, the street had been blown to pieces. It was now nothing more than a giant hole in the ground that the town was trying to figure out what to do with.

Levi and Emmett *hit it off*. Levi liked to drink, but he didn't like the bar scene. Nearly every night, he would join Levi on his porch and put down drink after drink. Levi would always call it a night around nine or ten, as he worked the early shift at a factory, but Emmett would keep going until well past midnight, even knowing he would have Nathan to deal with in the morning.

Spending time with Levi allowed Emmett to acquire the socialization he craved without going to the bar.

The third night that Levi and Emmett hung out and put back some drinks was a Friday. Levi could stay up well past his bedtime as he was off on Saturdays. Levi had also brought his fiancé, Shirley, over to join in on the fun. Emmett and Levi were *shooting the shit*, and Shirley was scrolling through her phone when the boy on the bike appeared.

Emmett's porch was one house away from the corner of Cauley Place and Grattis Drive. The boy on the bike appeared on Grattis Drive, approaching the stop sign. No streetlight was on the corner, so Emmett could only see the child from the few porchlights his neighbors had left on after dark.

"Look, Levi," Shirley was the first to notice the boy. "It's that weird kid on a bike again."

Emmett and Levi stopped mid-conversation and looked toward the corner where the boy on the bike had just turned around, heading back up Grattis.

"What's the story?" Emmett asked as he lit a cigarette. "That kid rode his bike up and down the street till midnight the other night."

"Beats the hell out of us," Emmett took a chug of his beer. "We used to see him do this every night when we moved in three years ago. He rides back and forth for hours on end. I never see the kid out during the day, only at night. It makes no sense to us."

"Do you know where the kid lives?" Emmett's curiosity had piqued. If the kid only came out at night, maybe his parents homeschooled him and didn't want him around the other kids on the street. He had read books and watched movies with overprotective parents who would do things like that. Maybe they sat on their porch, watched the kid ride his bike, and then ushered them back into their house. Thinking about it, he pictured them dressed in traditional Amish attire and had to stifle a laugh.

"We'll see him for like a week, and then it'll be months later, maybe a year, and he'll reappear," Shirley said. She was already bored with the conversation and returned to scrolling on her phone.

He could be visiting his grandparents for the summer, Emmett thought. *Maybe that's why they only see him one week out of the year.* That still didn't explain why the kid only rode his bike late at night.

Emmett didn't know why he thought about the boy on the bike so much. He had no clue why it had become such a mystery to him— a mystery he wanted to solve.

Because you are going nuts from not drinking ... really drinking, Emmett's mind pondered.

One beer later, the boy on the bike had stopped traveling back and forth on Grattis. Two beers later, Levi and Shirley decided to call it a night.

"If I don't fuck this one once or twice before bed, I won't hear the end of it," Levi remarked with a wink as he took Shirley by the hand. She punched him on the shoulder playfully, but Emmett believed Levi was telling the truth. The couple talked about sex non-stop and weren't shy to share the secrets of what went on *behind closed doors*.

Emmett also considered retiring for the night, but he still had another three beers in the fridge that he planned to put back. He didn't have Nathan in the morning. It was Shirley's day off, and she was taking him to visit her mother an hour away. With no responsibility, Emmett decided to get as drunk and stoned as he could from the skunk weed he had left. He quickly reminded himself to go to the dispensary to get more potent stuff.

I've got to get a job, Emmett told himself as he sparked a bowl and took a few deep hits. *I have way too much fucking time on my hands.*

The boy on the bike appeared again. He rode to the stop sign, turned around, and rode back into the shadows of Grattis.

Looks like an old Huffy. Emmett focused his full, stoned attention on the corner. *Like the one I had as a kid. I bet it has one of those banana boat seats.*

It was a red bike, that much Emmett was sure of. From what he could make out of the boy, he knew he was Caucasian and was probably around seven years old. That was why Emmett thought it was strange that the boy on the bike was out riding around in the dark. He couldn't imagine letting Nathan out alone at night at that age. He didn't plan on being an overprotective father, but he also didn't plan on being a stupid one either.

Emmett knew you always had to keep your eye on your children no matter where you lived. But he also knew you had to be extra careful in a place like Enigma Springs. People went missing all too often for his liking, which was startling for a town with just over two thousand residents. There were only two thousand and seventeen registered residents the last time he heard. He would be damned to hell if his kid became one of the missing.

Maybe it's a good thing you sit out here at night. If that kid's parents or caregivers aren't watching out for him, you can. He knew the kid was not his responsibility, but ever since Nathan came into his life, he noticed that he started paying attention more to other kids around him. He saw other people in his neighborhood doing the same thing. They were all watching out for one another's children, which is one reason why Emmett was happy he chose to move to Cauley Place.

Emmett's thoughts were broken when he heard a thud, metal, and flesh hitting the pavement followed by a child's cries. Emmett turned and looked to the corner of Grattis and Cauley Place, where he saw the boy on the bike lying in the middle of the street, curled in a ball with his bicycle on top of him.

Emmett jumped to his feet and immediately ran toward the boy on the bike. He could see him hunched over on the ground; it looked like he was holding his knee. Emmett hoped the kid hadn't broken a bone or crushed his skull. Emmett had noticed the boy wasn't wearing a helmet. Not that many of the kids in the neighborhood did.

Just as he was about to cross from Cauley Place to Grattis, a red car came speeding down the road with blinding headlights. There was no stop sign in the car's direction, and it was going too fast to stop before crushing the little boy beneath its tires.

Emmett's face went ashen white and his eyes widened.

"Jesus Christ! Stop!" he screamed, lifting one hand to his eyes to shield himself from watching the unthinkable. The car slammed on its brakes, but it was too late. The vehicle ran over the crumpled form of the boy in the middle of the road. Emmett didn't hear a thud, but he knew it had happened. He was momentarily frozen in fear and was sure he could feel a splash of hot urine running down his left leg.

"What the fucks the matter with you, asshole!?!" A large man came bounding out of the red car. "You nearly gave me a heart attack running up on me like that."

"The boy?" Emmett began running toward the man and the red car. "You hit a kid!"

"The fuck I did," The large man had a look of concern on his face and lifted a hand to his chest; he was on guard, not knowing Emmett, the crazy man who had yelled so loud that he could hear him from inside his car while speeding down the road. He noticed that Emmett's eyes were wide and crazy.

Emmett ran to the front of the man's car, panting with tears. He looked down, but there was no sign of the little boy or his bike. He fell onto his stomach, lowering his face to the road and looking under the car—still, no sign of the boy. His heart was beating so hard he could feel it pounding in his neck, and a nervous sweat covered him.

Where the hell is he? He was here! I saw him on the road. Emmett's mind was in overdrive.

"What the hell is the matter with you?" The owner of the car moved forward, staring down at Emmett. He maintained a reasonable distance, unsure if Emmett was crazy or on drugs.

"I ... I..." Emmett slowly stood; his legs were shaking. He looked from one side of the street to the other. "I'm ... I'm sorry. I thought I saw a kid in the street ... I'm sorry, man ... I'm sorry." He began to back away from the red car and head toward his house.

"You're fucking crazy, man," The driver of the car returned to his vehicle, got in, slammed the door, and sped off.

Once back on his porch, Emmett nervously lit a cigarette and stood staring at the corner of the street where he was sure he had witnessed the boy on the bike being hit by the red car. The street was quiet and empty, and there was no sign that the boy had been there at all.

Sleep did not come easy for Emmett that night. He knew with certainty that he had seen the boy on the bike crumpled in the middle of the street. He had heard his cries. He had listened to the fleshy and metallic thud when the incident occurred. He had seen the kid hunched over, holding onto his knee, crying out in pain.

People can hallucinate when they are having withdrawals, Emmett thought to himself, but he was still drinking beer every day. He would get the shakes now and then and night sweats, signs that his body was adapting to not having the hard liquor and cocaine it desired. He would have considered hallucinations a possibility if he hadn't been drinking beer nightly, but the boy had been there. Even the neighbors had seen him, so he knew he was real.

Maybe it's stress, Emmett considered. *You've been worried about getting a job. Maybe you fell asleep and dreamed the boy fell in the street? You know it's dark in that direction without streetlights.*

No matter how many theories and excuses crossed his mind, he didn't believe one of them.

The boy had been there. He had fallen to the street, crying out in pain. Then he had vanished. Vanished into the night.

Emmett woke far too early the following day. He figured he had slept an hour to an hour and a half. Every time he shut his eyes, the boy being hit by the red car would cross his mind, and he'd open them back up in a panic. He also kept getting up and peeking through the bay window curtains in his living room to see if the child was still there on the ground.

When he did sleep, it was restless. He dreamed he was on a busy street, perhaps in New York, and had taken Nathan for a walk. He had been distracted by two guys arguing, and Nathan was nowhere to be seen when he turned around. He had been taken! Emmett scrambled in the crowd, screaming his son's name. He had an empty and terrible feeling in the pit of his stomach and heart that he would never see him again.

Emmett woke covered in a blanket of sweat. The dream was still thick in his mind, and he ran straight to the bathroom and vomited.

By one that afternoon, Emmett was craving a drink. A strong one. He knew beer wouldn't satisfy his needs. He was mentally and emotionally battling himself for a good hour. At one point, he grabbed his car keys, headed outside, got into his car, revved up the engine, and prepared to head to the bar. He knew what he was about to do was wrong and would most likely spiral out of control. But he needed a drink in a *bad* way.

Wrapped around his rearview mirror were the first pair of Chuck Taylor's Emmett had bought Nathan when he turned two. The shoes immediately reminded him of why he was trying to embrace sobriety. He shut off the engine and headed back inside.

Get a fucking grip, man, he told himself. *You can't lose yourself, or you'll lose Nathan.*

Emmett went to his room and packed a bowl. He took a few hits, holding the smoke in to obtain a quicker high. Within minutes, he was good and stoned. He thought about taking a nap but was afraid he'd have terrible nightmares about Nathan going missing again.

Stepping outside, he decided to take a walk to clear his mind. He rarely exercised and thought the fresh air and physical activity might do him some good.

The moment he stepped foot outside the door, his feet started walking toward the corner where he was sure he had spotted the boy on the bike the night before. He couldn't help himself. As he walked over to where he was confident the little boy had fallen, his eyes dropped to the ground, looking for any sign that he had been there. Scrapes from the bike hitting the ground, blood from a scraped knee, anything.

"You trying to get yourself killed?" A man in a Ford pickup truck had stopped his vehicle in the middle of the street. Luckily, it was early afternoon, and he had seen Emmett standing there and had been able to slow down.

Emmett spun around and stared blankly at the truck. His mind had been consumed with the boy, and he hadn't even heard it pull up. He lifted a hand in acknowledgment and felt his face grow red with embarrassment.

"Sorry about that," Emmett tried to fake a smile. "Must have been daydreaming."

"No harm, but you might want to reconsider daydreaming if you plan on walking in the middle of the street." The man laughed as Emmett stepped out of the way, allowing the truck to pass.

Stick to the sidewalks, dumbass, Emmett told himself as he stepped up and over the curb and onto the sidewalk. He then started walking up Grattis, still lost in his thoughts.

Thirty minutes later, Emmett was pleased to discover that his mind was growing clearer. His nerves had calmed, and his thoughts weren't consumed by the bottle or the boy on the bike. With each step he took, the worries of the previous night began to fade. He smiled when he found himself humming under his breath.

You've been under a lot of stress. It would be best if you got away for a few days. Maybe rent a cabin by a lake and go fishing. Take Nathan with you, he considered.

His *California Sobriety* was not working out as he intended. He knew he should really stop drinking altogether. But it was such a large part of his life that he didn't know how he would adjust. He'd already lost most of his friends and couldn't imagine how lonely he would become without a bottle in his hand. Apart from Nathan and his roommate, Emmett's only friend was a cold drink.

He smiled as a group of kids came speeding by on their bicycles. They were around ten, and he could see the joy in their faces as they rode up and down the road. Two of the boys were even attempting to pop wheelies. One of them, wearing a red baseball cap, gave him a wave.

It was nearing five, and Emmett suddenly realized how hungry he was. He hadn't been hungry all day, but now he was ravenous. He turned around and started heading back down Grattis toward his own house. He was considering firing up the grill and putting on a few burgers. He had some hamburger meat in the refrigerator and needed to use it before it spoiled.

As Emmett continued walking up the street with great determination, he saw an old lady sitting in a chair on her porch. The porch was covered with hundreds of colorful flowers. She stood, walked to the edge of her porch, and waved at him. Emmett raised a hand and waved in return.

"You look like a man with many things on his mind," she remarked.

"It shows, huh?"

"Very much so." She stepped off the porch. "My name is Millie."

He stopped walking and focused all his attention on the lady. "Emmett, I'm pretty new to the neighborhood."

"Yes, you live on Cauley Place," Millie smiled, looking down the street in the direction Emmett resided. "I see you sitting on your porch enjoying drinks at night."

"Yeah, that's me."

"You tried to save my grandson last night," great seriousness rose in Millie's eyes. "He rides his bike up and down the street late at night."

Emmett felt a lump rise in his throat. He didn't know if he was about to vomit or scream. He felt sweat break out beneath his arms and on his forehead. He could feel himself trembling and was afraid he would pass out.

"Is ... is..." Emmett tried to speak but could only stutter. He stepped forward on wobbly legs and walked toward Millie. He needed answers. "Is the boy okay? I was sure he got hit by a car last night. I've never been so scared in my life. Please, tell me, is he okay?"

Millie frowned and motioned for him to approach her. He did so quickly until he was standing less than a foot from her. That is when she said the words that would haunt Emmett for days.

"I'm afraid to say my grandson is not okay, Emmett. He died two years ago."

Millie was sure Emmett was about to pass out. She placed a comforting hand on his left arm and directed him to follow her into the shelter of her porch. She made him sit in a chair and rushed into her house to grab him a glass of water. If nothing else, Millie was a caretaker, and she could tell he needed a little *motherly love.*

Emmett's mind clattered. Millie's words kept ringing between his ears: *He died two years ago.* He knew the lady was not pulling his leg. She didn't seem like the type to indulge in pranks. Suddenly, the mysterious accident from the night before made sense. The boy hadn't been hit by the car on the road because he hadn't really been there. Just the fragments of his prior existence had been on the road.

Ghosts are real? Emmett's mind questioned. He had never frowned upon those who believed that they existed. He didn't fully understand the logistics of the afterlife, and he believed in the possibility of life beyond death. *Did I really see a ghost? What the fuck is going on?* Emmett's heart continued to beat high up in his neck.

"Oh, Emmett," Millie's face was filled with great sympathy. "Steady your hands and take this glass."

"What?" He turned to Millie. For a moment, his eyes blurred, and he was unsure where he was.

"Water, it will do you good. Try to take a few small sips," Millie leaned over, passing the glass of ice water to Emmett. "Careful now; you don't want to spill it all over yourself."

Emmett's hands were still shaking, but not as bad as before. He managed to get a good grip on the glass and moved it to his mouth, taking a small sip. The water was satisfying; he could feel every cell of his body jumping for joy when the first sip entered his mouth. He sat the glass on a small table beside him and looked about the porch. It was riddled with hundreds of colorful flowers. He saw a few bees and butterflies dancing among the blossoms.

Millie moved to a chair beside him and sat down nervously, smiling. She reached out one hand and reassuringly patted Emmett on the knee.

"I want to know if I heard you right," Emmett struggled to speak. He was careful to whisper so as not to be heard by any passing neighbors. "Your grandson ... the boy on the bike ... he's not real?"

"Oh, dear," Millie leaned back in her chair. "He's very real, just not flesh and blood no more. He's not passed from this world to the next. He is trapped here for reasons I'm unsure of. But he has revealed himself to you, which means the world to me."

"The neighbors across the street from me have seen him too."

"But they have never interacted with him. He allowed you to see his fall. He's never done that before. Others have seen him pass up and down the street, but something about you made him feel vulnerable enough to show you his fall, even in the afterlife."

"I don't understand," Emmett's eyes begged for answers. He had never needed a drink more in his entire life.

"Let me start from the beginning, Emmett. I'll tell you what I know, the best way I know how to say it. You have to understand that it is tough for me to speak about, as he was my only grandchild, and who died under my care. Would you allow me to tell it?"

Emmett shook his head *yes* as he sipped the ice-cold water. This time, he nearly chugged it and felt a cold tinge of shock in his temples. Still, it was refreshing. He hadn't realized how much his body needed it.

"Danny was the sweetest child," Millie's eyes were wet, but no tears had yet to grace her cheeks. "His mother, my daughter, was an addict. Not only with the bottle, but also with pills."

I understand the struggle with the bottle, Emmett thought to himself.

"It was a long, hard road to convince her to seek help, but she knew if she didn't, she would lose Danny. She loved Danny, but she loved her vices even more. She was a single mother, and it was a long, rough road. Danny's father was never in the picture. I'm not even sure my daughter knew who his birth father was. I hate to say it, but she was *easy* in those days. If you get what I'm saying, she would do anything to obtain drugs. I hate to be so crude."

"I understand," Emmett nodded. He knew many women from the bars that would give you a handy or even a blowjob for another round of drinks or a couple of lines of cocaine.

"Danny was six when his mother entered rehab. My husband, Martin, was still alive then. He and I volunteered to take Danny into our care while she attended to her health. It was a great joy having a child in our home again. It had been several years since the walls of our home had that type of youthful joy. Each day was a blessing."

"I'm sorry to hear about the passing of your husband," Emmett said with complete sincerity. Emmett didn't want to interrupt Millie, as he wanted to hear the rest of the story, but he also wanted to show Millie he was listening intently.

"Thank you," Millie looked over her lawn and continued her tale. "It was Martin who bought Danny the bike. Danny never had a male role model, and Martin went out of his way to spend every waking moment with the child. Playing catch in the backyard, taking him fishing, showing him how to throw a football, and, of course, how to ride a bike."

Everything Martin had done with Danny was exactly what Emmett hoped to do with his own son. He smiled, imagining how much fun Danny had had with his grandfather. He was also considering how much joy Martin must have had to have obtained from teaching his grandson these things.

"Martin spent two days teaching Danny how to ride the bike and, of course, bike safety. He always wore a helmet. Martin was very strict when it came to protecting Danny's head. His sweet little head. He had the most beautiful green eyes and jet-black hair that made them stand out. He had the sweetest dimples and a smile that could melt your heart. I shit you not." Millie began to laugh.

"Danny was a very independent kid. He had to be with a mom like my daughter. We didn't know it at the time, but she had left him home alone all the time. Danny knew how to cook and provide for himself. He knew when it was time to take a bath and when it was time to brush his teeth, and he knew how to clean up after himself. He had an old soul. You could see sadness and tiredness in his eyes. Who knows what else that child saw when he was in the care of his mother."

"How is your daughter now?" Emmett told himself to stop asking questions.

"We'll get to that." Emmett saw a flicker of sadness in Millie's eyes when she responded. Perhaps the same type of sadness that had been in Danny's eyes.

"Once Danny learned how to ride the bike, demanding his training wheels be removed after only a few hours, his independence again came into play. Within days, he was riding up and down the sidewalk without assistance. Martin was so proud, as I was. He would go up and down the street, beeping the horn on his bike."

I didn't see a horn on his bike, Emmett thought to himself.

"He also kept wanting to go further and further on his own. But we would only let him go as far as the stop sign where Cauley Place meets Grattis. Where you saw him fall in the middle of the street," Millie turned her face toward Emmett and looked at him thoughtfully.

"I didn't want Danny to ride in the street, but Martin convinced me that Danny was responsible. Which he was. He never crossed the street without looking both ways and was always aware of his surroundings. As I said, Danny was wise beyond his years and very responsible. We allowed him to ride in the street only when we were sitting here on the porch, and each time he left the house, we would remind him of the importance of bike safety and being aware of drivers on the road."

Emmett was thinking about how protective he was when it came to his own son and knew it would be a hard decision to let him ride up and down the street without his supervision, let alone venturing into the road. He had already witnessed several older kids in his neighborhood who would often pull out in front of a car during their playful excitement.

Luckily, he had not seen an accident yet.

"The first time Danny fell in the street and hurt his knee, I was terrified, just like you saw the other night. I didn't want Danny to ride that blasted bike anymore, but Martin insisted that *boys would be boys*, and he would learn from each fall he had. I gave in, Danny continued riding his bike, and soon, he wanted to venture further. He had made a friend in the house next to yours. A little boy named Billy. After meeting his mother and father, we agreed that Danny could ride his bike to the house to play with the boy, but the moment the streetlights came on, he had to return home."

Millie stopped talking and looked at Emmett again.

"Sorry, I am rambling. You want to get to the *nitty-gritty* of it," Millie nervously smiled, then looked down at her hands resting in her lap. She nervously rubbed them together. "One evening, I came outside to wait for Danny to return home. The streetlights had just come on. I sat outside on the porch, waiting for him to arrive, and that's when I heard the most terrible sound I've ever heard. It was the sound of crashing metal. I heard tires squeal; I heard a terrible thud ..." Millie started crying. Emmett placed his hand on Millie's leg, letting her know he was sympathetic. "I still hear those sounds in my dreams. I'm afraid they will haunt me until the day I die. A reminder of those last minutes with my sweet little Danny."

"If it is too hard to continue, I will understand," Emmett tried to be comforting, but he hoped she would continue. He had to know what happened to Danny, and he needed to understand why he was seeing him ride his bike up and down the street at night. Why was Danny haunting him? This question he needed answers to above all else.

"No ... it's just, I miss him so much." Millie now had tears flowing down her cheeks. "I heard Danny scream. I heard him cry. I got to my feet, and I ran until it hurt. I have knee and back problems, you see. When I got to the street, I saw Danny crumpled in a ball, covered in blood. He had been crushed beneath the tires of a car. I ran to his tiny body and pulled him into my arms. I got there just in time to see the confusion in his eyes, and a moment later, I watched as all light vanished from them. My Danny was gone."

"That's horrible," Emmett had tears in his own eyes. His mind kept thinking about Nathan and how he didn't know if he'd survive if he had seen something like that happen to him. If Nathan died, Emmett was sure he would as well.

Millie wiped the tears from her eyes and smiled. She still had more to tell him.

"Martin died a week later. I believe it was from a broken heart. He destroyed what remained of Danny's bike and blamed himself for teaching him how to ride. His mother, my daughter, cut her wrists in the rehab facility after she heard what had happened. She blamed me and Martin, but I think she blamed herself even more. Danny wouldn't have been with us if she hadn't been in rehab, and he would have still been alive."

"Grief," Emmett replied.

"Yes," Millie wiped tears from her eyes and again focused them on Emmett's. A week later was the first time I saw Danny riding his bike up and down the sidewalk again. Danny was dead and buried, but there he was, riding his bike, smiling, and waving. He was dead, but his spirit was still here on this street, where it remains. You are not going crazy, Emmett. You are seeing my dear Danny. You are seeing him, and I believe he is trying to reach out and tell you something. Something he is unable to say to me."

Emmett was speechless.

Emmett's hand had started shaking again. He didn't notice it until he reached to grab the glass of water Millie had given him.

She also took notice of his shaking hand. She fully understood why he was shaking. She couldn't imagine what was going through his mind, but she knew he believed her.

"It's a lot to take in," Millie said. "Believe me, I thought I was going crazy the first time I saw Danny riding up and down the sidewalk."

"You and me both," Emmett laughed, and it came out in a stutter. He took a small sip of the water and placed the glass back on the table.

"It was the first time I was alone here in the house that I saw Danny," Millie revealed. "I was having trouble sleeping. I hadn't slept alone since I was eighteen and married Martin. Trying to lay there in the bedroom without my Martin was impossible. I tried drinking warm milk, reading a book, anything to make myself tired, but nothing worked. So, I came outside to sit on the porch here. I thought the night's fresh air would help me fall asleep. Instead, I heard the sounds of a bike pedaling, and the next thing I knew, Danny was riding right in front of the house. He had a smile on his face, and he waved one hand at me and laughed."

Emmett couldn't imagine what had to be going through Millie's mind when she saw him. He imagined how terrified she must have been.

"When I saw Danny on the bike, I was initially scared. A deep kind of terror crept up on me. I thought I was going mad. I thought I was sleeping, and it had to be a dream. But when I stood to run off the porch and chase after him, I felt pain in my knees and hip and knew I was not dreaming. When I stepped off the porch, I saw him hit the corner of Cauley Place and Grattis, and then Danny and his bike vanished into thin air. One moment, he was there, and the next, he was not."

"Has he ever spoken to you?" Emmett's voice was shaking just as much as his hands were.

"Only once." Millie shot Emmett a warm smile. "I don't believe Danny is here to speak to me. I believe he is here to comfort me. To let me see him at his happiest, riding his bike and having the time of his life. At first, seeing him did nothing but sadden me. I missed holding him in my arms and brushing his black hair from his eyes. I missed him. Everything about him."

"What did he say to you?" Emmett was both curious and nervous at the same time.

"He said ..." Millie's voice broke, and the tears in her eyes poured down. "He said ... I'm fine, Grandma ... I love you..." Millie placed her face into her hands and caught her tears and sobs.

Emmett again placed his hand on her leg to comfort her.

"Do you think Danny is trying to communicate with me?" Emmett asked once Millie had composed herself.

"I believe Danny is reaching out to you," She nodded. "I'm not sure why, but he allowed you to see him getting hit by that car. He's never done that before that I am aware of."

Millie and Emmett sat talking for a few more minutes. They

agreed to keep in contact with one another. She made Emmett promise that if Danny did speak to him, he would tell him how much she loved him and let her know what his message was. Emmett agreed.

Stepping off Millie's porch and heading home, he noticed how late it had gotten and how much time had slipped away while speaking to Millie. He pulled his phone out of his pocket and saw it was already six. He was starving. His appetite had returned even though his nerves were still shot. He was uncertain that Danny was a true spirit with a message for him. Emmett wasn't as scared as he had been the night before, but he was still uneasy, wondering what it could be that the boy might want to say to him, and questioning why.

Gareth had just gotten out of the shower when Emmett returned home. "You look like shit," he jokingly mumbled.

"Feeling like shit, too," Emmett said.

"If you've come down with a bug, stay the fuck away from me," he said as he headed toward his room. "I can't afford to get sick."

"Just haven't been sleeping well, man," Emmett explained.

"Nothing a few shots down at the bar can't cure," Gareth mocked his roommate, knowing how hard he had been working on his sobriety but not believing it would stick. He thought Emmett would be a *boozer* until the day he died and kept hoping and praying he'd *fall off the wagon* so they could go back to their nightly antics at the bar. He missed working alongside his roommate and hoped he'd return and start bartending again.

Emmett decided against making hamburgers and instead made a couple of ham and cheese sandwiches and ate half a bag of potato chips and two dill pickles. He then drove to a carryout next to his house to grab a case of beer.

If that kid wants to communicate, let's fucking do it, Emmett thought. He planned to sit out on the porch, get a good buzz, and look out for the Danny. He was nervous but didn't think Danny was trying to hurt him. At least, he hoped not.

After cracking open his first beer of the night and plopping down in a chair on his porch, Emmett called Nathan. They only spoke for a few minutes, with Nathan detailing what he had done throughout the day and how much fun he had. The call ended with them both saying *I love you*.

Emmett always had mixed feelings when getting off the phone with his son. There was always the feeling of sadness. He missed his son and wished he was with him. The second feeling was overwhelming love. He had never loved anyone as much as he loved his son. He thought about him all throughout the day.

After hanging up with Nathan, he started thinking about his life without his son. He couldn't imagine what Millie, Martin, and their daughter had gone through when they had lost Danny. His mind again went to dark places, thinking how he knew he would never survive if anything tragic happened to Nathan. He just hoped and prayed that he would meet death before his son ever died. He knew he wouldn't be able to take it if it were the other way around.

Emmett didn't know it, but he was caught in the world of dreams.

In the dream, he sat on the front porch, watching Nathan kick a small black and white soccer ball around and laughing as he played in the water sprinkler. Emmett reached to the table next to his chair to retrieve his cigarettes and realized he had left them on the counter in the kitchen.

"Stay there, buddy," Emmett called out. "Daddy's grabbing his smokes."

Emmett returned to the house, leaving the front door open, and approached the kitchen counter less than ten steps from the front door. That is when he heard a terrible thud and tires screeching from the front of the house. Emmett dropped his cigarettes, turned, and ran through the open door. All the air had left his lungs, and his heart was brutally pounding.

"Nattthhhaannnnn!" Emmett felt himself scream, but he didn't hear it. A white truck had stopped in the middle of the road outside his house. In the middle of the street, he could see little Nathan crumpled in a ball in his swimming trucks. In the gutter, he saw Nathan's soccer ball. He screamed again, running by the truck driver who had just exited his vehicle. The man was pale white and had a pained and terrified expression.

"I didn't see him," the man cried. "He came out of nowhere."

Emmett ran to Nathan's crumpled body. He grabbed him and pulled him into his arms. He bled from every orifice and was not moving in the slightest. The man from the truck pulled his phone from his pocket, calling for help. Multiple neighbors had moved from their porches to their front lawns and watched the scene with curious and horrified eyes.

"Nattthhhaaannnnn!" Emmett screamed again, shaking his tiny, limp body and holding him tighter to his chest. He cried and moaned, a sound that was terrifying and skin crawling.

"Wake up, Emmett," a child's voice said.

Emmett felt a cold yet comforting hand on his shoulder.

He turned around, and young Danny stood beside him on a bike. He smiled and when he did, a grotesque river of squiggling maggots fell from his mouth.

"WAKE UP!!!!!" Danny screamed.

Emmett lurched forward on his seat. It was night; he could see the moon and stars in the sky as he stood on his shaking feet. He was sweating, and his heart was pounding. He was recovering from the terrible dream he had just escaped from.

It wasn't a dream! It was a fucking nightmare! his mind corrected him.

"A fucking nightmare," Emmett mumbled as he slowly sat back in his chair. Next to him were eleven empty beer bottles. He ignored those and grabbed his cigarettes, quickly lighting one. He needed to calm down before he *lost his shit*. He was having difficulty shaking the image of Nathan's crumpled and bloody body in his arms, and the maggots spilling from Danny's mouth.

"Danny," Emmett whispered as he turned to the corner of Cauley Place and Grattis, where the boy on the bike always presented himself. The street was quiet, and there was no sign of Danny.

A set of headlights appeared on the corner, and a second later, Gareth pulled into the driveway. Emmett immediately picked up his phone and checked the time. It was three-thirty in the morning. Emmett couldn't believe he had been so out of it that he had slept that long on the front porch. Gareth was getting off work.

"What's up, fuckface?" Gareth called out as he came staggering out of his vehicle. Emmett could tell he was *shit-faced* drunk and probably fucked up on cocaine.

God, I miss cocaine.

"You missed a hell of a time tonight, man," Gareth stumbled onto the porch and sat in the chair beside him. He placed two fingers to his lips, motioning for Emmett to give him a cigarette. He was a social smoker and never bought cigarettes. He was known for bumming them. Emmett slid his pack over on the table between them. Gareth drunkenly pulled out a cigarette and lit it.

"I bet I did," Emmett replied with not much emotion.

"What the fuck are you doing out here so late?" Gareth blew a cloud of smoke in his direction.

"Told you, man, haven't been sleeping too well. Nightmares. Bad ones," Emmett answered as something caught Emmett's attention from the corner of his eye.

"Listen, man," Gareth began. "I know I've been giving you a hard time about not drinking, and we haven't had the chance to hang out and talk lately, but if there is something on your mind, you just need to vent ... I'm here for you, buddy. But right now, I've got to take a wicked piss." Gareth stood and walked by Emmett, entering the house and slamming the door.

Emmett looked to the corner of Cauley Place and Grattis, where he watched Danny riding his bike back and forth in the darkness of night. His heart once again attempted to claw its way out of his chest. Danny was on the corner once again. Emmett saw that he was wearing a tiny helmet, and this time, he noticed a little horn connected to the handlebars of his bike. Danny stopped on the corner, turned his bike around, and sped back up the road, disappearing from Emmett's line of vision.

Should I go after him? What does Danny want with me? He knew Millie believed Danny was trying to reach out for some mysterious reason. *Why did he choose me?*

He stood, stepped off his porch, and began walking toward the corner. His legs felt heavy beneath his frame. Emmett could feel sweat building on his forehead. He moved closer to the corner and felt flush with heat when he saw Danny speeding down the street toward him. Emmett stopped walking, frozen to his spot in the middle of the two streets. Danny waved a hand at him.

This is fucking insane, he thought to himself as he slowly lifted his hand and returned the gesture. Danny laughed and beeped the horn on his bike. He stopped on the corner and stared Emmett in the eyes. Emmett could feel them penetrating his soul. His skin was pale and nearly sparkling in the light of the moon.

Danny's smile dropped from his face, and Emmett watched in terror as a stream of maggots began running from the corner of the boy's eyes. He was crying a river of maggots. Emmett held his hand to his mouth, sure he was about to vomit.

Billy ... Danny opened his mouth, and the word filled the air, but it wasn't coming directly from his mouth. It was coming from all around Emmett, pounding in his ears. *Talk to Billy.* Danny's hand lifted and pointed beyond Emmett toward his house, or at least in that general direction. *Beware the bad lady.*

Danny's mouth shut. He stopped pointing, snapped his fingers, and suddenly vanished.

Another restless night lay ahead of Emmett. He couldn't get Danny out of his head. He didn't understand why, out of all people, he had chosen to reveal himself and reach out to him.

I'm a loser, Emmett thought as he stared at the ceiling in the darkness of his room, wishing he could fall asleep. At the same time, he was sure that even in sleep, he wouldn't obtain rest. He'd been having terrible nightmares for days now.

Billy was the little boy that Danny had been friends with before his death. Emmett was sure he knew who the little boy was. He had seen him a few times in his backyard while mowing the grass. He had a habit of kicking his soccer ball over the small fence in the backyard, but he never once tried to venture into Emmett's backyard to retrieve it. Emmett would toss it over the fence each time he discovered it. But he wouldn't have minded if the kid had crossed onto his property to retrieve his belongings.

Who is the bad lady? This was the final thought Emmett had before his eyes finally grew heavy, and he was instantly transported into the realm of nightmares.

Emmett jerked in his sleep. He could hear crying coming from the other side of his bedroom door. It was Nathan. Goosebumps covered Emmett's skin, and a nervousness flowed through his blood to the point that he was sure he would be sick. Emmett knew Nathan was not at his house that night, but he knew the crying came from his son.

"Nathan!" Emmett called out, pulling himself out of bed and rushing into the hall. "Nathan? Where are you, son?" He heard the crying again and ran toward the living room, sure that was where the sound came from. The moment he entered the room, he stopped, frozen in place. The living room had changed. It was not how Emmett remembered it. It was almost from another time, even though it was his living room.

There was a large oriental rug that covered much of the hardwood floor. An old brown recliner sat in the corner beside the bay window. The curtains were open, but they were not the curtains Emmett knew he had in his house. The curtains were yellow with orange and blue butterflies on them. It was dark outside. There was a small table next to the recliner where he saw a glass of urine or light-colored tea. Next to it were three open baby jars. Each one looked like they were filled with blood. It was even dripping from the sides of the jars, running onto the table.

What terrified Emmett the most was the forty-something woman sitting in the chair. Her face was jaunt with dark circles under her eyes, and her hair was thinning to the point that he could see bald patches. She wore an old, white cotton nightgown covered in dried food and multiple stains. There were holes in it as well, as if moths had been feeding on it. She reminded Emmett of someone in the final stages of cancer.

On the woman's lap sat Nathan. Not really sat—more like a held prisoner. She gripped Nathan's arm, and Emmett could see his son squirming in her grasp. Her other hand had a large spoon in it. She moved it to the table, dipped it in one of the bloody jars, and then pulled it out, moving it back to Nathan.

Nathan screamed, and Emmett could see his lips and face stained red. He was sure the creepy woman had been feeding him what was in the jars. He looked at the spoon she was moving toward his son's mouth and saw an eyeball on it. Veins hung off the spoon, and drops of blood were falling like rain. The woman quickly shoved the spoon into Nathan's screaming mouth.

"Noooooo!!!!!" Emmett bound forward. He was no longer frozen in place. But the moment he took his first step to rescue his son, he awoke in the real world and fell off his bed, hitting the hardwood floor below with a thud.

"Shit!" Emmett called out in pain. Sunlight was creeping in through the sides of the curtains in his bedroom window. His heart was still pacing from the realness of the nightmare. He looked over at the clock and saw that it was already noon. "What the hell am I going to do?"

After showering, Emmett was pleased to discover he had energy. He had felt drained ever since seeing Danny for the first time. Even though he had experienced the terrible dream the night before, he had also gotten enough sleep to feel like a new person. He also discovered that his appetite was coming back. He made some crispy bacon and a large four-egg omelet. He devoured every bit of it.

While eating breakfast, Emmett decided his first order of business would be to see if he could find Billy outside playing so he could speak to him. Emmett was nervous about doing this, knowing how it could look if his neighbors saw him conversing deeply with a little boy in the neighborhood. It didn't seem appropriate, but Emmett knew he had to do it. Danny had directed him to do so, and he was curious to see what the boy would say. Not that he had any idea of how to start a conversation about Danny with him.

Emmett considered walking down to Millie's and telling her about the words Danny had spoken to him, but he decided against it. He would only talk to her when he had something more substantial to tell her. Plus, he didn't want to worry the lady. She had enough going on in her life already.

Emmett pushed his mower into the backyard. The yard didn't need cutting, but he felt he would look less creepy if he at least appeared to be doing something in his yard when he conversed with Billy. He noticed that the boy always played in his backyard. He seemed like a loner.

He spotted Billy's black and white soccer ball to the left of his fence line. He didn't approach it. He'd wait for Billy to appear first. That way, he could quickly start a conversation with the boy. He didn't have to wait long.

Billy came running out of the back door of his house and went to the wooden shed moving to the side of it. He watched as the little boy pulled out a small soccer goal and moved it to the corner of his yard, where he always set it up. He waved at Emmett.

"Sorry, Mister," Billy called out. "I kicked my ball into your yard again!" The boy smiled, but it was not a happy one. It was an apologetic one.

"Not a problem, buddy," Emmett stopped pretending to pick weeds and went to the soccer ball. He retrieved it and walked over to the fence where Billy awaited. "Here you go." He tossed the ball to the boy.

"Thanks! I'm trying to get better with my high kicks, but I keep losing control of the ball," Billy explained.

"Do you play soccer in school?" Emmett pushed forward, trying to show the kid he was friendly.

"Not in school," Billy shook his head. "I play at the YMCA, though. I'm the second-best player on the team, I reckon."

Emmett laughed and then smiled. He liked the confidence the kid displayed.

"What position do you play?"

"Center Forward."

"You must be good if you are a Forward."

Billy dropped the ball to his feet, and Emmett thought he was about to display some of his footwork to impress him. Instead, he moved closer to Emmett and the fence. He looked back over his shoulder as if he was checking to see if his parents were around or if anyone was listening. Then he whispered, "Did Danny send you?" The seriousness and the tone of Billy's whispers sent chills running throughout Emmett's body.

"Yes," Emmett whispered. "How did you know that?"

Billy looked over his shoulder again, then returned his gaze to Emmett. "He comes to me in my dreams sometimes; only I don't think I'm dreaming. I think he is really there. He is sad.".

"Why is he sad?"

"Because he's dead."

"And he told you I was going to talk to you?"

"He wants me to tell you about the bad lady," Billy's face filled with concern, and his whisper lowered even more.

"Who is the bad lady?" Emmett asked the question, not knowing if he wanted the answer. Even in the light of day, he felt terror.

"She ..." Billy started to speak when his mother stepped out the back door. She had a nervous look on her face.

"Billy?" The woman called out. He jumped at the sound of her voice.

"Hey, Mom!" Billy faked a smile. "This is our neighbor; I kicked the ball into his yard."

Emmett raised a hand in greeting. "I'm Emmett; nice to meet you, ma'am."

The woman stared him up and down. He could tell she was sizing him up to see if he was a friend or foe. She was looking out for her little boy. "I'm Mrs. Smith."

Emmett could tell by the expression on her face that she was not happy that he had been talking to her son. Even though he needed answers about the bad lady, he decided not to press his luck.

"Anyway, I better get back to work," Emmett turned, starting away from his fence. "This lawn isn't going to mow itself."

He moved to his mower and noticed that Mrs. Smith was still staring at him. He didn't plan on mowing the lawn, but now he had no choice. He had to put on a show, or Mrs. Smith would think he was a threat. Little Billy had already returned to his ball and goal.

Emmett started the mower and began cutting his grass, wondering how he would find out who the bad lady was. Was it the woman from his nightmare the night before? She certainly looked like a bad lady, feeding his son eyeballs.

Did the bad lady hurt Billy or Danny? Does the bad lady want to hurt Nathan? Emmett wondered, and a shudder ran down his spine.

That night, Emmett found himself once again sitting on the front porch of his house. His eyes were directed toward the corner of Cauley Place and Grattis, eagerly waiting for an appearance of Danny. He had met with Billy, like Danny wanted, but did not receive much information. All he knew was that Billy knew who the *bad lady* was.

Emmett was halfway through a case of beer and was good and stoned. He had gone through more weed in three days than he usually went through in a month. He realized that was partly to replace his alcohol consumption with another vice. He really could go for a Jack and Coke. Maybe a double or a triple. He had also gone from smoking one pack of cigarettes daily to two to two and a half packs. He could feel his lungs burning each night he crawled into bed, and he would hack for a good hour after he first awoke each morning.

There was no sign of the Danny, and he was starting to think he would not be appearing that night. Part of Emmett wanted to see him while another part hoped he wouldn't show up. He just wanted the whole situation to end before he was forced to open a bottle of whiskey or snort an entire bag of cocaine.

Time to break the seal. Emmett's bladder was screaming for release. He stood to his feet, moved to the door, and placed his feet on the doormat when he noticed something near his feet. There was a piece of paper poking out from under the doormat. Emmett stepped back, lowered himself to the ground, and pulled the paper from under the doormat.

It was a folded piece of notebook paper. Emmett opened it and saw youthful writing in black. It was all written in large print with a few misspellings. Emmett looked at the bottom of the paper and saw it was signed: BILLY.

The little neighbor boy had left him a note.

Emmett forgot about the need to release his bladder as he sat back in his chair and began reading the letter in the dim light. Above his head, two moths flew around the lightbulb near the door.

MY MOM DOESN'T LIKE YOU. SHE DOESN'T LIKE YOUR HOUSE. THAT IS WHERE THE BAD LADY LIVED. SHE SAYS YOU COULD BE A BAD MAN. I DON'T BELEVE HER. YOU ARE NICE. THE BAD LADY GAVE US COOKIES. THEY MADE ME SICK. THE BAD LADY DIDN'T LIKE US PLAYING BALL OR MAKING NOISE. THE BAD LADY HURT DANNY. I STILL SEE HER SUMETIMES IN THE WINDEWS OF YOUR HOUSE. BE CAREFUL.
– BILLY

Emmett's hand shook, and he dropped the note onto his lap. He slowly turned his head, looking to the bay window. He had the uncanny feeling that he was being watched, not by Danny, but by someone inside his house. He felt like the bad lady was watching him.

Danny did not make an appearance that night.

Sleep did not come easy for Emmett that night. He lay on his bed, reading the letter from Billy over and over again. The *bad lady* was the lady who lived in the house before he moved in. He was sure of that now. It was just hard for him to believe. After meeting her father, whom he purchased the house from, he couldn't imagine his daughter being *bad*, let alone a person who could hurt a child.

You never know what types of secrets people hide. Just because her father was nice doesn't mean she was. She could have been a truly terrible person. People can lead two very different lives without being discovered. Emmett knew that for a fact.

If she was a bad lady, what did she do to Danny? Was she responsible for his death? Is that what Danny is trying to tell me?

Billy said he sometimes saw the *bad lady* in the windows of his house. That chilled Emmett to the bone. He told himself the little boy could have imagined things—seeing things that weren't there. But, at the time same time, he wondered if maybe her soul was attached to the house, the same way Danny seemed to be connected to his bike and the street corner.

Emmett fell asleep thinking about the *bad lady* and how she could have hurt Danny. And if she was attached to the house, would she be capable of hurting Nathan?

The following morning, Emmett found himself watching Nathan *like a hawk*. He would not let his son out of sight as they played in the living room. The house was small, and from the living room, he could see into the dining room, kitchen, and down the hall. The only place he couldn't see was the bathroom.

Nathan was potty-trained and drank so much juice that he ran to the bathroom every twenty minutes. Emmett grew nervous each time he was in the bathroom. He kept waiting to hear Nathan scream. If he did, Emmett knew it would because the *bad lady* had her grip on him and would be feeding him eyeballs.

He was so distracted by his thoughts that he couldn't even enjoy himself with his son. He felt terrible when he dropped him off at his mother's work. He felt like he had wasted the day thinking about the *boy on the bike* and the *bad lady* when he should have focused entirely on living in the moment and making memories with his son.

On his way home, Emmett stopped at the liquor store. He went inside and grabbed the largest bottle of whiskey he could. He didn't want to do it but couldn't help himself. He needed to get fucked up. He needed to get as shitfaced as possible to escape the world around him.

Emmett also stopped at the bar he used to work at, had two beers, and waited for one of the local dealers to show up. When they did, he approached them and secured some cocaine. He knew what he was doing was wrong. He had been doing so well with avoiding hard liquor and drugs. But the idea that there may be a *bad lady* lurking behind the walls of his home was pushing him over the edge.

Tears were in Emmett's eyes as he made the drive back to his house. He was disappointed in himself but was incapable of stopping.

Gareth was sitting on the couch when Emmett walked through the front door. He eyed the bottle of whiskey in Emmett's hand. He figured it was just a matter of time before Emmett would return to the bottle. He had also received a text from the bartender at work letting him know that Emmett had shown up. He was finally going to get his friend back, and they could go barhopping and chasing tail again.

"Rough day?" he asked.

"Rough week," Emmett responded as he moved to the kitchen and placed the bottle on the counter. He returned to his car and retrieved a case of beer, a two-liter of Coke, and a bag of hamburger meat.

Gareth curiously watched Emmett seasoning hamburger meat in the kitchen. He had already cracked open two beers and smoked one cigarette after another.

"Seriously, man," Gareth began as he turned down the television set where he had been watching an old war movie. "You need to talk?"

"I'm good, man," Emmett lied. He would have liked to sit down and tell Gareth everything about the *boy on the bike* and the *bad lady*. He would have loved to tell him about Millie, the story she had told him about Danny, and how he was terrified Nathan could be in danger in the house. He had not seen or heard anything in the house other than feeling like he had been watched one night. But no bumps in the night. No apparitions. He also knew Gareth would not believe a single word. He figured he wouldn't have believed them if he had been on the opposite side of the events he was now part of.

"Working tonight?"

"Yeah, I picked up a shift," Gareth answered.

Emmett grilled out some burgers, and he and Gareth devoured them. Afterward, Gareth headed off to work, and Emmett headed to the porch with a beer, a bottle of whiskey, a glass full of ice, and a splash of Coke and sat. He was ready to confront Danny.

It was just beginning to grow dark outside, but Emmett was already shifting in his seat. He shifted from side-to-side and kept looking at the corner. He kept expecting Danny to appear, but he knew it wasn't dark enough. Danny only appeared when darkness fully engulfed the neighborhood.

The glass of ice with a splash of Coke had melted entirely. The whiskey bottle had yet to be opened, but Emmett kept eyeing it, fighting the urge to pour himself a hearty glass. He had one hand in his pocket, fingering the small bag of cocaine he had acquired. He had yet to partake, but he was getting close to running inside and spreading a few lines out on the kitchen counter to truly gain the focus he needed to confront Danny.

Emmett decided he'd do whatever it took to get Danny to tell him what he wanted so he could end the nightmare he was living. He just wanted to be done with Danny and the *bad lady*. He needed to return his focus to getting a job and being an upstanding father to Nathan.

"I want you to stay away from my son," Mrs. Smith stood three feet from Emmett's front porch. He didn't even see her walk up his lawn. He had been consumed with his thoughts about Danny and the *bad lady*.

"Hello, Mrs. Smith," Emmett's voice was shaking. He could see Mrs. Smith's eyes judgmentally looking at all the empty beer cars and the bottle of whiskey sitting next to him. "I didn't think I did anything wrong. We were just talking about soccer."

"You were doing more than that, Emmett," Mrs. Smith moved a step closer to the porch. "You were talking to him about Danny. He told me you asked about him, and he told me he told you about the lady who used to live in this house."

"Billy told me she was a *bad lady*," Emmett revealed.

"Everyone that has lived in your house has been a bad person, but she was the worst of all. I'm sure she poisoned Billy and Danny the night that poor, sweet child was hit by a car. I couldn't prove it, and at this point, it's moot now that the bitch got what she deserved," Mrs. Smith said with a crooked smile playing across her face.

"Listen ..."

"No, you listen to me," Mrs. Smith stepped back. "Billy is finally getting over what happened with Danny and this house. You stay the fuck away from him, or I'll send my husband over here next time, and he is nowhere as nice as I am."

Emmett didn't even verbalize a response. He nodded as she turned and quickly walked away from the house. She stopped halfway down the sidewalk, looked over her shoulder, and shot Emmett the middle finger.

The sound of a horn filled Emmett's ears. It wasn't the horn from a car; it was the horn from a bike. Emmett turned his head and looked to the corner of Cauley Place and Grattis. There, in the middle of the street, was Danny. He was looking at Emmett, waving at him with one dead and clammy hand.

The bizarre interaction between Emmett and Mrs. Smith was no longer on his mind. Emmett's eyes were focused on Danny standing in the street, waving at him. He didn't turn his bike and ride back into the shadows of the street as he usually did.

This is it, the moment of truth, Emmett thought as he walked across the lawn, heading directly to the corner where Danny stood. His legs were wobbly like the night he had witnessed the ghost boy get hit by a car.

Danny stopped waving his hand and dropped it to his side. He had a serious expression on his face. His eyes were wholly transfixed on Emmett.

"I talked to Billy; he told me the *bad lady* lived in my house," Emmett began before he even made it to Danny. He didn't even care that one of his neighbors might see him talking to himself because they most likely wouldn't have seen Danny standing in the road. He believed that Danny had appeared that night to speak to him. To see if he talked to Billy or not.

"See," Danny's voice was monotone. His eyes were nearly black, but Emmett could feel them eyeing him.

"See what?" Emmett yelled. He was now closer to Danny than he had ever been before.

Danny dropped his hands from the handlebars of his bike and reached them out toward Emmett as if he were requesting a hug.

"See," Danny repeated. The moment he did, maggots began pouring out from the corners of his eyes like tears again.

"What do you want me to see?" Danny stepped right before the bike. He was sure it would vanish into thin air if he reached out to touch it.

"See," Danny reached out, and Emmett could feel Danny's cold hands touch the flesh of his own. He pulled Emmett's arm. "See!"

Danny screamed as he pulled Emmett down until they were staring one another in the eyes. Emmett's skin crawled as he watched the larvae roll out of the corners of his eyes. "See," Danny placed both hands on the side of Emmett's head and put his thumbs over

Emmett's eyes. Emmett immediately closed his eyelids, and a second later, he saw things as he had never seen them before.

Emmett was more disoriented than he could ever remember being. He was even more disoriented than he had ever been when he was nearing blackout drunk or stoned out of his gourd. At first, he could barely get his eyes to focus. He knew he was standing on grass, and it was daytime. But everything was moving fast.

"Kick it to me, Danny!" a young voice called out. Emmett immediately recognized it as the voice of the neighbor boy, Billy.

Emmett's vision lifted, and he was staring directly at Billy, who was a few yards away. He looked down and saw a soccer ball between his tiny feet. Emmett was not looking through his own eyes. He was looking through Danny's eyes. Danny had taken control of him and was showing him things just as he had seen them in the past before he was killed.

Emmett watched Danny's little foot pull back and kick the soccer ball to Billy. He began to dribble the ball and went to kick it into the goal. He pulled his leg back and kicked the ball with a vengeance. The ball went high into the air, flew over the goal, and crossed over the fence and into the backyard of the house Emmett now lived in.

However, Emmett did not live in the house now. The *bad lady* lived in the house. This was a vision from the past.

"What did I tell you, little shits?" the voice was crude and high-pitched. Danny turned toward the sound of the voice, and Emmett caught a glimpse of the *bad lady* for the first time.

The woman was five feet tall with a hunched back. She was wearing a pink bathrobe that had seen better days. She had long, scraggly, sandy blonde hair that needed to be washed. She had an oxygen tank with tubes running to her nose. Her teeth were stained brown, and Emmett assumed it was from tea stains, as he had been told she died in her chair drinking tea.

"Sorry, ma'am," Billy's voice called out. "It was an accident!"

"It's always an accident!" the *bad lady* lashed out. "If it happens again, I'll keep the damn ball! Anything on my property is mine!"

Danny shuffled his feet, and his eyes dropped to the ground.

"Get your ball and scoot!" the *bad lady* called out.

Danny lifted his eyes, and Emmett watched as Danny climbed over the fence, retrieved the ball, and retreated to his yard. The *bad lady* cussed under her breath. Danny's eyes lifted, and he watched as she vanished back into her house.

A shutter of brilliant white light flashed before Danny and Emmett's eyes. It reminded him of the bright flash from a camera. A second later, he was transported to a new scene. He was once again looking through Danny's eyes. He could instantly tell that he was climbing onto his bike. Danny began to pedal the bike quickly.

Danny was outside Billy's house, and the streetlights had just come on. Danny waved goodbye to Billy as he sped away. He turned his bike and rode by the house Emmett now lived in. He heard a crunching sound and watched Danny hit the brakes on his bike, bringing it to a halt.

"Oh, no!" Danny's voice called out as he dropped his eyes, and Emmett saw what Danny was seeing. The sidewalk outside the house was covered in broken glass. Danny had just ridden over it, and his tire popped.

"That'll teach you little shits," the *bad lady* stood on the front porch. She had a beer bottle in her hand that matched the same glass on the sidewalk. "This sidewalk is mine! Now shoo! Get going!"

Emmett could hear Danny crying. He was upset about his tire popping and was scared of the *bad lady*. She was a cruel woman.

Who the fuck does she think she is? Emmett thought to himself. *She doesn't own the fucking sidewalk in front of the damn house! Danny was just a kid, and she flattened his tire for no reason.*

The strange visions continued for what seemed like hours to Emmett. He saw Danny's grandpa help him fix the tire on his bike. He watched as Danny's grandma, Millie, tucked him into bed. Emmett felt nothing but love when he captured visions of Danny and his grandparents.

Whenever the visions would switch to Danny playing with Billy and seeing the *bad lady*, Emmett felt nothing but nervousness and fear. There was no love other than when Danny and Billy were playing in Billy's front yard or within the protection of Billy's house.

The visions grew confusing when they seemed to slow down to a single moment. A moment Emmett knew was critical. He could feel it in his bones.

"Hey boys!" It was the voice of the *bad lady*, but she was not screaming or scolding Danny and Billy. Emmett saw her through Danny's eyes. She was wearing a pair of khaki pants and a floral shirt. Her hair was fixed, but her smile was still brown. She was smiling at the boys. "You can get your ball! I can see it by my sunflowers."

Danny's eyes looked to Billy's, and Emmett could see confusion in Billy's eyes. The *bad lady* had never spoken to the boys with politeness. It was very unsettling.

"Okay," Billy said as he crossed the fence to retrieve the ball.

"Do you like my sunflowers?" the *bad lady* questioned.

"Uh ... yeah ... they are pretty," Billy stuttered.

"Thank you. I work hard to keep them looking this way. They make me happy," the *bad lady* spoke. "Do you boys like cookies?"

Danny's eyes focused on Billy's again.

"Yes, ma'am," Billy answered.

"Well, I just made some fresh chocolate chip cookies and sun tea," the *bad lady* said. "Why don't you boys join me in the sunroom, and we can have some."

Billy and Danny's eyes once again met. Both of them were nervous, but the idea of chocolate chip cookies delighted them both.

The *bad lady's* sunroom was quaint. There were hundreds of flowers, a small flowing fountain in the corner, and numerous comfy seats with floral patterns. There was also a small glass table where Emmett saw a plate of fresh cookies and a pitcher of sun tea. The *bad lady* poured the boys a glass of iced tea each, as both boys eagerly ate the cookies.

Danny's eyes surveyed every inch of the sunroom, and Emmett could see how beautiful it was. Back in his reality, there were only a few old lawn chairs and trash bags filled with empty beer bottles. He wished the sunroom looked like the *bad lady's*. He imagined that Nathan would enjoy sitting out there playing.

Another flash of light moved the scene to Billy's backyard, where the soccer ball was being passed around again. It was growing dark, and Emmett knew the streetlights would come on soon, beckoning Danny back to his grandparents' house.

Billy suddenly stopped dribbling the ball and looked at Danny with a pained expression.

"I feel sick!" Billy ran to the corner of the yard where the shed was set. He leaned over and began vomiting.

Though Emmett was looking through Danny's eyes, he also could feel what Danny was feeling. He felt his stomach rumble and then a tiny stab of pain. He could tell that Danny was about to be sick, too. The streetlights were coming on, and Emmett could hear Billy's mom calling the puking kid inside.

"I don't feel so good," Danny said with a shaking voice. "I'm going home."

Danny stumbled to Billy's front yard and got on his bike. Emmett started to see that Danny's vision was blurring. He got on the bike and had a hard time getting onto it and getting it going. When he did, he swerved back and forth on the sidewalk as he rode to the corner, turned, and rode by the *bad lady's* house. He looked at the house, but his vision kept going in and out. He could see Danny pedaling faster on the bike, crossing the street to pass over from Cauley Place to Grattis.

Emmett next saw the headlights of a car barreling down on Danny. He watched in horror through Danny's eyes as his little body was hit and thrown through the air. He felt the air go out of Danny. He heard his bones crunch and crack on the pavement. He felt tears and blood forming in Danny's eyes and rolling from his mouth. He listened to the cries of Millie screaming. He then watched Millie come to Billy and hold his dying body in her arms.

Another camera flash of light filled Emmett's mind, and he was back standing on the street corner. He was staring directly into the eyes of the boy on the bike, who had removed his hands and fingers from Emmett's head and face.

"See!" Danny cried out. "See!"

"See what?" Emmett was crying. He had just witnessed the death of Danny firsthand and couldn't stop thinking, *what if that had been Nathan?*

"See!" Danny hissed one final time before he vanished into a vapor of smoke.

Emmett stood from his hunched position in the street and stared at the spot where Danny had been moments earlier. A horn honked, and brakes squealed. Emmett looked up and saw that a car had stopped feet from him. He had nearly been hit again in the same spot where Danny had been killed.

Three days later, Emmett gathered Millie and Billy's parents, Mr. and Mrs. Smith, into his living room. He waited to arrange the gathering when Gareth would not be home. He didn't want him to know about the boy on the bike. He was certain he would think he had lost his mind.

It had been a near impossible task for Emmett to convince Mr. and Mrs. Smith to come to his home. Mrs. Smith had already shown great disdain for him. Only after Emmett revealed that he could prove the previous tenant of 217 Cauley Place poisoned both their son and Danny did they agree. Mrs. Smith was skeptical but agreed to come, but threatened Emmett that if he were fucking around with them, she would take action.

If Jerry, the father of the *bad lady*, and his wife were still in Ohio, he would have invited them as well. But they had already relocated to Florida. He planned to send them what he uncovered only after he showed it to the Smiths and Millie.

Millie was the easiest to convince to stop by. Emmett told her he had spoken to Danny and knew what he wanted him to *see*. She smiled with tears in her eyes and told Emmett she would be there.

Emmett had connected his laptop to the flat-screen TV mounted on the living room wall and purchased a couple of bottles of wine. He wasn't sure if the Smiths or Millie would be interested in drinking, but he figured it was at least polite to make the offer when hosting houseguests.

The Smiths arrived a few minutes before eight that night. Billy was with them. He shyly waved at Emmett and sat beside his mother on the couch. Mr. Smith introduced himself and shook Emmett's hand. He had a firm handshake. When speaking to him, he looked Emmett directly in the eyes, and Emmett could tell that Mr. Smith did not trust him.

Millie arrived at 7:30. She was very anxious to discover what Emmett had to say and was more than curious why Emmett had invited the Smiths.

"What's this all about?" Mrs. Smith questioned. She had crossed her legs and was anxiously shaking her foot. She was eyeing the room up and down judgmentally.

"Well, we are all here for Danny," Emmett began.

"You didn't even know the kid," Mr. Smith said. "You weren't here when the accident happened."

"I know," Emmett began again.

"Then explain to us why we are here," Mrs. Smith said in the most condescending tone.

"How about we let the young man say what he has to say instead of interrupting him? Let's give him a little respect like mature adults," Millie sat forward in the recliner and shot fire from her eyes as she spoke to Mr. and Mrs. Smith directly.

Billy smiled when she did so, and Emmett imagined this was the first time someone had ever talked to his parents with disrespect in his presence. He figured the kid was happy to see someone take a stand against them.

Mr. and Mrs. Smith looked shocked but fell silent and sat back on the couch, looking back to Emmett.

"When I first moved here, I began seeing a small boy on a bike. He would ride up and down the street and then vanish. At first, I didn't think much about it. But then, one night, I believed I saw this little boy being hit by a car in the intersection. But when I got to the corner, the boy was not there. This went on for weeks, until one day I took a walk and ran into Millie," Emmett quickly described his first experiences with Danny.

Millie leaned forward and directed her attention to the Smiths again. "I invited Emmett here to sit with me on my porch. I could tell he was troubled and had many things on his mind. I also knew he had seen Danny riding his bike up and down the street," Millie explained.

"With all due respect, Millie, your grandson is dead. He isn't riding his bike up and down the street any longer," Mr. Smith respectfully spoke.

Millie chuckled. "I'm not losing my mind. I'm older, but I can confidently tell you I have seen Danny riding his bike up and down the street. I have been seeing him do this since his funeral and to this very day. Others have also seen him, but he has only directly interacted with me and Emmett here. He interacted with me because of our closeness, but I was never certain why he had revealed himself to Emmett and showed him the accident he was in."

"I don't believe in ghosts," Mrs. Smith replied.

"Mommy, I see Danny too. He tells me things," Billy spoke for the first time since arriving at Emmett's house.

"We don't tell lies in this family, Billy," Mr. Smith sternly spoke to his son.

"I'm not telling lies," Billy solemnly swore.

Mr. and Mrs. Smith both looked from Billy then to one another. Billy was a good kid, and he had never once lied to them as far as they were concerned. Still, neither one of them believed in ghosts.

"Listen, whether you believe it or not, I want to show you something on my TV. It will only take a few seconds. But I want you to know this first. Danny spoke to me about the *bad lady* who lived in this house, and he wanted me to see something from the final day of his life." Emmett shook. He hadn't had a single drink all day. He wanted to be completely sober when he revealed what he had discovered.

"Danny showed me that the bad lady may have poisoned him and Billy here," Emmett continued. "But of course, there has never been any proof. Until now," Emmett turned from his visitors. He turned on the TV and clicked a few keys on his laptop. A few seconds later, the screen came to life, and the Smiths and Millie discovered the truth.

Three days earlier, after having the strange experience with Danny in the street, where he saw through his eyes, Emmett had returned to his house and had a one-person party. He consumed the entire bottle of whiskey and half the bag of cocaine he had acquired.

To hell with sobriety, he thought to himself. He needed to get the images of Danny's accident from his mind and the feelings he experienced whenever he was around the *bad lady*. He blacked out drunk and woke up in a pool of vomit and urine in the upstairs bathroom of his house, dry heaving with the worst headache of his life.

Emmett was in and out of consciousness the rest of the day. In his bedroom with the curtains tightly closed, he took small sips of water and nibbled on crackers. He took it slowly, sure he would throw up. Plus, whenever he opened his eyes and came into contact with direct light, he felt like he would pass out.

See, Danny's voice kept popping into Emmett's mind.

"What the fuck do you want me to see?" Emmett whispered into the emptiness and darkness of his bedroom.

Emmett started to recall that one memory Danny showed him involved the sunroom of his new home. He remembered thinking Danny wanted him to pay attention. He remembered all the beautiful flowers, the comfy chairs, and the table. He also remembered the fountain, cookies, and tea. He knew he was supposed to remember something else but couldn't figure out what it was for his life.

White flashes of light had taken him from one scene to the next as Danny showed him memory after memory. Emmett recalled thinking that it reminded him of flashes from a camera.

Emmett's eyes opened wide. He suddenly remembered something from the sunroom of his house. When he bought the house, he remembered the wireless battery-powered security camera installed in the sunroom corner. He remembered asking Jerry, the father of the *bad lady*, about the cameras, and he told them they came with the house, but he didn't know if they worked.

When Emmett opened the camera in the sunroom, he found that the batteries were acid-covered and smelled metallic. The cameras were cheap, and Emmett didn't think he needed them. The neighborhood was safe, and he didn't think anyone would dare fuck with him or his roommate.

He removed all four cameras he found. Two on the front of the house, one on the back, and the one in the sunroom. The one Danny wanted him to *SEE*. Emmett found the hard drive for the cameras, placed it and the cameras in a box, and put them in the attic when he moved into the house. He stored them away, thinking he could sell them on Facebook or eBay.

The fucking hard drive. Emmett needed to retrieve the hard drive and see if it had anything from the sunroom on it. His headache and stomach issues were no longer a concern. He retrieved the hard drive from the attic and attempted to figure out how to operate it. When he couldn't, he got in his car and headed to the bar he used to work at.

Peter was a computer technician who spent most of his time at the bar when he wasn't working. Emmett had shown him the hard drive and asked if he could pull the contents from the device and place them on his laptop. Peter agreed to do so if Emmett would pay off his tab at the bar, which was nearing two hundred dollars. Emmett didn't want to spend that type of money, but he knew if he didn't, he'd most likely be haunted by Danny until the day he died.

All three Smiths and Millie leaned forward, watching the security camera footage playing on the screen. The footage was from the sunroom, and it was also from the night that Danny died. Millie held her hand to her mouth as she saw Billy and Danny enter the sunroom and devour cookies and tea. She had tears in her eyes seeing Danny smiling and joking around with his best friend. They watched the footage until Billy and Danny left the sunroom, leaving the *bad lady* alone. She waved at the boys and flipped them off when their backs were to her.

The footage stopped, and Emmett looked at his guests.

"Did you notice that she didn't drink tea or cookies with Danny and Billy that day?" he asked.

"Now that you mention it, yes, but that doesn't prove that she did anything illegal," Mrs. Smith answered with curious eyes. She felt like Emmett had more to say or to share with them.

"That day you got sick, Billy, right?"

"I did. I couldn't get off the toilet all night, and I puked for two days; Mom thought I had the flu," Billy explained.

"Danny and Billy were poisoned by the lady that lived here. I don't know if she was trying to kill or make them sick. Billy, did you get dizzy and have blurred vision?" Emmett continued.

"I did," Billy answered.

"He staggered around like a drunk," Mr. Smith revealed. "We just assumed it was from his fever and sickness."

"I have one more thing to show you," Emmett moved to the laptop. "I went back on the footage before the boys arrived and found this."

He pushed another key and then stood back and allowed the others to watch as the *bad lady* entered the sunroom with her a plate of cookies and a pitcher of tea. She reached into her pocket and pulled out a bottle of pills. She placed a few into her mouth and appeared to begin chewing them. She then leaned over the pitcher and spat them into the tea. She seemed to be laughing. There was no audio on the video, so no one could be sure. She then stirred the tea and placed the bottle of pills back into her pocket before going to the back door and entering her yard, on her way to invite Danny and Billy inside for cookies and tea.

The video stopped, and everyone sat in stunned silence.

"I don't know what she put in the tea, but her father told me she died of a blood disease, so I assume she put some of her medication in the tea. I don't know what it was, but I believe it affected Danny like it did Billy. I believe he was disoriented when he left your house," Emmett motioned toward the Smiths. "I bet he didn't even see the car coming when he was hit by it."

"My Danny was always so safe." Tears streamed down Millie's cheeks.

Emmett and his visitors spoke for upwards of an hour about his discovery. They believed the *bad lady* had drugged the young boys, but with her dead, they didn't think they could do anything.

"I think Danny just wanted us to know what happened," Millie said toward the end of the conversation.

Mr. and Mrs. Smith still didn't believe in ghosts. Later that night, they both agreed that Emmett must have been bored and had been going through the footage left on the hard drive and discovered the drugging of the boys. They didn't know his angle but decided to watch him closely.

Millie hugged Emmett on the front porch as she headed toward the street. Before leaving, she told Emmett she loved him and thanked him, telling him that she believed Danny would be at peace now that the truth had been revealed.

Emmett sat on his porch that night with a smile on his face. He didn't even feel the need to drink. He enjoyed a few cigarettes and thought about everything he would do the next day when Nathan came to the house. He was ready to be the very best father he could be.

Right before heading inside for the night, where he would have the best sleep in years, something caught his attention from the corner of his eye. He looked over and saw Danny standing in the middle of the street. His bike was gone, and he wasn't wearing a helmet. His eyes were clear, nearly glowing from a distance.

Emmett stood to his feet, lifted one hand, and waved at Danny. The little kid raised his hand and waved back at Emmett with a smile. Emmett then heard Danny laugh the most youthful and joyful laugh he had ever heard, and the next second, he vanished into the night.

About Travis VanHoose

From a young age, Travis VanHoose found himself enthralled by the power of literary escapism, devouring the young adult horror fiction of authors such as Christopher Pike and R.L. Stine.

During his teen years, he became obsessed with the dark worlds and tales crafted by master storyteller Stephen King and surreal filmmaker David Lynch. He discovered that books and films could transport him to exciting places, freeing him from the realities of life.

VanHoose was always drawn to the dark, macabre, and the paranormal, which led him to dabble in short-form writing after being inspired by his sixth-grade teacher, Mr. Curtis, who told him he had what it took to become "one hell of a writer."

For years, VanHoose struggled to find direction in life. He pursued a variety of careers, serving as a naturalist, summer camp director, video store manager, psychic hotline operator, debt collector, and even as a youth minister for several years.

However, knowing his true passion was writing, VanHoose was never satisfied with such careers. He fought his muse until his forties when he finally put pen to hand and began working on his first novel, SEEING RED, which he published in paperback in September 2023.

These days, VanHoose finds solace and pure happiness in creating his twisted worlds and unique characters—releasing the dark tales that have haunted him throughout his life. By unraveling mysteries in his writing, he has discovered parts of himself he never knew existed.

VanHoose has several novels and serials in the works that he will rapidly begin releasing in early 2024—and hopefully for years to come.

ALSO BY TRAVIS VANHOOSE

Seeing Red

Skeletons in the Closet

Dead and Dating

Anya Bayne

Dead and Dating

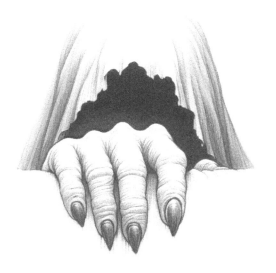

Anya Bayne

For: Aja Lace, who talked me into joining Anthologies, and for being a good friend as well as one heck of another author!
Thank you,
Anya!

Blurb for Dead and Dating

Ella Bellamy-Allard died one hundred and sixty years ago. She has been stuck in her family's plantation home all alone since the day she died. Her days are quiet and peacefully boring until a handsome stranger comes barging into her afterlife.

Kyle Murphy needed a change in his afterlife and decided to relocate to New Orleans, only to end up forced to share a house with a beautiful, young Karen-geist!

Can these two dead souls find love in their afterlives? Read along to find out!

PROLOGUE

'Poltergeists need a happily ever after, too! Here at Dead-N-Dating, we will find you the perfect incorporeal haunting mate to spend eternity with.'

Ella bit her lower lip as she concentrated on what she was typing on the computer screen. Lordy, this was still hard for her, even after a year of learning and practicing. She didn't think any of these things others took for granted would ever come easy for her.

Looking at the headline on her page, Ella smiled at the new website she had created. The idea of starting a dating service for the dead excited her. She knew many in the afterlife were as lonely as she had been before she met Kyle.

"What do you think, Ky?" Ella called over her shoulder to gain Kyle's attention as he sat drawing a picture. She had to admit the man was not only handsome but talented. Plus, he was outstanding in bed.

Kyle stood up, stepped over to stand behind her, and studied the screen. "I think it looks amazing, babe," he told her, then kissed her cheek. "Those computer classes are really paying off."

"If it wasn't for you, I would have been alone and stuck here for eternity." Ella smiled at him. "I am so thankful that you came barging into my afterlife."

"Baby, you didn't have an afterlife until me." Kyle gave a cocky grin. "And now look at you!"

Ella hopped up and showed him her short skirt and crop top shirt. "I know, and I look amazing, don't I?"

"Way better than you did in that heavy old '*Gone with the Wind*' style dress you used to wear. That thing had to be annoying as hell." Kyle told her honestly. "I mean, I thought you were beautiful from the first moment I saw you, but damn, you are sexy as hell now."

"The stays in the corset were very uncomfortable, but after the first fifty years or so, I hardly noticed them anymore," Ella told him, shaking her head. "But I definitely like these outfits much better."

Kyle slipped his arm around her waist, pulled her close, and kissed her. "I like you in them better as well. But I like you even better out of them." He ran a hand over her ass lovingly.

"You have always been so forward, Kyle," Ella told him, shaking her head as she blushed.

"Yes, but I had to be. Because you were such a prude." Kyle told her with a laugh.

"I beg your pardon, sir! I'll have you know. I was not a prude. I was just a well-mannered southern-born and bred lady." Ella told him, sticking her nose in the air.

"You were a spoiled brat!" Kyle told her with a laugh. "But a damned cute one, even when I wanted to turn you over my knee or strangle you."

"That is not how I remember it. As I recall, you were an overbearing brute!" Ella told him heatedly.

Barging In

Eloise strolled through the mansion that had been her home for the last one hundred and fifty-plus years. She had been born in a bedroom upstairs and died in this massive house. She had spent her entire life on this plantation. And here she remained for her afterlife. Eloise had watched as her family was forced from this place they had called home while she was stuck here. Wandering from room to room, seeing her beloved home change with each new owner as time marched on endlessly.

Walking over to the large window, she looked out over the vast estate and marveled at the many changes and things that remained the same outside the house.

How she missed the grand parties her family would throw, from formal balls to parties that would last for a week. Eloise missed her family most of all. Damn, those Yankees and their meddling in all their lives. They were why she was stuck here all alone and had been forced to wander through this house for years.

Now, her days and nights just blurred into an eternity of

boredom. "This must be hell!" she muttered, shaking her head sadly. She wondered what she had done to deserve this.

Eloise wandered back to the attic and laid down on the old dusty settee that had been moved up there years ago and forgotten. Oh, how she missed her grand old bedroom, with the large soft feather tick mattress. She missed so many things from her life. Tears began to slide down her cheeks as she silently cried.

Eventually, she must have dozed off because some awful racket and what sounded like an animal in pain woke her from slumber. Pushing up from the dusty cushion, Eloise frowned and looked around. Standing up, she stretched, then winced at the stiffness in her body. Lordy, she would give anything to have a comfortable bed again.

Slowly, she made her way out of the attic to the upstairs floor and began following the noise or what sounded like some form of awful music and what she would describe as bellowing, not truly singing. Reaching one of the larger rooms in the back of the house, she saw movement. Someone was in her home! How dare they trespass!

Taking a deep breath for courage, she marched into the room. "Who are you, and what are you doing in my house?" Eloise demanded loudly.

The man didn't seem to hear her over the noise from the odd-shaped box sitting on a crate in the corner of the room.

Suddenly, the man stood and turned around, then jumped. "Holy hell, who are you, and what are you doing here?"

"I *live* here." Eloise snarled at him. "This is my house. How did you get in here..." she trailed off and frowned. "Wait, you can see me? Like really see me and hear me?"

"Well, kind of." The man strolled over and turned off the noise. "There, that's better. Now, what are you doing here?" The man asked her with a deep frown.

"I *live* here. *What* are you doing here?" Eloise demanded, crossing her arms over her chest and raising her chin.

"I am moving in. This place is registered as an unoccupied dwelling." The man informed her with an annoyed frown.

"Registered? Registered with whom?" Eloise raised an aristocratic brow.

"With the local D.O.H., of course." The man shook his head as if she were dense. "Didn't you register with them that you live here?"

"I have no idea who or what you are speaking of, sir. But I have lived here for over one hundred years! You *cannot* simply barge in here and think to stay."

"I guess we will have to visit the D.O.H. to figure this out. Because all my things will arrive here tomorrow." He told her with an annoyed look.

"What in the name of all that's holy is this D- whatever you said. What do they have to do with my house?" Eloise snarled at him, waving her hand around and becoming annoyed.

"The D.O.H. and they clear us to live in houses. Every city has one. How do you not know this? Have you lived in a cave for the last hundred years?"

"Of course not! I have been living here for the last one hundred fifty years. So, what is this D.O.H.?" Eloise demanded once more.

"Are you saying you haven't left this house in over a hundred years?" The man looked at her, astounded.

"Well, no. Of course not. I died here. So, I am stuck here." Eloise furrowed her brows in confusion. "So, what is this D.O.H. you keep talking about?"

FRANKLY, MY DEAR

"THE DEPARTMENT OF OCCUPATIONS AND HAUNTINGS. Are you saying you have never heard of it?" He asked her, completely confused. "And you haven't left this house since you died?"

"Well, no. Of course, I haven't." Eloise spoke hesitantly. "We aren't allowed to leave. Are we?"

"So, you are telling me that no one from the D.P.R. ever came and talked to you after you died?" He asked her, shaking his head in wonder.

"I don't even know what that is!" Eloise growled at him, wholly annoyed and frustrated. "It's like you are speaking a foreign language. Could you speak in plain English, please?"

"I am speaking English!" He snapped back at her. "The D.P.R is the Department of Poltergeist Registry. And you are saying you have never heard of it?" He didn't believe her. All spirits knew what it was. She was most likely just a squatter who didn't want to take the time to go through the proper channels to get a place. Lord, he didn't want to deal with a Karen poltergeist or, as many called them, a Karen-geist.

Eloise tapped her foot and looked down her nose at him even though he stood more than a head taller than she did. "If I had heard of it, I certainly wouldn't be asking who they are, now would I? And you are not staying in my house!"

"Yes, I most certainly am. Because this is my place, I registered it with the D.O.H. last week. So, technically, it is my place, not yours, Scarlett!" He snapped at her.

"Scarlett? My name is not Scarlett. I don't even know Scarlett." Eloise frowned at him. "But no matter what, this is my house, and you need to leave and take your noisy box with you. I don't like it. The thing hurts my ears."

"Well, frankly, my dear, I don't give a damn!" He said, then laughed. When she just raised a brow and scowled, he shook his head. "You truly don't get it? Or are you just being a Karen-geist?"

"I beg your pardon? A what?" Eloise spoke haughtily. This man was the strangest creature she had ever had the misfortune of meeting. "For your information, sir, my name is not Scarlett. It is Lady Eloise Bellamy-Allard. My family has lived here since Orleans was settled. We have lived here for over three hundred years at least until you, damned Yankees and carpet baggers, destroyed our lives."

"Us what?" He raised a brow and frowned in complete confusion. "Now, who isn't speaking English?"

"Northerners! Do you not know what those are?" Eloise snapped at him.

"Look, Scarlett. I don't know anything about Yankees or Carpet baggers. I am originally from Chicago. My name is Kyle Murphy, and I registered with the D.O.H last week to stay here. This place was supposed to be an empty dwelling." Kyle snapped back at her. "If you are referring to the Civil War, well, toots, your side lost the war, which ended over a hundred years ago. So, get over it, move on with your afterlife, and enjoy it."

"How dare you talk to me that way, you filthy Irishman!" Eloise spoke in disgust. "For the last time, get out of my house. I don't care if you are the first person I have spoken to since I died. I don't like you. And I am not sharing my house with you. You *baudet*!" Eloise stomped her foot, then turned and stormed away.

"Why are all the pretty ones crazy pain in the asses?" Kyle muttered to himself as she stormed away. He was not about to leave.

He didn't care what she said. Kyle figured he had just as much right to be here as she did.

Eloise stormed up to the attic and began to pace as anger and hurt from his last words filled her. She wasn't crazy. And she most certainly wasn't a pain in the ass. He, on the other hand, was an overbearing jackass. Even if he was breathtakingly handsome, she thought with a sigh. Lordy, when the man had first turned around, her breath had caught in her chest. Then he'd opened his mouth and ruined it.

As her mama had always said, '*A man had to have more than looks to be worth a second glance. If he didn't use the brain, god gave him run the other way*'. Sadly, not only was he a damned Yankee, but an Irishman as well. He absolutely couldn't stay in her house. Besides, they were unchaperoned, and that was highly improper. She had no clue how to find this D.O.H. place and speak to someone. She hadn't been out of the house since a few days before the night she had died. Not that she clearly remembered that.

How was she going to make him leave? There had to be a way. Reasoning was obviously not going to work with him. Could she really venture out of this house? Kyle had said he was from Chicago, which she knew was a city in the North. So, it appeared that ghosts could travel away from where they had died. Why had she always thought she was stuck here? Why hadn't she ever tried to leave?

Eloise realized she needed far more information about being a ghost. And right now, she had someone she could ask. But could she stand being around him long enough to find out?

LOOK SCARLETT

KYLE PACED THE ROOM HE HAD CHOSEN TO BE HIS ART studio. How in the hell had that girl never left this house in her entire afterlife? Why hadn't she left? She acted as if she didn't know she could go anywhere. God, how long had she been here all alone? What if she wasn't a squatter and truly knew nothing about the D.O.H. or the D.P.R.?

He had so many questions. Damn, he should have handled that whole meeting better, but he'd been shocked when he'd turned around and saw the woman standing there. She was so damn beautiful, even in her '*Gone with the Wind*' style dress. And that begged another question. Why was she dressed that way? Both her clothing and mannerisms spoke of the old South. Could she genuinely have been stuck here since the Civil War?

If that was the case, then Kyle felt terrible for her. She really must be lonely. Damn it, he ran a hand through his hair. He needed to apologize and talk to her. Then maybe they could work this mess out. Striding over to the door he whipped it open only to receive a punch to the face.

"What the fuck?" Kyle bellowed, grabbing his nose as he saw stars.

"Oh, lord almighty, I am so sorry!" Eloise gasped as mortification filled her.

"What the hell did you punch me for?" Kyle snarled at her as his eyes watered.

"Well, I didn't mean to, of course. I started to knock when you whipped open the door." Eloise snapped at him.

"Why are you here?" Kyle growled at her.

"Because *I live* here!" Eloise growled back at him. "Remember, this is *my* house, *not yours*!"

"I didn't mean why are you here. I meant, why did you come back to this room?" Kyle snapped at her as the pain in his nose receded. That was the one thing about being dead. The pain didn't last long, and you rarely got sick.

"Well, I came here to try to talk to you and see if we could be civil until we could figure this whole mess out," Eloise told him with a frown. "I certainly didn't come to punch you!" She had never struck another person in her entire life. "I didn't know we could even touch each other. Or truly feel anything."

"You were serious when you said I am the first person you've talked to in over one hundred years?" Kyle asked her with a frown.

"Well, yes. I haven't spoken to anyone since 1864, to be exact. I don't even know for sure what year it is. I lost track sometime back. But I know it has been at least one hundred and fifty years since I spoke to anyone." Eloise told him quietly as she wrapped her arms around her waist.

"Holy shit! It's been one hundred in sixty years!" Kyle told her with a frown. "How did you not lose your mind?"

"Recently, I was accused of being crazy by someone." Eloise raised a brow at him.

"Uh... Heard that, did you?" Kyle rubbed the back of his neck, embarrassed. "I didn't really mean it. I was just upset and mad."

"Yes, well, it was still very hurtful," Eloise told him, sticking her nose in the air as if it didn't bother her.

Kyle could tell it had bothered her a lot. "Look, I'm sorry. I didn't mean to hurt your feelings."

"And I didn't mean to punch you or to be so rude when I found out you were here in my house. I was just surprised." Eloise told him honestly. "I haven't seen another person in years. And to know you could see me and hear me. I was shocked."

Kyle shook his head. "I can't imagine being all alone for that long. And staying in this house so long, it blows my mind." He paused and turned to look at her, raising a brow. "Why did you think you couldn't leave here?"

Eloise shrugged her slender bare shoulder. "I honestly don't know why I thought such a silly thing."

"Well, you aren't stuck here. You can leave any time you feel like it. Go anywhere you want. See the world if that is what you want to do." Kyle told her with a grin. "There is a whole world out there to explore."

Eloise shook her head. "I wouldn't know where to go or what to do."

"Well, where is some place you'd like to see?" Kyle asked her softly.

"I don't know, I have never thought about it. But now, I have so many questions." Eloise told Kyle with a frustrated sigh.

"I can try to answer some of your questions. I don't know if I can answer everything." Kyle told her honestly. The more he spoke to Eloise, the more he felt sorry for her.

"One thing I have wondered for years is, why didn't I go to heaven?" Eloise looked at her hands and spoke in a low, sad voice. "Did I do something wrong? I wasn't perfect, but I regularly attended church with my mama and papa. I wasn't always the kindest person, but I never hurt anyone. And I followed what the Bible and what the commandments said for us to do. So, why didn't I get into Heaven? Or is Heaven not real? Do all dead people become ghosts?"

Kyle laughed and shook his head. "Let's take this one question at a time. What do you say, Ella?"

Proper Southern Lady

"Why did you call me Ella?" Eloise asked him with a frown.

Kyle smiled down at her. "Well, you look more like an Ella than an Eloise. Especially all dolled up in that Cinderella-type gown. You could be a princess."

Ella smiled shyly as she tucked a curl behind her ear. "Thank you. No one has said such a nice thing to me in years." She laughed. "Well, more like a century and a half."

"Why don't we find someplace to sit and talk." Kyle offered with a smile. "We can't go to the D.O.H. until Monday away, so we are stuck here together for the weekend. We might as well make the best of it and get to know each other better."

"I suppose that is the best we can do. For now." Ella smiled at him. "But I'm sorry to say, there isn't much furniture left in the house. Only the things that remain in the attic."

"So, let's go up there for now," Kyle suggested. "Maybe later you can give me a grand tour of the place and tell me some of the history."

"I certainly can. My home has a plethora of history behind it." Ella told him proudly.

"It has a what of history?" Kyle frowned at her as he followed her to the attic.

Ella giggled, shaking her head and making her blonde wispy curls bounce. "A plethora of history. That means a whole lot of history."

Kyle felt his breath catch at the sound of her giggle. Damn, this woman was beautiful, and he was attracted. She wasn't at all the Karen-geist he had thought her to be. "Well, then, I am eager to hear it."

As they entered the attic, Kyle looked around. "What is all this stuff?"

Ella wrapped her arms around her slender waist, frowning as she looked at the items. "Like me, it's the forgotten things people have left behind."

Kyle shook his head. "I am sure no one meant to forget you. Maybe it was an oversight due to all the dead people they had to deal with at the time. Our country was at war, and thousands of people died during the Civil War." Stepping closer to her, he reached out and tucked a few wispy curls behind her ear. Then, he brushed his knuckles gently across her cheek. "How could anyone forget someone as beautiful as you, Ella?"

Ella leaned into his touch, revealing something she hadn't felt in so long she had nearly forgotten how it felt to be touched by someone else. "That is by far the sweetest thing anyone has ever said to me." She looked up at him with bright blue eyes filled with tears.

Kyle had the biggest urge to lean down and kiss her. But he didn't think she would react well if he did. She was old school, way old school, he thought, trying not to laugh at that. "Well, it's the truth." He spoke gruffly.

"Thank you, Kyle," Ella replied softly, then turned away. "I'm sorry, but I only have the old settee to sit on."

"There must be an old trunk or crate or something I can sit on. Let's look around." Kyle told her.

"There is, but it is over in the far corner," Ella told him with a frown.

"That will work." Kyle went over, found the chair, picked it up, and moved it across from the settee.

Ella stared at him in awed surprise. "How did you do that?"

"I picked it up and moved it." Kyle frowned at her.

"But how?" Ella demanded to know. "How come your hand didn't just pass through it?"

"Because I don't expect my hand to pass through it. I simply think about picking it up, then I do." Kyle told her with a grin.

"But you're a ghost!" Ella cried.

Kyle grimaced. "We are poltergeist, Ella, not ghosts."

"There is a difference?" Ella asked with a frown as she sat on the settee, spread her dress around her, then ensured her ankles were properly tucked back out of sight.

Kyle watched her and smirked. "I have never seen anyone make such a production out of sitting down before."

"I don't know what you mean." Ella frowned at him. "I sat down like any proper unwed lady would, sir."

"What does that mean exactly?" Kyle asked with a smirk.

"Well, a proper south lady will smooth the back of her gown to avoid wrinkles if she must sit. She spreads out her skirt to avoid wrinkles, especially when wearing silk or satin. She must make sure her ankles are well hidden from view because only an unchaste woman would ever show off her ankles, especially in front of a man she hardly knows. And I, sir, am no common strumpet."

Kyle wanted to hoot with laughter. Showing her ankles was indecent, but the tops of her breasts could show. What a backward society she had lived in. He thought, shaking his head. "Trust me, if your ankles show, they will be the last thing I'll notice." He winked at her.

POLITICALLY CORRECT

ELLA ROLLED HER EYES. "YOU WERE SAYING. WE ARE NOT ghosts? Then what pray tell, what are we exactly?"

"We are poltergeists, revenants, apparitions, or spirits. Not ghosts. That is kind of an offensive word. The word ghost makes you think of people running around in sheets draped over their heads with two eye holes cut out, making silly noises." Kyle told her. "Personally, I like the term revenant. However, poltergeist and spirits are the more preferred pronouns."

"I see. So, how exactly did we become spirits?" Ella asked, raising a brow. "Did we do something wrong?"

"No one really knows." Kyle shrugged. "Some revenants think it's because we have unfinished business. Like something we were supposed to do. Or longed for in life, but we died before we could do it." Kyle sighed, "And some think it aligns with the Norse idea of the afterlife. Only some go to Heaven, and we are in another part of the afterlife. Like the part for commoners. Or something." He winked at her, "But if this is the commoner part, I'll take it. We can travel the world and don't have to worry about paying taxes or bills."

"Do you have unfinished business?" Ella asked softly.

"Not that I remember," Kyle told her with a smile. "I would think if I did, I would remember."

"Do you remember dying?" Ella asked him quietly.

"Not really." Kyle shook his head. "How about you?"

"No, I remember the last day I left the house. Then I only remember waking up, hearing my mama crying and papa trying to console her. She was awfully upset. I tried to talk to her, but she couldn't hear or see me. For the longest time, I kept trying to talk to everyone. Finally, when they hung a black shroud over my portrait, I realized I must have died." Ella told him with a sad look. "How did you realize you were dead?"

"An agent of the D.P.R. came to see me and explained everything, then gave me a handbook that explained even more." Kyle shrugged. "He told me I needed to read it because it was essential. So, I figured I didn't have anything else to do. So, I sat down and read it."

"What did it say?" Ella asked curiously.

"Well, it explained that the living can't really see or hear us unless we exert a ton of energy. However, there are a select few who are able to connect with us, but no one knows why or how these people do it." Kyle explained. "The book talks about simple things like picking up objects and moving them. And other things we need to know about our new world around us and our afterlife."

"How do I get one of those books? There is so much I want to know." Ella bit her lower lip, then asked. "Is that how you knew you didn't have to stay where you died."

"Yes, but Dave, the guy that greeted me, explained a lot of it to me," Kyle told her and smiled. "We'll get you registered, and I am sure you will find out it's an oversight. They will make sure you get a copy of your own." Kyle couldn't imagine how they had missed her. But like he had said, a war was going on, and people were dying by the masses. "For now, I can be your guide, sort of, if you like."

Ella smiled brightly and clapped her hands, making her seem so young. "Oh, that is so exciting. To finally learn how to be a real ghost!"

Kyle raised a brow. "Revenant, or spirit. Remember, Ella, the word ghost is offensive to many of us."

"Oh posh, you know what I meant." Ella smiled at him and waved his words away. "And you hardly seem like the easily offended type."

"Well, I'm not, but you never know who is," Kyle warned her. "So, just try to remember to use one of those two words."

"I'll try." When he raised a brow at her, Ella waved him away. "I will, I promise." She looked at him eagerly. "Will you teach me how to pick things up?"

"Teach you? You mean you can't pick things up?" Kyle frowned at her. "Did you forget how to?"

"Well, no, at least I don't think I did." Ella frowned and looked down at her hands. "Maybe I did. I don't know."

"Okay, let's try something small." Kyle looked around and saw a children's book sitting on a shelf. Walking over, he picked it up and held it out for her. "Here, take this."

Ella reached out for it, and her hand passed right through it. "See, I can't!"

"Because you are making yourself go incorporeal." Kyle laughed softly.

"I beg your pardon. I am doing what?" Ella asked him, raising a brow.

"You are making yourself have no matter, no substance," Kyle explained.

"I don't understand." Ella shook her head.

Kyle studied her for a moment. "You said earlier that you didn't know we could touch each other. How do you enter a room if a door is closed?"

"Well, I don't. Because I cannot open doors." Ella rolled her eyes at him as if he were daft.

"So, there are rooms you haven't been inside of in years because the door is shut?" Kyle frowned at her.

"Well, yes. I have no way to get into them." Ella told him.

God, this girl was so totally mixed up. "Ella, we can make ourselves incorporeal, corporeal, or even semi-corporeal." He tried to explain.

"I don't understand." Ella shook her head.

How to be a
Poltergeist 101

Kyle pushed up from the chair and paced, trying to figure out how to explain this to her. Stopping, he looked at her. "Okay, so you understand what incorporeal means, right?"

"No, not really." Ella shook her head, frowning at him.

"God, I was never really good with science, I'm an artist." Kyle laughed, then looked around and picked up the small book again. "Every object from the living world has mass or substance. Like this book." He set the book down on the chair. "We, as revenants, can negate our mass because we actually have no bodies. We are energy. At least, that is how I understand it. A spirit is just energy." Kyle smiled at her. "Do you understand what I am saying?"

"No, I don't." Ella shook her head as she furrowed her brows.

Kyle thought for a minute about how to better explain it. Then grinned. "I'll show you!" He held out his hand to her. "Take me to a room you haven't been able to get into but want to." He nearly laughed when Ella reached out to take his hand, but hers passed through his.

The only thing that stopped him from laughing was the tingling sensation he got from her touching him. The woman didn't know she was doing precisely what he had tried to explain. "I guess just lead the way," Kyle suggested with a shrug.

Ella stood then, brushed out her skirt, and lifted the hem of her dress so that she would trip. Then, she left the attic with Kyle following her, shaking his head.

Lord, but the woman was mixed up and thoroughly confused. He wasn't even sure if he could help her get this down. But he was going to try his hardest.

"I wanted into this room since my papa shut and locked the door," Ella told him, sounding almost sad.

"Is there a key?" Kyle asked her with a frown. "Yes, my papa left one key inside the room and took the other with him when he and my mama were forced to leave the house," Ella explained. "But my mama didn't want anyone to be able to get inside this room. So my papa put a lock on this door and left the key on the vanity. Then, he took the other key with him."

"And no one has ever tried to open it?" Kyle frowned at her as they stopped outside a beautifully carved wooden mahogany door.

"A few have, but they usually get too scared to actually open it," Ella told him, shaking her head. Reaching up, she reached out a hand but stopped short of touching the wood completely.

"Well, can I unlock it from the other side with the key?" Kyle asked her.

"Yes, it should unlock from either side," Ella told him sadly.

"Alright, give me a minute to find the key and unlock the door," Kyle told her. Then he walked straight at the door and phased through it.

Ella gasped, then reached out and touched the solid surface. She pushed against it, but it wouldn't budge. "How did he do that?" she spoke in wonder. She could hear him moving around inside the room and frowned.

Kyle stepped through the door and paused. This room would be opulent if it wasn't for the dust and cobwebs. Fit for a princess. White sheets shrouded the dust-covered furniture, from what looked like a massive bed to an enormous armor and more. The walls were painted in what appeared to be a light shade of purple, the trim was gold, and a mural was painted on one wall. Kyle began looking under the sheets until he found the vanity, and just as Ella had said, there sat a metal key that had been painted gold.

Walking over to the lock, he quickly unlocked the door then called. "It should be unlocked now, Ella. Try opening it."

Ella reached for the door handle, but her hand passed through it. Over and over, she tried, growing more and more frustrated. Tears slipped down her cheeks. She wanted this part of her life back, and it was right in front of her. But like a cruel joke, it was just out of reach.

"Ella, open the door," Kyle told her again.

"I'm trying, but I can't!" Ella cried as she tried again and again.

Suddenly, Kyle appeared right next to her. Reaching out, he caught her hand in his. "Ella, stop."

"Why can't I open it?" she looked up at him with tears sliding down her cheeks.

The sight of those tears made his heart catch. Lifting Ella's hand to his lips, he kissed her fingers. "You can't open it because you believe you can't."

WHAT YOU BELIEVE!

"THAT IS THE SILLIEST THING I HAVE EVER HEARD," ELLA told him, shaking her head as she sniffed.

"Can you walk through the door like I did?" Kyle asked her, raising a brow in challenge.

"It is a door. Of course, I can't!" Ella told him with a deep frown.

"But you saw me do it," Kyle told her with a gentle smile as he fought not to laugh.

"Yes, but..." Ella started to argue, but he placed a finger over her lips.

"No, buts, Ella, if I can do it, so can you." Kyle took her hand in his before she could deny his words. "Can you feel that? Can you feel our hands touching?" He entwined their fingers. "If you aren't trying, it comes naturally. But if you think about it, you tell yourself you can't."

"Yes, I can feel you touching my hand." She smiled softly when he gently reached up, cupped her cheek, and ran his thumb over her cheekbone. "I can feel that as well."

"Keep your eyes closed." He lowered their hands, and Kyle touched their fingers to the doorknob. "Can you feel that?"

"Yes!" Ella spoke in wonder. "It's metal."

Kyle raised their hands and pulled their fingers apart but cupped his larger hand around hers. "Can you still feel my hand?"

"Yes, I can," Ella told him, then gasped as he lowered their hands again and wrapped their fingers around the doorknob. She smiled as he helped her turn the doorknob and open the door.

"Open your eyes, Ella," Kyle spoke softly near her ear, making her shiver.

Slowly, Ella opened her eyes then gasped. "Oh my lord, we did it." She turned and threw her arms around him and hugged him excitedly. "We did it! It's finally open!"

Kyle hugged her back. Damn, the feel of her pressed against him had him reacting with longing to kiss this woman and do oh so much more. "Yes, you did it." He smiled down at her. "Now, do you see what I am saying? You tell yourself you can't open the door or grab the object. But when you don't think about it and just do it, then it works. Like when you sit on that couch in the attic. You make yourself corporeal. But when you try to open the door, you tell yourself you can't and make yourself incorporeal, so your hand passes through the doorknob."

Ella shook her head. "So, you are saying I'm backward?"

Kyle laughed and shook his head. "No, just a little bit mixed up. But we'll get it straightened out if we work at it together."

Ella liked the idea of them working together. She was surprised at how much she was starting to like Kyle. He was as bad as she had first thought. "Thank you, Kyle."

"You're welcome, Scarlett," Kyle said with a teasing grin.

Ella rolled her blue eyes. "Why do you keep calling me that?"

"Because you are dressed kind of like Scarlett O'Hara from the movie 'Gone with the Wind,'" Kyle told her with a laugh.

"I don't know who this Scarlett is you keep referring to, or what a...what was it you said, is." Ella shook her head, frowning at him.

"Yeah, I guess all that is after your time," Kyle told her with a frown. "When my stuff gets here tomorrow. I'll show you what movies are and see if we can watch 'Gone With the Wind.' It's not my favorite movie, but you might like it." He told her with a shrug.

When she grew quiet after he talked about his things arriving the next day. Kyle decided to change the subject. "So, why is this room so important?"

Ella bit her lower lip and moved over to the vanity. Carefully, she pulled the sheet that was covering it off. Smiling softly, she ran her fingers over a little painted wooden box. When she tried to open it, her fingers passed right through it. "This is so frustrating." She stomped her foot, which only caused Kyle to smile.

"Why can't I do this?" Ella asked him, trying over and over.

"Tell me what this room is," Kyle asked her with a frown.

Ella took a deep breath. "This was my bedroom. It is where I died." Tears filled her eyes.

"Maybe that is your problem." Kyle strode over to stand behind her. "Let's try it together again." He slipped an arm around her waist and pulled her back against him as he covered her hand with his larger one. "Close your eyes, and just feel." He placed her small, delicate hand on the wooden box. "Can you feel that?"

"Yes," Ella whispered even as her heart began to pound in her chest, and she grew breathless from the feel of his large, hard body pressed against hers.

DAGNABBIT!

KYLE FELT HIS HEART POUND AT THE FEELING OF THIS woman pressed against him. "Ella, how old are you? Or were you?" He asked her softly, not releasing her.

Ella frowned in thought. "I had just turned eighteen the month before I died."

"Damn, you were barely more than a child." Kyle frowned in thought. "You barely got to live."

"I beg to differ. I was a full-grown woman. Betrothed and everything. I had a life, and I was getting married, at least until those damn Yankees interfered." Ella pulled away from him as anger filled her. She began to pace angrily back and forth. "When the war started, all the men were called to fight for and defend our way of life. So, Johnathan left with his brothers to help defend the South." She wrapped her arms around herself. "He died in one of the battles."

"I'm sorry. That must have been hard for you." Kyle told her softly.

"Of course, it was hard. Terribly hard, especially being forced to wear those awful black gowns. And not being able to attend any events for three whole months. That felt like forever. Land sakes, we weren't even married, yet my mama insisted I mourn like a proper lady. No less than three months." She rolled her beautiful blue eyes and sighed dramatically. "I was sure I would not survive it by the end of the first month."

Kyle bit his tongue. This girl was something else. "Okay, let's get back to what we were doing."

Ella walked over and tried to place her hand on the wooden box, but it slipped right through again. "Dagnabbit! Why won't this work."

Kyle couldn't help it as he started laughing.

Ella turned and glared at him with outrage on her face. "This is not a laughing matter, sir!"

"I'm not laughing because you can't do it." Kyle shook his head, "But your expression. You, a proper Southern lady, all but swore!"

"I did not! I would not!" Ella looked at him, horrified that he would suggest such a thing.

Damn, she was cute when she was frustrated. Kyle thought, smiling at her. The girl could be annoying as hell, but she was damn cute when she was annoyed and when she was super serious and biting her lip. "You did so when you said *dagnabbit*! By the way, this is not a word I have heard in years. I think it's been at least fifteen. My grandpa used to say it instead of God Damn it because my Gram would give him what for, for taking the lord's name in vain." Kyle laughed and shook his head.

"Oh, hush up with you." Ella waved him away. "You are not funny, sir."

Kyle got his mirth under control. "Alright, let's try it again. This time, try thinking about feeling the design on the lid."

Ella moved back over to the vanity and put her hand out, closing her eyes. Slowly, she lowered her hand to touch the jewelry box's top.

When she started to miss Kyle grabbed her wrist. "Going off course, Scarlett."

Ella suddenly felt the wood under her hand again. "I want to open it."

"So, feel for the lip on the lid, then open it," Kyle advised her softly with a grin. "See, there you go."

Music began to play, and Ella gasped. "I did it!" she turned and hugged Kyle excitedly, then blushed. "Well, I mean, we did it."

"No, Ella, you did it. I didn't touch it." Kyle told her with a grin. Reaching up, he tucked a lock of hair behind her ear. "I think you are getting the hang of this."

Kyle recognized the tinny tune as 'Fere Jacques.'

Ella swallowed nervously, then stepped back. "Perhaps." She shrugged a slender shoulder.

"The music box is beautiful. Tell me about it." Kyle urged her.

"My papa brought it back from France with him." She gave him a sad smile. "He gave it to my sister Emma as a gift for her sixteenth birthday." Biting her lip, she returned to the box and peered inside. With a shaky hand, she closed her eyes and began to reach inside. Then, she jumped slightly as she felt Kyle's hand over hers.

Kyle was sure she was after the locket inside the box as it looked like the only thing in it.

He grinned when she picked up the locket, opened her eyes, and looked at it. Carefully, she opened it and looked inside. Tears began sliding down her cheeks, and suddenly, the locket slipped through her fingers.

Quickly, Kyle caught it before it could hit the floor. "Got!" He said with a smile, then looked at the photos inside.

"Those are my sisters and my family," Ella told him sadly. "Emma, Elizabeth, and me. Then, of course, we were with our parents."

Kyle looked at the tiny photos. From her reaction to seeing the picture, he knew something terrible had happened to her sister. Carefully, he closed the locket. Then placed it back into the music box.

LEARNING NEW THINGS!

KYLE GRINNED AS ELLA PACED AROUND THE ROOM, annoyed and waving her hands in the air. "I did not agree with you about moving your things into my house." She snapped at him as the movers finished putting his things in the parlor. "I said you could stay here for the moment, not move into my house." Ella snapped at him. "This is highly inappropriate, sir!"

Kyle shook his head, "Well, it was already arranged, and besides, I am registered as the resident here, not you." He couldn't help but to tease her. "Maybe if you are nice to me, I'll let you stay."

"I beg your pardon? Allow me to stay?" Ella gasped in outrage then stomped her foot. "This is my house, not yours! You, sir, are trespassing upon my property!"

"Calm down, Scarlett. I was just teasing you." Kyle laughed and shook his head.

"Why must you insist on calling that? That is not my name, and you know as well!" Ella spoke through gritted teeth. "Infuriating Irish Yankee!" She spat those words and started to storm away, but Kyle grabbed her arm and pulled her back. "I'm just teasing you, Ella." He laughed, shaking his head.

"Well, it is not funny, in the least." Ella frowned at him, crossing her arms over her smile chest.

"I'm sorry if I upset you, Ella," Kyle told her softly. "How about I show you some cool things? I think you'll find this stuff truly amazing. The world has come a long way, baby, since you were last in it."

"Why on Earth would I want to see cold things. And how pray tell are you keeping them cold?" Ella frowned at him, confused.

Kyle threw back his head and laughed, really laughed, unlike he had in years. "Ella honey, you kill me."

Ella threw up her hands in frustration. "I cannot possibly kill you if you are already dead." She shook her head at him. This only caused Kyle to laugh harder. Damn, he could fall for a girl like her. One who annoyed him. Made him laugh and was downright beautiful. And Ella had all three things in the bag. "I didn't mean literally kill me, honey. That is just an expression. The same as cool. I didn't mean cold things. I meant..." He paused to search for a word she would understand. "Amazing things you have never seen before."

"Like what?" Ella frowned at him. "If it is like your loud box, then I would prefer not to see or hear them." She stuck her nose into the air. "It sounded awful and hurt my ears."

"You might find some things like that, but I think most of it, you will find amazing," Kyle told her, then took her hand and pulled her over to some of the boxes and crates. Quickly, he began opening them.

"This is a television," Kyle told her with a grin. "I was completely shocked that we could still watch T.V. and movies while dead." He waved his hand at the odd-looking thing, and Ella frowned.

"It is a what?" She bit her lower lip.

"Television, let's take it up to your bedroom and set it up since there is furniture in there." Kyle picked up the odd-looking square and carried it upstairs. "It will be easier to show you than try to explain it."

HALF AN HOUR LATER, KYLE SMILED. "OKAY, NOW IT'S TIME for the magic to begin."

"You can do magic?" Ella asked in awe from where she sat on the lounge he had moved to sit in so they could watch television.

Kyle shook his head. "No, it's another expression. As I explained, some words have taken on other meanings over the years."

"So, what does magic mean now, then?" Ella asked, eager to learn this new expression. Kyle seemed to know this ghost, oops, Poltergeist business really well. She thought with a smile. Plus, she loved these new expressions. Though she had heard him mutter a few while hooking up the thing he called a television that she was sure no proper Southern lady would utter.

"Well, I guess I would say something incredible, wonderous, unbelievable. That sort of thing." Kyle shrugged, then picked up the T.V. control and turned it on the box.

When the box lit up and images appeared on it, Ella gasped and reared back with wide eyes. "Oh my, how did those people get stuck in there? Are they trapped?" She looked at him, horrified. "This is terrible!" She spoke, beginning to sound distraught. "We need to help them."

Kyle quickly hurried over to her. "Ella, honey, they are trapped in there." He took her small hands in his larger ones and smiled at her. "They are perfectly fine." He assured her with a smile. "It is like photographs that move, and you can hear them talk." He stopped and thought for a moment. "Have you ever been to a play?"

Ella looked at him, confused. "Of course I have. I don't understand what that has to do with this?"

"You know how in a play, the actors pretend to be in a story?" Ella slowly nodded her head. So he continued. "Well, that is what they are doing, but it is like they took pictures of the actors, and those special pictures can move, and you can hear the things they are saying with those special moving pictures," Kyle explained to her carefully.

"Are they alive or dead like us?" Ella asked him with a frown.

"Well, it depends on the movie and actor or actress. Some are alive still, and some have died like us." Kyle explained to her.

"If they are dead, how are they taking those special pictures of them?" Ella asked curiously. "Are they making themselves capital?" She asked in wonder.

"You mean corporeal?" Kyle asked, and when he shook his head no, she looked more confused than ever. "Honey, these movies were made while those actors and actresses were alive," Kyle explained. "However, we do have Specter T.V. with stars... I mean actors who are dead. That takes way more explanation." He shook his head. "Let's get this down then we'll go on to more."

COUCH POTATO 101

ELLA QUICKLY GREW FASCINATED BY THE MOVIES. SHE watched, glued to the television, and asked questions occasionally. Kyle grew bored and began walking around the room, removing covers from the furniture. When he uncovered the beautiful four-poster bed, he whistled softly. The thing was huge and stood nearly waist high. He checked it to see if any rodents had taken up residence in the mattress. He was glad when he found it rodent-free. Even though he was dead, he still had an aversion to rodents. He had been like that since he was a child in Chicago. The back alleyways tended to have giant ones that had scared the hell out of him. Adjusting the pillows, he climbed onto the bed and laid back, tucking his hands behind his head. Oh yeah, this was the perfect place to lounge and watch T.V., he thought with a grin. "Hey Scarlett, why don't you come over here? It's way more comfortable." He called out to Ella.

"I...What?" Ella looked around and saw him lying on the bed, then shook her head. "No, I am fine right here."

"Suit yourself." Kyle lay there and watched the show. Before long, he noticed Ella's head slowly fall forward, then jerk back up as she fought to stay awake. Shaking his head, Kyle pushed off the bed, then walked over and scooped Ella off the lounge. He carried her over to the bed and laid her down.

Ella yawned, then shook her head. "I was fine. Why did you move me?"

"Because you were falling asleep, honey," Kyle told her. "Lay here and watch it, and if you fall asleep, you won't fall off the lounge and end up on the floor or in the basement." He said with a laugh as he teased her. When she didn't respond, Kyle looked at her and saw she was already fast asleep. Rolling onto his side, he studied her sleeping face. Damn, she truly was beautiful. Even in death, she was stunning with soft porcelain-colored skin, a sweet, heart-shaped face, and a cute, perfect little nose. When she was awake, he loved to see the fire in her China-blue eyes when she was pissed off at him. That was why he liked to tease and annoy her so much.

As he studied her, he realized that she was young, really young, and it made him feel like a pervert to even think about her in such a way. He had been in his thirties when he died. That made him far too old for this girl. And if he had found her in life, he would have never given her a second look. She was far too young for him. But then, his chances of meeting her had been slim in life. They came from two vastly different worlds. He doubted he would have made time for her back then if they had met. She would have most likely thought him to be a pompous asshole. Because he was. Looking back at his life, he regretted how he had treated people.

Kyle lay there looking at this beautiful girl and drifted off to sleep.

ELLA WOKE TO THE STRANGEST FEELING. THE FEELING OF something touching her almost wrapped entirely around her. Her eyes fluttered open, and she looked at her beautiful bedroom. What a strange dream she'd had. She had dreamed of being dead and meeting a dead man. She sighed as she looked at her familiar bedroom and felt relief wash over her. Thank goodness it had just been a horrible dream, she thought, then turned her head the other way, and a scream ripped from her throat.

Kyle woke with a start at the sound of an ear-piercing scream and jerked backward, then felt himself falling. He felt himself phase through the floor, then another, and finally land with a thud on a concrete floor.

The Ultimate Sin

Kyle lay on the concrete floor and looked up at the rafters above him. Thank God, he was already dead because, between her scream, which had nearly given him heart failure, and that fall, it would have killed him. He thought with a sardonic laugh as he shook his head.

Pushing up from the floor, Kyle brushed himself off, then looked around until he found a set of stairs. Slowly, he trudged up the stairs until he made it to the first floor, then began climbing to the second floor where Ella's bedroom was.

Ella lay in her bed, unsure what had happened. A man was lying beside her for one second, then disappeared. He was the man from her dream, or at least she thought he was, but he had disappeared so fast it was hard to say.

Climbing from the bed, Ella looked down at her gown, then looked around her room and spied the television. Kyle, it had been Kyle who was sleeping on the bed next to her. We'll next to her wasn't quite the word, more like wrapped around her. Holding her. Ella gasped. How had she gotten on the bed with him? And how had she ended up in his arms? Gasping, she covered her mouth as tears filled her eyes.

Walking over to the lounge, she sat down and buried her face in her hands as she began to cry.

Kyle walked into the bedroom and found Ella sobbing as if her heart was breaking. Hurrying over, Kyle knelt next to her. "Ella? Honey, are you okay?"

She shook her head and sobbed. "No!"

"What's wrong?" Kyle asked her, concerned.

"I... I... I know why I didn't go to heaven now!" Ella cried loudly.

"Why?" Kyle asked, confused.

"Because I am not a proper Christian woman!" Ella sobbed, shaking her head.

"Honey, I don't understand what you mean." Kyle shook his head, completely confused by her words.

Ella looked at him and sniffed. "I am no better than a strumpet, a... a harlot." She shook her head, upset.

Kyle was shocked at her words. "What makes you think that, sweetheart?" He asked and tried to soothe her.

"I am an unmarried young woman, and I laid with a man I am not married to." She wailed at him, horrified by her actions.

Kyle went to reply but then stopped and raised a brow. "Excuse me? You did what?"

"The Bible says it is a sin, a horrible sin, to lie with any man who is not your husband. And you are not my husband." Ella explained to him with her lower lip quivering.

Kyle fought not to roar with laughter. But he could genuinely see how young and innocent Ella truly was. Biting his lip, he fought for control and to keep from laughing. "Ella, honey, that is not what it means. What we did was not what the Bible means, honey."

Ella sniffed. "It's not? Are you sure?" she looked up at him with hopeful eyes.

"It's not. At all." Kyle assured her and blew out a breath as he ran a hand through his thick brown hair. "Do you know what sex is?"

She furrowed her brows at him. "What?"

Kyle frowned, trying to think what an aristocratic Southern Bell might know it as. God almighty, this was hard. "Let's try this way. Have you ever been kissed by a man or a boy?"

"Well..." Ella blushed and looked away.

"Okay, well, do you know what coupling is?" Kyle asked her, trying to explain this as delicately as possible.

"Is that one of those expressions you told me about?" Ella asked him with a frown.

"Well, kind of, yes. Coupling is when a man and woman make love. They perform the act of procreation." When she gave him a confused look, he pushed on. "The act of trying to make a baby. Do you know how people make babies?"

"Of course, a husband and wife lay together in a bed." She told him as if he was stupid. "It is why it's a sin to lay with a man who is not your husband."

"And what do they do when they lay together?" Kyle asked her gently.

"Well, they sleep." Suddenly, Ella looked horrified. "Ghosts can't have babies, can they?"

"What?" Kyle furrowed his brows, then shook his head. "No, of course not!"

"Oh, thank God." Ella let out a relieved sigh.

Kyle scrubbed a hand over his face. "Ella, laying with is an old expression for having sex with. When two people have sex. There is kissing, touching, and more involved. And there is nothing wrong with two grown-up people having sex. It is not a sin. Therefore, I am sure, you not going to heaven had nothing to do with you committing sins." Reaching out, he tucked one of her wispy curls behind her ear. "I think someone made a mistake. Because you are not a bad person."

FREEDOM

"Why don't we walk around for a few outside, and you can show me the property. Tell me about this place." Kyle suggested with a smile.

"Leave the house?" Ella asked with a squeak. Then she forced a smile. "Sure, why not." She gave a shrug of one slim shoulder. "I am not sure what has changed."

"So, let's go find out!" Kyle grabbed her hand and pulled her to her feet. "We can come back later and watch more television."

"But I was watching this. Can't it wait until after it?" Ella drug her feet. "It is an interesting play."

"Show, not a play." Kyle corrected her gently.

"Oh, yes, that is right." Ella laughed softly.

"Come on, let's go outside. It is a beautiful day." Kyle tugged at her hand to get her moving.

Ella reluctantly allowed him to tug her out of the room and down the stairs. As they neared the back door. She felt fear fill her. "Stop! Kyle, please stop!" she pulled backward.

Instantly, Kyle stopped and turned to look at her with a raised brow. "Ella, what's wrong?"

Shaking her head, she tugged her hand from his and wrapped her arms around her waist. "I can't," Ella told him, staring wide-eyed at the door.

"Can't what?" Kyle frowned at her.

Ella shook her head. "I can't go out there." She whispered with a sad look.

"Why not?" Kyle asked with irritation, lacing his voice.

"Be...Because... I'm scared." Ella looked at the door and bit her lower lip as fear filled her. She hadn't set one foot out of this house in over one hundred and fifty years. She wasn't even sure exactly what she was afraid of, but she was terrified. "I don't think I can do this, Kyle." She shook her head.

"You can. I promise nothing is going to happen to you." Kyle walked over and opened the door, then moved to the doorway and waited. "Look, I'm out here, and I am fine."

Ella shook her head. "What if I am really supposed to stay here? What if it's like my punishment or something, and that is why I have never seen anyone in all these years." She shook her head.

"Ella honey, I am telling you, there is no way you did anything to be punished for," Kyle told her gently.

"You don't know that for sure, Kyle!" Ella felt like crying again.

Kyle stepped over to her and cupped her face in his large hands. "I promise that's not true. Besides, I'm here, which ruins that theory, honey."

Ella jerked away from him. "What if you aren't even real? And I have finally lost my mind! Or what if you were sent to just tease me. Or... or you are here when you aren't supposed to be? Or it's a nightmare." She began to pace as she spoke.

Suddenly, Kyle grabbed her and pulled her against him. Then, as she gasped at his action, he cupped the back of her head and captured her lips in a searing kiss.

At first, Ella froze, but the feel of his hard, muscular body pressed against hers and the feel of his lips on hers made her body fill with a sensation unlike anything she had ever felt before. She heard a moan and suddenly realized it was her.

Kyle reveled at the taste of this young woman. He hadn't thought about it but reacted when he kissed her. She moaned and wrapped her arms around his neck as she started kissing him back. He pulled her tighter against him.

He continued to kiss her and distract her for several minutes. Damn, she tasted amazing and felt perfect pressed against him. Almost as if she had been made for him. Slowly, Kyle pulled back from their kiss and spoke again her lips as he brushed kisses across them. "Ella, honey, open your eyes."

Slowly, Ella pulled back with a dreamy sigh then opened her eyes. She blinked and frowned, realizing they were standing on the back veranda. "How? I don't understand... You tricked me?" She asked, horrified.

"Kind of, but it didn't start that way. I just wanted to show you that I am real and that you aren't dreaming or crazy. Then I realized you were so wrapped up in our kiss you didn't even realize when I picked you up and moved you through the door." Kyle told her with a laugh.

"Oh God, what if something had happened? What if..." Ella started to say, but he placed his fingers on her lips.

"Nope!" he shook his head. "Don't focus on any of that. Just on the fact that you are outside and free!"

MEMORY LANE

"COME ON, ELLA, COME WALK WITH ME." KYLE TOOK HER hand in his and tugged her to follow him.

Reluctantly, Ella followed him. They walked through what had once been a beautiful garden full of flowers. "This was once my momma's pride and joy, her flower garden. We would hold huge grand parties here on the plantation that would last an entire week. Every guest room would be filled, and people would come from all over to be a part of it." She pointed to what had once been a huge gazebo. "We would have dancing in there. And the scent of cooking food filled the air nearly day and night."

"Wow, that must have been amazing." Kyle shook his head in wonder.

"Yes and no," Ella told him with a smile and a shrug.

"What do you mean?" Kyle asked, furrowing his brows.

"Well, those parties, they weren't just for fun." She shook her head. "They were for men to gather and discuss business, and politics, that sort of thing, and for hopes of us young people, making decent matches."

"And if you didn't?" Kyle frowned as he asked, noticing a strange note in her voice.

"Then, our parents would arrange a match for us. No matter if we liked the person or not. Or how they treated you." Ella told him, then quickly changed the subject, giving him a fake bright smile. "Oh, but you should have seen the dresses. Papa used to ensure we had some of the finest gowns straight from Paris."

"You ordered clothes from Paris?" Kyle asked in surprise.

"Oh yes, a business partner of my papa's who lived in Paris would send Papa sketches of all the latest fashion to show us girls, then we would spend a whole week looking through them to decide on colors and materials to be used." She told him dramatically as they walked along. Lovingly, she brushed a hand down over her gown. "This was from the last time we were able to choose gowns. The gown I am wearing belonged to my sister Emma. This was one of her favorites."

"It's stunning," Kyle told her, looking her over.

"Emma looked better in it than I do. She was by far prettier than me." Ella replied, then bit her lower lip.

"I don't know how that is possible." Kyle shook his head. "You are beautiful, Ella."

"Oh, um, thank you," Ella spoke nervously as she fidgeted with a lock of her hair.

"You seem surprised to hear that." Kyle had seen the shock at his words in her expression. "Didn't you hear that often when you were alive?"

"No, not really." Ella shook her head, then shrugged her shoulder. "No one really noticed me until Emma died, that is."

"What do you mean?" Kyle frowned at the thought. How could no one notice this beautiful young woman? She was gorgeous, with her porcelain skin, pale blonde locks, and large China blue eyes.

"I... I would prefer not to discuss this." Ella spoke stiffly.

Kyle was a little shocked by the sadness and embarrassment he heard ringing in her voice. "Okay, let's go walk down by the water." He tugged at her hand to turn them in that direction.

They walked hand in hand for some time, in complete silence. Finally, Kyle broke it. "It must have been amazing growing up here. The place is beautiful, and there is so much space to move around."

"Summers were hot, but the rest of the year was perfect." Ella motioned toward a large open area. "Emma and I used to lay over yonder and stare at the stars for hours. I would lie there and listen to her tell me stories about the people and objects in the stars."

"You mean the constellations?" Kyle asked with a smile. "I'll bet you can see a billion stars from here!" He grew sad. "Chicago was always too bright to see many stars unless you used a telescope or went to the planetarium."

"I don't know what that is," Ella told him with a slight shrug. "I've never heard of a planny, whatever you called it."

"Well, you know what a telescope is?" Kyle asked her with a grin.

"Papa had one." Ella nodded as she thought of the one her father had when she was a child.

"Well, a planetarium has a giant telescope that can see way out into space. Past the moon and into the stars." Kyle told her as they walked along.

"And you can go look through them to see all that?" Ella asked curiously.

"Well, usually, it is on a big screen for everyone there to see. And sometimes, if there is a special event, they host whole gatherings."

"So, like your television?" Ella asked him excitedly.

"Yes, but the screens are usually bigger," Kyle told her. Then, she stopped walking as she seemed to freeze. "Ella, what's wrong."

"I...I...We need to go back to the house," she spoke the words, barely above a whisper.

"Why? What's wrong?" Kyle looked her over but saw nothing that seemed amiss.

"Please, I need to go back to the house!" Ella tugged at his hand. "I don't want to go any farther." Finally, she pulled her hand from his, then turned, picked up the skirt of her dress, and raced away from where Kyle stood, puzzled by her odd reaction.

THE CUTEST FACE

Kyle searched the house from top to bottom for Ella. He began worrying as the day grew late and turned toward twilight.

He was feeling a bit desperate when he remembered her talking about the dances in the old gazebo and how her eyes lit up. Kyle raced through the house and out into the garden. Stepping into the old structure, he paused as he looked around. At first, he didn't see her, but then he caught a glimpse of light blue material. Walking over to where he saw the material, he found her sound asleep in a corner. She must have cried herself to sleep from the look of her. Now, he really wanted to know what had made her so upset.

Carefully, Kyle scooped her up in his arms then took them both into the house. Carefully, he laid her down on her large bed and looked down at her, studying her. Damn, she truly was beautiful. But she was just so damn, young. He knew it was wrong for him to be attracted to her. But holy Hell, that kiss earlier, Kyle swore he felt it soul-deep.

Reaching out, he gently brushed a stray wisp of hair off her cheek. Carefully, he trailed his fingers over her silky skin. The urge to crawl into that bed with her and wrap his body around hers just to hold her was so strong. However, he thought he didn't relish the idea of falling, waking up, and hitting the basement floor again, and he fought not to laugh. Eloise Bellamy-Allard was turning out to be the oddest but most beautiful and fascinating woman he had ever met.

Deciding to let her sleep, he walked over to the lounge and settled in to watch T.V. quietly until he grew too tired to stay awake.

ELLA WOKE TO THE LOW MURMUR OF VOICES. SHE furrowed her brows as she looked around her bedroom in the gray morning light. How had she gotten to her bedroom? The last thing she remembered was running into the gazebo to hide so that she could cry in private. She didn't want Kyle to see her crying.

She didn't want him to think of her as pathetic or childish. Ella liked Kyle a lot! And he had not only kissed her and not hurt her, but he told her she was beautiful. Jonathan had never told her she was beautiful, and he had been mean to her and hurt her the two times he had kissed her. She didn't like how he had touched her. The memory of that sent a sick shiver down her spine.

Slowly, she sat up, looking around her bedroom. She saw Kyle sleeping on the lounge, which was too short for him. She would have laughed, but she didn't want to wake him, and she felt bad he was stuck sleeping there.

Quietly, she rose from her bed and moved across the room. She looked at the television and saw a movie playing, as Kyle had called it. Curious, she sat on the floor in front of the lounge and began watching it. Quickly, she got caught up in the story.

Kyle woke to the sound of a giggle and cracked his eyes open. He saw Ella sitting on the floor by him, trying to stifle her laughter. He assumed it was to keep from waking him. For a long time, he watched her. She looked so young and carefree. It only made him feel worse that he was interested in her. But there was just something about her that drew him.

"Hey, Scarlett, how long have you been awake?" Kyle teased her, trying to get a reaction out of her.

"Why do you insist on calling me that when you know perfectly well that is not my name?" Ella demanded to know. Why did this man have to be so handsome and annoying half the time? Why couldn't he just be handsome and sweet all the time?

"Because I know it annoys you, and when you are irritated, you scrunch up your nose, and you look so cute," Kyle told her honestly.

"I so do not scrunch up my nose!" Ella huffed out a breath in disgust. "You, sir, are makin' that up!"

"I am not!" Kyle sat up and shook his head, then reached over and ran his finger over the bridge of her nose. "It's right here!"

Ella quickly put her hand over her nose. "I do...not." She frowned as she realized she did indeed scrunch up her nose. "I shall try not to do so any longer. I apologize. I did not realize I was making a face. I shall attempt to be more lady-like in the future." She spoke primly.

Kyle sighed, running a hand through his hair. "I did not mean for you to stop, Ella. I think it is cute when you do it. I like it."

"But it is not lady-like to make faces." Ella shook her head.

"I don't care if you are lady-like or not, Ella. I like you just being yourself." Kyle told her honestly. He didn't want her to put on airs for him.

"I cannot be myself. Trust me, you would not like me." Ella spoke quietly and looked away from him.

"I highly doubt that, Ella." Kyle looked her over, then changed the subject. "Do you know what today is?"

Ella bit her lower lip and shook her head. "No, I don't even know what month or year it is."

LOST IN TIME

"WELL, IT IS MONDAY, SO WE CAN GO TO THE D.O.H. AND the D.P.R." Kyle gave her a bright smile, hoping the idea of straightening out this housing mess and finding out why she had never been registered after her death would excite her, but it seemed to have the opposite effect.

"That is great," Ella spoke in a tight strained voice, then pushed to her feet and paced the room.

"I would think you would be thrilled to get rid of me." Kyle gave her a bright, teasing smile.

Suddenly, Ella stopped. "I have been thinking. What if we don't go? What if we leave everything the way it is?"

"You mean, not notify them that you are here?" Kyle frowned at her.

"Well, yes. I mean, you and I seem to get on well enough. Why does anyone have to know I am here?" Ella spoke in a nervous rush. "I mean, will it truly change anything?" She asked in a high-pitched voice.

Kyle studied her for a long moment. "Well, maybe not. But I thought you wanted to know why you didn't get into Heaven. Maybe they will know. Plus, I thought you wanted to claim this house, and what if you decide you want to travel. And you need to learn the ins and outs of being a poltergeist."

"Does any of that truly matter?" Ella waved her hand around and paced nervously again.

Kyle pushed off the lounge, walked over to her, and caught her as she would have walked by him. Pulling her to him, he looked at her, then sighed when she lowered her eyes. He placed a finger under her chin and brought her gaze up to meet his. "Talk to me Ella, what's wrong?"

"W...what if I was supposed to go to, Hell?" She whispered the last word. Then, she licked her lips. "And why can't you just teach me to be a ghost? And can we just share the house? I don't want them to kick me out." Tears formed in her bright blue eyes as she looked up at him. "Where would I go? What would I do?" she whispered desperately.

"Oh honey, I won't let them do that to you. Trust me, I won't. I might not have been a very nice guy in life, but I promise I will take care of you." Kyle swore to her, feeling like a jerk for causing her so much worry. "If it comes down to it, I'll find someplace else to go."

"But... I don't want you to go." Ella whispered, wrapping her arms around herself. "I... I mean, I don't want to be here all alone again."

Her soft words touched his heart more than any other's had when he had been alive. "I promise everything will work out fine, honey." He attempted to reassure her. Kyle couldn't bring himself to tell her the truth.

ELLA FROWNED AS KYLE USED A LITTLE SQUARE THING, AND he pressed on it with his fingers, making it beep. Then, a solid wall section looked as if it changed to liquid. "What is that?"

"A portal to near where we need to go," Kyle explained patiently.

"A what?" Ella asked with a deep frown as she studied the wall with concern.

"A kind of doorway." Kyle took her hand in his. "Come on, we need to go through before it closes." He quickly tugged her through the liquid wall.

Ella gave a small shriek of shock. Then she stumbled onto a busy street that looked strange to her. She stared at all the people and things moving about around them. There was so much noise. "Where are we?" Ella looked around in shock, awe, and fear.

"New Orleans," Kyle told her with a grin.

"No, No! This isn't my home! My home doesn't look like this! What is all this?" Ella looked at all the things moving, as well as the people. This place was so crowded and noisy. "I want to go home. Please, I want to go home."

Kyle frowned. He hadn't thought about how much the world had changed in one hundred and sixty years, but looking at it from her perspective, he could understand her confusion and fear. "Ella, honey, look at me." He stepped in front of her, blocking her view, then he took her face in his hands. "Focus on me."

Ella looked at him with large, frightened eyes. "Please take me home."

"Just focus on me, and everything will be fine. I promise you'll get used to all this in time, honey." Kyle tucked back a lock of her blonde hair, then caressed her cheek softly. "A lot has changed since you were last out in the world. Just like the things I have shown you on television. I will try to explain anything you don't understand. Okay?"

Ella bit her lower lip, then slowly nodded her head. "Okay," she whispered the word to him.

"If something frightens you, just squeeze my hand, and I'll know you are having a hard time." Kyle caught her hand in his and gave it a light squeeze. "You'll get used to this in time."

"I'm sure you are correct." She took a deep breath and fought for calm.

A Strange New World

Walking down the sidewalk, Ella stared wide-eyed at everything, "Kyle, why is everyone dressed so strangely?"

Kyle smiled at her. "Because just like you told me, your father's friend would send sketches of the latest fashions from Paris. Clothing styles have changed considerably in the last one hundred and sixty years."

Ella stopped altogether and stared at a woman. "Is...Is that woman wearing trousers in public?" She spoke in awe.

"Yes, she is. Women can wear anything they want to now." Kyle told her, then he wondered what she would look like in modern clothing. *She would be stunning*, he thought with a smile. "We can go shopping after we visit the D.O.H. and see if we can find you some clothes that are a bit more modern. If you would like?"

"But I don't have any money," Ella told him with a frown.

"I can cover it, don't worry about it," Kyle assured her.

"You cannot pay for my garments. That would not be proper." Ella shook her head, sending her blonde ringlets bouncing.

Kyle wasn't sure how to explain to her that the world no longer held to those standards. "We'll talk about it later. Because we have reached our destination." He stopped them in front of a large plain looking building.

Ella looked at the building, then swallowed hard. She was still terrified that they would tell her she had to leave home. And if that happened, she didn't know what she would do.

Reluctantly, she allowed Kyle to lead her into the building and up to a front desk where an ashen, gaunt-looking man sat in front of an odd thing with a screen, much like Kyle's television, but far smaller.

"What can I do you folks for?" The man asked with a strange accent.

"Is Miss Baker available?" Kyle figured he would ask for and speak to the agent he had initially dealt with when he came to New Orleans looking for a residence.

"Hold on, let me see if Charlene is busy." The man reached over, picked up the phone, and dialed her extension. "Hey there, Char, got a couple of folks askin' to speak with ya. Are ya busy?" The man listened for a moment, then looked at Kyle and asked. "She wants to know who you are?"

"Tell her Kyle Sinclaire," Kyle told him, furrowing his brows.

"But Kyle, I thought...." Ella started to say, but he cut her off.

"I'll explain later, Ella." Kyle regretted coming here and that he hadn't taken her up on her offer just to stay in her home quietly together. But if he was going to be honest with himself, he knew he also wanted answers as to why this charming, beautiful young woman had not only been missed all this time but had been denied access to heaven. She would make the most beautiful angel ever. What had the higher powers that be have been thinking, he wondered.

"Oh, yeah, right away, Char." The man nodded his head as he spoke into the phone. When he hung up the phone, he looked at Kyle. "I'll take you to see Char right now."

"We appreciate it." Kyle nodded in thanks.

The man hopped up, then hurried around the desk. "Please follow me, Mr. Sinclaire."

They hurried over to an elevator that opened. Ella hesitated before stepping into the tiny looking room but squeezed Kyle's hand as he had told her to do.

When the doors slid closed, her grip tightened on his hand even more, and she made a soft sound. Quickly, Kyle pulled her to him and slipped his free arm around her, holding her close. Leaning down, he spoke softly in her ear. "Just close your eyes, honey, and imagine we are back at the house standing in your mother's garden, and it's beautiful again, just like you remember it being."

Ella nodded quickly, then buried her face against his chest as fear filled her. This tiny room seemed to move, and it made her uneasy.

As the small room came to a bouncing stop, Ella gave a squeak and gripped his shirt tighter.

"She okay?" The man asked, frowning at Ella.

"This is all a little strange for her," Kyle explained to the man as he slowly ran his hands over Ella's back to comfort her. He had to admit, at least to himself, that he liked the feel of her in his arms and that she sought comfort from him.

"What, she ain't never been in an elevator before?" The man snorted.

"In fact, she has not." Kyle snapped at the man, irritated that he was making light of Ella's obvious discomfort. "This is her first time."

"Shoot, who ain't been in an elevator in this day and age. When did the girl pass over?" The man eyed her clothing.

"A long time ago. But that is a whole different issue." Kyle informed him. "We need to speak to Miss Baker about an urgent matter."

"Char is waiting on ya, Mr. Sinclaire." The man assured them as he led them off the elevator and down a hallway. They stopped at the door, and the man knocked.

A pretty red-haired woman opened the door quickly. "Mr. Sinclaire, I didn't expect to see you here. Is there a problem with the property or the moving company?"

"Oh, there was definitely a problem with the property," Kyle told her with a frown as he tugged Ella into the room behind him. "Miss Baker, meet Eloise Bellamy-Allard, the property owner."

"What?" Charlene Baker squeaked. "That isn't possible. She must be some sort of squatter. That property has sat vacant for decades."

"Well, apparently it hasn't. Ella has been there since the day she crossed over in Eighteen-sixty-four." Kyle explained. "Which tells me that your department never checked the property like you should have."

"If she isn't registered, I can file paperwork and force her to leave the property immediately!" Charlene Baker narrowed her eyes at the younger woman.

What Could Go Wrong

Ella gasped, then tugged at Kyle's hand to make him release her. She had known this was a bad idea. Oh God, now, where would she go? Ella thought frantically as fear filled her.

"The hell you will!" Kyle snapped at Miss Baker firmly. "That is her house and needs to be registered as such."

"But Mr. Sinclaire, you..." Charlene started to say, but he cut her off.

"I know, but I want it listed in your system as her house," Kyle demanded.

"If she is in the system, that shouldn't be a problem." Charlene Baker told him demurely.

"We don't believe she is registered," Kyle informed her.

"What? That isn't possible. Let me check the DPR to see if she is there. What was your name?" The older redhead looked at Ella.

"Lady Eloise Bellamy-Allard." Ella told her.

Charlene tapped away at the keys on her computer, then frowned, shaking her head. "Is your name spelled E-l-i-o-s-e? Last name A-l-l-a-r-d?"

"Umm...yes," Ella replied hesitantly.

"This is odd. I have an Emily, an Elizabeth, and a Sarah, but nothing for you. I don't know how that is possible." Charlene frowned at her screen.

"Those are my sisters and my Momma," Ella spoke excitedly. "Do you know where they are?"

Charlene bit her lower lip. "Yes, they ascended."

"W...What does that mean?" Ella asked her hesitantly.

"They went to heaven, of course," Charlene told the younger woman.

"I'm glad," Ella told her in a small voice, but Kyle knew she was thinking the worst about herself.

Kyle stepped closer to her. Carefully, he pulled her to him. "Ella, stop thinking like that. I told you, it must have been a mistake."

"I...I don't want to talk about it, Kyle. I just want to go home." Ella shook her head and looked up at him with sadness shining in her eyes. "While I still have a home, that is." As she spoke, her lower lip quivered.

"Ella, I told you, I won't let anyone take your home from you," Kyle promised her. "But before we return home, we need to visit the DPR and talk to someone."

"I am contacting them now to find out why Miss Allard is not appearing in my system." Charlene frowned at her computer screen. When her computer pinged with a message, she read the message and scowled. "They are checking into it." She looked up at them. "In all my years doing this, I have never heard of an unregistered specter. I don't understand how no one knew."

"Well, as I said, she has been in her house since she crossed over," Kyle explained again.

"So, you never left your house?" Charlene looked at her in shock.

"Well, um, no. I didn't know I could." Ella shrugged her thin shoulders. "Not until Kyle came along last week."

"Oh, my stars, that is horrible!" Charlene stared at her wide-eyed. "You poor thing, no wonder you are dressed the way you are." She shook her head. "I will ensure this is fully investigated and dealt with."

"Good. Because Ella did nothing wrong, this mistake is solely on the DPR's end." Kyle snapped at her angrily.

"Oh, absolutely, Mr. Sinclaire. I am sure we can find an answer and come to a resolution that will satisfy everyone involved." Charlene Baker assured them. "I will not rest until I know this has been resolved. I might not be in the DPR, but I know all the right Specters to contact there."

"We appreciate your help, Miss Baker. Now, I think I will take Miss Bellamy-Allard to see a bit of this city." Kyle told the older woman.

"That is a marvelous idea. Perhaps, take her shopping and such." Miss Baker told him. "And I can see to it that the DPR helps reimburse you for any clothing cost."

"I'm sure I do not need that." Kyle frowned at the woman, who clearly knew he didn't need the reimbursement. "Come on, Ella, there is nothing more we can do today. Let's go look around the city."

Ella reluctantly took his hand and let him lead her from the woman's office and out of the building. "Kyle?"

"Yeah, honey?" Kyle asked as he led her down a sidewalk, looking for a clothing store.

"W... Why did you tell them your name was Sinclair? I thought it was Murphy?" Ella frowned at him.

"Can we talk about that when we get home?" Kyle glanced over at her. "Right now, I want to do some things for you. Spoil you a little, honey. You deserve it after everything you've been through."

"I suppose it can wait. But what do you mean spoil me?" Ella frowned at him.

Kyle found what he was looking for and grinned. "Come on, you'll see!"

Ghosts From the Past

Kyle tugged Ella into a shop and smiled. "Let's buy you some new clothes, then we'll get you a pedicure and a manicure. You'll love them both. I am told women truly enjoy them." Kyle grinned at her.

Looking around the shop Ella bit her lower lip, then shook her head as she reiterated. "I...I don't have any money, Kyle. How am I to pay for anything?"

Kyle winked at her. "Don't worry, beautiful, I have a platinum ghoul card. I have you covered."

"I don't know what that means, Kyle!" Ella felt frustrated as he spoke about things she had no clue about. Today had already been a trying day. Now, more than ever, she feared losing her home, and that woman Miss Baker had confirmed that her mother and sisters had gone to heaven, but she had been left behind. Ella wanted to go home, curl up in her bed, and be left alone.

Kyle saw the look on her face and could guess what she was thinking about. "Ella, come on. Don't think about any of that stuff." Reaching out, he cupped her cheek, then ran a thumb over her soft skin. "I promise you. You won't lose your home. I won't let that happen." Damn, he wanted to kiss her again so badly. But he held himself in check. "Let's get you some new things to wear, and let me spoil you a bit. It will make you feel better."

"But Kyle..." Ella began to argue, but the feel of his lips against hers made her words trail off.

Pulling back, he spoke softly, "Consider it all a gift. For your birthday, Christmas, whatever, but please, Ella, let me do this for you."

"Fine!" Ella gave in with a sigh, then looked around the shop. "I don't think they have any dresses or gowns."

Before Kyle could reply, a woman with long dark hair spoke in a loud voice. "Oh my God, is a costume party happening somewhere, or are they filming a new movie around here?"

"I don't know, we'd have to ask." Came a man's voice.

When the woman came hurrying over, she stopped and stared at Ella. "Oh my God, Weezie? Is that really you?"

Ella frowned at her. The woman looked familiar, but she couldn't place her. "Forgive me, but d... do I know you?"

"Well, I should say so. It's me, Georgia! You silly goose!" The woman lightly shoved Ella's shoulder. "We thought you had done ascended with the rest of your family. Wherever have you been hidin' yourself? Johnny and I were not fortunate enough to ascend."

"J...J...Johnny?" Ella raised a brow even as she felt sick to her stomach.

"Oh yes. Johnny! Come over here! You remember little Weezie, don't you?" Georgia called to a man across the shop.

Ella paled as the man came over, and she stared at him wide-eyed. "J...J...Johnathan?"

"Hey, Eloise, it's been a long time." He let his gaze roam over her.

"Um...y...yes, it has." Ella stuttered as she licked her suddenly dry lips.

"Why are you wearing that ratty old get-up? Is there something going on?" Georgia asked as she laughed and waved her hand at Ella.

Kyle could see that these two were upsetting Ella. He wasn't sure why, but he couldn't help but to feel protective of her.

"You look ridiculous, Weezie!" The woman laughed at Ella. "God, to think we used to be forced to dress like that! Isn't it ridiculous, Johnny?"

"It's something," Johnathan said as he stared at the tops of Ella's breasts, leering. "Where are you staying, Eloise?"

"I...I...um..." Ella stuttered once more, but Georgia cut her off, laughing loudly.

"Lord, you still stutter like an idiot. I would have thought you outgrew that long ago."

Kyle had heard enough. Grabbing a skimpy red dress off a rack, he stalked over to where Ella was standing with the couple. "Hey, beautiful, I found you the perfect dress." He threw the dress over the rack next to Ella, then slipped his arm around her waist and pulled her against him. Quickly, he captured her mouth in a searing kiss. As his hand cupped the back of her head. He felt her melt into him, and he was elated. When he finally pulled back from their kiss, he smiled as she stood there with a soft, dreamy expression. "Introduce me to your friends, sweetheart." He spoke softly to her.

Ella's eyes snapped open and met his. "Kyle." She whispered his name then smiled at him as she looked into his green gaze.

Kyle looked at the couple then said sternly, "Kyle Sinclair, and you are?"

"Like thee Kyle Sinclair?" The man furrowed his brows.

"Yes, that Kyle Sinclair," Kyle spoke harshly. He didn't like how this man looked at Ella in a predatory way. "So, how do you know, my beautiful Ella here?"

"Oh, we are old friends, and G.G. here is her cousin," Jonathan told him with a tight smile.

"I can't believe you would be dating our little Weezie here." Georgia gave a harsh bark of laughter.

Kyle could feel Ella stiffen at the woman's words. "I fell for Ella the moment I looked into her beautiful blue gaze." He didn't like this woman or her attitude toward Ella. "I knew right then that she was a special woman. I only wish I had met her when I was alive. But the divine had a different plan."

"Well, she did cross over more than a hundred years ago." Georgia gave a snort. "I'm surprised you didn't take off runnin' in the opposite direction the moment she opened her mouth."

Kyle felt Ella stiffen even more at the woman's words, then frowned as she pulled back and he watched her wrap her arms around herself as she ducked her head. He was curious about her reaction to these two people.

"You never did say where you were stayin', Eloise." Jonathan looked her over. "With your entire family having ascended, you are all alone." He gave her a wolfish smile.

"I...I...I'm s...s...staying at m...my house." Ella stuttered the words.

Kyle was puzzled by her reaction to these two people. This was not the tough, sassy Southern girl he had initially met. He was curious. "Speaking of home, we should finish shopping and head back home, sweetheart." Kyle caught Ella's hand and brought it to his lips, pressing them to her knuckles.

PITY LOOKS

ELLA LOOKED INTO KYLE'S EYES AND BLUSHED, THEN nodded but said nothing. God, she didn't want to sound like a simpleton around this man. But now he would look at her disgusted after hearing her stutter, like a fool. He would probably make fun of her like everyone else.

Kyle looked at the couple standing before them, then down into Ella's worried eyes. Reaching up, he softly stroked his fingers along her jawline. "Let's try on your new dress, then we'll grab a couple other things to go with it. What do you say, beautiful?"

Ella kept her mouth closed and merely nodded.

Kyle looked at the couple. "You'll have to excuse us. We have some things to do." With Ella's hand in his, he made to lead her away, then whipped back around as the other man reached out and roughly grabbed her arm, stopping her and making her cry out as he jerked her to a stop.

"Eloise, how do you even know him?" Johnathan demanded as he grabbed her.

Kyle glared at the man as he spoke in a low voice. Ella gave a soft whimper as she tugged at her arm. "Get your fucking hand off her right now." He didn't know what the deal was between Ella and this man, but he would be damned if he allowed him to hurt or bully her.

Johnathan looked at Kyle, then slowly released her.

"Don't ever touch her again. I mean it. Because I might not be able to kill you, but I know people who can and will do far worse to you." Kyle threatened the other man.

Johnathan frowned. "Fine, I'm not lookin' for any problems." He tugged his wrist from Kyle's grip even as he glared at the other man. "Come on, G, let's go!"

"But I didn't get my..." Georgia started to say, but he cut her off.

"We'll come back later!" Jonathan snapped at her.

"Fine!" Georgia spoke in a pouty voice.

Once the couple walked away, Kyle looked at Ella. "Let's find you a few new things."

Again, she said nothing but simply nodded. Kyle led her over to a rack of dresses. "Let's look through here and see if we can find you something you like, and we can look at jeans or other kinds of pants. Okay?"

Ella gave a quick nod of her head. Kyle sighed. "Ella? Honey, are you upset with me?" When she shook her head no, he frowned at her. "Then why won't you talk to me?"

"B...B...Because." Ella looked down at her hands as she spoke. "I... I'm embarrassed." She covered her face with her hands.

Kyle furrowed his brows. "What are you embarrassed about?"

"You heard them! W...what they said about me. Th...that I...I'm s...stupid." Ella let out a shuddering breath even as she blinked tears.

"You aren't stupid. They were idiots." Kyle growled the words low. Carefully, he reached up and cupped her soft cheek. "Ella, you are beautiful, smart and brave."

"No, I'm not any of those things." Ella tried to make him understand. "Th...th...they are...r...r...right." She told him sadly. "My whole life, everyone told me I was s...stupid."

Kyle had noticed her slight stutter when she seemed upset but had ignored it. But something about that couple had seriously upset Ella. Now, he wanted to know what. For now, he just wanted to finish their shopping and get back home.

"Let's get you trying on some of these clothes and see if we can find some things you like," Kyle suggested as he held up a white blouse and red skirt.

Ten minutes later, they were in the dressing room area. Ella stood in the tiny room and frowned, unsure what to do. She couldn't unfasten her gown and corset herself. So, how was she supposed to get out of them? She had no maid or servant to help her.

"Hey, are you okay in there?" Kyle tapped on the door as he spoke.

Ella bit her thumbnail, then sighed. "I...I, um.. have a little problem." She decided to be honest with him. Kyle seemed to be good at fixing problems.

"Do the clothes not fit?" Kyle was pretty sure he had picked the correct sizes. When she didn't answer, he sighed. "Talk to me, Ella."

"I...I can't get my gown and corset off by myself." Ella told him in a low voice.

TEMPTATION

Kyle sucked in a deep breath as those words washed over him. She needed him to help her remove her clothing? Damn, this was like every man's fantasy come true, but it was currently his worse nightmare. Because he was attracted to Ella, he wanted her more than he had ever wanted any woman, living or dead.

Swallowing hard, Kyle cleared his throat then asked. "What do you need help with exactly?"

Ella frowned. "I... n...need help to unlace my gown, a...and remove it. Then, unlace my corset and remove that as well."

Kyle looked around for a woman who could help but saw no one. Scrubbing a hand over his face, he sighed heavily. "Shit!" he spoke under his breath. *I can do this. I just have to try not to look at anything. Yep, then I will be fine.* Kyle assured himself. "Okay, we can do this. As long as you are okay with me helping you because I don't see anyone else who can help you."

"I...I suppose it is the only way." Ella frowned and wrung her hands. She jumped when Kyle stepped through the closed door.

Kyle looked at her stuffed in the small room, then joked. "Lord, you barely fit in here, Scarlett, with that big old dress." The bottom of her dress nearly filled the room.

Ella chewed on her thumb nervously. "M...Maybe we should forget this and go home."

She looked up at him from under her long lashes with those worried China blue eyes, and Kyle couldn't help thinking she was the most beautiful woman he had ever seen. *Damn, this is going to be complicated. But keep it impersonal, Sinclair.* He thought to himself. He had always been great at being impersonal in life, so he could do this in the afterlife.

"No worries. We got this, beautiful." Kyle assured her. "Now, turn around and let me see what I am working with."

Obediently, Ella turned around. To show him the laces in the back of her gown. "I can't untie or unlace it enough to get out of my gown. Can you get me out of it?"

Kyle swallowed hard. Damn, why did she have to phrase it that way? Fuck, he would love to strip her out of her gown and whatever she was wearing under it. His mind kept creating images of what he would like to do once he stripped her out of her clothing. He just prayed she wouldn't notice the erection he had going on. "Okay, I can say I have never helped a woman out of a dress like this. What am I supposed to do?" He studied the laces in the back of the dress. Slowly, he ran a finger down her back beside the closure.

"Y...You need to untuck the tie, then loosen the laces until we can pull the gown over my head." Ella explained to him quietly. "I will need you to do the same with my corset. You have to loosen the stays until I can remove the corset after you step back out of the room." She shivered at the feel of his fingers as they gently traced over the skin on her bare shoulder.

"Do you know how beautiful you are, Ella?" Kyle spoke the words in a low voice near her ear.

The feel of his breath brushing her ear made her shiver, even as her heart began to pound and her breath caught. No one had ever said anything like this to her. Only Kyle had ever told her she was beautiful. "Y...You don't mean that."

"I do, Ella. I know I shouldn't be thinking about you in such a way, but I can't help it. You captivate me, Scarlett." Kyle spoke quietly against the skin of her neck. Fuck, he wanted to taste her so badly.

"W...Why shouldn't you be thinking about me in such a way?" Ella asked him, frowning.

"Because you are so young, honey, and I am much older." Kyle softly brushed his lips against her neck and heard her quick gasp of breath.

Ella gave a soft laugh. "You aren't older than I am, Kyle."

"Sweetheart, I was almost forty when I passed over. So, now I would be almost fifty." Kyle tried to explain, but her snort of laughter had him frowning. "Why is that funny?"

"Kyle, I died one hundred and sixty years ago. So, I am way older than you are." Ella giggled softly.

Kyle frowned in thought. "I guess you're right. So, apparently, I have a thing for older women." He laughed softly. "I really want to make love to you, Ella."

Ella gasped and shook her head. "But you don't love me, Kyle. And we aren't married."

"We don't have to love each other or be married, Ella, to have sex." Kyle shook his head.

"That would be a sin, Kyle," Ella spoke on a gasp.

"What do you care at this point?" Kyle asked her, frustrated. "It's not like Heaven is waiting!"

Ella gasped, then whirled around to glare at him. "How could you say that?"

Kyle ran a hand through his hair, then scrubbed his hand over his face. "I'm sorry, Ella. I shouldn't have said that."

"I want to go home! Now!" Ella stomped her foot as anger surged through her.

"Ella, let's just try on the clothes, then we'll go home." Kyle tried to reason with her.

"No, I don't want your stupid clothes!" Ella spat at him, furious.

"Fine, then let's just go home for now." Kyle snapped at her. Grabbing her hand, he opened the dressing room door and saw several women. Staring at them. Kyle only wished that what they most likely thought had happened had indeed happened.

How did one deal with a raging hard-on when you lived in a house with no shower because specters didn't need to bathe like the living did. If this wasn't so uncomfortable, he'd laugh at the situation.

APOLOGIES

ELLA WOKE UP THE FOLLOWING DAY ALONE IN HER bedroom. She hadn't seen Kyle since they returned. Angry at his words, she hurried away from him, not wanting to talk to him, then paced for almost two hours in her bedroom. As she paced, she began to think about what he was saying. Kyle was right in a way. She wasn't getting into Heaven now. Ella knew she had missed her chance. So, why not enjoy her afterlife if she could? She didn't plan to get wild, but now she didn't have to worry so much about being a proper lady. And maybe that was why she hadn't gotten into Heaven since she had been so wild in her childhood years. Ella blew out a breath of frustration. Ella figured she would most likely never know the truth.

Sighing, she climbed from her bed and moved around the room. Something on her vanity drew her attention. Walking over, she looked at the stack of neatly folded clothes and the piece of folded paper lying on top.

Picking up the note, she opened it then frowned. How she wished she could read what it said.

Biting her lower lip, she made a decision. She would find Kyle and ask him to tell her what it said. Holding the note, she strode through the mansion, searching for Kyle.

When she couldn't find him in the house, she feared he had grown truly angry with her and left her. Sadness filled her. But she knew there was one place she hadn't looked. Outside! Walking to the door, she reached for the handle then pulled back. Fear filled her. "You've gone outside before, silly goose. And nothing happened." Oh, but how she wished Kyle was there to distract her by kissing her. The thought of Kyle filled her with determination. Striding over, she whipped open the door and gave a yelp of surprise.

There stood Kyle! Elation raced through her. "You didn't leave me!" Ella threw her arms around his neck, pulled him down, and kissed him.

Shocked, Kyle didn't pull away but fell into their kiss. He couldn't believe Ella was actually kissing him. When they finally pulled apart, he laid his forehead against hers and brushed kisses over her lips. "Does this mean I am forgiven?"

"Forgiven?" Ella raised a brow in question.

"Yeah, for being a jackass yesterday," Kyle spoke the words against her lips. "I'm so sorry for hurting your feelings, honey."

"Y...You were right, Kyle." Ella admitted hesitantly. "It's not like I still have a chance to get into Heaven now. So, what does it matter if I behave like a proper lady?"

"My momma was right when she told me I would never get into Heaven. But when Emma died, I just knew she would go to Heaven. And I wanted to be with her again so badly that I changed my ways. I tried so hard to do everything Emma always did. But Momma was right. Heaven only took beautiful, proper young ladies who weren't sinners." She reached up and wiped at her tears. "Heaven doesn't want s...stupid ugly girls like me." Ella pulled away from him and wrapped her arms around herself as she cried.

"Ella, oh honey, you are not stupid, and sure as hell aren't ugly." Kyle stepped over to her. "If you ascended right now, you would make all the other angels jealous. Do you know why?"

"No, why?" Ella asked him in a small, sad voice.

"Because you would be the prettiest angel up there." Kyle turned her around to face him. Placing a finger under her chin, he raised her face. Leaning down, he kissed her tears away.

Ella gave a small smile. "Thank you, Kyle. It is very nice of you to say such a thing."

"Do you think I am lying?" Kyle frowned at her.

"I know you are just being nice. And I appreciate it." Ella frowned and wiped at her tears.

"Well, that is the first time anyone has said that to me in a long time." Kyle shook his head.

"Said what?" Ella asked him curiously.

"Called me nice. That's not how most people described me when I was among the living." Kyle shook his head.

"Why not?" Ella was bewildered. How could anyone think Kyle wasn't nice? He had been so kind, patient, and gentle with her. Then, when they ran into Georgia and Johnathan, he protected her. No one besides Emma had ever cared about her.

"I wasn't the nicest man when I was among the living, Ella. I was too focused on making money and making a name for myself. I didn't really care about people and what happened to them." Kyle told her honestly.

"But you care about me, right?" Ella gave him an unsure look. "Or has it all been a lie?"

"I do care about you, Ella." Kyle smiled at her as he reached up and cupped her cheek. "I wish I had met you while living. You would have changed my life." Hell, he might have changed his life for this woman and actually had a life worth living.

"Will you do something for me, Kyle?" Ella asked him in a low, hesitant voice.

"Anything, honey, just name it," Kyle told her seriously.

She held up the piece of paper with his note written on it. Ella just hoped he wouldn't laugh at her. "Can you read this to me?"

Kyle took the note out of her hand. "You can't read?"

Ella looked away from him, embarrassed. Then, she shook her head. "No, I tried really hard to learn, but my momma said I just wasn't smart enough."

"I don't believe that, Ella." Kyle shook his head in disbelief.

"It doesn't matter. Can you just read this to me, please?" She asked him with a frown and held out the note again to him.

Something Special

Kyle took the note and sighed heavily. He didn't want to read aloud what he had written in the note. Because writing it had been hard, but now reading it to her would be harder. "I'll just tell you what it says." He ran a hand through his hair nervously. He had never been one for expressing his feelings. "Basically, it says. I'm sorry for being a jerk yesterday. I went and bought you some clothes and I hope you will accept them along with my apology."

"But Kyle, you were right." Ella spoke softly as she ducked her head shyly.

"Wait, what did you just say?" Kyle stopped and stared at her. "Did you, a woman, just say I was right?"

"You were." Ella told him honestly.

"Holy moly, it's a miracle!" Kyle teased her.

"I don't understand." Ella shook her head confused.

"You are a woman, and you admitted you were wrong and I was right!" Kyle laughed.

Ella rolled her eyes at him and smiled. "Now, you are just being silly."

"Hey, a man has to take his victories where he can with a woman."

Kyle winked at her. "Plus, my being silly made you smile, that beautiful smile of yours."

Ella blushed, tucking a wisp of hair behind her ear. " Do you really think, I am pretty? Or are you just saying that to make me feel better?"

"No, I don't think you are pretty. I think you are positively beautiful." Kyle smiled at her, then took her hand. "Come with me, I want to show you something." He began dragging her through the house, then up the stairs to her bedroom.

"This is my bed chamber, Kyle." Ella shook her head.

"Not the room silly." Kyle pulled her across the room, then stopped in front of an object covered by a sheet. He ripped the sheet off and smiled. "This!"

"A looking glass?" Ella frowned at the free standing mirror.

"No, not that." Kyle grabbed her hand again and tugged her forward, then spun her toward the glass. "This is what I want to show you."

Ella looked in the mirror and saw the room. "What am I looking at?"

Kyle wrapped his arms around her and pulled her back against him. "Watch." He breathed the word against her ear making her shiver.

Ella's eyes widened as she saw both her and Kyle's reflection appear in the mirror. "Oh my gosh how? How did you do this?"

"It's kind if hard to explain. But do you see what I mean? You are so beautiful, Ella."

She bit her lower lip as tears filled her blue eyes. "I look like Emma."

"No, honey, you look like Ella, and she is absolutely beautiful, smart, brave and unique." Kyle whispered those words against her ear. "Now, let's trying on your new clothes. Because as beautiful as this gown is, I think the new clothes will be far more comfortable."

"Okay, can you undo my stays?" Ella asked biting her lower lip.

"Absolutely, honey." Kyle quickly released her and stepped back determined not to react to the thought of undressing her this time. Swiftly he untied the laces, then began loosening the closure. Once, he had it lose he frowned. "I can't pull the string out of the holes, because it appears to be one big loop.

Ella laughed and shook her head. "That's because, that is what it is. So that the tie stays with the gown."

"So how do we get this off you?" Kyle frowned as he studied the closure. He was usually good at solving puzzles, but this one stumped him.

"Just pulled the sides apart as far as you can and remove the panel, then we need to pull it up over my head." Ella instructed him.

"Can't you just step out of it?" Kyle asked with a frown.

"No, it won't go over my petticoats and crinoline." Ella shook her head.

"Your what?" Kyle frowned deeper studying her gown that was now half open.

"My crinoline and petticoats." Ella told him, then sighed. "That is what is under the skirt of my gown."

"Can't we just lift part of you gown and untie it, then you step out of everything?" Kyle frowned at the dress. That would seem so much easier than trying to get all this satin material over your head." Also he wouldn't have to touch her or anything for very long. Because no matter what he told himself undressing her even in this fashion, made him yearn to strip her bare so that he could touch her and taste her. He wondered if sex in the after life was as good as sex in life?

TEMPTING THE DEVIL

FANTASTIC NOW, HIS MIND WAS BACK TO BEING STUCK ON the idea of having sex with her. "Let's try it my way, and if it doesn't work, we'll do it your way. What do you say?" Kyle suggested gently.

"I suppose it cannot hurt anything." Ella shrugged her shoulders. "But the ties are in the back, so you must lift my gown and petticoats up, then untie me," Ella told him with a frown. "I cannot possibly reach the ties."

"No sweat, I got this." Kyle was sure it couldn't be that hard. He lifted and bunched up what felt like ten yards of light blue satin, then began digging through layers of petticoats. Within moments, he grew frustrated. "Good God, how many layers of this stuff is on you, woman?"

"I don't know. I used to have a servant who helped me dress." Ella told him. "I just let her put the stuff on me, but my momma always picked my gowns."

"You have never dressed yourself?" Kyle looked at her in shock.

"No, my momma wouldn't allow it," Ella informed him as if this was normal.

"I can't imagine what that would be like." Kyle shook his head. Having been dictated to your whole life. To not have any choices in your life. "Well, now you are free to make choices, honey. You can wear whatever you want, whenever you want. Go where you choose, and do anything you want to do."

Ella bit her lower lip nervously. In some ways, that all sounded amazing, yet the notion of that many choices was overwhelming, to say the least. She had never made her own choices.

"What if I make a mistake or choose wrong?" Ella spoke in a worried voice.

"Then you learn from it. Ella, there is a whole world out there for you to discover." Kyle assured her gently as he finally found the ties to her petticoats. Once that was untied, he found the tie to her crinoline and unfastened it. "Okay, let's see if we can push these down and have you step out of them?"

Once those were removed. Lying in a pile around Ella's feet, Kyle quickly helped her push the silky gown off, leaving her standing in her corset and knickers.

"Good lord, woman, how did you ever use the bathroom with all this stuff on?" Kyle shook his head.

"The bathing room? Well, I didn't wear all this when I bathed, of course!" Ella laughed and shook her head.

"I mean the out-house or whatever you called it." Kyle shook his head.

"Oh, the water closet! A servant used to help me." Ella explained to him. "She would help to hold my dress out of the way. And my knickers are not sewn together."

"Wait! What did you just say?" Kyle grinned as he looked over the beautiful woman standing before him in a corset, a pair of Capri-type pants, and silk slippers. As Ella went to answer that, Kyle stopped her. "Nope, don't answer that!"

Ella's shoulders snagged. "D...Did I do s...something wrong?"

Kyle laughed. "Not in the least. This is all on me." God help him, but the thought of her wearing crotch-less underwear, basically, was more than he could handle. Already, he wanted her so bad his body burned with desire. He was fighting the urge to touch her more intimately and attempting to seduce her. Lord, it would take very little to push him over the edge. Seeing her dressed in only this corset had his body humming with need.

"Kyle, can I ask you a question?" Ella spoke softly as she stood there, biting her lower lip nervously.

"Anything, honey, go for it," Kyle told her with a grin.

"What is it like when a man and woman, you know..." She trailed off and ducked her head in embarrassment.

"When they have sex?" Kyle knew the last word came out in a husky voice.

"Umm... y...yes, that." Ella stuttered nervously.

Kyle blew out a breath and ran a hand through his thick black hair, then over his face. "Well, if it's done right, it is pleasurable for both the man and woman."

Ella closed her eyes and asked in a barely audible voice. "W...W... Would you have s..sex with me?"

THE SWEETEST TASTE

KYLE DIDN'T KNOW WHY, BUT HEARING THOSE WHISPERED words from her nearly brought him to his knees. Fuck, he would give anything to have her. But she was so innocent, and a part of him genuinely believed the higher powers had made a mistake and she belonged in heaven. How the hell was he supposed to resist this kind of temptation? He wouldn't have hesitated or cared if this had been him in the living world. But now? Now, death had changed him in so many ways. Now, things mattered. This beautiful woman before him mattered.

Ella felt a sinking feeling in her chest as he remained silent. Of course, he didn't want her. No one ever had. No one had ever really loved her except Emma. With a shaky hand and a quiver in her voice, Ella tucked a loose lock of hair behind her ear and shook her head slightly. "N...N...N...Never mind. F...F...F...Forget I asked." She turned away from him as she fought the tears that threatened to fall.

"Aww God, Ella. You don't understand what you are asking of me." Kyle shook his head. "Besides, you hardly know me."

"Y...Y...You d...d...don't have to explain. I understand you don't want me." She shook her head and started moving away from him, but forgot about the material around her and started to fall.

Instinctively, Kyle reached out and grabbed her, pulling her to him. The moment, her body came into contact with his, he felt all his good intentions fly out the windows. He looked down into her sad face and sword softly, then claimed her mouth in a hungry kiss.

Ella moaned softly into his mouth. She felt him lift her out of the tangle of clothing and knew she should stop Kyle from kissing her. She knew in her heart that he didn't honestly want her, but she just wanted this. The feelings this man created inside of her. Jonathan had never been able to make her feel this way. She had only ever been scared of him and disgusted by him and what he had done to her.

Kyle slid her down his body until she was on her feet, then pulled back long enough to command in a deep, growling voice. "Wrap your legs around my waist, baby."

Before she could reply, he scooped his hands under her butt and lifted her. Still lost in the euphoria of his kiss, Ella did as he commanded and wrapped her legs around his waist. She gasped into his mouth at the feel of him pressed against her intimately. The feeling of the hard wall against her back was uncomfortable, but she didn't care at that moment. All she cared about were the sensations this man was making her feel.

Kyle began moving against her soft feminine core and growled deeply in his throat. He was going to take her, but he feared once would never be enough with this angel. Pulling his mouth from hers, he kissed along her jaw and back by her ear. "Tell me you really want this, Ella. Please, honey."

"Yes, yes, Kyle, I really want this," Ella spoke breathlessly. "Please."

"Oh, Thank God!" Kyle spoke in a husky voice against her ear. He began kissing her neck, then worked his way down to the tops of her breasts. "I need to get this damned corset off you."

"Just loosen the stays," Ella instructed him with a soft moan of pleasure as he nipped at the top of one of her breasts.

Kyle began tugging at the strings on the back of her corset. When he felt something rip, he didn't care because he didn't plan to let her put all these ancient, old, torturous clothes back on. He would ensure she had more clothes than she knew what to do with. As the top of her corset came free, he nearly crowed in elation, but he was more interested in freeing her beautiful breasts. Tugging down on the edge of the binding, he growled low in his throat as one luscious breast popped free. Not even waiting to free the second one, he began kissing, licking, and suckling her perfect glob and reveled in her cries of delight. Damn, this wasn't nearly enough, he thought. Pulling his mouth from her breast, he looked at her. "I want to touch you, Ella." He wanted to hear her cries of passion as he pleasured her.

"Oh God, yes!" Ella begged him as her hands fisted in his dark hair and brought his mouth back to her breasts.

Carefully, Kyle slipped a hand between them and found the opening in her knickers between her legs. Damn, this was convenient. He barely thought until his fingers brushed over her already damp center. He slid a finger between her nether lips, finding her wet and eager. Gently, he slipped one long finger inside her tight sheath, even as his thumb found her tiny pearl and began stroking her.

Ella had never felt anything so amazing. She arched her back and cried out in pleasure at the sensation his touch was causing. Then she felt herself falling....

FOR THE REST OF THIS STORY, I INVITE YOU TO JOIN ME AND see what happens with Kyle and Ella!

You can find links to this story and more at Linktr.ee//Magickmoonink or on the website at www.Magickmoonink.com

ABOUT ANYA BAYNE

Anya Bayne grew up with a love of all things Spooky and Magickal. She is fond of all the monsters and legends. Her passion for History, Mythology, English, and Writing prepared her for a career as a full-time author. Now, with her faithful white wolf and the support of family and fans, she can live her dream of writing as a career. And she can bring those monsters to life with her words in the pages of her books!

Spectral Hunger

Aja Lace

Spectral Hunger

Aja Lace

Dedicated to my husband, my heart—my family, my soul—and my extraordinary editor, Kate Seger's shimmering ethereal heart.

Blurb for Spectral Hunger

When love vanishes, how far would you bend reality to bring it back?

Kandis disappears without a trace, shattering her girlfriend Sabina's world. Thrust into a mind-altering realm of shadows, magic, and questions, she must confront malevolent forces beyond her imagination. In a desperate race against time, she grapples with unspoken fears and discovers an untapped power within herself—one that could reunite them or twist their future into a nightmare.

When a jarring encounter illuminates a horrible secret, it cuts her to the marrow. Will devastation consume her, or can she rise to read the truths between the lines of lies? With each step, reality shifts, and nothing is as it seems, forcing her to question everything she knows about love, sacrifice, and the nature of her beliefs.

Dive into this chilling tale, where the line between the ordinary and supernatural blurs, a place where the power of love faces its ultimate test. And in a world where things are not always as they seem, Sabina must push beyond the boundaries within her mind to reshape their future—but at what cost?

ONE

KANDIS HAS THIS LAUGH—VIBRANT AND INFECTIOUS. IT bubbles up from deep within her, a pure sound that never fails to hook my lips and tug them into a smile, no matter how rough the day has been. At least, that's how it used to be. Nowadays, the echo of her laughter haunts the hollow spaces of our home, a ghostly reminder of better days. For the past three months, she's been different, so quiet and serious, a stark contrast to her vibrant personality. When I try to talk to her, she shuts me out, and it's so unlike her.

It makes me wonder what's going on with her. What's wrong with her? It seems like the change came out of nowhere, which makes it all the more baffling, and I don't know what to do. Why won't she talk to me? Standing in the kitchen, leaning against the smooth granite countertop, I sip on my steaming coffee before it has a chance to cool. It burns my tongue, but I don't care. Damn it, I do everything for her, and this is how she shows her appreciation?

I shake my head, and the half-finished canvas in the corner catches my attention. It's my latest piece, which I've been pouring my soul into. Why can't she understand how important this is to me? She's always trying to pull me away from my work after her hospital shifts, as if my art isn't just as demanding and vital as her job. Maybe if she were more supportive of my passion, we wouldn't be having these problems. Whatever.

The mug warms my hands, but not the chill seeping into my bones, and a shudder works through me. She's late. Not the 'caught in traffic' late or even the 'lost track of time' late. No, it's the 'should've been home over three hours ago' kind of late—the type that turns your anger into a puddle of worry in the desert, where all the parched, anxiety-riddled butterflies congregate in the heat of summer.

I call the hospital to see if maybe she's working overtime and forgot to call me, but my hopes are crushed by her coworker's words. "Sorry Sabina, looks like she clocked out on time."

Okay. Well, her shift ended at 6 am, and it's now 9:30 am. What. The. Hell. Kandis? Unlike me, she's always on time, so there's that.

Damn it. Trying hard not to freak out here. Sure, we've been having some problems, but I don't think things are so bad that she wouldn't come home, call, or at least send a text. Doubt creeps in, and I can't help but wonder if she's cheating on me. No. No. She's not like that. A drama queen, sure, but a cheater? No, that doesn't seem plausible. If there's one thing Kandis is good at, it's being loyal.

Sometimes, I find it comical the way she clings to me like a puppy dog—ever the faithful one. Other times, it feels downright annoying. Don't get me wrong, I love that she's into me, but it can be a little suffocating. Hence, the reason we've been fighting. Okay. Okay. I may have told her to stop being so clingy and let me have some time to myself. Hell, what can I say? My work-life balance is shit, and sometimes I get snappy. So shoot me. Besides, I don't see anything wrong with asking for some alone time. What's the big deal?

Feeling on edge, I run a hand through my hair. *Okay, you're not working late. So where the hell are you?* Light flashes from the screen as I swipe into my phone for the thousandth time. No messages. No missed calls. Did she come home, and I missed it? Maybe. I am a deep sleeper.

Sighing, I flick my gaze to the front door. Shit. The chain smiles at me, a dangling U still locked in place. And that means she never came home. Nope. Otherwise, I would've heard her pounding on the door to be let in. Damn it. Cracking my knuckles, I wrack my brain for an idea of anywhere else she might've gone. The sound of the clock ticking on the table burrows under my skin, making me contemplate kicking the stupid thing out the window. Whatever. Focus. I pinch the bridge of my nose, chewing the inside of my cheek. Maybe she stopped for breakfast or a coffee? No. No. Neither would take three hours. Hmm.

Two

As my stomach growls, I glance at the empty kitchen, and it reminds me of our breakfast routine, which now seems like a distant memory. Our apartment feels too quiet, void of her hummed tunes that used to mingle with the sizzle of eggs in the pan. I picture her dancing around in her pajamas, a wild mop of curly hair bouncing with each step. That image used to be my dawn. Now, it's just a wistful longing as I glance at her abandoned stool across the island.

I text her again, but the third message sits unanswered and glowing on my phone's screen. Rrr, it makes me want to scream. *Why won't you answer?* With each passing minute, her silence twists the knot of worry tighter in my belly, and I don't know what to do with myself. Trying my best to ignore the gnawing sensation of stomach acid threatening to etch its way up my throat, I turn on my computer and scroll through social media, but that doesn't last long. Stupid politics. Slamming my laptop shut, I stomp into the kitchen and warm up a frozen breakfast burrito.

THE DAY DRAGS ON, THE SKY SHIFTING FROM THE SOFT blush of dawn to a gloomy overcast. It's as if the weather resonates with the brewing storm inside me. What if she left me? No. No. I turn on the TV, trying to distract myself from the endless questions punching at my consciousness. But the talk show hosts and annoying commercials do nothing to ease my mind, so I tap the power button, and the queries continue assaulting me. Maybe she's punishing me for telling her I want space? Could be. By late afternoon, I'm pacing the length of our living room, phone pressed to my ear, calling all the local hospitals, friends, anyone who might have seen her.

Damn it, Kandis. Where are you? I call the police, and they put me on hold for five minutes. Unbelievable. After getting passed around the station a few times, I'm told they can't do anything because it hasn't been long enough. What a colossal waste of time. To them, she's an adult who probably stepped out for some air. But they don't know Kandis like I do. She wouldn't just leave. Would she? My stomach swirls, and I swallow hard. Ugh. I want to believe everything's okay with her, to believe she wouldn't just up and leave. But now, I'm not sure.

Sighing, my gaze bounces around the apartment, but nothing seems out of place or missing, except her. Everything feels wrong, yet it all looks right. Her tablet sits on the coffee table where she last used it to watch TikTok videos. And her plush-looking pink slippers rest at the foot of the couch. Yeah, no way those would still be here if she left me. But what if I don't really know her at all? The question sticks with me, twisting in my guts as the hours tick by.

Day drifts into evening, and I'm a screenshot of despair, curled up on our bed, inhaling the fading scent of her sweet perfume on the pillows. Sighing, my gaze drifts around the room, taking stock of her belongings, when something grabs my attention—her oversized heart-shaped locket on the dresser. My heartbeat thuds in my skull as I leap to my feet and retrieve the necklace. Wanting to feel close to her, I tug the chain over my head and huff back down on the bed.

What if she abandoned everything and is never coming back? The thought is too much to bear, so I pop a muscle relaxer and try to push the anxiety away. It's not long before I melt into the cushions and drift off to sleep.

After a few hours, I wake with a start. And that's when I feel it— the air shifts, charged with an energy that pricks at the hairs on the back of my neck. What the hell?

Sabina.

My name, a whisper, so soft it's almost swept away by the silence of the room. With my heart hammering against my ribs, I bolt upright.

THREE

Sabina.

Again, my name is in the air, gentle as a breeze. And there, in the dim glow of streetlights filtering through the blinds, stands my girlfriend—Kandis. But it's not really her. No. It's an ethereal version of her. Looking like a specter caught between realms, pale and translucent, she shimmers into full view, curves and all. This can't be real. Am I dreaming?

With desperation on her tongue, she murmurs, "Please, help me."

She sure sounds real. Whether or not I'm losing it is unclear. But I leap to my feet anyway, and a strangled gasp escapes my lips. "What— what's happening?"

Her form flickers along with her voice, and she sounds unstable. "I can't... took me. It's bad, so bad. You need to find..."

"Who took you? Find what?" Panic claws at my chest, a cold sweat breaking across my skin.

Suddenly, a train's horn blares through the night, and her figure wavers like a flame in the wind. When she opens her mouth, static surrounds her words. "Find the... follow... help me!"

Reaching for her, for anything solid, I lunge forward. "Please, don't go!"

My hands close on empty air, and she's gone, leaving nothing but the echo of her plea and a chill that sinks deep into my marrow. So, I do the only thing there is to do. I start looking, tearing through our room for anything out of place, any clue of what she could be talking about. When I stumble upon her journal, tucked away behind some clothes in the back of the closet, the first spark of hope flickers in me. But why did she hide it? The pages are filled with scribbled notes, strange entries, drawings, and a name that, for some unknown reason, makes me shudder. Probably because it's written over and over again. Nico Vale.

Anxiety settles over me like a wet blanket, making my muscles quake with the need to take action, and I grip the journal tight. What am I supposed to do? Call the police again? The thought feels ridiculous. No. No. They'll think I'm nuts.

After pacing myself into absolute exhaustion, I slide onto the sofa and stare at the wall. I have to do something. But what? What can I do? Those thoughts vibrate through me, shaking me to the core, but I'm helpless to come up with any answers. Somewhere around 10 pm, I nod off again, and that's when the dream takes me—a swirling vortex of shadows and whispers coiling around my consciousness.

Where am I? Wading through a thick fog, each step feels like molasses, but I push forward. The sound of a crow cawing fills the air, and somehow it seems like an ominous warning. Spinning around, I find nothing there except the shimmering darkness surrounding me.

As I take another step, my foot squelches against the soft, muddy ground, and clouds of steam float upward, similar to heat radiating from a hot spring. What the hell? Out of nowhere, Kandis's face appears in the puffs of murk, and then a brilliant white light blasts away the darkness.

With a pleading expression, she opens her mouth, her voice echoing through the air. "Do you know what's in a face? What's in a name? You have to know!"

I wake with a jolt, the familiar darkness of my room a stark contrast to the unknown world of my slumber. What was that? The afterimage of her desperate gaze lingers, a ghostly imprint burned onto my retinas. What did she mean? My breaths come in ragged bursts, and despite the chill in the air, I'm slick with sweat.

FOUR

AM I LOSING IT? MY MIND IS A MESS OF COBWEBS AND confusion, so I toss a throw pillow off the couch and then rub my eyes. Yep, I've lost my marbles, and none of this is real. No. No. Feeling beyond rattled, I try to shake the image of Kandis from my mind, and the world sways a bit. Oh yeah, the muscle relaxer.

A bit of relief spreads through me, and I run a hand along the shaved part of my head. Yeah, that's got to be it, probably a medication-induced hallucination or dream. But still, I can't stop thinking the incident has some kind of meaning. Hell, maybe it's my subconscious mind telling me something. Or maybe it's something more, a whisper from beyond. I shake my head, trying to dislodge the thought. I'm an artist, not a mystic. But then again, isn't art just another form of magic? Whatever. Trying to think it through, I chew my lip for a moment, and then it hits me.

The journal—I need to look at it again. Maybe I missed a detail in it somewhere, a crucial piece that might point me to her. My trembling hands flip through the pages, the scribbles dancing before my eyes until I settle on the last entry. Nico Vale is scrawled in cursive for the hundredth time. Shocker. Not.

Along with the name is an address, looking like it was etched into the paper with a heavy hand, as if she wanted it to stand out. Where is this place? In a flash, I punch it into Google Maps. Huh. A bar. Continuing my search, I tap in Nico Vale and scroll for a while, but nothing pops up. *Who is he, babe? A friend? An enemy?*

I rack my brain for any mention of him, but the name doesn't click with my memory. It's not like she's ever been good at telling me stuff about her life, though. Most of the time, she's a vault of secrets when it comes to talking about things before me, but I never want to press her. I know she had a rough upbringing, so it's always been a sensitive topic for her. What I've gathered over the years is that she grew up in a cult-like situation in the southern part of Utah, and it was super traumatic at times. So, yeah, I figured she'd talk to me about things when the time was right for her.

The clock's ticking is a relentless reminder that time is a luxury I don't have right now. Nope. I need to get to the bar before it closes. So I get dressed in haste, my movements robotic. Jeans. Hoodie. Sneakers. The essentials for a search. I pause only to grab my keys and phone.

The night is an abyss. The city's usual glow and the full moon's light are smothered by the clouds. Brr. As I step outside, the air bites at my exposed skin, but it's the worry gnawing at my insides that eats up the silence and spits out a buzzing sound.

I hop in my Toyota Tundra and head to the address scribbled in the journal—a rundown bar on the east side, the kind of place where secrets are currency and questions are met with looks of stone or a fist. It's a dive I've heard Kandis mention in passing, a footnote in her life that's now the headline of mine. The door groans on its hinges, a protest to the invasion of the outside world. But the bar's patrons don't bother looking up—they're ghosts in their own right, nursing drinks and drowning memories.

"Nico. Is there a Nico here?" The words come out with way more confidence than I feel.

This is so stupid. Shit. No one so much as glances up, so I raise my voice and repeat myself.

FIVE

My words rip through the tavern at a much higher decibel than I meant. This time, it's like I dropped a stone into a still pond, the ripples reaching out to touch every ear, but only one man reacts, his shoulders tensing just so. He's at the far end of the bar, cloaked in the dim light that doesn't quite reach him. As I approach, his features become clearer—sharp and dangerous, like they're cut from the dark. There's something familiar about him, an echo of Kandis's descriptions of people who 'just have the aura.'

Oh shit. It's more than just an aura. I recognize his profile from the drawing in her journal. At least, I think it's him.

"Nico?" I say again, and this time, he turns, his eyes locking onto mine with an intensity that pins me to the spot.

"What do you want?" His voice is smooth, the kind that could make lies sound like truth.

"Hi, uh. I'm Sabina, Kandis's partner and—" Before I finish, something unreadable shifts in his expression, and the words stick to my tongue.

He motions for me to sit, so I do, though every instinct screams to run. Irritation chases off the fear because I hate that feeling. Piss off fear.

As I slip into the seat, words spill out of me like Niagara Falls times ten. "I know we don't know each other, and uh, I don't know how you know Kandis, but uh, she's missing." Trying to slow my roll, I suck in a breath and run a hand over my face, but it doesn't help. "She didn't come home this morning, and that's not like her at all. And, uh, I found your name in her journal... like multiple times." He cocks his head, but doesn't say anything, so I continue. "And there was a picture, well, a drawing of you. Anyway, I don't know where she is, who you are, or what the hell is going on."

My words hang in the air for a few long seconds, and a part of me wants to tell him about the weird encounter with the Kandis-like apparition thing, but I stop myself there. Don't want to come off as a total lunatic. And hell no, I'm not admitting that a muscle relaxer caused me to have some trippy hypnogogic dream thing. No way. It wasn't real, so no point in bringing that up.

Something resembling curiosity sparkles in his deep-set eyes, and he leans back. "Missing, huh? I'll be damned. Well, this is a strange turn of events, but that seems about right for her." His rich tone floats through the room, reminding me of an echo, and I can't help but wonder why it sounds like he rehearsed those words.

And what the hell is he talking about, 'a strange turn of events that seems about right for her?' What does he know? My muscles tremble like they're begging to take action, but I do my best to ignore the hostile urges raging through me. This guy better start talking, or I'm going to freak the fuck out.

Pushing my anger to the side, I force a nod. "Yeah. I called the police and was told they can't do shit because it hasn't been long enough. Blah, blah." I suck in a breath, and more words rush out. "Whatever. I have to find her. So what do you know? And how do you know her?"

For a long moment, he gives me a blank stare and then sighs. "I'm sure you know Kandis has... depth. And you must realize there are things she keeps from everyone, even you." He taps his fingers on the counter, smiles and continues talking. "You think you know what love is?" His eyes gleam. "True love, the kind that changes worlds, demands more than you can imagine. It requires sacrifice and courage to face your deepest fears so you can protect the ones dearest to your heart."

Frustration vibrates through me, and I grit my teeth to keep from lashing out. What the hell is he going on about? I crack my knuckles, and questions burst out of me. "Who are you to her? And why the hell is your name and picture plastered all over her journal?" I press, but he shakes his head.

"It doesn't matter. And it's not my place to speak on this matter. But..." He pauses, searching my face. "I can give you a nudge in the right direction." A wicked-looking smile spreads up his face, and he leans back. "You don't know her as well as you think you do."

SIX

OH, GIVE ME A BREAK, REALLY, NICO? THAT'S THE BEST you can come up with? Heat creeps up my neck, prickling along my skin, and it's all I can do to not scream obscenities at this idiot. Ugh, I hate people. Willing myself not to freak out on him, I pinch the bridge of my nose and take in a slow breath. Cryptic words from a cryptic-ass man. Just great.

Guess I shouldn't expect anyone Kandis knows to actually communicate any better than her. Sigh. I glare at him. Can't help it. Yeah, maybe I have a little problem with my temper, but whatever.

My stare-down doesn't persuade him to spill the tea, and he just chuckles. A deep, resonant thing that works its way under my skin and makes me itch. So annoying. After downing his beer, he tugs a pen from his jacket pocket, scribbles something on a napkin, and then slides it across the counter—another stupid clue, another piece of the shit puzzle. It appears to be an address and a time.

"Be careful." His tone has a dark edge. A warning or a threat? I'm not sure. "Some truths can't be unlearned. And with that in mind, better hurry; you don't have much time." As his thick caterpillar brows crawl up his forehead, he taps the note.

I want to ask more, demand that he tell me everything, but the finality in his voice says the conversation is over. *Whatever, man.* Sighing, I leap to my feet and snatch the napkin off the counter. It's hard to suppress the groan in my throat, but somehow, I manage to. What the hell is wrong with people these days? Is it really that hard to answer a few questions? Apparently, it is for this guy. I've got to get out of here before I punch him in the throat.

"Thanks. I guess." What I want to say is, "Thanks for nothing, fuckface." But I restrain my tongue, along with the urge to roll my eyes.

Stepping back into the night, the cool air feels different now, charged with an electric touch of something I don't understand. As Nico's words circle in my brain, 'Some truths can't be unlearned,' a darkness sinks into my stomach, and I wonder what Kandis has gotten herself into. The city is almost silent, but my heart thunders in my chest, a storm waging war against the unknown—the chaotic rhythm of hope motivating me to figure this shit out—an unspoken promise that I'm not giving up. *Kandis, I'll find you.*

Hoping to burn off some of the violent urges rampaging around in my system, I stride down the road for a block. Okay, far enough. As a bit of calmness washes over me, I head back to my SUV and hop in. The address leads me to a part of town where the streetlights flicker, and the shadows stretch across the pavement like long, hungry cannibals of the light. It's the sort of place where you can feel a whisper tickling the back of your neck even when nothing's there but the shadows—the imaginary creatures of the night that creep along the road carrying secrets and warnings alike.

I pull my jacket tighter around me, as much to ward off the chill as to cloak myself in something that feels like armor. No, I'm not scared. Not at all. Lies. All lies. Guess what I should say is that I refuse to give in to the feeling—fear will not dominate my existence. My phone vibrates in my hand—another text from our friend Lila asking if there's any news. I type back a quick 'nothing yet' and slide the device back into my pocket. Probably should tell her what Nico said, and give her the address in case anything happens, but I don't want to deal with her histrionics. Yeah, Lila belongs in a Soap Opera, so let's just leave it at that.

SEVEN

THE BUILDING LOOMS BEFORE ME, LOOKING DERELICT AND draped in ivy that seems to hold the bricks together by sheer will, and I wonder how long it's been here. I'm grateful when the clouds dissipate because the moon is shining with full force tonight, and combined with the streetlight buzzing behind me, it feels like day. The number Nico gave me is etched into a metal placard bolted to the weathered wooden gate, the digits almost lost to rust and time. The place looks abandoned. Huh. My hand hovers over the handle, hesitation clinging to me like a bitter taste on the back of my tongue, and disturbing images fill my mind's eye.

What if a bunch of overgrown sewer rats are living in there or something even worse—like an evil presence seeking to possess a human. I draw a slow breath, puffing my cheeks out on the exhale, and somehow, it helps me rationalize my fears. *Stupid. That's stupid, Sabina.*

Kandis is the reckless type, so she'd barge on in. I need to stop freaking myself out and be more like her. Envisioning her strengths helps push me into action. My fingers graze the cold metal latch, flicking it up. And then, to avoid touching the wood, I toe the bottom corner of the gate until it swings open. Phew, disaster averted. Yeah,

I'm talking about splinters—they suck. The hinges groan, and somehow, it feels like a warning, but I'm not letting it stop me. Nope. It's not long before I'm opening the battered front door and stepping into the building.

Inside, the foyer is blanketed in darkness, except for the dappled light streaming in through the windows, but the moonbeams lose their battle against the shadows the further into the house I go. No rats so far, so that's good. A stairwell curls upward, inviting me to come explore, but it feels more like a dare. What is this place, and why did Nico send me here? Dust motes dance in the streaks of light before me, and I wave my hand through the air.

Hell, let's be real. The guy's a total stranger, so why the hell would I even come here? A cough bursts from my lungs, and I let it out. Nothing like choking on your own saliva. Back to the hair-brained idea of coming here on a whim. Well, what else could I do? It's not like the cops are helping look for Kandis, so never mind the whys.

The steps creak under my feet, a chorus of groans and whispers that scratch at my nerves. I tell myself it's just the old building, but somehow it seems ominous, like the house is screaming at me to leave. Maybe I should give up and go home. Fear shivers through me, and for a split second, I consider turning around. Wouldn't that be the smart thing to do? Instead, I swipe into my phone, flick on the flashlight app, and then continue creeping up the stairs.

At the top, the hallway stretches on, a narrow thing lined with closed doors. This place reminds me of an old hotel. Eerie. One room at the end of the hall captures my attention, the door gaping at me like a mouth frozen in mid-yawn, as if the ink-black darkness has been waiting a lifetime to swallow me whole.

I step forward anyway, fear be damned. Waving my phone around, the light spills into the room and pushes back against the creeping shadows, revealing a room that's a stark contrast to the dilapidation outside. It's clean, almost sterile, with furniture placed in a meticulous manner. Odd. Nothing seems out of place.

Suddenly, I catch a whiff of some Lily of the Valley perfume—it's Kandis's favorite. Sniff. Sniff. Sniff. I breathe the sweet, floral aroma in like a crime scene dog on the trail of death.

EIGHT

"KANDIS?" THE NAME FALLS FLAT IN THE STILL AIR, AN offering to the silence that somehow feels humiliating, and I groan.

This is so stupid! Of course, she isn't here. No one's here except me and my imagination. As soon as I think that, it almost feels like the room responds, the air growing heavier, the walls closing in. This is ridiculous. It's just my mind playing tricks on me. Sighing, I do my best to brush the strange sensations off and continue exploring. Oil paintings of women holding various types of flowers line the walls. Beautiful.

A dark, velvet-lined clawfoot bench rests beside a set of mahogany shelves. Well, that's strange. No vandalism or anything. How can all this stuff still be here if the place is abandoned? It's an unanswerable question, one that burns in the back of my mind with the heat of a blow torch, but I can't think about that right now.

Taking in my surroundings, I spin in a slow circle. A desk sits in the corner, with stacks of papers spread out across it in an organized fashion. Feeling curious, I step forward, and my phone light spills onto a shocking scene—a photograph of Kandis, her smile as luminous as ever—and a gasp rips out of me. It sounds more like a double gasp, and I almost choke again.

Beneath the picture is a note in handwriting I don't recognize: "Follow the firefly to the fen, where the water whispers and the reeds keep secrets."

Cryptic. Maddening. It's a riddle that scratches at the edge of my understanding, taunting me to continue with the promise of some magical revelation. What. The. Hell?

A floorboard creaks behind me, shattering the silence, and I spin around. Gasping, my heart leaps into my throat, but I find nothing there except the empty room and the unnerving feeling of being watched.

"Who's there?" My voice comes out sounding tough, but I can't suppress the tremble in my muscles, and the light vibrating from my phone gives me away.

The air shifts, a chilling current that makes goosebumps prickle along my skin, and I shudder. Something deep inside me is screaming that it's her again—the specter-like version of Kandis—the wannabe hallucination I blamed on a muscle relaxer. The idea that she might be visiting me here, in this strange place, is a presence that's both comforting and terrifying.

Her soft voice floats through the air, or maybe it's in my mind. I'm not sure. Either way, I go still.

Sabina, you're close.

It's her. At least, I think it's her. Regardless, the whisper is a thread pulling me forward, and whether or not I'm going to come undone all the way in the end is a conversation for another day.

"Close to what?" Good thing this isn't a library because the question comes out with more force than I intended.

One word vibrates through me. *Truth.* It's a breath on the back of my neck, and the room seems to exhale along with it.

What am I supposed to do? The photograph is begging for me to understand, to figure it all out in the blink of an eye, but none of this makes sense, and I'm way out of my element. Still, something tells me it's time to go, and so I do. Questions spiral around in my head, but one takes center stage. There are gazillions of fireflies around here, so how am I supposed to know which one to follow?

Stomping out of the building, the door clicks shut, and I stagger down the porch steps. Damn it. I'm losing it. Running my hands over the stubble on the back of my head, I wonder if it's time to check myself into the psych ward.

NINE

EVEN THOUGH IT SEEMS MY MARBLES HAVE BEEN scattered across a sea of despair, somehow, the night air feels less oppressive, the shadows less menacing. As if I'm being guided by an unseen force, a path lit up with whispers and dark glimpses of a world beyond my own. Yeah, I know that sounds bonkers.

In fact, maybe I'm not just losing it—maybe I've straight up lost it —like a drunk newbie gambler at a craps table. Maybe I bet my life savings against the odds, and the house won. Feeling dazed beyond comprehension, I stagger up to my SUV, still pondering what to do. Guess I'll travel to the place where land and water meet in a lover's embrace. Seems like a fitting place to start. It's close enough to get to, but far enough away to still feel untouched, a perfect hideaway. That's probably why all the high school kids go there to get frisky after prom. Anyway, it's a gorgeous lake on the outskirts of town, a camping spot filled with lore, where spirits are said to dance and sing their silent songs. It's where I first met Kandis.

She was partying with her friends by the water, dancing around, looking as wild and carefree as ever. And I was camping with some of my artsy friends, taking advantage of the quiet ambiance to work on one of my pieces. Well, I was trying to. But it was kind of hard to paint a still lake with her around. She was distracting, mesmerizing, really, and I watched her for half a day from our camp spot before getting the nerve up to go talk to her.

Wish she were here to talk to right now. Sighing, I rev the engine and make my way out of town, driving on habit more than anything, my mind drifting in and out of memories. After winding through the back roads, I find the secluded spot with no problems at all. It's as if it's only been a couple days since I last visited the lake, instead of many years. Time sure has a way of zooming by.

Feeling eager to look around, I hurry to park and then burst out of the vehicle. The reeds rise up like they're grasping for the stars; the ground beneath my feet is soft and yielding. Whoa. Swaths of fireflies hover around the edge of the lake, like eerie pulsing lights of marsh gas from the legends, and somehow, the flickering draws me in with its hypnotic rhythm.

Cupping my hands around my mouth, I suck in a deep breath and scream into the darkness. "Kandis!" But it's not in an expecting-an-answer kind of way—no, this is more like an I need to fill the silence kind of thing.

The light dances, retreating as I move forward, and somehow, it reminds me of a mirage that's just out of reach—always just out of reach. It looks so cool. Before I know it, a lone firefly bursts out of the pack and flutters right in front of my face. Gasp. Is this the one? When it moves, I move, and we inch forward. No way, this can't be the one.

Feeling a bit ridiculous, I shake my head. How about, no way this can't be happening? The thing zips in front of me once more, and I'm convinced. Whatever. A whisper floats into my mind again, but this time, it's my own voice. *You're losing it, stupid. Chasing bugs in the middle of the night.*

Shut up! Telling myself to shut up doesn't quite make me feel sane, but I do it a few more times, anyway. *Shut up! Shut up! Shut up!*

See, yelling at yourself is absolute proof that you're insane! Did you ever stop to consider that maybe you cracked up and killed Kandis? Hey, lightbulb moment here. Maybe you tied some bricks to her feet and tossed her into the la—

"Shut. Up!" The words rip out of me, slicing into the silent night like a sharp blade, but thankfully, it seems to do the trick.

My mind goes quiet. Phew. Thank goodness.

Sighing, I continue following the firefly, and now I'm beyond convinced this is the one—indoctrinated into the mystical firefly cult is more like it. It's leading me, or perhaps I'm chasing it. Either way, it feels meant to be.

TEN

THE WIND PICKS UP, BLOWING A LONG STRAND OF HAIR IN my vision, and I swipe it away. *Damn it. Stupid hair, stay out of my face.* It's times like these that make me regret not shaving my entire head. Oh well, it's another compromise I make for Kandis because she likes me best with long hair. Shave the underneath for me and leave the top long for her. Not my ideal hairstyle, but oh well. I do it for her.

A memory barges into my brain, and I'm transported back in time, chasing Kandis along this very path again. Her laughter fills the air, and I wonder if the breeze found a way to capture her essence—the sweet sounds that used to warm me. Now, it's both a calming presence and a ferocious sword, making me feel less alone, yet cutting me to pieces at the same time. A scream builds in my throat, but I do my best to strangle it. Ugh.

I can't do anything to stop the conflicting sensations spiraling through me. So I roll with the discomfort. Literally, but it's not on purpose. No, I trip over a rock, roll down a hill, and tumble off a small ledge headed right for the edge of the water. Shit.

With a yelp, I splash face-first into the wet peat. Ha. At least it was a soft landing. Chuckling, I pull myself upright and wipe the slicked hair from my face. For a moment, I gaze out across the dark water, feeling stunned, and then it hits me—my phone—my light source. Oh no. No. No. Please let it be back up there and not in the water. I shoot to my feet and crawl back up the hill like a swamp monster on a rampage. As I crest the top, a sigh escapes my lips because the phone is lighting up a patch of wilderness, so all is not lost. Phew. Thank goodness.

After scooping it up, I spin around in search of my little firefly friend, and it's not long before a lone flicker captures my attention again. Right on. Glad I didn't lose you either. As soon as my gaze lands on the flashing bug, it zips down over the hill where I just came from. Huh. Wondering what it's up to, I stumble toward the edge with squelching steps to take in my surroundings. The flickering light dances across the darkness, floating through the air as it zigzags toward the lake.

Suddenly, the fen opens up to me, a mirror of the night sky, and all the stars of the universe are reflecting off the still water. Gasp. The firefly continues to float into the distance, flickering in a way that taunts me to venture after it, and so I do. Feeling like I'm on the threshold of something important, something out of this world, my heart punches into my ribs, and I slide down into a sitting position. This is nuts. Ignoring my rational side, I scoot downhill on my butt, with the secrets of the unknown luring me forward. Stumbling up to the water, I pause to catch my breath.

"Show me." The words come out like a whisper to the night. Somehow, I hope they'll make it to Kandis, and she'll understand.

If not her, then maybe whatever magical energy or entity is dwelling in this place will hear me and respond in a helpful way. Even though it's outlandish—okay, ridiculous, but whatever—I'm still full of hope. What else can I cling to? Nothing.

As the firefly's light pulses, the water stirs, and I step forward, ready to plunge into the depths of darkness to find some answers—to find my love. The reeds part like curtains, and the path before me looks as clear as glass. This is it. I feel it in my heart that it's time to take a leap of faith. To trust in my instincts. *But you're losing it, remember?* Shut. Up. Refusing to listen, I stomp that voice down, before it can change my mind. This is the moment where a dream turns into liquid, and the flow becomes a revelation. At least, that's what I'm hoping for.

ELEVEN

THE FEN'S SURFACE RIPPLES LIKE IT'S BEEN WAITING JUST for me, ready to spill its guts, and that damn firefly keeps darting over the water, a silent siren luring me deeper into the heart of darkness. *Okay, little bug, I see you.* Of course, like an idiot, I follow it. My feet squelch with each step, the marshy ground threatening to swallow me whole. Fitting, right?

The reeds make soft noises around me, speaking some secret language of the night. And I strain to understand, to catch some meaning, some clue from their rustling speech. Bet they're whispering of hidden things, of sorrows drowned and truths buried.

Real cheerful stuff, I imagine.

"I'm here, babe." I try to sound brave as my voice echoes out into the void. "I'm here, and I'm not afraid."

Liar, liar, Speedos on fire. My heart's dancing like it's at a techno rave, a cocktail of adrenaline, doubts, and questions coursing through me. This is insane. Running a hand across the back of my head, stubbles prickling my fingertips, I contemplate giving up and going home. Because what the hell am I even doing out here? But I cling to the image of Kandis—my love, my other half—out there somewhere, needing me. My teeth sink into my bottom lip, and I shake my head.

Suddenly, the firefly stops, like it knows I've made up my mind and is agreeing with me. Thanks, little bug. I inch closer to the water's edge, peering into the murk. For a split second, something flashes below the surface—a strange glowing shape, too damn symmetrical to be natural. What the hell is that?

Before a rational thought can talk me out of it, I kick off my shoes and wade in. The water's embrace is terrifying and startling, like the last gasp before tumbling into a frozen lake. I do my best to ignore the unsettling feelings, mud sucking at my feet as if a billion hands are groping for purchase, trying to drag me down into the darkness. Sorry, not happening.

My hands slice through the water, searching for—well, for anything. And when my fingers brush something hard and cold, I latch onto it, yanking it free from the muck. What the...?

It's an oversized silver locket. Tarnished, yet so familiar. Whoa. I shake my head, trying to dislodge the thoughts crystalizing in my brain. It's Kandis's necklace. The one she took off and left on the dresser when we started fighting months ago. A gasp rips out of me, tearing through the night. Yep. No doubt in my mind.

Wait, didn't I put the locket on before falling asleep earlier? A gnat tries to land in my eye, but I swat it away. *Maybe I took it off in my drugged state.* I nod because it's the only thing that makes sense. *But how in the world did it get out here?* The question eats at me, but I have no answers. So I file it away for another time.

Unease swirls in my stomach, making me want to vomit. This is some unbelievable supernatural crap, that's for sure. Feeling like a lunatic, I struggle to keep from screaming, from crying, from running far away from here. But a memory stops me from doing all the above. An image of Kandis when I gave her this locket—her face lit up like a kid strolling through a candy factory. I lick my lips and shake the memory off.

Man, this is insane. Am I dreaming? My gaze slices through the darkness, searching for what, I don't know. Answers maybe? Something to tell me this is all a nightmare? Probably. But nothing happens. Beyond the buzzing bugs and crickets chirping in the distance, the night is quiet.

Of course, my brain isn't. No, it's busy pondering this absurd situation, and how her necklace ended up all the way out here. And most of all, I can't stop wondering how in the world I managed to stumble upon it—in the middle of the night. What the hell? I swallow hard. No big deal, a little bug led me to it.

Suddenly, a chill vibrates through me as memory surfaces. Something weird Kandis mentioned one day out of nowhere. She said, 'Sabi, sometimes I feel like there's a whole other world just beyond our reach.' I'd laughed it off then, but now... it makes me wonder. But only for a second, and then I scoff, casting my disbelief out into the night. Because this can't be real.

Even though it seems outlandish, well, beyond that really—it's insane—something still tells me this is all real. It's really happening. As if to punctuate the moment, the little firefly buzzes in front of the locket, calling my attention back to the curious thing. So, I flip it open with trembling fingers. And there she is, my girl, smiling up at me from a tiny photo of the two of us, framed by the locket's delicate edges. Wow, look at us. How happy we were. I sigh and continue examining the miniature picture.

Behind it, a tiny scrap of paper, folded and faded. I unfold it, the damn thing almost dissolving in my wet hands. The words are so small, but somehow, I manage to read them.

"Where water meets the willow's root, and the moon reveals the hidden path, you'll find the key to the locked door."

Great. A riddle within a riddle, served with a side of what-the-fuck. My mind's spinning, trying to make sense of it all. Willow's root? Moon's path? I tilt my head back, searching the ink-black sky for answers, but the moon is just a sliver, hiding behind a patch of clouds like it's scared of what it might find here, too.

TWELVE

I WADE BACK TO SHORE, CLOTHES CLINGING TO ME LIKE perspiration on a humid day. The locket's a dead weight in my fist, heavy with promises I'm not sure how to keep. I don't wait for the moon to show its face. Time's a river, and I'm caught in the rapids. But a piece of the riddle makes sense to me—the locked door part—it's in our apartment above the stairs.

To be honest, we tried to open the attic door in the past, albeit not very hard, just pushed on it with broom handles. But it never budged, so we figured it was painted shut or something and left it at that. Plus, it's positioned high above the staircase, which makes it a bit difficult and dangerous to reach. Guess it wasn't worth it to drag the ladder out, or maybe we just didn't want to risk falling. At one point, Kandis was super curious about it, but too nervous to climb the ladder, so she asked me to do it.

I told her no. Well, it was something along the lines of, "Babe, hell no. Not worth it. I guarantee there's nothing up there but insulation. So if you want to get fiberglass shards embedded under your skin, by all means, have at it."

I knew that last line would change her mind. Kandis is neurodivergent, and to say her tactile senses are heightened would be an understatement. Yeah, I guess it was a strategically timed statement on my part, meant to manipulate her so she'd leave me alone about it all. But whatever, it worked.

She grimaced and shook her head. "Ew. No thanks."

And that was that. Once in a while, she'd joke that the door was sealed by magic, and we'd laugh. Stupid, naive us. Now, I wonder if maybe she wasn't right.

Guess it's time to find out. So I sprint back to my vehicle, heart thudding in my skull, breaths ripping into my lungs in ragged spurts. Squealing the tires, I race home, making my way inside and up to the staircase.

The unopenable door is there, same as always, mocking me from above with its stupid, stubborn lock. This time, I'm determined to try harder to get to it, to get it open. Because something's telling me there's more than insulation behind it. So I drag out a ladder from the closet, the one I use to change the lightbulbs and dust the window sills perched up high.

Teetering on the rickety old thing, I examine the attic door. Huh. Strange. There's a familiar shape etched into the wood—an oversized heart—just like Kandis's locket. No way. I hold out the silver necklace, comparing it to the carving. Well, I'll be damned. Feeling like a total idiot, I press the locket against the wood. Half of me expects the door to laugh in my face.

But then a soft, unmistakable, clicking sound fills the air—along with my gasp—and the door swings open like some kind of creaking, spring-loaded trap door. My heartbeat drums inside my skull, but I do my best to ignore it and peek into the room. It's like stepping into another world. Dust motes dance in my phone light's beam, swirling in the air, twirling skin-flake specters in the night. I shine the light around, expecting to find nothing but insulation and more dust. But that's not the case, at all. No, it's an actual legit room.

Something catches my attention, a shimmer of gold, and I gasp. What the hell?

Thirteen

Paintings upon paintings line the walls, circling around the room. A couple dozen, for sure. All Kandis. But they're not simple portraits. No, they're something else. Something more. A gallery of multiple horrific moments, frozen in time, emotions captured within the oil-like screams scraped across the canvas. Haunting. But at the same time, they sparkle, making me wonder if there's some kind of magic in them.

Somehow, it feels like there's a secret here, a whispering of something inhuman, something inhumane. Perhaps it's something dark, something wicked hiding behind her silent scream—an obsession beyond reason—a thing with no up or down. I scramble around the attic, studying each portrait in great detail. Whoa. As my jaw drops, I swivel around, absorbing the view. Such masterpieces. Whoever did this, possesses a talent that puts my skills to shame. This is way past the point of impressive, it's damn near impossible.

In the center of the small room, an unfinished painting rests on an easel. It's Kandis, but wrong. Her gaze is hollow. The usual vibrant auroras swirling through her irises are muted, hiding behind an overcast sky. Her smile is gone, replaced by a twisted grimace—a scream made visible.

Reaching out, my hands tremble, and I touch her face. Part of me expects the canvas to be warm, to pulse with some kind of evil life. Nope. It's just paint and cloth. Still, the thing has a static electric charge, making goosebumps prickle along my skin.

And then, a soft noise drifts into my ears, and I still, tuning into the sound. A faint whisper that stirs the stagnant air. Feeling certain it's her, I whirl around, but she's not there. Just her voice, clinging to my heart.

Sabina.

"Babe?" Feels foolish, talking to myself, but I can't help it.

Another whisper vibrates through the air, a voice that sounds like goodbye.

"No!" The word rips from my throat, raw and desperate. "Not goodbye, damn it. I'm here. I'm still here."

Silence. Deeper than before. A void that swallows my words, my hope, my everything.

I sink to my knees before the easel, locket clutched in my fist, tears swimming in my vision. The paintings are silent voyeurs, privy to my failure—my inability to read between the lines, to understand the premise hiding in her eyes. Rrr. Irritation vibrates through me, and I grit my teeth.

Damn it. I know there's a story here in this stupid hidden room. But what the hell does it mean? A mixture of emotions washes over me, twisting in my stomach—feeling left out, lied to, but the biggest one is embarrassment for being clueless. Not sure what to think or do, I ball my fists, nails biting into my palms. Why would she hide all this from me?

A flicker of light captures my attention again. The unfinished painting, a contradiction of shadows and light—those hollow eyes shimmering in a way that seems impossible, making me feel like her heated gaze is burning right through me. Sucking in a breath, I crack my knuckles and shake my head.

"Did you come up here with some secret lover?" Heat flashes through me, kindling the suspicious part of me to life. "Let some other artist paint you?" The words seethe out of me, flames licking up my neck, and I glare at her painting. "What the hell did you start here, huh?" My fingers slip through my hair, balling at my scalp. "Whatever it was... whatever it is, this isn't how things end." I raise my voice, fire burning on my tongue. "This is bullshit. You don't get to disappear on me without a word."

I kick a box, and paint supplies scatter across the floor. Damn it. Okay, now I'm just acting unhinged.

"I'll figure it out, Kandis. I'll fill in the colors. And I will find you."

Not sure if that's a promise or a threat. Maybe it's both. Sucking in a breath, I do my best to calm down and think things through, but it doesn't work.

Fourteen

My breaths are shallow, ratcheting up my nerves, and it feels like my heart is stuttering. Shit. I can almost hear Kandis telling me to chill out. Fighting the urge to roll my eyes, I crack my neck, releasing some tension.

Still feeling wound up, I grit my teeth and pace the room, trying hard to mellow out. But it doesn't work, and heated words explode out of me, slashing into the silence. "Yeah. Yeah. I spazzed out again. So what?" Sighing, I gather up the paint supplies from my outburst and put them back in the battered box. "Doesn't change anything." I lower my voice, but violence is still simmering under the surface. "I still don't know where the hell you are."

And what am I supposed to do with that? The unknown is killing me, making me want to hurt someone. Somehow, I have to take a step back, study the situation from all angles. Find a different perspective and use it to get a clearer picture. Feels about right. Because that's what this is—a portrait of a disappearance.

So, maybe it's time to examine the shadows and light. After all, I am an artist. The clues are my palette, the riddle is my paintbrush. And I may not be a Picasso, like the creator of the portraits here, but it doesn't matter. What's important is for me to put the pieces together and find my girl.

This exhibition isn't over. I'm not done. Not by a long shot.

The attic air presses down on me, thick with unanswerable questions that stick to me like tree sap. I can't tear my eyes from the paintings, countless gazes staring back at me from all angles. Each one portraying another version of Kandis, frozen in time, emotions raw and on full display. What the hell? It's impossible to wrap my mind around this situation. Who would do this? I spin in circles, expecting to find some rogue stranger lurking in the shadows, holding a paintbrush and a can of paint—maybe even a machete or other threatening object. The air buzzes with something I can't quite understand, a hundred mosquitos just out of sight? I don't know.

What I do know is that confusion is scraping at my consciousness, digging for answers, and making me question my own sanity again. Kandis doesn't paint. I'm the artist here—the painter—it's what I do for a living. My fingers trace the edge of the unfinished painting resting on the easel. An unsettling hollowness radiates from her expression, and the smile splayed out on her heart-shaped face is all wrong. Creepy. It's like a stranger is wearing my girlfriend's skin. A chill skitters through me, leaving goosebumps in its wake, and I shudder.

"What were you mixed up in?" The question hangs in the air, unanswered. Of course it does. I'm talking to myself like a certifiable nutjob.

Leaning in, I examine the picture closer, focusing on the details in the brush strokes to get a feel for who this artist might be. There's something... strange here. It sinks into my marrow, haunting me, like an ache from a bad flu. And it's not just the unsettling factor of having a room full of secret portraits. No, it goes beyond that.

FIFTEEN

YEAH. I'M PRETTY SURE THERE'S SOMETHING OFF ABOUT this unfinished painting—something unsettling in the brushstrokes and colors. They're too vivid, too alive. Dark energy seems to radiate from them in waves, giving me the creeps and making a small part of me want to hide.

Of course, I'm not going to because that's just stupid. Not wanting to be a wimp, I stomp down the scared little kid inside me. The one who used to squeeze her eyes shut against the darkness as soon as the lights went out, huddling under the blanket hoping for morning—the young version of me that always believed a monster was under the bed.

I crack my knuckles, forcing myself to toughen up. Damn it. The only thing that abolishes fear is to stop feeding the beast, to stop believing in monsters. Okay. So that's what I have to focus on. Still, my forced bravado doesn't stop the nagging feeling that something magical is going on here. Duh. How else could I explain the locket? It's a war inside my head. Magical portraits are the only things that make sense. Well, there's always the losing my marbles thing. But whatever, I'm leaning toward the magic.

And isn't that what Kandis always said she loved about me? My ability to see beyond the ordinary, to believe in the impossible. 'You're my window to wonder,' she'd say. Well, I guess it's time to throw that window wide open. But it's not something that makes me happy, that's for sure. I may be able to see the aesthetic things as an artist, but can't say I've ever believed in mystical crap. No, that's Kandis's thing, not mine.

Great. My teeth sink into my bottom lip, and I run a hand through my hair, fingers snagging on a tangle. What's next? A talking lizard to guide me on my quest?

All humor aside, I can't shake this feeling of dread. The locket in my hand grows warmer, almost humming against my palm. Weird. I hold it up to one of the paintings—a portrait of Kandis laughing in a field of wildflowers. For a second, I swear the scent of fresh grass is wafting through the air, along with the echo of her laughter.

What in the actual hell?

Stumbling back, my heart pounding like a vampire is at my throat, I spin in circles again. This is insane. All of it. Kandis showing up in ghost form, the locket, clues, and this strange room full of freaky paintings. Ugh. I should call the cops again and tell them everything—

Yeah, right. They'll think I'm crazy. Nerves buzzing, I shake my head. Hell, maybe I am.

But the love of my life is missing. And whether or not I'm off my rocker, these paintings must mean something. I just have to figure out what, and where they came from. Yeah, I know that sounds ridiculous. But what else can I do? Sit around twiddling my thumbs? With a heavy sigh, I tilt my head back, studying the skylights.

Hmm. Maybe some weirdo was stalking her and got in through the windows, painting her from up here? Well, there is a ladder outside going to the roof, and our apartment is on the top floor. I tap my chin, trying hard to think this through. No that's stupid and sinking into paranoid, ultra-creep-festival material. Besides, the windows are way too small. *Yeah, get a grip. Stop. Feeding. The Beast. Remember?*

Hmm. My thoughts bounce back to wondering what else I can do —what normal, rational actions will help me find Kandis. Crap. She doesn't have any family that I know of to call, so not a lot of options to choose from on that front. Already spoke to Lila, her best friend, and she hasn't heard from her. So that circles me back to the things I've already done: called her work, the hospitals, and the worthless cops.

Trying to calm myself, I take a deep breath, puffing out my cheeks on the exhale. *Okay, Sabina, dust off your artist brain and get creative. Think. Think. Think.*

SIXTEEN

Hmm. I wonder what Kandis would do if she were in this situation? The sound of a dog barking in the distance catches my attention for a second, but then I tune it out and go back to my thoughts. Well, hell. That's a no-brainer. She'd dive in headfirst and embrace the weirdness.

Right. That's doable. I can be reckless and impulsive like her. For her.

I spin toward the paintings, studying them from all different angles. There's got to be a pattern, a message hidden in the images. My eyes dart from canvas to canvas, searching for... something. Anything.

And then I see it. In each painting, she's holding something. A book. A flower. A key. Objects that seem random at first, but upon closer inspection, it appears they're repeating. The same items, over and over, in different positions.

It's a code. I nod, hope spreading through me. It has to be.

As my brain scrambles to connect the dots, to make sense of it all, I grab my phone and snap pictures of each painting. My hands are trembling, but I force myself to be thorough. Never know, every detail could matter.

Click. Click. Click.

Huh, that's weird. At the last painting—the unfinished one on the easel—I pause. There's something strange about this one. The object in her hand is different from the other portraits, and it's not quite solid. Almost like the artist started to paint it and then changed their mind. Hmm. Weird.

Chewing my lip, I lean in closer, squinting in the dim light. And then something colossal registers in my brain. Faint pencil marks underneath the paint. A rough sketch of what the finished painting was supposed to look like. I scrape my thumbnail across the paint, and some of it flakes away, revealing a few words and an arrow pointing up at the lines.

Scrape. Scrape. Scrape.

More paint flakes chip away. My breath catches in my throat, and I cock my head. Because there, before my eyes, is a map. One that looks a lot like the walking trail looping around the woods—the place where I found the locket in the fen. No way. I drum my fingers on the easel and continue studying the canvas. It can't be from her. Oh, but it is. The words scribbled below the map are in Kandis's handwriting. No doubt in my mind. And the message is made out to me.

> *"Sabi, find the brush that fits your hand to paint the light within our love. Inside the locket, your creation shall dwell, just like the power in the crystals above. When time distorts in the land of dark, all will seem lost, but that's only the start. To see the end, you must open your heart, and that's how you'll know it's time to sting like a wasp."*

As much as I want to laugh and write all this off, something about her message feels important, ominous even. It's like a flashing neon sign warning of a crash up ahead, and there's no way I can ignore it.

"Oh, Kandis." My tone is soft, my voice cracking. "What's going on here?"

Find the brush that fits my hand? Hmm...

An idea comes to me, and I scramble over to the box of paint supplies, rifling through it to find a paintbrush that feels right in my hand. *This is nuts, but whatever.* After squirting some paint on a tray, I crack open the locket and pull out the small picture of us, flipping it over. Doing my best to channel the light in our love, I dip the edge of the brush into a blob of paint and tilt the thing, letting a few hairs whisper across the back of our miniature picture.

Yes. This feels like the right thing to do. Doing my best to capture the essence of my love for Kandis, I transfer those parts of my heart onto the tiny paper, delighting in the image as it manifests. And finally, when the piece of art satisfies the silent muse inside me, quieting my drive to paint, I place the tiny portrait back inside the locket, snapping it closed.

After cleaning the paintbrush, I toss it into the box and go back to studying the canvas. As my fingers trace the faint lines on the map, I'm almost certain the thing is depicting the same area as the fen. Whatever this is, wherever it leads, I know one thing for certain: If there's any chance to find her, I have to take it. Nodding, I run a hand through my hair, determination coursing through me. *Alright babe, guess I'm off to follow this stupid map.* For a second, I place my hand on the side of her face, soaking in her beauty.

Stepping back from her portrait is hard, but not impossible. So I spin around to study the attic one last time, my gaze darting about this weird shrine to my missing girlfriend. What a nightmare. Sighing, I climb down the ladder, my mind racing with possibilities.

A wave of exhaustion crashes into me as I drift through the living room. No time for sleep. I make a silent vow to keep going, no matter where the strange map takes me. Because damn it, she's out there somewhere, and I don't care what it takes—I will find her. Sighing, I crack my neck, the sound punctuating my thoughts. Even if I have to yank her from the paintings myself, she's coming home again.

The car keys clink together in my palm as I scoop them from the hook by the door. Something tells me a pep talk is in order. Alright, guess it's time to gear up. I suck in a breath and head out the door, feet thumping against the ground with each step. Yep, I've got a map to follow, and my future wife to find.

A faint smile spreads through me because she'd love to hear those words. Shit. Six years together. Is it time to bust one out and get off the pot? I don't know. After all this is over, and she's safe in my arms, maybe I'll finally get the nerve to propose. Maybe not. Guess I'll unpack that bag when I get to it. Either way, I'll love her the same. Nodding, I slip into the SUV, revving the engine. And to hell with anyone who tries to stop me.

Seventeen

THE DRIVE BACK TO THE WOODS IS A BLUR OF streetlights and racing thoughts. My hands grip the steering wheel so tight my knuckles are white, but I barely notice. The map from the painting is burned into my brain, a roadmap to... what? Answers? Kandis? Or just more questions?

I park at the edge of the woods, the same spot where that damn firefly found me. The trees loom ahead, a wall of darkness that seems to whisper, "Turn back, turn back." Fat chance.

Sighing, I grab my backpack—stuffed with a flashlight, water, and the locket—and plunge into the woods. The flashlight's beam cuts through the darkness, but it feels weak, pitiful against the vastness of the night.

"Alright, Kandis," I mutter, orienting myself from the map seared in my brain. "Where the hell are you taking me?"

The forest is alive with sounds—the rustle of leaves, the hoot of an owl, the snap of twigs under my feet. Each noise makes me jump, my nerves frayed and sparking like a live wire. Pushing deeper into the woods, I follow the path and it's slow going, the undergrowth thick and unforgiving. Branches claw at my face and arms, leaving stinging scratches. Ouch. Great. By the time this is over, it'll look like I lost a fight with a rosebush.

After what feels like hours of stumbling through the dark, I break through into a clearing. And there, in the center, stands a willow tree. Its branches sweep the ground, creating a curtain of leaves that sway back and forth in the night breeze.

"Where water meets the willow's root," I breathe, the words from the riddle coming back to me.

As I approach the tree, my heart punches into my ribcage, blood rushing in my ears. Funny, my breaths are so ragged and loud, I'm almost surprised they don't wake the whole forest. Damn, chill out body. The locket in my pocket pulses in time with my heartbeat, growing warmer with each step.

When I reach the base of the willow, something tells me this is the spot. A small pool of water, dark and still, is nestled between the roots. Yep. The moon, finally free from its shroud of clouds, casts a silver light over the scene.

"And the moon reveals the hidden path." The words are more breath than anything.

I crouch down, peering into the pool. At first, there's nothing but my reflection, distorted and wavering. But then—there. A glint of something beneath the surface.

Without hesitation, I plunge my hand into the icy water, goosebumps prickling along my skin. My fingers close around something solid, something that sends a jolt of electricity up my arm.

I jerk back, pulling the unknown object out, water streaming from my hand. It's a key. Old, ornate, and maybe even magical. Okay, I can't be ignorant. The thing is practically humming with something mystical, an unfamiliar, powerful energy, making the hairs on the back of my neck stand up.

"Okay." I nod, turning the thing over in my hand. "I've got the key. Now where's the damn door?"

As if in answer, a gust of wind whips through the clearing. The willow's branches part, revealing a sight that makes my jaw drop. There, carved into the trunk of the tree, is a door. A door with a keyhole that looks like it was made for the key in my hand. No way.

I'm slow to approach, half expecting the door to vanish like a mirage. But it remains solid, real, waiting. My hand trembles as I raise the key to the lock. This is it. Whatever's on the other side of this door has to be the next step to finding Kandis. Sure, it could be dangerous. It could be insane. But I don't care.

"I'm coming, babe." My voice is steady despite the twisting in my guts. "Whatever it takes."

I insert the key and turn. The lock clicks, a sound that seems to echo through the entire forest. Okay, that's weird. The door swings open, revealing a swirling vortex of light and shadow. Whoa.

Without letting myself think twice, I step through. The world spins, reality bends, and I'm falling. Falling, and falling, and falling...

Into what, I've no idea. The door slams shut behind me, and I'm engulfed in the unknown. *Shit, here goes nothing.*

Eighteen

The world stops spinning, and I land hard on my ass. *Smooth, Sabina. Real graceful.* I blink over and over, trying to clear the stars from my vision. *Where the hell am I?*

My vision is blurry, so I pat myself down, scanning my body for injuries. *Phew. All good.* As my eyes adjust, the view comes into focus. Is this some sort of... cavern? The walls shimmer with an otherworldly light, pulsing like a soft heartbeat. It's beautiful in a way that makes my skin crawl. Struggling to my feet, I brush off my jeans. The air here is thick, heavy with a scent I can't quite place. It's sweet, almost cloying, like rotting fruit.

"Kandis?" My voice echoes off the crystalline walls. No answer. Of course not. That would be too easy.

I take a tentative step forward, and the ground beneath my feet ripples like water. What the actual fuck? I freeze, heart pounding, waiting for the floor to open up and swallow me whole. But nothing happens.

Okay. Okay. I can do this. Just... don't think about it. I force myself to keep moving, each step sending waves of light pulsing through the floor. Wild. It's like walking on a giant mood ring.

The cavern stretches on, twisting and turning. Wandering, I lose track of time, the monotony broken only by the occasional shift in the light's color or intensity. Am I going in circles? Suddenly, a sound stops me in place. A voice. Faint, not much more than a whisper, but it's unmistakable.

"Sabina..."

I whirl around, searching for the source. "Kandis? Kandis, where are you?"

The voice comes again, stronger this time. "Sabina... help me..."

I break into a run, following the sound. The cavern blurs around me, the lights pulsing faster, matching the frantic beat of my heart. Rounding a corner, I skid to a halt. There, in the center of a large chamber, is Kandis. She's suspended in midair, surrounded by tendrils of darkness that writhe and twist like living smoke.

"Wait! Stay back!" Her voice is shrill, worry lines etching across her face.

"What the hell?" The words burst out of me, more gasp than anything, and I step forward. "What can I do?"

She shakes her head, a frown twisting her expression. "No. Get back. I'm... I'm not safe." The words hang in the air, a promise or a lie? It's hard to tell.

I don't trust her right now, and it's not just the shadow tendrils surrounding her. No. It's because she called for help, yet doesn't want it once I'm here. Why? Unsure of what to do, I wring my hands. Feels like a trick. I whirl around, thinking maybe someone's in the shadows, forcing her to refuse my help. But nope. No one's there. I turn to face her, confusion swirling in my mind.

I'm struggling to comprehend the scene, but it's way out in horror show territory. "What do you mean?" I can't wrap my mind around her declaration or anything about this nightmare situation.

More words rush out of her, stabbing into my chest. "Baby, I'm sorry. There's something you don't know about me...something I hid from you."

Suddenly, the shadow tendrils pry her mouth open, forcing their way down her throat. She chokes, and I gasp. What the...? For a split second, time seems to stretch out into the cosmos, and I'm too stunned to move. The sound of Kandis gagging on the stream of shadows flowing down her throat tugs me back, freeing me from my paralyzed state, and I lunge forward.

"Kandis!" As the scream tears out of me, an invisible force slams into me, knocking me back. Oof. I hit the ground hard, the air rushing from my lungs.

Her eyes flutter open, and they're completely black, like two bottomless pits sinking into her face. "Sabina." Her voice is distorted and wrong. "You shouldn't have come."

I push myself up, wincing at the pain in my ribs. "What are you talking about? I'm here to help you."

She laughs, a hollow sound that echoes through the chamber. "Help me? Oh, Sabina. You don't understand. There's no helping a creature of the night."

A creature of the night? I try to reason with her, or whatever the thing is that's wearing my girlfriend's face. "Babe, just come home with me. We can work this out."

"No!" Her voice—the thing's voice—tears through the cavern, ripping into my eardrums, and I wince. She smiles, a wicked, haunting thing, all teeth and malice. "Don't you see? I've never been more alive."

The tendrils of darkness ripple under her skin, spreading through her like an oil-slicked vascular system, etching lines and patterns across her body. As the strange shadows begin seeping from her fingertips, she shudders. Oh, shit. A look of ecstasy washes over her exotic features, and she throws her head back.

"Babe, what's happening to you?" My voice cracks, and I shake my head. "This isn't you. This isn't right." Now, I've no doubt in my mind this thing possessing her is pure evil.

She glares at me, a cruel smile twisting on her lips. "You're right. This isn't the Kandis you knew. I'm so much more now. And soon, you will be too."

The darkness surges forward, reaching me with grasping tendrils. No. I scramble backward, fumbling for something, anything to defend myself with.

My hand closes around the locket in my pocket. Shit. It burns hot against my palm, pulsing with a light that pushes back the encroaching shadows. Yes.

She hisses, recoiling from the light. For a moment, just a heartbeat, a flicker of my real girlfriend flashes in her eyes. Scared. Trapped.

"Fight it!" I hold the locket out like a shield. "I know you're in there. Fight!"

Looking wounded, her face contorts, and she clutches her head. "Sabi... I can't... it's too strong..."

The darkness slithers through the air, and then lashes out at me with violent speed. Everything and nothing slams into me, pushing me back a few feet. I dig my heels into the dirt, holding my ground, and my arms tremble under the force. As the thing tries to pull the locket from my grasp, the light gutters as if the shadows are trying to snuff it out, but I'm not giving up. Hell no.

For an unknown amount of time, I'm caught in a tug-of-war between light and dark, love and corruption, and there's no end in sight.

Gritting my teeth, I raise my voice. "I'm not giving up on you." Horror swirls through me, and I step into the pressure, pouring every ounce of my strength into the locket. "Do you hear me? I'm not letting you go!"

A deafening roar rips through the chamber—light and shadow collide. My gaze narrows, and I brace for... whatever the hell comes next. I know in my heart it won't be good, but one thing's for certain: either we'll leave here hand in hand, or we'll die trying.

Nineteen

The world explodes in a spectacle of light, like every color in the universe is painted in the air. I'm thrown backward, my head cracking against the crystalline floor. Stars burst behind my eyelids, and then darkness creeps into the edges of my vision. No. I can't black out. Not now. Not when I'm so close.

Forcing my eyes to stay open, I will the flashing dots to disappear. As they evaporate, all I can do is blink over and over. Blink. Blink. Blink. The smell of dust and smoke threatens to strangle my breath, and I cough. Still, the chamber is a war zone of swirling darkness and pulsing light. And in the center of it all is Kandis, her body arched back, an agonizing expression carved into her face as the two forces battle for control.

"Kandis!" My voice is ragged, throat raw. Struggling to my feet, the room sways, and I do my best to stomp down the despair. The locket burns white-hot, searing my palm, but I refuse to let go. It's the only weapon I've got.

Staggering forward, I fight against the maelstrom of energy that threatens to knock me off my feet. Each step is a battle, like balancing on a ball. But I push on.

Her eyes snap open, and for a second, they're normal. Terrified.

"Sabi." Her voice is a shriek. "Run. Please. I can't... I can't control them. They want me to feed."

"Bullshit." I shake my head, pushing forward. "I'm not going anywhere without you."

The darkness surges, wrapping around her like a cocoon. Oh no. Her face contorts, shifting from the Kandis I know and love to something... other. Something wicked and violent.

"You fool." Her voice is part hiss, part growl. "You have no idea what you're dealing with. This power is beyond anything you can imagine."

Kandis's message whispers in the back of my mind. *To see the end, you must open your heart, and that's when you'll know it's time to sting like a wasp.* Suddenly, a light bulb moment flashes through me, and I know what to do.

"Yeah?" Smirking, I step forward, raising the locket. "Well, imagine this."

Hope this helps. I rip the locket open, and a blast of pure, brilliant, blinding white light erupts from it, slamming into the darkness surrounding Kandis. The shadow creature shrieks, throwing its tendrils into the air, and I can't help but smile. Ha. The light ricochets around the room, eating away at the shadows like acid through metal. And as it carves a path straight to my girl, I lunge forward, my hand outstretched, reaching up to her.

"Babe, grab my hand."

For a heart-stopping moment, she looks frozen in time. But then, a scream tears from her throat, the horrifying sound rips through the cavern, like echoes of the dead, and she reaches out. Our fingers brush, then clasp together. The instant we touch, it's like a circuit completing. Energy surges between us, and the world goes white.

I'm falling again, tumbling through space and time. Flashing memories assault me—Kandis and I meeting for the first time, our first kiss, our first fight. But there are other memories, too, ones that aren't mine. Dark rituals in hidden places. Secret powers awakening. A hunger that can never be satisfied.

With a jolt, I'm back in the chamber. Kandis is in my arms, her body limp and trembling. The darkness is gone, leaving behind a silence so profound it rings in my ears.

"Babe?" The word comes out soft as a breath, and I brush a lock of hair from her face. "Babe, can you hear me?"

She stirs, her eyes fluttering open. Peeking out through thick lashes, her gaze is both bright and rich at the same time. Twin pools reflecting spring meadows—a liquid spectacle that captures all the light and sends a familiar swirl around her irises, making me sigh.

"Sabi?" Her tone is curious, face twisting with wonder. "What... what happened?"

A laugh bubbles out of me, the sound bordering on hysterical. "Good question. We definitely need to talk, but that's not important right now. What matters is you're okay. Are you?" I scan her body, checking for injuries.

She tries to sit up and grimaces. "Um... everything hurts. And I feel... different. Like there's something inside me that wasn't there before."

A chill vibrates through me, and I grit my teeth, trying not to wince. "We'll figure it out." Forcing confidence into my tone, I level my gaze on her. "We'll get through this, babe."

She nods, and then gasps. Eyes widening into saucers, she takes in our surroundings. "Um. Sabi... where are we?"

Before I can answer, a low rumble ripples through the chamber. Fissures spiderweb across the crystalline walls, and chunks of dirt from the ceiling rain down around us.

"Shit." I leap to my feet. "It's collapsing. We gotta go. Now."

I tug Kandis to her feet, and we stumble toward the exit, dodging falling debris. Oh no. The ground ahead is crumbling apart, revealing a yawning chasm of absolute darkness.

"There!" She stabs a finger in the air, pointing at a glimmer of moonlight peeking through a hole in the far wall.

Our ticket out. We make a mad dash for it, leaping over widening cracks and sliding under falling stalactites. Just as we reach the hole, a massive tremor rocks the cavern. Oh, shit! The ground gives way, sending us into free fall. Down. Down. Down.

My hand shoots out, grabbing onto the edge of the crack. Kandis dangles from my other arm, her grip white-knuckled, face a mask of desperation.

"Don't let go." The words sound rough as sandpaper, but so what? My focus is on more important things. Grunting, I try to pull us up, muscles screaming in protest.

"Wasn't planning on it." Her voice is sharp, and despite everything, a hint of amusement flashes on her face. There's my girl.

With a final, Herculean effort, I haul us through the crack and out into the cool night air. We collapse onto the soft grass, gasping and trembling as the sound of the cavern collapsing fades away. For a long moment, we just lie there, clinging to each other. I press my face into the nape of her neck, kissing her delicate skin, and breathing her in— the sweet scent of her Lily of the Valley perfume tickling my senses, making me feel at home. Then she turns to me, her gaze glistening with unshed tears and a thousand unasked questions.

"Sabi." Her tone is almost as delicate as her features, all rose petals and dandelions. "What do we do now?"

Sighing, I roll onto my back, gazing up at the star-filled sky, and then back at the woman I love. The woman I almost lost to... something. Something horrible and unfathomable. A thing so wicked and twisted it's unnamable—a monster so vicious and violent it belongs only in a nightmare. And the sad part is, the residual shadows flickering in my girl's gaze speak volumes that *it,* whatever *it* is, isn't over.

"Now?" Somehow, I manage a crooked smile. "Now we go home. And then... then we figure out what the hell just happened. And how to deal with it."

As her fingers lock with mine, I challenge the cosmos. Bring it on, universe. We've got this.

Right?

Twenty

The drive home is a blur of streetlights and silence. Kandis sits in the passenger seat, her face pale and drawn in the dashboard glow. Feeling half-afraid she'll disappear if I look away for too long, it's hard to stay focused on driving.

"Eyes on the road, Sabi." She runs a hand along my thigh, a ghost of a smile on her lips. "I'm not going anywhere."

I snort, tightening my grip on the steering wheel. "Yeah, well, excuse me for being a little paranoid after... everything."

The words hang between us, heavy with all the things we haven't said yet. All the questions we're both too scared to ask. But I'm fine with that, as long as she's by my side.

We pull up to our apartment, and for a moment, we just sit there, staring at the familiar building. Wow. A surreal feeling crashes into me, like none of this is real, but I shake it off.

"Home sweet home." I kill the engine and sink into her sparkling gaze. "Ready?"

Nodding, she takes a deep breath. "As I'll ever be."

As we make our way inside, I can't help but notice how Kandis hesitates at the threshold. It's almost like she doesn't recognize the place anymore. I grab her hand, squeezing it tight. She smiles, and some of the tension eases from her shoulders.

Once inside, the surroundings seem to overwhelm her. She wanders from room to room, touching things as if to reassure herself they're real. Not sure what to do or say, so I trail behind her, hoping she'll start talking. But I don't want to push her. And at the same time, I'm hoping she won't start talking. Because as much as my brain wants her to explain things, to be honest, my heart is terrified of what she might say.

Finally, she stops in front of the ladder that's resting under the gaping attic door.

With a questioning look, she flicks her chin up. "Shall we?"

Forcing a smile, I nod. "After you, beautiful."

She returns the smile, all pearls and grace. We climb up into the attic, new territory for us as a couple. Curious how she'll react to all the paintings, I position myself in a good spot to study her face. She takes in the room, gaze flicking over the paintings. Her paintings.

Stepping up to the unfinished painting on the easel, she runs her fingers along a canvas. "Kinda feels like I'm looking at someone else's memories. Like I was watching myself paint these, but it wasn't... me." She spins to face me, looking curious. "You ever feel like that when you paint?"

A chill runs down my spine, and I'm not sure what to think. But whoa, that was unexpected. Guess it's better than a rogue creeper. Still, something doesn't feel right.

I cock my head, my tone lilting at the end. "You painted them?" The thing hanging between us is eating at me, begging to be free, and I can't contain it any longer. I run a hand across the back of my shaved head. "Babe, what aren't you telling me? What are you hiding?" The words come out sharper than I intended, slicing through the air, and she winces.

Damn it. Once again, I let my anger get the best of me and snapped at her. As she wraps her arms around her body, guilt slips onto my shoulders, weighing me down. Why am I always such a jerk to her?

Willing myself to calm down, I suck in a breath and force

compassion into my words. "I'm sorry. Please, can you talk to me? I promise not to get mad."

Lies. All lies. But is a lie for the greater good still considered wrong? I don't know. Guess I'll have to unpack that later.

Looking vulnerable, tears swim in her eyes, but it doesn't stop the words from sighing out of her. "I don't know, Sabi. It started about a year ago. I spoke to you on the phone, and um... you were staying late at the studio to work on some piece. Grumpy as usual." She sucks in a breath and flicks her gaze around the room again.

With hesitation on her tongue, she continues. "Well... I guess... I uh... felt alone." Her lip quivers, and so does her voice. "I really wanted to be a part of your world. But you'd never let me in." Sighing, she seems to collect herself. "Suppose I was bored." As she pauses to scratch the side of her nose, dread fills me, along with a flush of jealousy.

"Yeah, I'm really not liking where this is going." My tone has a bite, but I can't help it.

She glares in my direction, but doesn't call me out, just shakes her head. "So, I pulled out the ladder and came up here."

The fire is still burning inside me, but it's down to campfire level instead of inferno. "How the hell did you get in?" I crack my knuckles, waiting for her to respond.

"Um... how do you think? The door." She laughs, the tinkling sound drifting across the room like bells on a breeze. "Pretty funny, it wasn't jammed or painted shut like we thought. Obviously. I made it up here." She shrugs, all casual like. "Suppose it just needed a good push."

Huh. Well, that's just strange. Something doesn't add up. What isn't she telling me? "Did you use the locket?" Needing to know, the question blurts out of me, like it has a mind of its own.

Her brows furrow, and she cocks her head. "My locket? What are you talking about?"

"Never mind. Please... just finish." I wave my arm through the air, gesturing at the paintings. "Was all this stuff up here?"

She gives me the side eye and continues. "Uh... No. I mean, yeah. Well, some of it was."

A few seconds tick by, and I raise a brow. "And?"

She sucks in a breath, and words exhale out of her. "Thought maybe if I learned to paint, we could spend more time together. So I bought some supplies and ventured up here."

As if on cue, a shadow flickers across her face. Uh, oh. For a moment, her eyes go black, and I'm back in the cavern, facing the thing that tried to take her from me.

"Whoa!" I step back, my hand going to the locket still hanging around my neck. "Babe?"

She blinks, and her eyes are normal again. But there's a look of horror on her face that breaks my heart. I lick my lips and am about to speak, but she beats me to it.

"Oh god, Sabi. This is what I was afraid of." Tears tumble down her cheeks, and she shifts her weight from foot to foot.

To hell with the shadow thing inside her; I can't keep from comforting her. Closing the distance between us, I pull her into a tight embrace, breathing soft words into her ear. "I don't know what to say, babe. But we'll figure it out. I promise."

We stand there for a long moment, holding each other in a room full of questions. As the silence stretches on, I can't help but feel the inevitable truth is creeping closer. But I wish we could stay like this forever, locked in each other's arms.

Suddenly, she stiffens, her heart thudding against my chest. "Sabi." Her voice is tight and trembling. "We're not alone."

I whirl around, my heart leaping into my throat, and there, standing in the doorway, is the figure from her journal—the man from the bar—Nico Vale. He's tall, dark, and radiating an aura of power that makes goosebumps prickle along my skin.

He smiles, and it's like watching a predator bare its teeth. "Well." His voice is smooth as buttermilk and cold as ice cream. "Isn't this a touching reunion?"

Kandis steps in front of me, her stance protective. "What are you doing here? We had a deal."

He tsks, shaking his head. "Now, now, my sweet. Is that any way to greet a special friend? Especially after all the trouble I went through to... awaken you?"

Flames lick up my neck, raging out of me. "What the hell did you do to her?" My voice is a snarl, my heart is in free fall. I step around her, moving forward fast, ready to attack. But she grabs my arm, holding me back.

His smile widens. "What didn't I do to this sweet little thing?" His laugh is a thick, noxious, rumble, like the suffocating exhaust from a rusted muffler. "In bed? Everything." He steps up to her, cupping her cheek and chuckles again. His smile is all sharp teeth and danger.

"Don't touch her!" My vision tunnels, adrenaline ripping through my veins.

Smirking, he throws his hands up in a mock placating gesture, and continues talking. "Beyond that, I showed her the truth of her power. Opened her eyes to the reality of our world." He spreads his hands. "I offered her a gift. She chose to accept it."

"Liar. It wasn't like that at all," she hisses, but there's a tremor in her voice that makes me wonder. "I... I... was bored and lonely. And you... you saw me at the art store upset, and you took advantage of me in my emotional state." Her voice breaks, and she pauses for a second to collect herself. Shaking her head, she spins to face me. "Sabi, I never meant for this to happen. You know I love you."

She reaches out to touch me, and I swat her hand away. "What the fuck? How could you?" My voice is almost as raw as my heart.

"Please, please let me explain." She wraps her arms around herself, reminding me of a flower trembling in the rain, tears dripping from her quivering chin. "He told me I had the aura of a true artist. Said I just needed some instruction, some lessons, and I wanted to believe him." Moaning, she drops her face into her palms and shakes her head. "For you." The words are muffled, almost indecipherable, as a sob wracks her body.

An uncomfortable moment passes before she pulls herself together enough to continue. Sucking in a breath, she exhales the truth, her voice cracking. "I wanted to impress you. But the lessons got out of hand." She peeks up at me, eyes shimmering and rimmed in pink. "Oh god. I'm so sorry." Her voice is starving, hungry for sympathy.

Nico's hands come together in a slow clap. "Perfect, my sweet little puppet." His voice takes on a sing-song quality, his gaze fixed on my girl. "Yes. I heard those words before, too. Oh, god. Oh, god, Nico."

Oh, hell no. Blood rushes in my ears, and my vision tunnels. She grabs my arm, trying to hold me back, but I break free from her grasp.

My fists ball, and I launch myself at the bastard. "I'm going to kill—"

But as he throws a hand up, an invisible force warps around my throat, slamming me to the ground and pinning me there. Ouch. Shit.

He steps around to the front of the unfinished portrait, and the air seems to thicken around him. "The process isn't complete, you know." His tone is cool and calm, but his expression screams violence. "What you're feeling now, my dear, is just the beginning. Soon, you'll understand. You'll embrace your true nature."

"Like hell she will." My voice is a wicked growl. "You're dead, fucker."

He throws his head back and laughs. A rich thing that vibrates through my body, making me shudder. "Oh, you petty, naive thing. Your threats mean nothing to me. And, so you both know, the fun you two had back in the caverns, well, that was just the first act, my dears. The real show is about to begin." He waves his finger through the air and makes a tsking noise. "Don't forget, water is good at spilling secrets." Smirking, he levels his gaze on me and continues speaking. "When you try to drown your emotions, they always find a way to resurface." *What?*

He snaps his fingers, and suddenly, the room is plunged into darkness. I reach for Kandis, but my hands close on empty air. No. No. Acid rises in my throat as she cries out.

"Kandis!" The hold on my throat evaporates, and I leap to my feet, stumbling forward. "Babe, where are you?"

The darkness recedes as fast as it came, and I spin in circles, eyes adjusting to the dim light of the attic. Blink. Blink. Blink.

No. Kandis is gone. And so is Nico.

But on the floor, written in what looks like fresh blood, is a message:

"The game isn't over, Sabina. It's only just begun. And as you come undone, know that brick by brick, she's sinking under. At the bottom of love's despair is a power that's beyond rare. A darkened cloak I plan to wear."

My gaze is frozen on the message, my mind reeling. What in the actual fuck is going on? My muscles are vibrating, and so is my heart. Whatever this is, it's something much bigger, much darker than I ever imagined. Shit. *How did you get wrapped up in this, babe?*

I pace the room, my feet thudding on the floorboards. Now we're both caught in the middle of this shit show. I clench my fists, determination solidifying in my mind. Fine. If it's a game he wants, it's a game he'll get. And there's no way in hell I'll ever let him win. Feeling out of my mind with nervous energy, I shake my head. She's mine.

"Hold on, babe." The words breathe out of me, a whisper on fire, blazing through the empty room. "I'm coming for you."

TWENTY-ONE

THE ROOM SPINS AROUND ME, NICO'S WORDS ECHOING IN my head like a twisted mantra. 'The game isn't over. It's only just begun.' What kind of sick, twisted—

No. Focus, Sabina. Don't let anger rule you. Kandis needs you.

I force myself to take a deep breath, then another. The coppery scent of the blood message turns my stomach, but I push past it. Time to think. What do I know?

Nico Vale. The name that's been haunting her journal. Her "mentor." The bastard behind all this. And now he's taken her again, right when I thought we were safe.

"Screw you, Nico." I raise my voice, pacing the attic. "You want to play games? Let's play."

Running my hands along the back of my head, I pause, a question tickling the back of my mind. If the painting I made out of love for Kandis could blast away whatever that thing was back in the cavern, what would a portrait of my anger for Nico do? A compulsion to paint washes over me, and I nod, stepping over to the box of art supplies. *The muse has spoken.*

Suddenly, the world tilts as if reality is bending and reflecting out from a funhouse mirror. For a sickening moment, it feels like I'm about to be yanked into another dimension or something else twisted and insane. Whoa. But then everything snaps back into focus. I'm still in the attic, still alone. But now I'm holding something. Another paintbrush. *Weird.*

What just happened? Maybe a moment of vertigo, and as it struck, I just happened to grab this brush from the box? Wanting to believe that's the truth, I nod. But if Nico and Kandis could disappear in the blink of an eye, maybe a brush could appear the same? The thought of more unexplainable, magical things popping in and out of dimensions or time or whatever the hell, is just way too mind-bending. Nope. Can't think about that now. Telling myself that doesn't stop the talons of panic from clawing at my insides.

A shot of adrenaline slams into me, and my heart flutters, ratcheting up my stress levels. No. No. Doing my best to shake the thoughts away, I focus on the paintbrush. This one looks old, the bristles worn and soft. But the most curious thing of all is the paper that's wrapped around its handle. Huh. What's that?

"Okay." My voice cuts through the silence. "I'll bite." The vowels extend out, as if somehow, maybe, they can make sense of this incomprehensible situation.

Weird. I unroll the paper. It's a note, written in Kandis's familiar scrawl:

> Sabi, if you're reading this, things have gone very, very wrong. I'm so sorry I kept so much from you. Thought you'd be safer this way, but now I see it was a mistake. The truth is, I'm part of something bigger than both of us. Something old as time itself. It's beyond powerful and dangerous.
>
> Nico isn't who he claims to be. The power he offers comes at a terrible price. I tried to make things better, but... he tricked me, and now everything is in chaos. Find Lila. She knows more than she lets on. And whatever you do, don't trust anyone else. With that in mind, take a

chance and follow your heart. I love you, Sabi. I'm sorry for dragging you into this. But if anyone can figure this out, I know you can.

Stay safe. Stay smart. And when the time comes, please remember: the light is strongest in the darkest places.

<3 K

I read the note three times, my heart pounding harder with each pass. She knew. My teeth sink into my lip, and I shake my head. She knew something like this might happen. And she left me a lifeline.

"Dammit, babe." My voice is a ragged breath, a mixture of frustration and love warring inside me. "Why couldn't you just talk to me?"

But there's no time for whys or what-ifs. I've got a lead. Two, actually. The paintbrush and Lila.

Abandoning my plan to paint, but still feeling like the brush may be important, I tuck it into my bag and head for the door. Yet, as I get to the other side of the room, something makes me still. The attic suddenly feels... different. Charged. Like the very air is holding its breath.

Whirling around, I scan the room again. Suddenly, the door slams shut behind me, and I jerk my head toward it, gasping. Nothing there. But across the room, where there was nothing before, a shadow is lurking in the corner. But not just any shadow. This one moves. Pulses. Almost like it's alive.

I'm frozen in place, and the shadow is growing. Stretching. Taking shape.

And then a figure steps out of the darkness, tall and imposing. For a heart-stopping moment, I think it's Nico. But no. This is someone —something—else.

"Hello, Sabina." The voice comes from everywhere and nowhere at once. A haunting sound, an explosion of gravel and smoke bursting through the air. "We've been waiting for you."

The shadows swirl around its feet, reaching for me with tendrils of charcoal and burnt rubber. No. I back up, fumbling for the door latch.

"Stay back." The tremor in my voice gives me away. "I don't know what you are, but I'm not in the mood for any more bullshit."

The figure chuckles, a sound that makes my arms hairs stand at attention. "Oh, but you are. You just don't know it yet."

The thing steps forward, and the shadows surge, darkness spreading over the room. Oh, shit. I yank the door open, ready to bolt.

But before I can move, the figure speaks again. "You want to save Kandis, don't you? To understand what's happening to her?"

I freeze, my hand on the edge of the door. "What do you know about her?"

The figure's smile is all nightmares and wickedness. "Everything. And nothing. The question is, Sabina... how much are you willing to risk to learn the truth?"

I should run. Every instinct is screaming at me to get the hell out of here. But Kandis's face flashes in my mind, her eyes black and alien in that cavern. Was this what she meant by 'The light is strongest in the darkest places?' And is this the 'chance' I should take?

Guess I'll follow my heart and see. Sucking in a breath, I square my shoulders, steeling myself for what's to come. "Tell me."

An impossible chasm of sharp teeth and violence opens up before me as the figure's smile widens. And then it fills the air with words, sounding more like screaming gusts of wind than anything. "Very well. Let us begin."

Darkness rushes forward, enveloping me in its cold, suffocating nothingness. Oh, shit. As the world fades away, one thought echoes in my mind:

What have I done?

Twenty-Two

The absence of light is absolute, pressing against my eyeballs like a physical thing. Damn. I can't see, can't breathe, can't—

And then, fast as it appeared, the darkness is gone.

Gasping as if I've been underwater for hours, my gaze darts around, and I try to make sense of my surroundings. Where the hell am I?

It looks like some kind of study, all dark wood and leather-bound books. A fire crackles in a massive stone fireplace, casting wicked-looking shadows on the walls. It'd be cozy if it wasn't, you know, creepy as all get out.

The voice full of gravel rumbles through the air behind me. "Welcome, Sabina."

I whirl around, my heart punching to get out of my chest. The figure stands still, wreathed in shadows. But now I can make out more details. It's tall, impossibly tall, with limbs that seem too long and joints that bend in ways they shouldn't. Its face is... well, let's just say it doesn't look soft to cuddle with.

"Who are you?" I stomp the ground, proud that my voice only shakes a little. "What is this place?"

The figure moves—glides, really—to a high-backed armchair by the fire. "Who I am is not important. What I am... now that's the real question."

Great. More riddles. Just what I need.

"Look, I don't have time for games." It's a struggle to keep my voice even. "Kandis is in trouble. Nico has her, and I need to—"

"Yes, Nico Vale." The words are rough, tone dripping with disdain. "A pawn who thinks he's a king. But he has no idea of the forces he's meddling with."

That gets my attention. "What do you mean? What forces?"

Looking more and more solid by the minute, the figure leans forward, firelight casting its face in sharp relief. Creepy. But I resist the urge to look away.

"The shadows, child. The real shadows—the True Darkness. Not the pale Stark Shadow imitations Nico and his ilk play with, but the ancient, primal darkness that existed before light itself." As the thing sighs, a whistling gust of wind blows through the room, and then it continues speaking. "The True Darkness encapsulates the planet, creating harmony between light and dark—it's what separates night from day." The thing's voice increases in volume, a howling sound that echoes through the room. "If Nico completes his ritual, some of the false shadows will be released into the atmosphere, and this will disrupt the natural balance of the True Darkness."

A shudder vibrates through me, and I wrap my arms around myself. "And what the hell does this have to do with Kandis?"

"Everything." The figure rises, moving to a large mirror on the wall. With a wave of its hand, the glass ripples like water. "Can you imagine what will happen to the plant life if light and dark are thrown out of balance? Beyond that, come have a look into the future. I want to show you what will happen in a few short hours."

Cautious, I approach one step at a time and peer into the mirror. At first, it's just my wavering reflection, smooth skin surrounding twin pools that seem to spiral off into the endless chasms of my pupils. But then the image shifts, and I'm looking at Kandis.

She's in a dark room, strapped to some kind of altar. Nico stands over her, chanting in a language I don't recognize. And the shadows...

oh shit, the shadows are everywhere, swirling around them both like a living storm.

"What the hell's he doing to her?" The words are more of a shriek than anything. For a moment, I'm unable to tear my gaze from the horrifying scene.

"He's trying to complete the ritual." The figure chuckles, a hollow, ominous sound. "Binding her to the Stark Shadows for an eternity. Making her into a vessel for their power, so he can control her and use the darkness to dominate the world."

Gasping, I spin to face the figure, flames burning through me. "How do I stop it?"

The figure's laugh is like bones grinding together. "Stop it? Oh, my dear girl. You don't stop it. You complete it."

"What? No! I'm not letting that bastard—"

"You misunderstand." The figure waves a finger through the air, tsking me. "You're going to participate in a different ritual. An alternative to Nico's flawed and incomplete one. And if he finishes, Kandis will be lost forever, consumed by a power that should never be controlled. To do this, he'll weigh her down, sacrificing her soul to the Stark Shadows. As she drowns, they'll fill her, completing the ritual. And as long as she's submerged in the dark waters, he'll have control of the Stark Shadow's hungry power."

Not liking where this is going, I swallow hard. "And the alternative?"

Once again, the figure's smile is all teeth and shadows. "You complete the true ritual. Bind her not to the false Stark Shadows, but to the True Darkness. Give her the power to control it, rather than be controlled by it."

Do I listen to Kandis's instructions or not? She told me not to trust anyone but Lila. Shit, what do I do?

Glaring at the thing, I cross my arms over my chest. "And why the hell should I trust you?" My voice is a branch snapping. "For all I know, you're just another monster trying to use us."

The figure nods, looking... pleased? "Good. You're learning. Trust no one, question everything. But ask yourself this, Sabina: what choice do you have?"

I turn back to the mirror, watching as she writhes in pain on that altar. My heart. The woman I love, being tortured by a madman who thinks he's a god.

"Fine." The word tastes like dirt. "Tell me what I need to do." My body feels covered in mud.

The figure waves its hand, and a book appears on a nearby table. Whoa. It looks thousands of years old, the cover made of some kind of dark, scaly leather that I really don't want to identify.

"Simply put, you'll need to paint the picture in a different light. Reach through time itself to create a balanced future. It's not something I'm at liberty to explain. But everything you need is in the book." The thing smiles again, a flash of danger, and it makes my skin crawl. "The true ritual, the ingredients, the words of power. Pay attention to it all. But be warned, dear one. This knowledge comes at a price."

Ugh. Of course it does. Because nothing in my life can ever be simple.

"What price?" Stupid. Why do I even ask? Already know the answer's going to suck. But oh, well. Whatever.

The creature's grin widens, splitting its face in a way that defies any familiar anatomy. "Why, your humanity, of course. To wield the power of True Darkness, you must become one with it. Are you prepared to make that sacrifice? To give up everything you are, everything you might have been, for her?"

She writhes within the mirror, and the pain etched on her beautiful face stabs me in the heart. Damn it. It's hard not to think of all we've been through, all the moments—good and bad—that have led us here.

"Yes." I nod, never more certain of anything in my life. "I'll do whatever it takes."

Looking satisfied, the figure chuckles. "Then it's time for you to begin. Your guest will show you the way."

My guest? As I reach for the book, the room around us begins to fade. The last thing I see before darkness claims me again is Kandis's face in the mirror, her eyes opening to reveal nothing but endless, swirling shadows. Oh shit.

TWENTY-THREE

I COME TO WITH A JOLT, MY HEAD POUNDING LIKE I'VE BEEN on a three-day bender. The attic swims into focus around me, looking exactly as it did before... whatever the hell that was. Was it real? A vision? Some kind of funhouse mirror acid trip flashback?

The weight in my hands sort of answers the questions. The book —that ancient, creepy-as-hell book—is here, its cover pulsing under my fingers. Great. Because that's not unsettling at all.

"Okay," I mutter to myself, struggling to my feet. "I've officially lost it. But hey, at least I'm committed to the crazy train now."

Stuffing the book into my bag, I try not to think about how it seems to radiate heat against my hip. Whatever. Focus. I need to find Lila. Guess I shouldn't have ignored her call earlier. Oh well. If Kandis's note is right, Lila must know something. If not, she'll think I'm insane. But hell, maybe I am.

I make it halfway down the stairs before the vertigo hits. The world tilts sideways, and suddenly I'm on my ass, tumbling down the last few steps. Fan-freaking-tastic.

"Sabina?" A voice calls out—familiar, worried. "Oh my god, are you okay?"

Stars dance through my vision, and then Lila is standing over me, her face a mask of concern. Oh, shit. Speak of the devil. If there were a devil.

"Lila." My voice sounds hoarse, and I grunt into a sitting position. "What are you doing here?"

She kneels beside me, helping me to my feet. "I've been trying to reach you for hours. When you didn't answer... I got worried."

Hours? I glance at my phone. Holy shit. It's been almost a full day since I went into the attic. What the hell?

"I'm fine." The lie tastes like melted plastic, but I ignore that and brush myself off. "Just a little clumsy. Listen, we need to talk."

Her gaze narrows, darting to my bag where the book is barely concealed. "You found it, didn't you? The book."

Freezing in place, my hand tightening on the strap of my bag, I study her face. "How do you know about that?"

She sighs, suddenly looking much older and more tired than usual. "Because I was hoping you wouldn't. Come on, we can't talk here. It's not safe."

Before I can protest, she's dragging me out of the house and into her car. The engine roars to life, and we're peeling away from the curb like a horde of zombies are on our tail. For all I know, they are.

"Lila, what the hell is going on?" I demand as she takes a corner way too fast. "How do you know about the book? About any of this?" And how the hell did she just show up right when I was about to go find her? Huh. Seems a little too convenient, but whatever. I'll unpack that later.

For a long moment, silence hangs in the air. Really? Her gaze is fixed on the road, knuckles blanching on the steering wheel. I crack my knuckles, resisting the urge to say, "Come on, any day now."

Sighing, she licks her lips, and then spills the tea. "Because I was like you once. Young, naive, and in love with someone caught up in things they didn't understand. And I made a similar choice to the one you're about to make."

My heart skips a few beats. "What are you talking about?"

Her laugh is bitter, edged with old pain. "The ritual, Sabina. The one to 'save' Kandis. Let me guess—some shadowy figure offered you the secrets of True Darkness, right? Told you it was the only way to free her from Nico's control?"

I nod, not trusting myself to speak. Somehow, it feels like a big *oops* is in order on my part. She curses under her breath.

"It's a trap." Her voice is hard and sharp around the edges. "All of it. Nico, the Shadows, that book—they're all part of something bigger. Something that's been playing this game for centuries."

"What game?" Ugh. Not sure I even want to know the answer.

She pulls the car to a stop in front of an old, abandoned-looking warehouse. "The game of light and dark. Of balance and chaos. And we're nothing but dust on a shelf waiting to be cleansed from the Earth."

She turns to me, her eyes blazing with an intensity I've never seen before. "But we don't have to be. We can fight back. We can end this cycle, once and for all. But I need to know—are you with me?"

Ugh, I want to believe her. But should I? The image of Kandis strapped to that altar floats through my brain, and I can't help but think of the pain she must be going through. Of the shadows swirling around her, hungry and cruel. Of the choices I've made. And most of all, the price I'm willing to pay.

Kandis told me to trust Lila and no one else, so that's what I should do. I suck in a breath and nod. "I'm in." At first, my voice is steadier than I feel. "Whatever it takes to... to end this."

She nods, a grim smile on her face. "Good. Because we're going to need all the help we can get."

She gets out of the car, and I follow her toward the warehouse. As we approach, a shimmer catches my attention, symbols carved into the metal doors—disturbing symbols that look like the ones from Kandis's paintings.

Pushing open the door, Lila raises her voice. "Welcome to the resistance, Sabina." The hinges groan as she steps forward, calling over her shoulder. "Hope you're ready for one hell of a fight."

As the door thumps closed behind me, I'm taken aback by two things—the size of the place, and the fact that it's filled with people, all looking at us with a mixture of hope and apprehension. Books, weapons, and what appears to be magical artifacts are scattered everywhere. What the hell? Feeling way out of my element, my heart punches into my ribs, and I have to fight the urge to scramble out of here.

Sucking in a breath, I square my shoulders. Nope. No turning back now.

Twenty-Four

The warehouse is a hive of activity, people buzzing around with purpose, their faces set in grim determination. Dang. It's like walking into a war room from some fantasy novel, except this is all too real.

"Feeling overwhelmed yet?" Lila smirks, a hint of dark humor in her voice.

I half snort or whatever the opposite is. A grunt? "Overwhelmed doesn't even begin to cover it."

Chuckling, she leads me through the chaos, nodding to people as we pass. I catch snippets of conversations—talk of ley lines, shadow incursions, something called the Veil. It's like they're speaking a whole other language. People poring over books and reciting different number combinations. Weird.

I'm too curious to be patient and stay quiet. "How long has all this been going on?"

"Longer than you'd believe." She stops in front of a large table covered in maps and weathered-looking scrolls. "The battle between light and shadow is as old as life itself. We're just the latest players in a very, very long game."

Great. No pressure or anything. As my gaze flicks around the room, I crack my knuckles.

A man approaches us, tall and lean with silver at his temples. His gaze locks onto mine, and I resist the urge to squirm under his scrutiny. *Okay, you can stop staring at me now, old man.*

"So." His voice reminds me of a rumbling car. "This is her? The one who's going to save us all?" He throws his head back, laughing like a maniac. Yep, I already don't like him.

I bristle at his out-of-place humor. "Look, I don't know about saving anyone except my girlfriend, Kandis. That's my priority here."

The man arches a brow. "Is that so? And you think you can just waltz in here, demand our help, and then walk away once your girly friend is safe?'

"Marcus." Lila's tone has an edge of warning, but I'm already stepping forward, anger bubbling up inside me.

"Listen here, buddy." The words are more snarl than anything, and I jab a finger at his chest. "I didn't ask for any of this. I never asked to be dragged into your little secret war. All I want is to get Kandis back." Gritting my teeth, I step closer to him. "So yeah, that's my priority. You got a problem with that?"

For a tense moment, we have a glare down. And then, to my surprise, he breaks into a grin. *Yeah. That's what I thought.*

"Oh, I like her." Chuckling, he slaps a palm against his thigh, grinning at Lila. "She's got fire."

Sighing, she waves him off. "Sabina, this is Marcus. He's our resident grump, old man, and loremaster. Marcus, play nice. She's been through a lot and isn't going anywhere."

He nods, his expression softening at the edges. "My apologies. We're all a bit on edge these days. But she's right, kiddo—you've been thrust into something bigger than you can imagine. And whether you like it or not, you're part of it now."

I run a hand along the nape of my neck and sigh, the fight draining out of me. "Yeah, I'm getting that. So, what now? How do we take down Nico and whatever that shadow thing was?"

Lila and Marcus exchange a look. "It's not that simple." She chews her lip for a second, and then the truth tumbles from her lips.

"Kandis... she's been touched by the Stark Shadows. They're deep inside her. Rescuing her physically is only part of the battle."

I cock my head, studying her face. "And the Stark Shadows are... what exactly?"

"They're shadows that were manipulated thousands of years ago to feed on light in an attempt to prolong life. But shadows are meant to coexist with the light, not consume it." Looking wound up, she waves her hand through the air, flashing some kind of signal at someone across the room, whatever that means. After a second, she sighs and continues speaking. "Stark Shadows go against all laws of nature and magic. An aberration of the gravest kind. They feed off the spectrum of light humans are unable to see."

Whoa. Okay. Now, that's beyond creepy.

Too much to think about, so I change the subject. "So, we bring Kandis back... and uh... what's the other part of the battle you were mentioning?" The words come out, even though the answer seems obvious. Hope I'm wrong.

Her face is grim. "Saving her soul. Nico is already in the process of binding her to the Stark Shadows. No doubt they're already gnawing away at the luminous essence that makes up her soul."

Well, shit. That's what I was afraid of.

"Okay." I suck in another breath, and words sigh out of me. "So... how do we do that?"

Lila reaches for my bag, firing up my instincts, and I jerk back from her. What the hell? She gives me a knowing look.

"The book." She snaps into the air. "The key to everything is in there, but it's beyond dangerous in the wrong hands. So maybe you should hand it over, before the thing dooms us all."

I shake my head, not ready to give it up. "And in the right hands?" I give her the side eye.

Marcus cuts in with sharp words, a contradiction to his smiling face. "In the right hands, it could turn the tide of this war—unless you want to stand in the way of that." He steps closer, lowering his tone. "But if you're with us, then you should know using it comes at a price. Are you prepared for that?"

I think of Kandis, of the shadows swirling around her. Of the shit storm raining down on us. And duh, it's not a hard decision.

"Whatever. I'm here, aren't I?" My voice is solid, determination roaring to life. Sighing, I tug out the book and hand it to Lila.

A mixture of satisfaction and something unreadable flashes in her eyes. Sadness maybe? She swipes a forearm across her glistening forehead and steps over to a long, wooden picnic table in the center of the room. Of course, Marcus and I follow her.

"Alright." She sets the book on the tabletop and smiles, lines crinkling around her eyes. "Then let's begin. We don't have much time."

She opens the book, and the air around us seems to thicken, making it hard to breathe. Whoa. But whatever. I'm more concerned with the glowing symbols on the pages, and the way they're pulsing in time with my heartbeat. And yeah, that's not creepy at all. Blood swooshes in my ears, ratcheting up my stress levels, and I swallow hard.

As her brows furrow, she thumbs through the pages and then stops. "The ritual to bind the Stark Shadows." Leaning forward, she taps the worn paper. "It's the most dangerous, most terrifying ritual known to mankind. And if we're not careful, we could all perish from it in horrible ways."

Chuckling, Marcus folds in on himself, and then a string of words pour out of him. "Come now, Lila, don't scare the girl with your theatrics." He winks at me and continues talking. "Anyway, it's what Nico is trying to do to Kandis." Now he taps the book. "But this here is a more controlled version. You'll be connecting to the ether with the conduit 369—the three digits that align you with the power to create —the secret code to manifestation—the energy, vibration, and frequency flowing everywhere and connecting everything."

I open my mouth to question him, but he continues talking. "The three signifies death and rebirth. It's the beginning and end of all things. A timeless energy that's in constant motion. Six is the gravitational pull holding matter together. Some call it the nature of the beast, which is a figure of speech, meaning it's the essence within reality that makes reality itself. And nine is the vibration of the universe, the collective power of existence spiraling out through the cosmos in endless fractals of light."

After pausing to suck in some air, he scratches his temple and exhales more words. "Now, the trio of numbers combined make up the vortex of creation for traveling the ether. The thing you'll be connecting to while using your belief and your artistic gifts." Smiling, he claps me on the back. "Alright, kiddo, you'll hear us chanting and reciting those numbers as we perform the ritual that will draw the Stark Shadows in."

"Say what?" I gnaw at the inside of my cheek, my mind spinning.

Lila traces circles around a complex diagram. "Yeah, don't worry about all that stuff. All you need to know is that it's like a counter-ritual—one that can free her, and potentially seal the Stark Shadows away for good."

"What's the catch?" I study her face, looking for any hint of deception because there's always a catch.

Marcus's voice fills the air, his tone solemn. "It requires a deep sacrifice. A willing vessel to contain the insatiable desire—the unfathomable hunger that only the darkness understands."

Lila nods and drops the world on me. "Basically, you'll have to consume blood to keep from going mad. If you don't, then the world is pretty much doomed. The Starkness will become uncontrollable, siphoning the life from anything and everyone it finds."

The implications hit me like a punch to the throat, stealing my breath for a second. "You mean... like a fucking vampire?"

She nods again, her gaze meeting mine. "Yes, something like that, but even more terrifying."

This is it. The price the shadow figure mentioned. My humanity. "Can I think on this?"

She shakes her head. "If we don't do this before the sun breaks at dawn..." She glances at her watch, and continues with a clipped tone. "In thirty-six minutes, to be exact. Nico wins, and we all lose. The ritual will be complete."

Marcus steps forward. "Kandis will be lost to the darkness forever with a different kind of hunger coursing through her, much worse than what the vessel, you, will face. The hunger inside her will not be for blood. It'll be for death."

Lila sighs, running a hand over her face. "That's true. Nico will use the Starkness to reshape the world to his liking, one death at a time. And once his ritual is complete, we'll never be able to find Kandis in the dark waters—so there'll be no way to fix things—Nico and the Starkness will be unstoppable."

"Shit." I'm too flabbergasted to say anything else.

Marcus puts a hand on my shoulder and squeezes. "Look at the bright side, kiddo. At least you'll be able to control your urges. All ya gotta do is sip on a little blood, and you'll be golden."

I study Lila's face, searching it. For what? I don't know.

She gives me a weak nod. "Essentially." As a smile spreads up her face, a flash of sharp fangs emerge, retracting so fast, I stumble backward with a gasp.

Okay, so that's what she meant about her deal with the shadow thing. Shit. Well, why couldn't she stop all this then? It doesn't make sense.

She sighs. "I know what you're thinking. And I couldn't stop them for a couple reasons. First of all, I wasn't in love. Second, I don't have a line to the ether like you do."

"What the hell are you talking about? The ether?" I shake my head.

Marcus cuts in, talking fast. "Look, kiddo, she's saying your artistic abilities—talents if you will—give you direct access to the ether. And that's what you'll tap into in order to manifest a Stark Cell."

"What the hell's a Stark Cell?"

Lila raises her voice. "It's the one thing, the one place that can trap the ancient Stark Shadows and hold them at bay."

I crack my knuckles, trying hard to ease some tension. "But? I feel a 'but' coming..."

She looks annoyed, and words rush out of her. "Yes, there's a catch. You can either stop Nico or the Stark Shadows. Obviously, the Stark Shadows are by far the most dangerous, so it should be them." She chews her lip for a second, and then her tone gets serious. "Now, once you get back with the Stark Shadows in tow, you won't have much time. So you'll have to be fast and create the Stark Cell to contain them over there." She points at an easel surrounded by painting supplies.

Marcus slices a hand through the air. "And you'll see Nico and your girlfriend during the ritual. But you best leave her be for now. Don't go all hero on us, trying to save her, yet. There'll be a time for that later. You have to leave her behind for now."

Lila nods. "That's right. You won't be in there long; just connect to the Stark Shadows, draw them out, and then you'll be back." She scratches her ear, and more words tumble out of her. "Also, you should know, in order to create the Stark Cell, you'll have to sacrifice something else."

Oh great. There's more. Just keeps getting better and better.

Marcus leans in, lowering his tone. "The Stark Cell will consume your artistic abilities. So you'll only get one shot at this."

"And..."

Lila winces, her tone softening. "Once created, it will pull you and Kandis into it, and neither of you will be able to leave the Stark Cell until the other conduit is closed—until Nico is taken out."

Shit. "Okay. I feel another 'but'..."

Marcus chuckles, and I try not to glare at him. And then he fills the air with his rough tone. "You'll both have to wait for us to find another creative like you, which could take years. In the meantime, you're gonna have to feed from Kandis to keep from losing it in there. Otherwise, you'll slowly go mad, kiddo."

"Drink Kandis's blood? She'll freak out!" The words burst out of me, more shriek than anything.

He nods. "Yes, and it'll be painful for her. Every. Single. Time."

Lila rolls her eyes. "Painful? We're talking beyond agonizing. She'll scream, cry, whimper like a wounded animal. It'll feel like acid coursing through her veins, and honestly, she may hate you for it."

He pats me on the back. "It's for the best, kid. For the greater good." Running a hand through his hair, he gazes into the distance for a moment and then continues. "Look, at least you'll both be alright, and you won't be able to hurt anyone... else in there."

"It'll keep Kandis safe though, right?"

Lila smiles, and it looks genuine. "Right. As long as you're successful."

"And if I'm not?"

She taps her watch, reminding me we're limited on time. Sighing, she waves an arm through the air and raises her voice. "You'll unleash chaos and destruction upon the world."

"What?"

He waves her off, amusement sparkling in his eyes. "Ha. Don't worry, kiddo, she's just being dramatic. If you don't succeed, the world will darken a few shades, that's all. Nothing we can't handle."

Huh. The shadow thing made it sound way more apocalyptic just like Lila. Whatever. I like Marcus's version better.

She rolls her eyes and scoffs, crossing her arms. "Tell that to the artists before."

With morbid curiosity, I cock my head. "What do you mean? What artists before?" But yeah, I'm not liking this conversation at all.

"Now, don't go gettin' your britches in a bunch." He's smiling, but his tone has a nervous edge. "Yeah, it's dangerous, and if you screw up, things won't be good for you... or for Kandis." His expression drops a bit, making me nervous. After a long, drawn-out sigh, he fills the air with his casual tone. "Look, nothing good ever comes without risk. Sometimes, it's best to leave it at that."

"No, she needs to know what she's up against. If you don't focus. If you get distracted—"

He smirks. "If you so much as fart—"

Oh, my hell. I give him the side eye, but a small chuckle bubbles out of me. Must be my nerves trying to keep me from overloading on stress.

"Marcus." The word is more growl than anything. She gives him a sharp look and raises her brows. "Sabina, this is serious. If you screw up, you'll be ripped to shreds and scattered about like confetti. Are you hearing me?"

Shit. No pressure at all. "Yeah. Okay, okay. I get it." Sweat beads on my brow, and I swipe it away. "Could've gone without all those details. Just saying, I mean, the other version was way more appealing —the less I know the better and all, but whatever."

"She's right though, kid. Really no sugarcoating this crap stick. You'll be stepping into a steaming pile, and that's that."

Man, they really have to beat it into me. "Okay. I get it." Sighing, I crack my knuckles, steeling myself for what's to come. "So how does this work? How do I create this Stark place?"

She sucks in a breath, perches a hand on her hip and exhales the dirt. "Stark Cell. During the ritual, we'll enchant a paintbrush for you. One you'll use to create the Stark Cell after you come back. Marcus, did you find a brush?"

"Hey, no need, Marcus. I brought one." All eyes are on me as I dig out the paintbrush from my bag and hand it to Lila.

She smiles and nods. "Alright, perfect. This works." Waving the brush through the air, she uses it to punctuate the words as they spill out of her. "Remember, it can only be used by you. If anyone else tries to paint with it, they'll invite all the shadows of the world into themselves."

Marcus leans in close, lowering his tone. "That means no getting cleaver and asking someone to paint you out of the Stark Cell."

"Okay... I imagine that'd be a bad thing."

"Yep. Wouldn't end well at all. For either of you." He claps a hand on my back, and something unreadable shimmers in his eyes. Hope maybe? "So, this is where you make a choice, kiddo. Are you in or out?"

His words reach my ears, but I don't give myself time to think it over—hell, there's no contemplating the lengths I'll go to to keep Kandis safe. She's my heart, and I'll tear the world apart to be with her.

Squaring my shoulders, I level my gaze on him. "Fine. Whatever. Yeah, I'll do it." The words burst out of me, a challenge to the universe, a threat to the darkness. "I'll take her place and make this right." I nod, feeling like some kind of impromptu speech is in order. "It has to be me. And to be clear, this is my choice, my life, my girlfriend. I'm doing it for her."

Marcus puts a hand on my shoulder; his touch is gentle, his voice a soft rumble. "You understand what this means, don't you? If you succeed, the Stark Shadow's desire will be bound to you. Forever."

I swallow hard, an audible sound that grates on my nerves. "I understand. But Kandis is worth it. She's worth everything."

Lila and Marcus share another look, something unspoken passing between them. A glimpse of shared pain flashes in their eyes, a hint of a history that makes me curious. And I can't help but wonder, how many others have stood where I'm standing now, ready to sacrifice everything for love?

"Alright." She slaps the book closed, tucking it under her arm. "Are you absolutely sure?" She cocks her head and searches my face. "Once we start, there's no turning back."

I think of Kandis's laugh, of her smile. Of all the moments we've shared and all the ones we might never get to have. And I know, with absolute certainty, that this is the right choice.

"I'm sure." My voice is even, my heartbeat erratic. "Let's do this."

As Lila and Marcus start gathering supplies, I press my palms to my eyes, sending a silent prayer out to the universe.

Yeah, I've been a shit girlfriend. I understand that now. But this is how I make things right.

TWENTY-FIVE

THE PREPARATIONS FOR THE RITUAL ARE A BLUR OF CHALK lines, burning herbs, and words in languages I can't even begin to comprehend. Feeling like a fraud, I stand in the center of it all, unsure of what to do. This is a strange world I don't belong in. But I'm rolling with it.

"You ready?" Lila cocks her head and raises a brow, lines of concern etching into her face.

Not trusting myself to speak, I nod. Ready? Hell no. But I'm doing it anyway.

Marcus approaches, holding a goblet filled with something dark and viscous. Yuck. I try not to think about what it is.

But he bursts my ignorant bubble and tells me. "Drink this. It's mine and Lila's blood." His voice is a grave covered in gravel. "It'll open your mind to the Starkness, making you receptive to the energies we're about to channel."

Grimacing, I take the goblet, my stomach turning. "Bottom's up, I guess."

The thick, warm, crimson liquid burns going down, tasting like some kind of vile, copper regret. For a moment, I gag, but nothing else happens. And then suddenly, the world sways to the side, colors bleeding into each other like a watercolor painting left in the rain.

"Whoa." I stumble back and start to fall, but Lila catches me, her touch anchoring me to reality.

"Stay with us, Sabina." Her voice sounds muffled, like she's screaming underwater. "Focus on Kandis. On why you're doing this."

Kandis. Right. I squish my eyes shut, picturing her beautiful face. Her brilliant smile. The way her eyes crinkle when she laughs. The world steadies a bit, and I nod.

"Okay." My voice sounds strange, like an echo across the Grand Canyon. "I'm ready."

Marcus and Lila take up positions on either side of me, their voices rising in a chant that seems to vibrate through my very bones. As my teeth chatter, the symbols on the floor begin to glow, pulsing in time with my heartbeat. Everyone is chanting unfamiliar words interspersed with the numbers 3, 6, and 9.

And then I feel it. The Stark shadows—the Starkness coursing within them—within me. Whoa. They're everywhere, pressing in from all sides, hungry and cold and so, so wicked. I'm drowning in darkness, gasping for a breath.

"Don't fight it." Marcus's voice cuts through the chaos, a scream drifting through time. "Let the Starkness in. They must merge with your mind, become part of your soul, and then you'll be able to control them."

Easier said than done. Every instinct screams for me to run, to fight, to do anything but let this primordial darkness into my soul. But an image of Kandis surfaces in my mind, a look of suffering on her face, and that's all it takes for me to force myself to relax into the Starkness.

My muscles go slack; all sense of time evaporates. The darkness surges forward, and suddenly, I'm not in the warehouse anymore. A vortex of nothingness whisks me away. I'm everywhere and nowhere, floating in an endless void of swirling darkness.

And there, in the distance, is a pinprick of light—Kandis.

Willing myself closer, I reach for her, but something's wrong. The light flickers, and she starts to fade in and out, her screams echoing through the chasm.

Her name rips out of me, my throat ragged and raw. "Kandis!" But the darkness swallows my voice, a silent scream on a starless night. "I'm here! Hold on!"

Pushing harder, I struggle against the current of Starkness holding me back. I'm close now, so close our fingers almost touch.

But then another figure appears. Nico. He stands between us, a cruel smile twisting on his face.

"Look who's here trying to save the day." A chuckle bursts out of him, vibrating my eardrums, and then he fills the air with his condescending tone. "You're too late." His voice tears through the darkness, thunder rippling through the fabric of time. "She's a sweet little mouse caught in my trap. And soon, her body and soul will be squeaking only for me."

"Like hell. The only squeaking will be from you, when I use my sneakers to stomp your ugly face into oblivion." My voice is all snarl, and I lean into it with every ounce of my will. The Starkness responds, swirling around me with nothing but violence.

Nico's gaze widens, a question on his tongue. "No... How... how are you doing that? You can't control them!"

Unbridled power courses through me, lighting me up from the inside. It's intoxicating, terrifying, and all mine. "Guess you don't know everything, asshole."

I lash out, tendrils of Starkness slithering through the air, and as they coil around Nico, a shudder vibrates through me. Oh, yes. This feels good. He struggles, but it only tightens the grip of my Starkness. A smile spreads through me, and I can't help but laugh. The sound slices into the moment, and with one simple thought, I fling him into the depths of the nothingness.

As everything starts to collapse in on itself, the thought of leaving Kandis here alone, horrifies me. But Marcus and Lila told me not to try to save her now. They said I must come back and create the Stark Cell first. Shit. I shake my head. What if something goes wrong, and she's stuck here forever? For a moment, I go to war with myself, my hands curling in my hair. And then, I make a desperate, love-struck decision to follow my heart. Not leaving her behind, I don't care what happens to the world. I'm not abandoning her here.

So I lunge forward, reaching for her light. "Take my hand!"

For a heart-stopping moment, nothing happens. Then, slowly, her light grows brighter, and her fingers lock with mine, warm and soft, so utterly real.

"Sabina?" Her voice is gentle, brows furrowed. "What's happening? Where are we?"

"It's okay." I pull her close. "I've got you. We're going home."

The void begins to dissolve around us, reality bleeding back in. Blink. Blink. Blink. And I'm back in the warehouse with Kandis in my arms, solid, alive, and completely mine.

But something's wrong. The Stark Shadows aren't receding. What the hell? They're growing, swirling around the two of us, hungry and insistent.

"Lila!" My voice rips through the room, harsh and high-pitched. "What's happening?"

Her face is pale, her eyes wide. "The ritual... it's not complete. You've freed the Starkness from Kandis without a vessel to contain them! You were supposed to leave her there and create the Stark Cell!" She shakes her head and raises her voice. "There's no time! It's you or her."

Shit. The realization hits me like a boot to the forehead. Of course. There's always a price. Maybe I should've listened to them and left her behind, but the risk seemed too great. I'd rather walk alone for a thousand lifetimes knowing she's safe than let her live a second of her life in possible danger. I'll do anything to protect her. Even if it's me I have to protect her from. A wall of Stark Shadows creeps across the room toward us, and now that the consequence of my choice is staring me in the face, I know what must be done.

For a breath, I study Kandis, drinking in her beauty. She's confused, scared, but here. Safe and alive. That's all that matters to me.

"I love you." I press a kiss to her forehead. "I'm sorry."

And then I let go, stepping past her and into the Stark Shadows.

She screams, but I can't look back. The Starkness surges into me, engulfing everything that makes me who I am.

The last thing I hear is Kandis screaming my name, and then the darkness swallows me whole.

Twenty-Six

Darkness. Cold, suffocating nothingness. Again. It's everywhere, seeping into my pores, filling my lungs, becoming a part of me. I can't see, can't breathe, can't think—

And then, suddenly, I can.

The world snaps into focus, sharper and clearer than ever before. The warehouse materializes around me, but it's... different. Stark Shadows cling to every surface, pulsing with life. Somehow, I'm connected to them, all of them, like they're extensions of my own body.

"Sabina?" Kandis's voice, trembling and uncertain. I whirl to face her, and she gasps, a sharp sound, cutting at me like a knife to my heart.

My reflection flashes in a nearby mirror, capturing my attention, and I stumble back. My eyes glow—two globes of ice spiraling around indigo skies—my skin pale as moonlight. Tendrils of Starkness writhe around my body like wisps of smoke.

"Oh, shit." My voice sounds strange, like an echoing specter. "What the hell?"

Lila steps forward, her face a mask of guilt and sorrow. "You're the vessel now. This wasn't how it was supposed to go. We told you to leave her there until after you created the Stark Cell."

Gritting my teeth, I shake my head. "No. I couldn't just leave her there. I couldn't risk her life. The place was collapsing around us." My voice is a gust of wind, attacking the silence.

Tears well in Kandis's eyes, and her voice cracks. "How long will she be like this? Is it... permanent?"

Frowning, Marcus nods. "The Stark Shadows aren't meant to be contained like this. They'll consume her, bit by bit, until there's nothing left of who she was."

"No!" Her tone is shrill, and she begins to sob.

"How long?" The words seep out of me, soft and weighted.

He turns to face me, leveling his gaze. "Days. Maybe weeks, if you're strong." His voice is gentle, almost pitying. I hate it.

Kandis pushes past Lila, reaching for me. I step back instinctively, afraid of what my touch might do to her.

"No." She shakes her head, voice breaking and tears tumbling. "No, this isn't right. It should've been me. Sabina, why did you—"

"Because I love you." The words come out harsher than I intended. And the Starkness roils inside me, hungry and impatient. "Because I couldn't let you suffer."

More tears stream down her face, and it takes every ounce of willpower not to reach out and swipe them away. "We'll fix this." Her tone is fierce, and she nods. "There has to be a way to reverse it."

Lila shakes her head. "I don't think there is." Sighing, she continues, her gaze fixed on me. "Once the Starkness takes hold, there's nothing we can do. But maybe you can fight it somehow."

The hopelessness of it all hits me like a crushing blow. This is it. This is how my story ends. Not with a happily ever after, but with a slow descent into darkness.

But as I study Kandis's face, a warmth spreads through me because she's safe and whole and alive. So I don't regret it. Not for a second.

"It's okay." Smiling, I lower my tone. "You're safe. That's all that matters."

She shakes her head, flames burning in her cheeks. "No, it's not okay! I won't accept this. There has to be something we can do."

The Starkness responds to her hostile tone, surging inside me, and I double over. Ouch. Damn it, that hurts.

"Sabina!" Kandis rushes forward, but Lila latches onto her shoulders, holding her back.

"Don't touch her." Lila's tone is sharp, a warning on her tongue. "The Starkness... they're unstable. Unpredictable."

Fighting for control, I suck in a breath and straighten my spine. Words stutter out of me, peppering the air, a breathless staccato of syllables and elongated vowels. "She's right. I don't... know... how long I... can keep them... contained. Have to leave. Now."

"Leave?" Kandis's voice breaks. "Where will you go?"

I shake my head, trying to ignore the whispers of the Starkness, urging me to give in, to let them take over completely. "Somewhere far away. Somewhere I can't hurt anyone... when I... while it happens."

Marcus steps forward, holding out a small, ornate box. "Take this. It's a binding charm. It won't stop the process, but it might slow things down. Give you more time... to... I don't know."

I take the box, feeling its power thrum against my palms. "Thanks, but not sure what good slowing it down would do."

Lila tosses me a bag. "Supplies." She nods. "And information. Everything we know about the Starkness. Maybe... maybe you'll find something we missed." She swallows hard, an audible sound that gets under my skin. Sucking in a breath, she tries to give me hope. "We'll keep searching for a way to help you."

I nod, not trusting myself to speak. This is it. This is goodbye.

Spinning to face Kandis, I drink in the sight of her one last time. "I love you." My words are thick with emotion as I pour every ounce of my heart into those three words. "I always have and always will. Remember that."

She surges forward, crushing her lips against mine, so desperate and salty with tears. For a moment, the world falls away, and it's just us. Just love.

But then the Starkness stirs, hungry, jealous, and so violent. My body responds, and I jerk back, pulling away to protect her.

"Goodbye." It's a faint breath, a whisper on the breeze. And before anyone can stop me, I command the Starkness to take me over.

The world dissolves into darkness, and I'm gone.

I reform somewhere far away—a desolate beach, the waves crashing against rough coral-lined shores. Alone. I allow myself one moment of weakness. One moment to scream my rage and grief to the uncaring sky. Damn it. The sun dips below the horizon, painting the sky in shades of fire and rainbows. Night is coming.

So what? Let it come. I'm ready.

Just as I'm about to step into the unknown, everything freezes. And then a familiar whispering voice fills the air along with a spectral-looking form. It's Kandis. Again.

She hovers in front of me, horror frozen on her face. "Sabi... You have to wake up now."

"What?"

"Nico... bricks to my feet... in the fen..." Her voice sounds distorted, and I hold my breath, trying my best to fill in the blanks.

"I don't understand."

She leans in close, her form wavering, but her voice is clear. "If you don't wake up now, you won't be able to stop it all from happening!"

I shake my head, and a wave of nausea rolls over me. "What are you talkin—"

"Wake up! Now!" Her shrill tone rips through me, making me feel flayed alive.

And then suddenly, the world around me starts to dissolve, like paint trickling down a canvas. Oh, shit. Before my mind can make sense of any of this, I'm jerked back to reality, gasping and covered in sweat.

Whoa. The room around me materializes—our room. My hand darts out, patting the side of the bed Kandis sleeps on, but it's empty. And so am I. Shit, was I dreaming? But it felt so real...

My heart skips a few beats, and I bolt upright. Oh, no. My hand darts to my throat, finding nothing there but the locket, and I gasp. So it wasn't all a dream. Or was it? Did I get her locket from the dresser or the fen?

I grab my phone, swiping into the calendar. It's still the same day?

The day Kandis disappeared. Well, it's nighttime. 9 pm. Before I went to the fen. I can't believe it. No way. But all my texts to Kandis are still glaring at me from the sent folder, unopened. My call log shows all my attempts to find her. Shit. She's still missing. My heart sinks to the ground, dread filling me. So I punch in her number, letting it ring several times, and when the voicemail picks up, the thing is full.

Shit. Shit. Shit.

Did I make it into the attic? Racing out of bed, I make my way down the hall, but the ladder isn't there to greet me. With confusion twisting in my guts, I drag the ladder from the closet and climb the thing faster than ever. This can't be happening. There's no heart-shaped carving in the door. Shit. I try to open the door, but it doesn't budge. Damn it. Needing to know what's in there—what's real—I slam my shoulder into it, over and over.

At last, the door pops open, and I burst inside. Pausing to take it all in, I flick my gaze around the room. My breaths rip out of me in ragged bursts, my heart fluttering in my chest, each beat feeling almost as ratchety as my nerves. Damn it. The paintings are all here. I crawl across the floor, scrambling toward the easel, and slam into it. The unfinished painting topples to the ground beside me, and I pick it up, cradling it to my chest for a moment.

Sucking in a breath, I lean back, admiring the shimmer of beauty captured in her eyes. What the hell is happening? The scene behind her is empty now, different than before—a white wall of nothing embracing the vivid lines surrounding her face, a stark contrast to her half-clothed body. It looks as if she's come undone, frozen in mid-scream, not too far off from how I feel. Why would she paint herself like this? Wait, was that part even real?

Struggling to make sense of everything, to decipher dream from reality, I chew my lip. But the endless questions continue swirling through my mind. So I examine the painting, wondering why she looks so sad. Is this how I made her feel? Alone, incomplete, hidden away from the world?

"I should've been better to you." As the words breathe out of me, remorse seeping from my soul, the most unthinkable thing happens—she blinks.

It shakes me to the core, and I gasp.

"Babe?"

She blinks again, making me do a double take. Whoa. Okay. I'm beyond shocked now. Flabbergasted? Insane? I'm not sure. All I know is that this is some freaky shit, like some kind of horror show made real. I swipe a hand over the painting, an electric charge running through my fingers on contact. How the hell is she inside the canvas? I cock my head, examining the thing from all angles. Is she trapped in there? My pulse quickens, and I swallow hard. Maybe it's some kind of dimensional shift?

For a moment, I chew on my thumb's cuticle, pondering all the possibilities. Hmmm, maybe it's a real-life Philadelphia experiment. Feeling scrambled, I run a hand over my face. But isn't that just a conspiracy theory? My teeth sink into my bottom lip, and I shake my head.

This is way too much to wrap my mind around. Sighing, I can't help but wonder what the hell is going on? Huh. Maybe it's the devil, but then again, I don't even believe in god, so the devil doesn't seem plausible. Hmm. Has to be some kind of strange magical force at play here. It's either that or my marbles were scattered at sea, and I'm just a lost ship floating through the fog.

My hand traces the outline of Kandis's face, and a shiver ripples through me. Should I check myself into a psych ward? The room swirls around me, making my stomach lurch, and I sway to the side. Desperation claws at my insides. Damn it, I have to figure this out. They say all the answers can be found within madness, so I just need to reach on in and pluck the right one out. The solution to end all this. The right brush to paint things in a better light, to...

Thunder claps in the distance, and I startle, my heart leaping into my throat. And then something appears—Kandis is here again, shimmering in the painting—a ghost captured on the canvas. Static buzzes through the room, like a million bees are living in the walls.

Her voice echoes out from everywhere and nowhere all at once. "The light in the darkest places... you've seen the path..."

I swallow hard, my mouth dry as a desert. "What are you saying?"

"Nico... he did it. This is me... this is me... after... after he drowned me."

"No!" The word is more of a gasp than anything.

"You must...paint into the past to save our future... find me in the past."

The moment fades, along with her presence, leaving me alone in silence. And before my eyes, the painting transforms into the image I saw in the dream. That's it. Suddenly, I understand what's happening. All of this has been some kind of precognitive thing. A premonition. Shit, I sure hope that's it. Because if it's not, then I'm definitely insane. I push the thought away, choosing to focus on the possibilities —on the idea of bringing her home.

Yes. A spectral version of her came from the future to help me stop all the awfulness from happening—an echo from the future. Okay, so she said Nico drowned her. The horror of that cuts me to the core, but I push on, determined to see this through. But she's alive now; I feel it in the marrow of my bones, so all the terrible shit hasn't happened yet. And that means it doesn't have to end that way either. I nod, a bit of hope creeping in.

What did she say? Paint into the past to save our future? Yeah, that's it. I bite my lip, almost hard enough to draw blood. But how do I paint into the past? Willing myself to figure this out, I flick my gaze around the room and sift through my brain for a solution.

Like the scent of lily on the breeze, an idea comes to me, awakening my senses, and I leap to my feet. A solution or delusion? I'm not sure. Hoping for the former, I slide the painting back onto the easel, and a smile spreads through me. Who cares? One thing is certain; either way, I'm diving into it headfirst.

Twenty-Seven

The attic is so quiet as I stand before the unfinished painting of Kandis. Maybe the problem all along was my inability to show my love, to listen without speaking, to look without judging—to truly see her and accept her for who she was—who she is. On top of that, the last thing I ever wanted was to put her in danger, but by pushing her away, that's exactly what happened. My ignorant actions led her straight to Nico. And now, to fix it all and save my girlfriend, I have to actually listen to her and follow my heart—just like I did in the dream—I must pull her from the darkness. Sighing, I nod, determined to believe this will work.

Dust motes dance in the pale moonlight streaming through the window, casting an almost otherworldly glow on the canvas. Her eyes, hollow and pleading, seem to follow me as I rush around the room, gathering supplies. *I've got you, babe.*

My leg bounces up and down as I rifle through a box of paintbrushes. Where is it? The scent of old paint and turpentine hangs heavy in the air, mingling with the musty odor of long-forgotten secrets. Ah, here it is. And damn if it isn't the same brush from my dream. So weird.

"I'm coming for you." The words drift out of me, a declaration to the silence, but I feel it in my heart she can hear me.

My fingers tremble as I pick up the brush. "Just hold on, babe. I promise, this time, I'm going to make things right." A tear tumbles down my cheek. "I'm sorry for always pushing you away and not paying attention to you." I shake my head, trying not to crack into pieces. "And for never showing you how much you mean to me—how much I love you. But I'm going to show you now. You'll see it, I swear."

A tortured laugh bubbles to the surface, and I let it out. Laughing more at myself than anything because how do you paint love? The usual irritation slithers through me, the serpent that always strikes when something doesn't go my way, but I grit my teeth and stomp it down. Screw you, irritation. I won't let you taint everything good in my life anymore. No. I have control now.

Feeling like I just made progress, a smile spreads through me, and I go back to contemplating my plan. The ritual was a dream, a premonition. So maybe what I learned in it can make a difference now. If I focus my mind on the ether, maybe it's possible to create the perfect scenario. Guess I'll have to see.

But how do I capture something so intangible, so powerful, in mere pigments and brushstrokes? The task seems impossible, yet something deep inside tells me it's the only way to save her. Running a trembling hand through my hair, I let out a slow breath. Maybe sometimes it's best to let our hearts guide the way.

As I bring the brush to the canvas, something shifts inside me. The dream, the premonition, the knowledge of what could be, flows through me and into the paint—illuminating the truth inside belief— the magical 3, 6, and 9 fueling manifestation. Colors swirl and blend, taking on a life of their own. And I start on the back of the canvas, marking out a plan that will make everything right. Slipping the locket over my head, I leave it dangling from the corner of the easel.

Flipping the picture over, I paint our first meeting—the spark in Kandis's eyes when she looked at me, the nervous flutter in my stomach. The way her hair captured the light, like every star in the universe was shimmering within each strand. How her pouting lips, so plump and soft, pleaded for me to kiss them at the end of our first date. The brushstrokes are quick, passionate, mirroring the excitement of our new love.

Next comes the laughter—our shared jokes and silly times. Years upon years of joyous moments together. The paint here is bright, vibrant, splashed across the canvas in brilliant arcs. Unending rainbows and prisms mirroring my love for her humor—the happiness she gives me—the most selfless, precious, and priceless gift.

Then our tears—the fights, the misunderstandings, the moments where we lost each other to distance. These strokes are darker, heavier, but interwoven with threads of gold. Like her hair, the shimmer in the dark is proof that strength comes from persevering, from putting the past behind us, releasing grudges, and living in the moment together.

I paint the quiet moments, our lazy Sunday mornings, and comfortable silences. Focusing on the peace of simply being in each other's presence. Being present for each other. These are soft, gentle brushstrokes, creating a sense of warmth and safety.

Of course, the fear of loss comes next because, within love, there's always both light and dark. I switch to darker colors, pressing down with a heavy hand, painting something thick, tangible and capable of holding the weight of the world in each stroke. Sweat beads on my forehead as the painful memories flow through me, the moment I realized Kandis was gone, the desperation of my search. The paint here is chaotic—all harsh lines and jarring colors.

But then, hope—the moment I found the first clue, the thought that somehow things would work out. The lines are soft, interwoven, everything is connected. The colors reach out from the shadows, drawing the eye to the vibrance and beauty and away from the gloom of the dark. These strokes expand, stretching out like an exhale of possibilities. As if reaching for the sky, the soft breaths of color promise new days and brighter times.

Next comes my depiction of the shadows that threatened us— Nico, the ritual, the darkness that tried to consume us both. The fact that none of it was real doesn't matter. Because, from it all, I learned some important lessons and found the truth surrounding belief. Hope—the thing that holds the light and always guides us home—

illuminating our love, our bond, the strength we find in each other. These strokes are soft and full of air, whispering of a spectacular dawn after a starless night.

Hours pass, or maybe days. Who knows? Time loses all meaning as I pour out my heart and soul, giving in to everything we are, transferring it all onto the canvas. My arms ache, my eyes burn, but I don't stop. Can't stop. Not until it's finished.

And then, suddenly, it is. Or so it seems. A portrait of emotion.

With a gasp, I step back, marveling at my creation. It's us, Kandis and me, but more than that. It's every couple who's ever loved, every heart that's ever yearned. It's light and shadow, joy and pain, all spiraling together in a swirling dance of vibrant colors and emotions.

Love, in all its messy, beautiful, and utterly terrifying glory.

My heart thuds against my breastbone, making me smile because it's a pain that keeps me present. Beyond that is a surreal feeling spreading through me, taking me over. And then, out of nowhere, the painting begins to glow. At first, it's subtle—a soft luminescence that seems to come from within the canvas itself. But it grows stronger, brighter, until it's almost blinding. A flash of brilliance under a black light. Whoa.

The figures within the painting start to move, to breathe. Kandis's eyes, once hollow, now shine with life. She reaches out, her hand pressing against an invisible barrier that separates our worlds, and my mouth drops open. For a moment, I think she'll pop out of the painting, and all will be well.

But it's not enough. Damn it. She's still trapped, her expression a mixture of hope and desperation.

And then I understand. The ultimate act of love isn't just creating something beautiful. It's sacrificing to protect the ones dearest to your heart. Just as the dream was trying to show me. Nodding, I bite my lip. Well then, sacrifice it is, my darling.

Without hesitation, I press my hand against the canvas, matching it to hers. This is it my love—my world. The paint is still wet, smearing beneath my touch, but I don't care. As my gaze connects with hers, sparkles dance in her irises, and I smile.

"That's my girl." My voice sounds thick as molasses. "I love you, babe. More than anything."

My hand slips from the painting, and I go to work, scrambling to capture everything inside me. To release myself onto the canvas, an exhale from the deepest part of my heart. I paint a picture of my existence, of how I want to be for her—better than the me from yesterday.

The world twists, colors swirling around me like a funhouse gone mad. With each stroke of the brush, pieces of the truth inside me come to life, each molecule of me sliding across the canvas. And then, with a loud popping sound, Kandis is birthed from the spiraling colors. It's disorienting, terrifying, and exhilarating.

Our fingers touch for a brief, electric moment as we slide past each other. A lifetime of memories, of feelings, of unspoken words passing between us in that instant.

And then I'm inside the canvas—but she's free.

The world inside the painting is strange, dreamlike. Whoa. Colors are more vivid, edges even sharper. The brushstrokes are beneath my feet, the texture of the canvas in the sky above.

Kandis presses her palm to the painting, rainbow tears spilling from her thick lashes. "Sabi!" Her voice sounds muffled, like a scream underwater. "No! What have you done? How is this possible?"

I place my hand against the barrier, tears trickling down my face, but I'm not sad. Not really. These are happy tears. This feels right, in a way that words can't do justice for. Suppose the cliché *actions speak louder than words* just may be true.

I give her my best smile. "I painted myself in here, but it's okay."

"How?" The word rips out of her, and she shakes her head.

The desperation in her tone makes me feel compelled to continue trying to soothe her. "This is how it has to be. How it was always meant to be. I had to do this to protect you from Nico."

She gasps. "No. Oh god, you know?" She searches my face, gaze bouncing between my eyes. "You know about him." She sags in on herself, deflating like a punctured balloon.

I nod. "Yeah, I know all about it. About him. And then some."

Her hand shoots to her mouth, and she tilts her head down for a second. "Oh, Sabi. I'm so sorry!" Sadness etches a frown on her colorful face, paint dripping from her chin.

"You've nothing to apologize for. It's not your fault."

"I should've told you about him sooner."

"No. You couldn't, babe. I understand that now. You were just trying to protect me. It's not your fault."

Strangling a sob, she sucks in a shuddering breath and exhales a question. "How did you know about us... about everything? Did Lila tell you?"

The thought of her in bed with Nico makes my stomach twist, but I do my best to project a calm tone. "Yes, and no. Well, I saw it in a dream, a vision, or whatever it's called. We can only break the cycle by breaking the cycle."

She presses her forehead to the canvas, her face a mask of anguish. Still, she's more beautiful than ever, vibrant and alive in a new way. It was worth it. All of it was worth it for this. As soon as I think that, the veil between us ripples, the colors melting from her face like a liquid sunset spilling into an ocean of eternal suffering.

A shudder ripples through me as her voice drifts through the air, a rainbow's melody on a summer breeze. She nods, an earthquake on the horizon. "I'll find a way to free you." The promise in her words is clear, even as her voice cracks. "I won't leave you here. I'll... I'll paint myself—"

"Shh, babe. You can't come back. I took the paintbrush. See, it's here with me." I hold up the brush in my hand.

"I'll use a different brush." Her shriek stabs into me.

"Babe, it doesn't work like that." It does, but I'm not about to tell her about manifestation right now; I can't risk something bad happening to her.

"What are you talking about?" Oh yeah, she doesn't know all the details yet.

Lowering my tone, I try to sound soothing. "It's okay, sweetheart. Don't worry about that right now." Damn it. Wish I could touch her face one last time.

Determination washes over her face, highlighting her prominent cheekbones. "I'm not sure how this happened or how to get you out, but I'll search the world to find a way." She nods, a tsunami of color crashing into infinity.

"I know you will. And I'll be waiting. No matter how long it takes." I step closer to the fading veil and raise my voice, needing her to understand the seriousness of the situation. "None of this will matter if you don't follow my instructions on the note."

"What? What note?" Her voice echoes through the atmosphere, a ripple in time, stretching out through this strange dimension like a bubble in the ocean.

"It's on the back of the painting. Please, listen. You have to wear your locket at all times. It'll stop Nico from getting to you. He's planning to corrupt you with Starkness, which will lead to your death."

"Starkness? My death?" She cocks her head. "What?" Her voice warbles.

"Starkness... the darkness within the Stark Shadows." Raising my voice further, I focus on enunciating my words, hoping she can hear and understand me. "It's all in the note. You have to help me prevent what I saw from coming true. Follow the note, and make sure to wear your locket at all times. It's hanging on the side of the easel. Promise me, you'll never take it off again."

She nods, two shimmering lakes reflecting the blazing sun in her gaze. "Okay. Yes. Yes. I promise." More rainbows spill from her lashes, melting down her face. "But I'm going to get you out. I swear it."

I love her drive. But the truth is, I want to be in here—I need to be in here—at least for a while. And I have big plans to make the world safer from in here.

As the glow of the painting begins to fade, I try to soak in the sight of her, committing every detail of her beautiful face to memory. The curve of her smile, the depth of her eyes, the way the colors glimmer in her gaze. The light winks out from the veil, stealing both my breath and my girl. Sighing, I spin away from the eternal sunset, stepping deeper into the painted world—the Stark Cell of my making.

And now that I know she's safe, safe from the Starkness of ignorance inside me, and safe from the threat of Nico and his stupid ritual, I'm ready to face whatever comes next.

Because that's what love is. It's sacrifice, hope, and protecting each other—no matter what stands in the way—even if it's yourself.

As I walk, the painted world shifts and changes around me. New landscapes form with each step, born from our love and shared memories. Not sure what will happen now, but I'm not afraid. How can I be when I'm surrounded by the physical manifestation of our love?

I don't know how long this will take or what challenges may come on the horizon. But I know it'll all work out for Kandis and me. Because manifestation is real—it's all tied to belief. And that means it's possible to be better than who I was yesterday. For now, I'm going to put this improved version of myself to good use, painting away all the dangers from the world to make our future bright. So this isn't the end of our story. It's just a new chapter. Because I'm a believer.

And somewhere out there, in the real world, Kandis is fighting for me. For us. Just as I fought for her. That thought warms me, gives me strength. And I'll continue fighting for her and her protection. Lifting my chin, I square my shoulders and step into the unknown.

I'm a lover, a fighter, and an artist—I may not be a Banksy, but this is my masterpiece—a depiction of eternal love.

THE END... FOR NOW.

Connect with the Aja Lace

Share your thoughts, stories, or your favorite tea blend with the author. Reach out at ajalacestory@gmail.com or follow on Facebook, Instagram, and TikTok @AjaLace.

Discover more captivating reads by this author on her website: ajalace.com

Don't miss out! Join Aja Lace's newsletter to be a part of the fun! No FOMO here: https://linktr.ee/ajalacestory

Or use the QR Code below.

About Aja Lace

An introspective sloth by day and a word ninja by night. Aja Lace draws inspiration from the peaks and valleys of life. When not lost in the world of fiction, she can be found sipping tea, pondering life, and contemplating the universe.

ACKNOWLEDGMENTS

I want to offer gratitude to the cosmic forces and the earthly muses that guided the creation of this story. The most heartfelt thank you to Laura Martinez for making this anthology possible. Without a doubt, I'm beyond grateful to my talented editor, Kate Seger. Thank you for helping me get out of my head and find the missing pieces. Your insights are worth more than gold and magical fairy dust.

In crafting this tale, I let intuition guide me to the place where imagination consumes me. Each word typed is a heartbeat, each scene a breath from inside my mind.

A Ghost from the Past

Pepper Anne

A Ghost from the Past

Pepper Anne

GHOST TOWN

LARRY CHESTERFIELD RODERICK TRAVELED FROM Missouri to Texas in search of Texas tea. Once he crossed the Louisiana state line into the Lone Star State, he traveled west in search of his fortune. In 1896, he stopped in a tiny spit of a town that was later named after him, called West Chesterfield. Among the windblown tumbleweeds and two mesquite trees, he struck black gold where he landed. He staked his claim in a Wildcatters Paradise. People traveled from all over testing their luck in the quickly growing boomtown. It did not disappoint.

They gambled and won, while others traveling with the railroad stayed on for work as it came to Texas. Jobs were plentiful because the railway system brought with it an exponentially amount of money to the thriving town. What once was a population of none, expanded to 10,000 due in part to the revenue from the combination of the railroad and rock oil. West Chesterfield had become a profitable place to live. It had easily been classified as one of Texas' famous boomtowns.

As the population continued to grow to over 40,000, more businesses moved in and homes were built. The land that offered hope and promise was now becoming a well sot out place to live.

Eventually, the oil dried up, and money from the railroad that helped bring more revenue to the town became bare. The wildcatters that once flocked to the area went in search of other places. The businesses that once thrived in West Chesterfield were suddenly closed thanks to the decline of the economic resources. Everything that once thrived was now closed. As many lost interest, the population dwindled to nothing. As quick as people were to flock to the West Chesterfield, they were equally anxious to abandon it for better opportunities, and so they did.

By the time 1965 rolled around, the Vietnam War was in full swing, and West Chesterfield was a designated ghost town. The only sign of life that ever existed were the empty buildings where dilapidated businesses were once located, and homes full of life with families in them had been abandoned.

In 1985, a developer named Bryce Kittle wanted to breathe life back into the ghost town. With it he brought opportunity for growth for a company that was looking for a place to expand into other regions. Kittle, like other investors, had profited off Exxon Mobil in the eighties. After making his fortune, he pulled out from the large conglomerate and invested his profits elsewhere.

Erin Grady was a silent partner for Exxon Mobil. He and Kittle were good friends. Grady favored the idea of a small town. He believed it would be the ideal place for Exxon Mobil to be able to branch out in. So, he followed in suite with Kittle, brought jobs and the hope of growth to West Chesterfield once again.

Kittle got the idea about moving there from his Aunt Lula. She told him stories about her cousin Myrna, once removed, who lived in West Chesterfield before it went bust. Myrna was a free spirit, sort of a prankster, and a fun loving kind of gal. She was trendy and well loved by all.

The flare of bell-bottoms, miniskirts, go-go boots and oversized sun glasses were a hit during the sixties era. There was no shortage of peace signs. It was a generation of modern free thinkers, labeled as hippies who were spreading love, while thinking up groovy ideas. There were trendy chicks making fashion statements by burning bras and screaming for equality. Their voices were heard loud and clear. Lula described Myrna as a fully fledged hippie, and she was.

Kittle learned about Myrna through Lula's stories she shared with him. There was a mystery surrounding Myrna's death and that was what really piqued his interest the most about the free spirited gal. He was fascinated at the stories that he'd heard. When Lula opened up about her disappearance, Kittle was all ears.

Lula spoke about her Myrna often. Lula's voice would tremble when she spoke about the last time anyone remembered seeing Myrna. At times, her voice would tremble and trail off, as if she wanted to change the subject. Kittle never pressed the issue with her and he always felt she would share more with him when, and if, she was ready. But deep down, he wanted to know the mystery surrounding Myrna's disappearance and what happened to her, just like everyone else that knew her.

Before, when Lula shared the stories about Myrna with him, she would laugh about the memories of the good times they had together. She shared funny stories with Kittle of when they were together. But Kittle noticed the times when Lula talked about Myrna and her voice began to tremble. She would quickly shy away from the subject and stop sharing. It seemed to him as if she was holding something back, maybe protecting a secret, though Kittle honestly couldn't say what.

Lula spoke about her and Myrna's Aunt Sally and how she adorned them. But what puzzled Kittle the most was the mystery surrounding Myrna's death. It wasn't until years later, when Lula became ill and was on her deathbed, that she opened up to Kittle even more. She told him what their family believed might have happened to Myrna. But in the end, no one ever learned the fate of Myrna of what really happened to her. And Kittle realized it wasn't until that moment when he understood why Lula was so emotional when she spoke about Myrna.

Ghosts from
The Past

Myrna was 23 when she and Bill first met and he was 24. They were at the West Chesterfield's street dance hosted by the city's Chamber of Commerce when he saw her from across the way. Bill was smitten from the very start. He walked up and asked her to dance when the song, "I Fall to Pieces" by Patsy Cline was played, and Myrna said yes.

Six months later, they were engaged. Two months after that, they got married. Their family and friends remarked about their short engagement, but the pair didn't care. They wanted to be married so they eloped.

Bill's family profited from the oil business, like many others. By most standards, they did quite well. Considering Bill and Myrna were both born at the end of the Great Depression and the Dust Bowl, they're families managed to survive the catastrophic downturns of the economy. They experienced their share of struggles. Everyone did, but during the Great Depression there weren't too many who couldn't help but go without, some more than others. They struggled, as most did. Bill's family managed to do very well for themselves.

When Bill and Myrna married, his parents gifted the newlywed's money to build their own home and in 1961 that's just what they did.

They built a single story ranch style home in West Chesterfield on ten acres of land that they inherited from Myrna's Aunt Sally. She was childless and thought of her nieces as her very own. She was fond of each of them, Myrna and Lula. She only had the two and adored each one equally. After Bill and Myrna married, Sally handed them the deed to the ten acres. They decided they would build a home and settle in West Chesterfield, so they did.

Six months after moving into their new home, Bill was killed in a plowing accident. He was plowing the field on the property with his tractor when he hit a big pit of quicksand. The mixture of water, clay, sand and salt creates a liquid known as quicksand. But it wasn't the quicksand that killed him, though everyone during that time firmly believed if you're submerged in it, then it would kill you.

Matilda, Sally's younger sister and Myrna's mother said, "It'll swallow you right up if you land in a pit of it. So, be careful if you see it, and don't fight it if you fall in, because it'll overtake you and you'll drown."

Of course the cartoons and movies based in the sixties and seventies had everyone convinced it was the absolute truth, when in fact it was not. If Gilligan or the Skipper on Gilligan's Island wasn't falling into a pit of it, somebody else was and cartoon characters portrayed the exact same message as the movies. Many were convinced that if they were to fall into a pit of quicksand, it would take the individual trapped in it to be able to grab a hold of a strong tree branch to be pulled out of it. As it turns out, quicksand is dense. If an individual falls into a pit of it, they will indeed float in it instead of drowning.

But Bill's cause of death was not from the pit of quicksand he was later found in. As he drove his tractor across the quicksand, he ran over a live electrical wire that had somehow fallen into the pit. It of course was not visible, because if it had been, one would have believed that Bill or anyone else would have avoided it altogether. But that wasn't the case because the instant he ran over the power line, there was a big explosion causing the tractor and plow both to ignite. Everything went up in flames and Bill was electrocuted.

The explosion was so loud, and the force from the repercussion caused the windows inside the house to violently shake. Myrna was in the house when she heard it. She was terrified. She tore outside, in a fast run headed to where she heard the noise to check on Bill, but it was too late. In an instant, her life went up in flames and it would be forever changed. All she could do was look at what was unfolding in front of her. Her loud and piercing cries were followed by uncontrollable sobs.

The sound from the explosion could be heard from miles away. When several neighbors who lived nearby heard it, they rushed to Bill and Myrna's house to see what had transpired. They found Myrna lying in a fetal position on the ground lying within feet of where the explosion just happened. She was in shock from what she had just seen. Neighbors were trying to move her away from where she lay for fear that there might be another explosion. Nobody knew what caused it, but they didn't want her or anyone else to get hurt from it.

Within minutes, first responders were on a scene racked with pure terror, mass confusion and chaos all around them. They prepared for moments like this. It was all in the training exercises they endured, but they later claimed they'd never witnessed anything as horrific as this. As they tended to the scene, nearby neighbors watched in sheer horror as the events played out before them. What followed in the aftermath was a scene that none of them would soon forget.

When the firefighters discovered the power line to be the cause of the explosion, they took even more precautions. When they saw it was still intact and was a live wire, they told the Chief of Police, who was also on the scene, to get people away from the area immediately. The concern, of course, was that the wire could cause another explosion. Everyone was trying to avoid anymore fatalities. Time was of the essence. They managed to contain the fire and remove the power line, but it took hours before the scene was cleared and safe.

Bill and Myrna were just young newlyweds, still starting out. The residents of West Chesterfield loved them as if they were their own. It was, after all, a small community. Everyone came together during difficult times and this was one of them. Myrna was hysterical. It took hours for her to calm down. She was rushed to the nearest hospital where doctors administered sedatives to help her sleep.

Myrna and Bill had only been married for six months when he was killed in the accident. She went from being a newlywed to a widow within a matter of seconds. She was devastated beyond belief.

After the funeral, she began to sell off parts of the land. She sold a few acres at a time, but kept the house and the acre that it was on. Every day was a constant reminder of what had happened months prior, making it more and more difficult for her to want to live in the home they built together.

As summer turned to fall, she managed to pull herself together, but only slightly. Halloween was fast approaching and she was determined to get through the holidays. Myrna wanted her friends around her, so she invited them to come over and pass out candy to the trick or treaters. She couldn't be alone in the house, especially on Halloween. And she didn't want to be, either. She was trying to surround herself with others. After all, she was a grieving widow.

Friends and family recalled how she looked forward to passing candy out to the trick or treaters. Lula and Myrna's friends showed up to enjoy the festivities. When Lula later repeated the story to Kittle, she told him the most requested candy from the kids that year was fruit stripe gum, now and later candies and lemonheads, a well loved treat. She exclaimed they were the most popular candy of the sixties.

"Kids flocked to every house in the neighborhood that had a lit porch light on it to get their candy! It's a good thing we bought extra, because they were coming to that house nonstop that night!" she told him.

The last time anyone remembered seeing Myrna was that Halloween night on October 31, 1961, after the candy was handed out and everyone went home. Lula recalled seeing Myrna standing in the entryway of her front door waving bye to everyone as they got in their cars to leave. There had been no set plans for the following day. They assumed they would see her the next day, around town or in passing.

No one had a clue where she'd gone to or what happened to her after they'd left. Did she leave on her own free will? Was she hoping to start over somewhere else without a trace? Had this holiday been too difficult for her to want to try to celebrate another one, especially in that house? Had she been abducted, or was foul play of any kind? If so, who could have done this? She certainly didn't act any different than before. Her spirits seemed to have picked up some and she was laughing with the rest of the girls during the evening. No one noticed anything out of the ordinary that raised any flags.

Her disappearance was a mystery to everyone. It was out of character for her. Her family filed a missing persons report, because they wanted answers.

No one knew whatever became of Myrna. Friends and family wondered if she was even still alive. The authorities investigated her disappearance, but without a crime scene, or suspects to interview, their investigation was limited at best. It was still a missing person's case, but with no leads, there just wasn't much to go on.

But Kittle's interest in West Chesterfield remained and he wanted to see what, if anything, he could find out about Myrna.

GHOSTS IN THE BACKGROUND

One afternoon, as Kittle was settling into his office located east of the square in West Chesterfield, he received a call from a man named Gavin Knox claiming to have something that might be of interest to him. His father, Hubbard Knox, was an old friend of Bill's. He came across an unopened box with a return address on it from William B. Mayes in West Chesterfield, TX that was in the attic of his parent's home after his mother passed away. Knox made a few phone calls and found the only surviving relative to Bill was Kittle, so he decided to call him.

Knox explained that his father died in Vietnam while in the service, so he didn't think he ever saw the box. His mother must have put the box in the attic when it arrived, not thinking much of it at the time and just never went back to it.

Inside the box were two tightly wrapped bottles and setting on top was a letter inscribed: *This is the last of the stash and I hope it's good. I have a few cases hidden beneath the trapdoor under the old red rug on the floor located in the hall. Myrna and I agreed it was our last batch, as she just found out she's expecting. We haven't told anyone yet, so you're the first! We decided to take up farming so I bought a tractor and plow and plan to give it a whirl later this afternoon when I return back from the post office. The radiator on the John Deere has been overheating, and it stalls from time to time, but Myrna and I agree it's safer than peddling moonshine.*

Take care, my good friend, and I'll see you soon.

Bill Mayes

Kittle made arrangements to meet Knox later that afternoon. When he heard the word trapdoor under the red rug, his mind started racing. He never recalled seeing a red rug in the house before. He picked up the phone to make one last call before heading out the door. He called his good friend Maybellene Rigby. If anybody could get the information he was looking for, and on such short notice, it would be her.

Maybellene Rigby, named after Chuck Berry, her grandpa's favorite rock and roll rhythm and blues singer for his hit single, "Maybellene", was West Chesterfield's local historian.

West Chesterfield had always been full of rich history. The story about Myrna's disappearance was the most popular one with the local residents. The fact that Maybellene and Kittle were such good friends, and that he needed a favor, especially one tied to the house owned by Myrna Mayes was one she simply couldn't resist.

Maybellene implored Officer Rowdell (pronounced like wow, but with an r) Chuckles to help her. Everyone called him Rowdy, because he preferred it that way.

A month after Rowdy's longtime girlfriend, Merlinda, dumped him, he and Maybellene started dating. Nobody knows why Merlinda dumped Rowdy, and if the truth were told, Rowdy didn't know either. He also didn't know where she ended up at after the fact, because Merlinda left West Chesterfield shortly after the split. She always said she wasn't meant to live in a one horse town. Most of the old timers would gather at the local diner drinking their coffee and contemplate her reasons for dumping Rowdy the way she did. It wasn't really any of their business, but it didn't stop them from gabbing about it. They were convinced Merlinda had a new beau in a neighboring town. Nobody was for certain though, but it gave them all something to talk about, and they surely did. Nonetheless, they were all in agreeance that Maybellene was by far the best fit for Rowdy.

Maybellene pulled the records for 3419 Newberry Lane from the assessor's office, which was located in the downstairs basement of the old William H. Taft Courthouse, named after the 27th U.S. President and tenth Chief Justice of the U.S. He was also known as the only individual to serve in both offices and had the records to prove it. The assessor's office also had copies of the blueprints and the plat map showing the homestead on lot number 689. That was exactly what Kittle was looking for.

While Kittle was busy meeting with Knox and picking up the box Knox called him about, Maybellene called to let him know that she and Rowdy were on their way to Myrna's. Just as Kittle had said, there was a key under the doormat on the back porch that she and Rowdy found. As they went inside, they made their way to the hallway located between the living room and bathroom where they found a rug on the floor. Only it was a green and white one. Rowdy lifted the rug and exactly where the blueprint had stated it would be, was a trapdoor leading to a downstairs basement.

He lifted the hidden latch and pulled the door open. As he looked inside he saw a set of stairs that led to a larger room. He made sure the trapdoor was left wide open and would not shut after he and Maybellene went inside. As they made their way into the room they saw an old refrigerator still plugged in to the wall. It appeared to be a man cave of some sort with chairs off to one side, pictures hanging on the wall, a small round table in the corner surrounded by 2 chairs and a rocking chair off to the side by itself.

On the floor next to the rocker were the skeletal remains of what looked like a woman. She appeared to be sitting with her back leaning up against the wall with one arm beside her and the other one draped over the arm of the rocking chair. There was also a pair of cut off jeans with writing on them on the skeletal remains with a Halloween shirt that a peace signs on it.

For Rowdy and Maybellene both, they knew who these remains belonged to. They were able to identify her because according to the outfit she was wearing the night of the Halloween party at her house, she still had on the same clothes she was described as wearing when they left her after the party.

The confusion as to why she was in the enclosed area was easily answered. After investigating the latch on the door, it was discovered that the door can only lock on one side and is only able to be opened from the outside instead of from the inside. So, if the door closes while someone is inside it, they are unable to open it, as was the case for Myrna.

So who closed the trapdoor? After looking closely in the downstairs basement it was discovered that Myrna's diary was in a well hidden place that no one would be able to see if, they hadn't' found her body and if they weren't looking for it. However, is the case, when the coroner searched through the pockets of her jacket that was lying beside her on the ground, he noticed a black diary with several entries that read:

Oct. 29th, 1961 - I have felt Bill's presence around me ever since the explosion on Aug. 31. I've seen him appear to me several times, and I know he's watching and waiting for me. In my dream last night, he reminded me to get the last of the moonshine we left in the basement. So, I plan to go down there after the party Halloween night.

Oct. 30th, 1961 – Lula and the girls will be over tomorrow night to help pass out candy. Bill came to me again last night in a dream and told me he would see me soon. He told me to carry my diary with me when I go into the basement. I'm not sure why.....Maybe he doesn't want anyone to know about the moonshine. I'm not really sure.

Oct. 31st, 1961 – The party tonight was great! I enjoyed seeing the girls and spending time with Lula. I'm writing this in the basement and brought my diary with me, just as Bill asked. When I set foot inside the dingy room, I heard a loud slam and then a click. I looked above me and realized the trapdoor was slammed shut. Then I heard Bill's voice yelling, 'It's time, my love. I'll see you soon.'

Nov. 2nd, 1961 – I'm still stuck in the basement and terrified that no one will ever know where I am. This will be where I die. I now know, it was Bill's ghost who slammed the door shut and is the one who is keeping me from getting out.

Nov. 8th, 1961 – I am still stuck in this dingy basement. I am hungry. I've eaten the last of the Eggos, been through the snacks and got thirsty so helped myself to the moonshine. But now I'm beginning to get weak and am tired. I believe this will be my last entry. Last night I saw Bill again and he asked me to dance. But how is it possible to dance with a ghost?

The diary said it all. She did in fact only have enough food and water to last her for a little over a week. Between the foods they kept in the basement along with the moonshine, she was able to survive but not long enough to be found. The fact was, the only ones who were aware of the trapdoor were her and Bill and of course if anyone had even considered looking at the blueprints he drew up. But why would they? She was stuck inside a room she despised and in the end it was what caused her demise.

Next to her skeletal remains was an empty mason jar that once held moonshine in it. There was also a toaster plugged into an outlet in the wall and beside it was a yellow Eggos box. According to Rowdy, who liked to crack jokes at the most importune times, commented that, "From the looks of things, and with that Eggo box right there, Myrna was 'Leggoing her Eggo', before the catch phrase ever caught on. As her cousin Lula did say, she was one trendy gal! May she rest in peace."

About Pepper Anne

Pepper Anne is a 7th generation Texan, where she and her family currently reside. She had diligently worked with private investigators, which helped flush her narratives with detailed excellence in her true crime books.

She has protected her identity because there are people who are not too happy that she published this story, warning her to stop, and hacking her computer, but she refused to give up. Her life and her family's lives were even put in jeopardy. This only put more resolve into her to continue writing the truth of what happens.

Pepper's goal is to bring the real story behind the stories we've all heard about. She is making sure that we hear all sides to the story so that we may make our own decisions of right and wrong and justice.

While her ultimate focus is, and always will be, true crime, some stories are too hidden to bring to light which is why she's decided to also dabble in writing crime fiction where the stories are inspired by real crimes.

You can connect with Pepper on her website and sign up for her newsletter about her upcoming releases at https://www.pepperanneauthor.com.

Living My Best Afterlife

Janet Lee Smith

Living My Best Afterlife

Janet Lee Smith

BLURB FOR LIVING MY BEST AFTERLIFE

In death, she found a new life. Now all she needs is justice.

Murdered and brought back as a ghost, I discovered the afterlife was more than just a myth. My one mission? To find out who ended my life. But as I delve into the mystery, a new question emerges: If I uncover the truth, will I be ready to move on? Or will I choose to stay in a world where, ironically, I'm living my best life? Maybe being a ghost has its perks after all.

To my wife, whose unwavering support and encouragement fuel my every endeavor, even when my plate is overflowing. These past 20 years with you have been a journey of joy and love, and I eagerly anticipate many more to come.

ONE

As I walked around my old neighborhood, Paradise Falls, I couldn't help but remember the moment I figured out I was now a ghost. I "woke up," floating over my body, with a knife sticking out of my chest. It was clear someone had murdered me.

If I had tears, they would have been falling. Why didn't I ever see how beautiful this neighborhood was? When I thought about it, the answer to that was easy. My life was so busy, I never took the time to appreciate the surrounding beauty.

The tree-lined streets had vintage lamp posts which cast a warm, inviting glow each evening as the sun set. The homes, a mix of cozy cottages and historic Victorian houses, boasted beautifully maintained gardens bursting with colorful blooms and fragrant herbs.

On any given day, I'd find friendly neighbors chatting on their front porches, children playing on the neatly kept lawns, and the soft chiming of a nearby church bell marking the passage of time. There was a local bakery with an inviting aroma of fresh bread and pastries. It served as the neighborhood's social hub, where my neighbors gathered for coffee, pastries, and friendly conversation.

Everyone except me. I was constantly on the go. Don't get me wrong, I loved that bakery. Especially their coffee rolls. I would get one every morning with my chai latte. But I wasn't a part of the social aspect of it all. I would run in, grab my latte and a coffee roll, and run back out. Occasionally, I would wave or smile at a neighbor sitting at one of the tables, but most days, I was in my little world thinking about all I had to do that day.

Would I spend the rest of eternity regretting my life's choices? Wishing I had truly lived instead of focusing on work? Time would tell. One thing I knew for sure was the first thing I wanted to do was find out who murdered me. This might be harder than it sounded because I had no memory of anything after I went for a walk the night before.

In the short time I'd been dead, I'd done a lot of thinking about this. I was 34, which was plenty of time to make enemies. The question was, did anyone hate me enough to kill me? I couldn't think of anyone I had hurt so much that they would go to such a length.

Sure, I had made enemies. Probably more than I realized. But killing me would be extreme. The first person I planned on stalk... err following... was my ex-fiancée, Thomas. It's always the significant other, isn't it? The thought of Thomas doing this would have made me sick to my stomach if I were still alive.

Luckily, I was dead.

I left him at the altar. No phone call, no email, nothing. Not a nice thing to do. Do you know what else wasn't a nice thing to do? Screwing my best friend. I know leaving him like that could cause some negative feelings toward me. But would it be enough for him to kill me? Especially since he didn't love me. If he did, he wouldn't have done what he did.

The night before our wedding, I went over to his house, even though we planned on following tradition and spending the night apart. When I got there, I just walked in. After all, the next day, it would be my house, too. I had a key for the past two years, so it wasn't like I never walked in before. I was on top of the world. After all, I was about to marry my best friend.

When I called his name, he didn't answer. Parked right in front of his house was his car, so I knew he was home. Maybe he went to bed early. After all, we had a big day coming up. As I got closer to the bedroom, I heard moaning. Then my best friend screamed his name. My heart shattered into a million pieces.

Hearing her scream was enough for me. I ran for the door and left without confronting either of them. I couldn't do it. I had to get out of there. As soon as I was outside, the urge to vomit hit me, and I ran to the side of the house. My dinner came up faster than it had gone down.

Once my stomach was empty, I went home, grabbed my packed bags, and went to the hotel we were staying in for our honeymoon. They would let me check in a day early if I paid for it. Paying for the extra day wasn't a problem. When my parents died in a car accident the year before, I became a very wealthy woman.

Was my money why Thomas had asked me to marry him? He was never interested in marriage until after my parents died. He had not only cheated, but he also had to take it to the next level and fucked my best friend. How had I never seen how much of a jerk he was?

He showed up at the hotel the next day, about an hour after our wedding was supposed to happen. I didn't know if he figured he and Jo could go on our honeymoon or if he thought I might be at the hotel. I didn't care either way. I had a feeling he would show up, and I was ready for him. When he opened the door, I was standing on the other side, ready to pounce.

"Couldn't show up for the wedding, but you made it for the honeymoon, Charlotte? That's kind of low class, isn't it?" Pure venom laced his voice, and spit flew at me. I had never seen him so angry. What he didn't count on was my being more furious than he could ever imagine. He would not put this back on me.

I laughed in his face. Couldn't help myself, really. I glanced behind him like I was looking for someone. "Where's Jo this morning?" I wish I could say I didn't feel any satisfaction when the blood drained from his face, but it would be a lie. "What's the matter? You're looking kind of pale." A twisted smile graced my face.

"At home? She was at the church, ready to walk down the aisle before you at our wedding. Did you forget we were getting married today? Did it just slip your mind?" He recovered quickly. I had to look really close to see the fear on his face. But it was there. There was no doubt in his mind that I had found out the truth.

"Whose home would Jo be at? Hers or yours? Because when I went to your house last night, she was there. In your bed. Well, maybe not in your bed. I didn't go far enough to find out where you were fucking my best friend."

If I hadn't already known he and Jo were sleeping together, his face would have confirmed it for me. He had the truth written all over it. He slumped to the floor, pulling out everything he had learned in his acting classes. Hell, tears rolled down his face. He was good; I had to give him that.

"I'm so sorry, Charlotte. She came over and hit on me. She did everything she could to get me into bed. What was I supposed to do? I tried to fight off her advances, but she wouldn't give up. It's never happened before last night, I promise." That was typical. The woman came onto him, and he was too weak to stop it. Please. I wasn't falling for that.

Last night, I didn't think I'd ever laugh again. Now, I laughed for the second time in less than ten minutes. "I'm not sure where to begin with that bullshit. We were getting married today, Thomas. If you loved me, you would have been able to say no. If that's what happened, which I don't believe at all."

I took a minute to gather my thoughts. "You know, I shouldn't even be surprised. Not once did you mention marriage before I received my inheritance. That's why I was so surprised when you finally did. This also wasn't the first time you cheated, although I will admit it's the first time since we became serious about each other. How many times did you blow me off to go out with your friends? That should have been a red flag for me. But no, I looked the other way. Now, I wonder if you ever loved me at all."

I took a deep breath while he got to his feet. The tears stopped as quickly as they began. "I also don't believe this was the first time you slept together. As much as I don't trust Jo right now, I'm pretty sure she wouldn't sleep with you the night before our wedding if she weren't already sleeping with you."

"Of course she would, Char. She's a slut, you know that."

I slapped him hard across the face. He reeled back and looked like he wanted to hit me. I was almost hoping he would, so I could justify beating his sorry ass.

"You would think, after three years of being together, you would not slut shame any woman in front of me. She wasn't a slut when you fucked her, was she? She is a grown woman who can sleep with whomever she wants to. Including my fiancée. Sorry, ex-fiancée." As much as I wanted to hurt Jo right now, she was a grown woman, and I wouldn't allow someone to shame her because of who she slept with, even my ex-fiancée.

"Let me in so we can talk, Char. It was a mistake. Let me fix this." He tried to push his way into the room. But there was nothing to talk about. Why he thought he could fix things was beyond me.

This time, my laugh held no humor. "Stop. You won't be coming in here. Don't ask for a key. They've been told not to give you one. You slept with my best friend. That's not a mistake, and you cannot make it right. It's over, Thomas. I never want to see you again."

I slammed the door in his face and started crying. I loved him. None of this was easy on me. Although I knew it needed to be over, it still wasn't easy.

There was another reason my mind went right to Thomas besides him being the most likely person because of our former relationship. From what I had pieced together, my murder was on the day of the wedding. I never had the time to change the beneficiary on my life insurance policy. That's not true. I had time. I just didn't think of it. It was a 2-million-dollar policy, with Thomas as the beneficiary.

As much as I hated what he and Jo did to me, the thought of Thomas murdering me hurt my unbeating heart. I hoped it wasn't him, although I couldn't think of anyone else who may have done it.

Two

Being dead and a ghost took a lot of getting used to. It had been a week since my murder, and I still wasn't sure I was used to it. What I hated the most was all the time on my hands. Especially after spending my life doing something almost every minute of every day.

There was a lot we thought about ghosts that simply wasn't true. For instance, while I might not have had a solid body, my body still worked the same way. For example, my hands didn't just go through something when I touched it. We could also open doors. It made sense since people talked about doors opening and closing by themselves.

I spent most of my time focused on finding my killer. Because my first suspect was my ex-fiancée, I had been following him around. He thought he was getting my life insurance. Would my insurance company pay the claim, knowing someone murdered me? Surely, they would wait until the authorities completed their investigation.

I figured out the first night that he loved going to a bar in the next town. He had gone there every night since my murder, and I followed him. Each night, I stood outside the bar, but that wouldn't help me find out anything. Tonight, I was going inside the bar. How had I ever thought this place was fun? It was crowded with drunk people and full of smoke.

"Hey, beautiful. Never seen you here before. New to the afterlife?" When I turned around to find out who was talking to me, I saw another ghost who was clearly full of himself. He needed to be brought down a peg or ten. If I was being honest, some women would find him attractive. He was handsome in a sleazy way, though. That was never my type.

"Is that how you ended up here? Because of cheesy pickup lines? And by here, I don't mean the bar. Did someone off you because of your lackluster flirting skills? Most women wouldn't do that, but some might." My words seemed to excite him. God, he was a creep.

"Sassy, I like it. Can we go out for dinner soon?" That was another thing I didn't realize about ghosts. We could eat. Gaining weight wasn't an issue, as we stayed the way we were when we died. Luckily for me, because my appetite as a dead woman was insane. Hunger was never this much of an issue when I was amongst the living.

"I like you. You still asked me out after I told you what I thought of you. Not my type, but I've only been dead a week. Having some friends would be nice." As soon as I said that, I saw my new friend looking over my shoulder at something behind me.

Turning around, I was still feeling my human nerves. Hey, I was murdered; it made sense I would be a little nervous. Standing behind me was a beautiful, statuesque blonde with the prettiest green eyes I had ever seen. If I were ever to want to be with a woman, it would be her.

"Hi, Sophia! What brings you here tonight?" the guy asked.

Damn, I needed to ask him his name. I looked at him again. "You? What is your name? Calling you 'that douche' in my head isn't working for me." I put on my best fake smile while I asked.

"I thought you would never ask. It's Romeo."

Staring at him incredulously, I asked if he was serious. His name couldn't be Romeo. If it was, he certainly didn't match his name. Life as a ghost might be interesting, after all.

He looked at me with a smile on his face. A smile that on some men would have been skeevy, especially on him since his overall look was skeevy, but somehow it was sexy. "Serious as a heart attack, which is how I died. No one killed me because of my horrific flirting skills." He pretended to tip an invisible hat as he bowed.

Smirking at him, I couldn't help but ask him if he was sure about that. Maybe he wasn't so bad after all. He took my insults well without being a jerk about them.

Turning back to Sophia, I put my hand out to her. "I'm Charlotte. It's nice to meet you, Sophia."

Instead of shaking my hand, she drew me into a hug, whispering in my ear, "You've met Romeo. Be careful; he acts harmless, but trust me, he isn't." Once she said that, she broke the hug and talked as if she had said nothing. Maybe I was wrong about him not being so bad. "It's nice to meet you, too, Charlotte. It's nice to have someone new around here. Recently deceased or traveled here from somewhere else?"

I wanted to ask her what she meant by what she said about Romeo, but with him standing right beside us, it wasn't possible. "Someone murdered me last week, and I'm trying to figure out who did it. My first guess is my ex-fiancée. Whoever killed me did so before I changed my 2-million life insurance policy and he was the beneficiary. He often comes in here, so I thought I would follow him around for a bit."

Looking around the bar, I couldn't help but wonder where he was. He was usually here before now. "What's his name? What does he look like?" Sophia asked. That was a good question. Maybe they'd seen him around. Why didn't I think of asking them?

"His name is Thomas. He's about 6'1, has dirty blonde hair that he likes to wear in a man bun, and weighs about 210. Usually wears a suit, including a tie." Sophia looked like she wanted to vomit. "Looks like you know him?" I asked, afraid of what she was about to tell me.

THREE

Sophia's face was white as... well, a ghost. As pale as she was a few minutes ago, as soon as I told her about Thomas, there was no color left on her face. This couldn't be good. I took hold of her hands, sensing that the touch might help her relax. Although, I also needed someone to calm me down. Deep down inside, I knew I wasn't going to like what I was about to hear.

"Sophia, whatever it is, you can tell me. I have no feelings for him anymore. If I'm being honest with myself, I haven't had feelings for him for the last six months or so. The day before our wedding, the day I found him in bed with my best friend, I went to his house because I felt like I wanted to call it off but wouldn't admit it to myself. I was hoping being near him would make me feel better about it all."

Looking like she was going to cry, she took a minute to pull herself together. I looked back at the door and pointed to it. We both headed outside. The bar was loud and looked like it was full of obnoxious people, so I didn't want to talk to her there. Plus, I needed some place quiet to talk. Humans might not see or hear us; however, that didn't mean it went both ways.

There was a park across the street from the bar. It was small but lush with greenery, with a water fountain in the middle. The sounds of water gently falling filled the air. Pointing over to it, I held onto her hand and began walking over to it. Hopefully, the quiet setting would calm us both down.

I saw Romeo walking behind us. "Stay here. We don't need you for this conversation."

He smirked but said nothing and walked back into the bar, probably hoping another ghost would show up. The look on his face said he wanted to get lucky tonight. It wouldn't be happening with me. Even if I found him attractive, I was in no mood for sex. Especially not after Sophia's warning.

The air was permeated with the scent of spring flowers. The smell brought back many happy memories, and for a minute, I wished I was still among the living. Letting that thought go, I sat on the bench, Sophia sitting at my side.

"Like I said over there, Sophia, you can tell me anything. The look on your face when I told you about Thomas told me you knew him. Let me guess, he cheated on me with you? If that's it, it's not a big deal now. It wouldn't be the first time. Why I said I would marry him will forever be a mystery to me." I never had major concerns before my death. We had our problems, but every couple did. Had I become paranoid?

This time, a lone tear fell down her face. She wiped it away and then appeared to steel herself for this conversation. "You're right. I knew Thomas. Not in the way you think, or at least not in the time you think."

Okay, so he didn't cheat on me with her. That was one woman he didn't cheat on me with. I was telling the truth when I told her it wouldn't matter if he had, but it was good to know he hadn't. I just met Sophia, but there was something about her I liked. Staring at the fountain, I waited for her to go on with her story. After a couple of minutes, she continued.

"My dad died when I was young. Thirteen years old. Since I was an only child, it was my mom and me for the next four years. When I was seventeen, my mom was diagnosed with aggressive breast cancer.

The disease spread through her body, and she died when I was eighteen years old."

Chills ran through me. Sophia didn't have to continue for me to know what happened. But she needed to tell this story, so I sat in silence while she pulled herself together.

"My mom had inherited a lot of money from her parents, which she had left in the bank. Since my dad had died and I was her only child, her money went to me, even though she hadn't had a will. Thomas came into my life about a week after probate ended, and the money was mine."

Sophia's story was like mine, but not exactly the same. Whereas Thomas entered her life after she received her inheritance, we had already been dating when I received mine. However, he had never spoken about marriage until I received my inheritance. When that happened, he wouldn't stop talking about us getting married until I finally said yes. I had two sisters who had also inherited part of our parents' estate, but we each inherited a lot of money.

Sighing, I told her my story. "This all sounds familiar. When I was 21, my parents died in a car accident. A drunk driver hit their car when they were coming home from a concert. They both died on the scene. I met Thomas shortly after their deaths, but before the probate process had begun. He never spoke about getting married until after I received my inheritance."

Sophia gasped, and I sat there looking around the park, willing the tears that threatened to fall to stay away. Once I could pull myself together, I spoke again. "Sounds like we have a lot in common. Which worries me. I'm afraid he's looking for his next victim. This makes the need for me to figure out if he was my killer and find some way to put him behind bars more urgent."

She chuckled without humor. "I'll help you figure out if he murdered you, but how will we alert the authorities if he did? While we still have most of the same abilities as we did when we were alive, talking to the living is not one of them. At least I haven't found a way yet."

She was right, of course. We wouldn't be able to tell the authorities. "If he killed me, we must figure out a way. He may meet victim number three any day. This brings up another thought. How did you die?"

She suddenly looked agitated. "Like you, I don't remember. The thought of being murdered never occurred to me. Until now. So, what's the plan, my new bestie?"

FOUR

I ALMOST VOMITED HEARING SOPHIA'S STORY. LUCKILY, while we could eat, we didn't get sick. Sophia was right. We could do most of what we did when we were alive, except get sick and have the living see and hear us. Therefore, we usually found an empty house to live in. No one wanted to find their showers mysteriously running, only to find no one in the room.

We didn't have to do anything; we could spend our time roaming around. Some ghosts did nothing but wander. However, most of us liked to live as close to our old lives as possible. It was a slight comfort to see those we loved. Most of the time. It was hard when someone we loved got hurt. But it was better than not seeing them at all.

I wished I had not eaten lunch today. Although we didn't get sick, my stomach still churned. I was sure it was a phantom pain, but it felt real. Our stories had enough similarities for us both to know he targeted us. Of course, this also meant he probably never loved either of us. I didn't know how to process all of this.

Sophia's story had me convinced that Thomas had killed both of us. We would figure out how we both died and somehow give the information to the authorities. This had to stop. No other woman would die at his hands.

"Where do we start, Soph? We can't let this go. We have to be sure either he killed us, or he didn't. He may have already met his next victim." I thought again about how we'd notify the police and may have found a way.

"We'll worry about how we'll let the authorities know once we have the proof we need. If we find any physical evidence, we can always leave it at a police station someplace. Let them figure out what to do with it. That's all we can do to try to stop him."

Sophia was right. We were severely limited in what we could do to alert the authorities, but her idea could work.

I was deep in thought when I realized Sophia was still speaking. I hoped I didn't miss anything as I once again focused on her words. "Yes, stopping him needs to be priority number one. He's probably at the bar right now, so why don't we head to his place? We'll be able to look around without him knowing. He may not see us, but he won't miss drawers opening or doors closing."

I couldn't help but giggle at the thought of scaring my ex-fiancée. He liked to act tough, but that was all an act. Taking one last look around the park, inhaling a lungful of the fresh air, a plan formed for me to come here often. We both got up at the same time and locked our arms together.

Since we were close to his house, it was a short walk. Which was good because I didn't like walking any more in my afterlife than I did when I was living. His car was parked right out front. "Let's check into some of the windows to make sure he isn't here. He would sometimes have someone pick him up."

Heading toward the back of the house, we looked in the bedroom window first. I was curious if he was with anyone. I wasn't sure if Sophia was feeling the same, but she followed me to the window.

Sitting on the bed was a packed bag. Not suspicious at all. Nope. Nothing to see here. Looking in the rest of the downstairs windows, we realized he truly was out. None of the lights except his bedroom one was on, and when he was home, he didn't shut off any lights.

"I think we should begin in the bedroom. A bag on his bed says he's going somewhere. I wonder why and where to?"

Agreeing with her, I followed her to the front door, where we both walked right in. We could walk through walls, doors, etc., even though we were solid. It was weird, but it came in handy when doors were locked and we wanted to get in some place.

Once we were in the bedroom, my new friend went to the bathroom while I went right for the bag. Looking through it, it was obvious he had a trip planned. Going through the bag, at first, all I found was normal packing stuff. Toiletries, clothes, shoes, etc.

Before I took everything out, Sophia came out of the bathroom looking like she was the one feeling like she needed to vomit. "I found this sitting on the sink," she said as she handed me a piece of paper.

It was one of those strips of photos that come out of a photo booth—Thomas and a woman. A much older woman. If we were talking about another man, this might not be suspicious. However, Thomas hated the very idea of dating an older woman.

The photo felt like it might burn me. Dropping it on the floor, something told me this had to do with his trip. I started grabbing everything out of the bag and throwing it onto the bed until I was at the bottom of the bag.

Sitting under his clothes was a folder filled with paperwork. Chills ran throughout my body. It was then we heard someone coming in the front door. First, I grabbed the envelope, and then Sophia and I walked through the bedroom wall. Luckily, the bedroom was on the first floor. It would have hurt falling from the second floor. Yeah, ghosts felt pain even though we didn't get sick.

He would notice someone went through his bedroom, but who cares? Let him call the police; he wouldn't be able to prove anything. Also, what would they do, arrest two ghosts? Good luck with that!

When we had things in our hands or on our person, they disappeared. This meant no one could see them. This came in handy, especially when you broke into a home and were trying to get away. We ran down the street as I led the way to my house. Since I'd only been dead a week, it was still empty. They'd probably sell it eventually, but for now, it was still my home.

FIVE

Since my old place wasn't far from Thomas' house, we arrived in no time. The downtown area was crowded with people, so we had to slow our run down to walking; however, we still got there quickly. "We're going to the house you owned when you died?" the other woman asked, appearing to be trying to make small talk.

"Yup! I'm not sure what I'll do when the house is eventually sold. While there are other empty houses to stay in, I'll miss this one. I grew up in it, and it held many memories of my parents. Leaving it will be difficult."

Our conversation ceased as we got lost in our own thoughts. Not needing a key to get in places came in handy. A key had been hidden near my back door, but the lock was changed. I had called my sisters before my death and told them I found him cheating on me, so I was sure they did it to keep him out of the house.

I still wasn't sure how I died, other than being murdered, but I did know that whoever did it made it appear as though it was some kind of accident. What kind remained a mystery to me so far. There would be plenty of time to figure it out. It's not like I had no time to figure this out; I had nothing but time.

Luckily, the lights at the front of my house and in the yards of my old neighbors illuminated my house at night. Unfortunately, ghosts didn't have the eyesight of other supernaturals. No light meant we couldn't see. Couldn't read paperwork if we couldn't see!

My new friend and I got comfortable in my living room, and I opened the envelope, hoping it contained the information about how I died. Convinced Thomas took my life, I realized how abhorrent the thought was. It almost broke my dead heart all over again.

My hands shook as I opened it and handed it over to Sophia. "Can you do this? Looking at it makes me want to vomit." Yes, I wanted my killer to be brought to justice, but now that I might find out what happened, I wasn't sure I wanted to.

"Sure." I noticed that she winced as she took it, probably having thoughts similar to mine. Sophia never thought she had been killed until I brought it up; now she looked afraid she might find out Thomas killed her, too. We were both a hot mess.

The thought that I went from a boss babe when I was alive to a woman who was afraid of a bunch of papers in death did not escape me. Being dead didn't mean I wasn't still a boss babe! "No, I'll do it. This was my idea; it's only fair I be the one to do this." Looking it over one more time, she placed it in my hand. "We're going to be okay. No matter what we find tonight, we're going to be fine. What doesn't kill you makes you stronger! Sorry, bad joke." She giggled nervously.

Pulling everything out of the envelope, I placed the papers on the coffee table and randomly picked up a sheet. The first one I grabbed was a letter he had written after Sophia's death. "Take a look at this. It was meant for you." After carefully taking it out of my hand, she began to read it out loud.

"My heart is broken when I think about you being gone. It will not be easy to go on without you. You were my first true love, and I'm not sure I ever want to allow it to happen again; I can't handle the pain of losing someone else." Stopping as tears fell down her face, Sophia wiped her eyes.

Pulling herself together, she began again. "We argued so often about your fear of doctors, but you never gave in. I can't tell you how much I wish I had pushed you harder so they could have found your heart problem. It's possible you'd still be alive today. It's something that I'll always regret not pushing you to go. I love you, and I always will."

She wiped her eyes once more. "So that's what happened to me. He shouldn't regret this. After what happened to my mother, I was petrified of doctors. What I didn't know couldn't hurt me, right? No matter what he did, I never would have agreed to go."

"Now you know the truth, my greatest hope is it was someone else who murdered me. Going through my afterlife knowing he cheated on me with my best friend is doable. If he killed me, I'm not sure how I'll handle an eternity with the knowledge he did this, too."

SIX

My body trembled as I pulled more sheets out of the envelope. Why was I so nervous about finding out if Thomas killed me? Learning someone you loved murdered you, even if they cheated on you and things were over, would be a real kick in the gut.

Going through the documents, I looked for something I thought would pertain to myself, so I was able to discard a lot of them. Most were general papers anyone might have. Pay stubs, some bills, and a few copies of checks. Nothing out of the ordinary.

When I was halfway through the pile, I gasped. "What is it, Charlotte? What did you find?" Sophia asked as I dropped the paper I was holding on the table.

"It's a letter from some woman threatening to kill me. A woman Thomas was once involved with, seemingly before me. If I were a betting woman, I would say he dated her in between being with the two of us. He went to the police. Why didn't he come to me?"

Tears fell down my face. I was no longer sure my former fiancée had done this. "Maybe he was trying to protect you? He would have known you would be scared if someone threatened your life." She wasn't wrong.

Memories of times with Thomas flooded my mind as I looked around my living room.

The fireplace we spent many nights in front of, cuddling as we fell asleep, waking up chilly because the fire went out, and we never put the heat on. The stereo where we played records whenever we decided to have an impromptu dance-a-thon. I looked at the door and saw the spot where he went on one knee to propose when we got home from dinner with my sisters.

He didn't wait to close the door; as soon as we were both over the threshold, he got on one knee. When I realized he wasn't following me, I looked back, and there he was with a small robin's egg-blue box in his hand. I had never been as happy as I was at that moment.

There were no indications of issues in our relationship, but there must have been there for him to cheat on me with my best friend, right? Was it possible he had been telling the truth?

Not about Jo coming onto him as he tried to fight her off. I didn't believe that part for a minute. He told me it only happened once; was he telling the truth? Should I have listened to him? Would I still be alive if I had? So many questions I might never have answers to. It wasn't like I could talk to him. When I heard Sophia call my name, I realized I was lost in the past. Shaking my head, I tried to clear the memories from my head.

"Were you saying something? I'm so sorry, I was lost in memories." She came over and sat next to me, placing her hand in mine.

"I know this isn't easy, Char. Remember, the answers you want may be in these papers. Although we haven't known each other long, I can tell you're strong enough to handle this." She was right; I could do this. At least it looked like my ex didn't kill me.

"You're right, I can handle this." Picking up a lined sheet of paper with one hand and wiping my eyes with the other, I steeled myself for whatever I would read next. A quick perusal of the letter told me this was what I was looking for. "You aren't the only ex he wrote a letter to after death. This is a letter to me."

Shaking, I began to read the letter out loud.

"My dearest Char. I'll never forgive myself for the pain I put you through. One of the things I'll always regret is not convincing you to listen to me the last time we spoke. If I had, maybe you would have believed me when I told you I only slept with Jo once.

"I'm not trying to defend myself; once was one time too many. Blaming it on Jo and calling her a slut was lower than I believe I have ever gone. It wasn't her fault. I had been having cold feet when Jo came by to check on me."

Tears sprang to my eyes as I read. Sophia came over and brought me tissues, and I quickly dried my eyes. I could get through this.

"She was always friends with both of us, so her visit wasn't unusual. What was unusual was that I gave in to my nerves. I've never allowed myself to be so afraid that I would mess up my whole life. When I slept with Jo, that's exactly what I did.

A few days later, when I went to your house to talk to you, I found you on your bedroom floor lying in a pool of blood. Taking you in my arms, I felt for a pulse, knowing there wouldn't be one. I feel like my life ended when yours did, Char."

My voice trembled at the thought of Thomas walking in and finding me dead. I could feel the pain in his words. It seemed as if he had poured everything he felt into that letter.

"A few years before I met you, I had been engaged to a woman who made me happier than I had ever been up until then. This is something I should have told you, as you had a right to know, but I couldn't bring myself to do it. Talking about her hurt too much.

"Sophia was an incredible woman, who died of a heart attack. She never went to the doctor, no matter how much I begged her to. Now, I've lost both of you to death, albeit a different type of death, and I don't think I'll be able to love another woman. Not after loving the two of you."

How could I have ever thought he killed me? Cheating on me the way he did was wrong, but that didn't make him a murderer. Hell, it didn't even mean he didn't love me. One thing was clear to me as I read his letter: he did love me.

"There's more I kept from you. Something very important. If I had told you, maybe you would still be alive today. After Soph died and before I met you, I briefly dated an older woman. It was all fun and games for me as I was trying to get over Sophia's death.

"Unfortunately, she began to display obsessive, stalkerish behavior. I ended it right away and never saw her again. What I didn't know was she was watching me. The stalkerish behavior she displayed when we were dating was nothing compared to the lengths she went to after I broke up with her.

"Finally, she came to me one day and told me if I didn't break up with you, she would kill you. I didn't take her seriously, but I should have. One thing I did was go to the police. They told me since she hadn't done anything physical, there was nothing they could do."

My mind was a jumble of thoughts. She threatened to kill me, and there was nothing the police could do. I couldn't help but wonder if I would still be alive today if they had at least investigated the threat.

"The police chief came to your funeral, you know. He wanted to apologize for not doing anything. I wanted to throat-punch him. You were gone. The second woman I loved with everything in me was gone.

"We are working together now to bring her to justice. I couldn't save you in life, but I will make sure she spends the rest of her life in jail.

"You'll always be in my heart, Char. The love we shared is what is getting me through life these days. Remember the teddy bear I bought you for Valentine's Day, our first year together? I sleep with it every night. It makes me feel closer to you.

"Wherever you are, I hope you and Sophia found each other and are now friends. You two would really like each other; you're so much alike. Goodbye, for now, my love. Until we meet again."

The letter fell from my hands as sobs overtook me. Sophia took me in her arms, gently rocking back and forth. Why didn't I allow him to tell me what happened? Why didn't he tell me about the threats against my life? Those two mistakes could have changed both of our lives if we had handled them differently.

SEVEN

FOR SOME REASON, I FELT THINGS DEEPER NOW THAN I ever did in my past life. It's not that I was a cold human being. I just wasn't very emotional. Now, my feelings were all over the place. They had been since I died. A few minutes after reading the letter, I managed to pull myself together. My heart still felt like it would never recover completely. Sophia pulled away from me. "How are you doing, Char?"

I wasn't sure how to answer her. "That's the question, isn't it? Am I okay? Yes. Although I'm not sure I'll ever get over this. Which is a hard pill to swallow since my afterlife will be for eternity. There are so many what-ifs running through my head."

My new friend shook her head, looking like she understood what I was saying. Of course, she did. She must have had a lot of questions of her own running through her head. "Now that I can relate to. There is one key question in my mind. Why didn't I go to the doctor? Would it have saved my life? I'll never know. Just the thought that I died due to my own actions is a tough pill to swallow."

Needing to do something, I went to the kitchen to make some tea. Times like this made me grateful that ghosts could still do much of what we did as humans. Having to roam around with nothing to do, the way ghosts are often depicted, would drive me insane.

"Would you like some tea?" I asked Sophia. For what seemed like the thousandth time, I was grateful that my sisters had not emptied my house yet. They would at least be cleaning out the cabinets and fridge soon. After all, the food couldn't stay here forever.

It was hard to break lifelong habits and eating and drinking fell under that category. Eating and drinking could be challenging for ghosts because it wasn't like we could eat while other people were around. It would be weird to see a fork on a table suddenly disappear when we picked it up. But when no humans were around, we could be ourselves. I always kept my kitchen well stocked, so there was plenty of food here for now.

"Tea sounds good. Do you ever put on records, or are you afraid the music would be heard by the neighbors? You have some of my favorite records here."

Music was something that I could go for. "We're not too close to any neighbors, and it's a dead end, so random people don't come around much. Put on what you want. Listening to music would be fun."

When I got to the kitchen, I concentrated on making the tea. Having something to think about besides the letter from Thomas helped me calm down a little. My emotions were still all over the place, but I could forget things for a few minutes.

The sounds of an 80's love song flowed through the kitchen. Her taste in music matched my own. My body started to move to the music, which helped me relax. Music always did have that effect on me, no matter what was going on in my life. Nothing had changed in that area in my afterlife.

A few minutes later, the tea was ready, and I placed some non-dairy creamer, sugar, and honey on a tray and went back to the living room. Sophia was dancing almost like I had been. She stopped and turned around when she heard me enter the room.

"I hope this song is okay. It's one of my faves." Smiling, I put the tray on the coffee table. "It's perfect. I was just dancing in the kitchen. You can keep dancing. The tea isn't going anywhere." She swayed to the music again, this time looking at me and crooked her finger, asking me to dance with her. If I was being honest with myself, I hadn't felt this free in years. So, I went and danced with my new friend.

By the time we were done, we had danced to both sides of the album. We fell on the couch, laughing and trying to catch our breath. "I haven't had this much fun in years. I'm so glad we met," I told her, and I meant every word.

"Same. On both counts. We would have been unstoppable together if we had met in life. Thanks for the tea. The way we were dancing, I can't believe we stopped moving long enough to drink it."

"I think you're probably right. You're welcome. The fact that I had food and drinks in the house came in handy. I was going to get rid of it all since I would be going on my honeymoon." When I looked at her, she seemed deep in thought. I soon found out why.

"Now that we've figured out how we both died, and we know Thomas is working on bringing your killer to justice, what are we going to do with the rest of our afterlife?" I looked back at her with a smirk on my face because I already figured this out.

"How about starting our own ghostly P.I. agency? We can help other ghosts who need to know how they died to find the answers they seek. We work well together, and our detective skills helped us figure out how we both died. What do you think?"

"I think that is a great idea! How will this work? How will we get clients? Word of mouth? It's not like we can hang signs or post ads on the internet." That was a great question, but not something we had to figure out right then. After all, we had all of eternity.

The End

FOLLOW JANET LEE SMITH

https://www.facebook.com/AuthorJanetLeeSmith
https://x.com/J_Smith_Creates
https://www.tiktok.com/@janet_lee_smith_author
Email: janetleesmithauthor@aol.com

ABOUT JANET LEE SMITH

Janet Lee Smith, a nearly 60-year-old native of New Bedford, MA, harbored a decade-long aspiration to become an author. Despite repeatedly delaying this dream, she finally took decisive action at 51, putting an end to procrastination and transforming her writing aspirations into reality. Celebrating 15 years of marital bliss with her wife, Shanna, Janet has shared her life with Shanna for over two decades. Their home is a lively abode, housing their playful canine companion, Daime, and their dignified feline friend, Star. Janet and Shanna cherish the unique dynamics of their household.

OTHER WORKS BY JANET LEE SMITH

Satan, is That You?

Heartstrings: Stories of Love & Desire

Whispers on the Wind

Daphne Moore

Whispers on the Wind

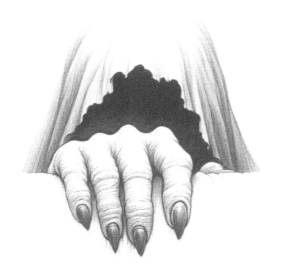

Daphne Moore

BLURB FOR WHISPERS ON THE WIND

Elena Caldwell, a skilled necromancer, has spent years hiding from a tyrannical government that seeks to harness her powers for their dark ambitions. Deep in a remote valley, she lives in solitude, shunning the outside world—until she encounters a ghost who becomes her unexpected companion and friend. As she begins to find solace in this spectral bond, Elena's past catches up with her, and the government tracks her down, threatening to tear apart the fragile peace she's found. Now, Elena must confront her fears and fight for her freedom before her powers are twisted into something monstrous.

For Dorothy, who knows all about terrible bosses

WHISPERS ON THE WIND

WITHOUT MY WILLING IT, THE MAGESIGHT SURFACED, AND the world became a constellation of flame. The warm glow of the lives burned in hollows of trees and under snow, accented by a brighter flare from the bear denning near last year's avalanche. Nearer to me, the glimmer of the fish slumbering in the steam.

All those souls remained neatly in place, except for the quicksilver flicker of the ghost trailing me.

I shook my head, calling back regular sight so I could finish setting up the solar charger. I'd blocked out the web of life around me as I set up the first three solar chargers, but the ghost approaching had triggered my internal warnings. Since up to this point he or she had been harmless, merely observing me, I returned to my task.

Only fitting the protective case to the charger remained. Clipping the case on the charger and smoothing the protective layer over the solar cells took only a moment. After examining it for a moment, I nudged it to the right. The tumble of rocks glazed with ice and dusted with snow glittered in the afternoon sun.

The chargers' locations had to be carefully selected, places where the telltale reflection of the cells would be mistaken for rock or water by searchers flying overhead. When the blinking green light informed me the battery was charging, my breath puffed out in a cloud of relief.

The batteries provided the power that kept me from freezing in my home. Not a luxury.

Shadow fell over me and I shivered. Clouds were piling up again, signaling more snow coming. I started home, rubbing my mostly numb fingers together.

Even on days like this when I was cold and hungry, this was freedom. Precious, still new to me and worth anything to keep, even when the loneliness crushed me.

When the lack of company became too much to bear, I spoke with the spirits of the water and trees. The effort made them happy and helped me figure out the little favors they wanted in exchange for their work in gently nudging other humans' attention away from this little valley.

But they weren't very good at conversation. I'd had training in communicating with them, and we still misunderstood each other often.

When the magic came back in the early 2000s, people tried to bargain with spirits as soon as they figured out it was possible. After a few bargains that went awry with results ranging from funny to horrifying, humans learned the smaller and better defined the bargain, the better. Spirits were very literal.

Right now, what they wanted from me was to tell them stories, which I did once a week from the mouth of my cave. Luckily, I read a lot, and so they were learning all about soldiers fighting bugs in space. Explaining things stretched the telling out too. That was all they asked, and I was glad to pay their fee, since no one but me and the wildlife had been here since I arrived.

The ghost didn't count, since it existed here before I found this refuge.

Pushing through knee deep snow, the snow dropping into my boots and melting just enough to make life a misery, I wished for climate control in my clothing. That luxury I missed in the winter even more than deep fried food. I'd never learned much about weather before I escaped.

But the electronics in that kind of clothing could be detected at a distance, so I made do with layers of wool and a puffy jacket.

I'd almost frozen my first winter here, even with cold weather gear. If I hadn't had my magic, and used it even though I was terrified of discovery, I would have died. Even three years later, I used as little magic as I could. My old job in the Bureau of Magic's black ops department meant they would hunt me until I died. And beyond.

At the dawn of the new magical age, someone in Homeland Security figured out necromancers would be useful to interrogate prisoners who died by their own hand or while being apprehended. That idea was handed down to the Bureau of Magic, and soon the Bureau ran the only school in the US that trained necromancers in the use of their magic.

Like other magical schools, they paid a substantial bonus to parents to have their children attend it year round.

In short, they got us young and raised us right. Don't question, don't think, use your power for the good of the country, sacrifices have to be made, you can't make an omelet without breaking eggs...I don't think they left a cliche unspoken. The job the Department offered when you turned eighteen paid well, and there wasn't really any other market for unclean magic than the Department of State.

Who, gossip said, trained their recruits in assassination techniques using their magic. At least the BOM was the devil I knew.

It wasn't like the people being questioned were good people.

And then I learned I didn't know it at all.

I kicked the snow. Sensing the ghost brought back those memories. But now, since I wasn't bound by orders and fear to harass it and torment it until it gave me information, I could let it be if it didn't want to approach me.

The wind picked up, driving puffs of loose snow into my face. My cheeks and lips, even covered by the thick scarf, had gone numb.

Pausing by a white tipped pine, I eyed the stream I needed to cross to get back home. Even though I was freezing, I needed to chop some ice to use for food and washing. A chitter above me caught my attention and I tilted my face back just in time for the squirrel to spring away, dumping snow from the green branch square on my face.

Thanks, buddy.

I missed the luxuries of modern life so very much, especially running water. Or even feeling safe enough to use magic to break the ice. Unfortunately, necromancy was an uncommon talent. Someone attuned to its magical signature could home in on it easily, if they detected it being used.

Even when I didn't use my power to heal or harm the soul, my magic still bore the scent of my talent. There was nothing I could do to make myself safer other than remain as isolated as possible.

I'd chosen the Cabinet mountains because I'd done search and rescue there, so I had memorized locations there in case I needed to go back fast. The area was mostly unpopulated, since the terrain and the weather extremes kept most of the land developers out.

The people who did live here unofficially were all very good at avoiding the drone sweeps and government agents sent here to remove unapproved primitive settlements.

Better living like this than paying for the sweets and luxuries I craved with shreds of my soul. Loosening my shoulders and grimacing in anticipation of the muscle aches I'd have later, I pulled the handax from my belt and got to work.The storm was coming fast, I could all but taste it in the air, and I only had a day's worth of water at the cave.

At least this life built muscle. I hadn't had a lot before I came here. It also built calluses, and achy joints...

Stop it, Elena.

By the time I got the full pail to the hillside, my hands and feet were stiff with cold and my cheeks completely numb. I hip checked my way past the windbreak. Inside, out of the wind, the lingering warmth within the cave wrapped me in a fiery blanket, stinging all the exposed flesh.

Ow. I'd let myself get far too cold.

The pail clunked to the floor as I peeled my gloves off. Clumsily, I punched the button to start the heater cycling, then kicked banked coals and put a log on the hearth. The double heat would help faster and a crack at the top of the cave helped clear the smoke.

The ice would melt on its own while I stripped, wrapped myself in a blanket, and waited for the burning to stop. The water in the teakettle would be warm soon and I could have a cup of herbal tea while I waited. Possibly some anti inflammatories too, but I hoarded them like the gold they were.

To distract myself as the water warmed and my skin ached I checked the wards. Veins of silver and gold twining above and below the cave, sunk in stone and earth, the magical construct shielded the cave from magical detection and attack. They were the first thing I'd made when I got here, paying the price of power and exhaustion to gain concealment and efficiency combined.

I'd barely been able to gather the energy to eat for a week after. But so worth the trouble.

Here, in my home, I could use my magic. Even safe, I tried not to, but without use, skill atrophied. And even if my magic was viewed by the world as a terrible thing, it was part of me and I liked using it.

So I was extra careful on the few occasions I left this part of the forest and traded with Old Ginger. I traded with him once a year, at different times of the year, and used a wisp of magic to disguise myself. The risk of the power used for the illusion was less than the risk he or someone else trading there would recognize me from missing persons bulletins.

It wasn't paranoia when there were people hunting for you.

The kettle whistled and I dropped dried chamomile and mint in my big ceramic cup, pouring the boiling water over it. The scent rose in the air, a reminder of summer and green days. I sat in my wooden chair next to the hob and breathed the aroma in.

Since nothing was feeling any better, I sent threads of my magic coiling through my body, nudging gentle repair to the skin cells, deadening the nerves screaming at me. A bit of frostbite, nothing to worry about. Good. I'd need to be more careful next time. Covering the energy I was expending meant eating more, but I had enough supplies to cover a few mistakes.

A generous dollop of honey in the tea took the edge off hunger and thirst as I rose to put together my meal. In my small space I meticulously organized everything— everything had its place, and on the food shelves cans of beans did not fraternize with hardtack.

Neither of them had anything to do with the ramen or the freeze dried tofu, the meal I kept back for emergencies.

I poured some of the remaining hot water into a bowl to rehydrate a few blocks of the freeze dried tofu and saved the rest back for a bowl of instant ramen when the tofu was ready. The tofu would provide protein and the ramen the needed calories without me needing to do a lot of prep. The seasoning packet was pure salty goodness and a treat in itself.

Food and my relationship with it had made for a rich vein of mockery from my boss before I left. He'd taken the extra weight I carried as if it were an offense to the divine and to humanity to behold it.

My mind bubbled like magma, spitting a toxic cloud of memories out.

"Tubbygirl, I thought vegetarians were supposed to be thin. How'd you screw that up?"

The pungent odor of my boss's cologne and gum hit me at the same time as his voice. Musk and mint, ugh. Tall and with the build of an athlete who'd tried to keep in shape, he thought his above average looks made him attractive to all women. His presence curdled my stomach. I hadn't liked my old boss, an older woman who channeled the warmth and charm of a hostile pit bull. She'd transferred out a year ago to spread joy in the department of defense.

Her replacement, Howard Graves, made me remember her fondly. She'd been cold and indifferent and demanding; he was nasty, petty and for some reason had decided to make me his super special project.

The brightly colored invitation he dropped on my desk made me wince. Another baby celebration; my colleague Anya must have succeeded in her IVF.

Management made no secret of the fact they wanted us to reproduce, preferably with other necromancers. It was a rare talent, and they always wanted more. A confirmed birth was worth a hefty bonus for both the parents and their manager, and it appeared he'd decided he wanted to increase the number of bonuses he collected. Since I was the only unattached female in the department, he'd focused on me.

He made constant suggestions on my ways to improve my looks, exercise techniques, just about everything was fair game. It was like he wanted to remake me into an older version of his wife. A brittle waif-like blonde, she was quite beautiful and very distant when I met her at the office holiday party. I'd liked parties before; it gave me a chance to socialize with the only people I knew.

Now, I had to schedule time every evening for a crying jag to blow off steam.

"Good morning." I returned my attention back to the form I was filling out on my computer, hoping this was a drive-by insulting.

"Don't get comfortable. You've got a new project to work on this morning." Graves sat on the corner of my desk. It brought him unpleasantly close to me, invading my personal space with abandon. I shifted backward several inches, stiffening.

Something about his tone made my skin creep today. Triumphant, possessive...I couldn't put my finger on it, but my hindbrain interpreted it as a signal to get far away from him.The same with his expression; I wasn't good at reading people, but it made me want to put a wall between us.

Keeping my voice level and calm, I replied, "I'm not supposed to have another project for at least three months."

'Projects' were coded office speak for interrogating the ghost of a person who had been killed when they were captured, usually a terrorist or traitor. Over the past decade I'd interrogated too many of them, and I hated the task beyond words.

He popped another stick of peppermint gum in his mouth. "Sucks to be you, Tubbygirl. There's one who's going to be dead in about five minutes. You know him. Danny Esposito. If I recall, you used to be lunch buddies. So you'll be able to say goodbye and then establish a nice quick rapport with his ghost."

His entire body was a sneer, from mouth to toes.

I saved the form, buying time to think through my shock. Danny had just graduated from college with a general degree in magic; he had no real specialty but was strong in divination and illusions. He'd only worked here for a year.

"Danny just transferred out a week ago. What is he charged with? What do you mean about to be dead?"

He leaned forward.

I scooted my chair back into the desk with a thump.

He didn't stop, still leaning until his face was only a half a foot from mine. His words hit me in a blast of venom and mint. "I knew you were dumb, but I never thought you were dumb enough to actually believe that all the people you've questioned died while being apprehended. Your friend Danny took some classified information with him, so he's a traitor. We can't have that. We need to know who his handlers are. We need to know who he told. And you're going to find out for us. Management has decided you're going to be brought on board, which puts you directly under me."

"No." I stared back at him. My stomach was churning as I digested his words, and there was only one answer for this. "I quit."

"Having a spine isn't a good look on you." He clamped one of my wrists in one meaty hand and squeezed, pain zipping down my arm. He fished in his jacket pocket and pulled out a mage cuff.

Stunned, I gaped at him. Mage cuffs were a restricted tool, used only for violent offenders or mages with a pattern of behavior dangerous to themselves or others. They came in grades, because they cut the offender' access magic to a minimal amount. The shock of being totally cut off often killed, so they were matched to the known grade of the prisoner.

He slapped a mage cuff on that wrist in a practiced move. The enspelled and deadened iron tingled unpleasantly on my wrist. If it was possible, my blood would have gone even colder. But it was already ice. The cuff bore the silver-blue metal inlay of a level three.

That was one grade above the power level in my personnel file. He'd picked it to make me hurt.

I'd never thought my laziness would help me out. The bonuses for testing into a new higher grade never seemed worth the effort of arranging the time off and traveling to be tested. Graves had no idea of my actual grade...though I wasn't sure either. I did know it was higher than the two on record. And three, since this cuff didn't seem to cut off the flow of magic.

"Ow!" I yelped, loud enough to be heard through the office. I wanted to see what my friends would do.

After a moment of quiet, the normal pace of office life resumed and Graves laughed at me as he grabbed the back of my shirt and rose to his feet, yanking and twisting to get me to follow him.

Since I was supposed to be without magic now I followed stumbling. People turned away from us as he pulled me to the door and into the hall. My eyes stung.

Not even worth a pause in the conversation.

I could overcome the cuffs with some effort. But what would I do afterwards?

Rescue Danny, at the last, if he was imprisoned here.

I needed facts before I made my final decision. I was afraid, yes. But fear wasn't the best basis for decisions.

Quick marching toward and then down the stairs, I continued yelping in pain, letting my voice quiver. It wasn't hard. I wanted to cry as people in the hall and stairwell ignored what was happening, colleagues I'd worked with for years. Who I'd thought liked me.

Possibly I was as unobservant as Graves implied.

In the detention area, Howard shoved me into a barren room. The wards flared on the door as I passed them, again calibrated to my supposed power grade. It cost more for higher security; he must have been trying to trim the budget.

I caught myself against the wall and turned to face him.

"You've got the cell next to Danny Boy so you can think." He chuckled, the twist of his mouth dark and grim. "You'll 'get the facts' on what happens when you don't toe the line. And don't think about trying to leak to the press or run away. You're complicit in the murders of thousands of people. Every person you've interrogated. Ignorance is not an excuse, so think about that long and hard while we finish prepping the lethal injection."

He slammed the reinforced door shut.

There was no way to communicate through the wards embedded in the walls to verify if Danny was there and this was all some strange kind of test. I had to make a decision now, a major, permanent one, with little in the way of facts. It was hard. I didn't like making any kind of decision off the cuff, even what was for supper.

Lining up the facts that I did have only took a moment. Danny was my friend, even if the friendship had been limited to work. I had no intention of either being killed or standing by while he was killed. Since apparently, I couldn't quit, I was going to have to break out of here. Breaking Danny out at the same time was only logical.

Would I be able to hide him? No. Danny was an adult and a fully trained mage. I needed to assume that he would be able to take care of himself once I got us free.

Sitting, bracing myself against the wall, I closed my eyes and focused on the cuffs. Even at low power, they burned and itched and made thinking hard.

Back in the day, I'd been friends with one of the people who worked on the magic layers of their design. We'd swapped awful workplace stories over beers. Since I had the security clearance needed to know about the project she'd brainstormed with me about ways to attach the alert if the working were interfered with to the effect that nullified the prisoner's ability to use magic.

I'd asked not to be credited at the time, since I didn't want people asking me to do similar work later as part of my job. It was fun as an exercise, not as a day-to-day chore.

The weakness of the design, which I'd mentioned to her at the time, was that if you were able to dismantle the alert, it didn't reestablish itself. It required the prisoner to be wearing cuffs below their grade, so we hadn't thought of it as a major flaw.

Thank goodness we'd been lazy.

Drawing in power, I used a tendril to pick the knot of the alert off the restraint and pulled it free, then flattened it like a shoelace. The magic dissipated in a whiff. It took me much longer to do that than it had at the cafe table, the discomfort of the cuff rising.

Pain sucked.

Once I'd neutralized the alert, I turned my attention to the nullification effect. Designed to be twofold, a portion of the working caused pain when power was drawn, and the rest acted as a resistor, preventing the power from reaching the person restrained.

While it would hurt, burning out the resistance would be the quickest way to deal with it. I braced myself internally, then pulled all the power I was capable of drawing into myself. The pain as the cuffs glowed bright was worse than anything I'd experienced.

The cuffs winked out and I panted. Knowing what would happen, I didn't think I could make myself do that again.

Also, based on the math we'd discussed back when, I must be grade five or above. Interesting to know.

I tasted blood. Blotting my lower lip, which ached where I'd bitten it, I straightened my shoulders. It was showtime.

Now or never, Elena.

Keeping the power I'd drawn in even though it felt like I was going to fly apart at the seams, I gently probed the spells woven into the walls. They weren't warded against any significant amount of magic. It made sense. These cells were normally used for questioning of bodies rather than live people.

If they were using them now for living persons held here were in mage cuffs, management had decided to cheap out on the defenses. Typical.

I'd figured out the working to teleport a few years back as an evening project to while away time. Despite that working being classified, if you got your hands on the original edition of Magical Instruction and actually read it and did the work, figuring out that working was child's play.

While I wasn't strong in any magic but necromancy, I wasn't powerless either.

There were several locations that I could anchor the transportation working to; my apartment, a few wilderness locations, my father's home. The apartment would be monitored, of course. Should I leave the few photographs I valued to ensure a clean break? My copy of Magical Instruction was there as well.

They planned to kill Danny. A clean break would be best, but I couldn't abandon the text. I needed it if I was going into hiding. It was the best reference in the world, and the first edition contained much more information than the later editions. It was very hard to find and cost the earth, as well.

I'd try bringing it to me before I 'ported to the apartment, though.

My memorized wilderness locations came from places I'd camped for fun and a few wilderness search and rescue operations I'd participated in. While I wasn't close to my family, camping together was a way we tried to bond. I knew where they stored their camping food and gear. I'd pay them back someday.

Plan decided, I examined the wall with the purpose of destroying it. No living components for me to rot. That meant I needed to use a blast of magical force, but luckily I had plenty of power pulled in.

The wall evaporated under the blast, reduced to powder. Danny, dark eyes huge and face bruised from cheekbones to chin, tear tracks cutting through dried blood on his face, flinched against the wall when he saw me. A quick step in and I grabbed the cuffs, hitting the deactivation code. It was easy to turn them off from the outside.

Danny had been honest about his rating; his cuffs were far more powerful than mine.

I touched his arm and 'ported the two of us to a campground two states over. Insects sang around us in the deep wooded trail, undergrowth stretching around us. We dropped several feet when we materialized. I never teleported directly to a spot on the ground if I could avoid it. Air didn't change as often as vegetation.

"They planned to kill you. What did you do?" I reached out to steady him as he swayed and he jerked away, wild eyed.

"You didn't know they were just executing people? I tried to tell the media." Shaking, he stepped further away from me. "They yanked me in there, threatened my family. You say they planned to kill me. What kind of monsters are you all?"

Ah. So, he hadn't actually been my friend. That hurt.

Did I not have any friends? Maybe it was better that I be alone.

I'd deal with it later. Keeping my face expressionless took a lot of effort. "I didn't know. You're on the Appalachian trail right now, near the border to West Virginia. I can give you my debit card to use, but they'll track it."

He shook his head, stepping further away. "No. I'll handle it myself."

Your funeral.

I blinked myself back to the present, my eyes stinging, and poured the warm water over the ramen and reconstituted tofu and dumped the entire seasoning packet in.

Who said memories dulled with time? They lied.

There was no knowing if Danny had made it out safe. I'd teleported to my cave, found that indeed, the working was reversible and taken my book back from the apartment, and went about making it really hard to find me, starting with laying the wards in these stones. I used the same working to take the camping equipment from storage.

It didn't work if I didn't know both objects and location intimately, which was good. That should prevent them from being taken away from me.

The supplies made the first spring and summer liveable, if not comfortable. I spied using my scrying stone on the surrounding area, identifying where others camped and made their living.

Watching showed me where people traded pretty quickly, and how to approach the place as well.

I walked toward the sturdy but weathered old cabin with care. I'd observed it over the course of several days and spent the additional magic to listen as well as I prepared to make the exchange. This cabin housed a trading center which supplied necessities to the people who lived in scattered camps in this area of the mountain range. While I wasn't desperate for resupply, I wanted to get more of several items necessary for the winter. I'd read that the winters here were fierce and I wanted to be sure I didn't run out of food or power for my camp stove/heater. I had some rechargeable batteries but I wanted more.

From a day's worth of eavesdropping, I knew that the name of the man who ran the trading post was Old Ginger. Which was strange because he was young and dark-haired, though I did gather from observation he had a spicy temper. He had a cold face and a mouth that clamped like a snapping turtle's, dressed in old fashioned clothing without climate controls.

When coming to trade, people approached from the north, along the trail, and always called his name when they reached the half-fallen oak tree that had been struck by lightning. Wrapped in an illusion that added more weight to my frame, thick gray streaks to my hair and gave me a still red scar on my cheek, I approached, following the steps the others had taken.

I'd brought camping meals with meat in them to trade. They'd been jumbled in with the vegetarian meals when I took all the camping supplies from the family storage. The meals were shelf stable for a long time and presumably would be a trading item people would be eager to get. My backpack bulged with them.

"Old Ginger! I want to trade!" I called the words and then waited.

After a moment the faded red door opened to the halfway point. Old Ginger stood there, partly obscured by the door. The shotgun in his hand was completely visible. Cold brown eyes squinted at me, like a gunfighter assessing an opponent. "I don't know you."

"Yes. I have things to trade." I really wanted to create a magical barrier between me and the shotgun, but that would reveal me as not a normal person hiding here.

"What do you have to trade?" His harsh voice had a faint accent, which sounded to me like central europe.

"Camping meals." I didn't move to open the backpack, not desiring to get shot.

The shotgun didn't move. "Why you willing to trade them?"

"I don't like the way these ones taste." I put some impatience in my tone.

He tilted his head examining me, eyes narrowing further into so narrow a squint I wondered how he could see, and then said, "Set one on the ground and back up ten paces."

I followed his instructions.

He approached slowly, keeping me covered. Then he crouched and inspected the meal.

"Huh. It isn't even expired." The shotgun no longer directly pointed at me but it was obvious that it could be brought to bear at any second. "That's worth trading for. What do you want?"

"Lentils, dried beans, solar recharger or batteries, freeze dried tofu."

Old Ginger sneezed a laugh. "Can't help you with that last. Set the meals down there," he pointed at the ground, "then back away and I'll tell you how much credit I'll give you."

I did so. He examined each meal, carefully scrutinizing the packaging for expiration date and tampering. Insects buzzed in the background, the shadows had lengthened, and I'd sweated through my shirt before he was half finished. I wondered if this was a technique he used to drive down the amount I'd accept from him.

"Ginger!" The hoarse shout came from behind me. We both jumped. Me to the side and Old Ginger to his feet, shotgun ready. I kept moving, finally stopping next to the oak.

Twigs cracking and pebbles spraying announced the arrival of two men carrying a stretcher with a youngster on it. The man leading yelled, "I think he's dying. Get the medkit, Ginger. I'll pay whatever you charge."

"Set him down." Ginger hurried to the side of the stretcher then swore.

The older man who had carried the back end of the stretcher focused on him with desperate eyes.

"He's a goner," said Old Ginger, his tone curt but not unsympathetic.

The younger man snarled. "Get the damn medkit!"

Old Ginger shrugged. "You're wasting trading credit, but whatever."

They jogged toward the cabin.

The older man tried to split his attention between me and the boy on the stretcher, then gave up, kneeling and starting to cry. He too wore old style clothing, without climate control. I decided to buy some as well.

I moved closer to them. The form on the stretcher was just a kid. He'd been caught in some kind of rock fall, or under a tree. He was pale, blood trickling from the side of his mouth, chest indented and an obviously broken leg.

"I have some medtech training. Do you mind if I look?"

A jerky nod from the older man. He breathed unsteadily, choking as he said, "Take a look, sure."

Crouching next to the boy, I loosed a quick and dirty diagnostic working. Most of those who practiced healing magic refused to acknowledge that it was a subset of necromantic talent, that would be used to harm or heal. I'd trained in it as I had with the other parts of my talent. While not as powerful as a dedicated healer, I wasn't a slouch either.

The working told me with magical intervention, the boy could survive. He had a collapsed lung, a spleen on the verge of rupture, a bruised heart, a leg broken in two places and worms. If I healed the worst of the internal injuries, it would stabilize him. Then he would be able to heal the rest, especially after they stabilized his ribs and splinted the leg.

Though he'd probably limp for the rest of his life. Assuming infection didn't set in.

Thank the stars he was unconscious. He'd be screaming otherwise.

I put my fingers on the side of his throat as if I were taking his pulse. Sending a pulse of magic to encourage healing in his spleen and heart, which responded with gratifying speed. Under it all, he was healthy. The lung was a bit trickier, but within my ability, and destroying the worms and eggs was simplicity itself.

His color improved. A general transfer of energy helped with the crashing blood pressure and temperature drop that shock had brought on. I hadn't lied when I said I had medtech training. Better to heal if you know what you're doing.

"He's going to need that leg set." I removed my hand from his pulse.

The boy's eyelids fluttered and he opened his eyes, seeming dazed. The old man shouted, "Max!"

The two men ran out of the cabin, covered in dust, and skidded to a halt next to us, Ginger carrying an ancient medkit the size of a suitcase in his hand.

His eyes fixed on the four of us. "I smell magic."

Damn.

The smart thing to do would be to kill everyone here and move again. Like necromancy, healing was a rare talent.

I didn't want to slaughter someone I'd just finished healing. Lying should work. From everything I'd seen, these people did not like talking to strangers.

"I've got a teeny bit of talent, not enough to make any money at it. I used it to stabilize the kid until you could get the medkit over to him. You want to make something of it?" I snapped, baring my teeth in a snarl as if I were ashamed.

Many games of poker over the years had taught me I wasn't good at bluffing, but this was higher stakes.

Killing led to more killing. I didn't want to go on a rampage until I was the only living person in this entire area.

"Dad?" whispered the boy.

"Thanks ma'am," the older man said firmly. "Even iffin it was magic, thank you."

"He needs his leg set," I said.

"I know how," said Ginger.

He still eyed me, eyes wary and assessing, but he didn't say anything more about magic.

My appearance didn't match the wanted bulletin. When I scried my parents' house, I'd watched for it to show up. The bulletin showed me as I was, average height, overweight, with a hooked nose and several moles by my mouth and on my cheek. They'd done several iterations on what they thought I might wear as a disguise, all of them more attractive versions of myself.

Which was not the illusion I wore. Possibly Old Ginger had sensed the illusion magic as well, which would be why he'd come out with the shotgun. Who knew?

I stood by as Old Ginger set the boy's leg. After, when I was allowed to stand in the doorway of the shop and point at what I wanted, the older man paid for my new set of clothes, beans, lentils and some dehydrated milk. While I desperately wanted the candy Old Ginger had on display, I didn't buy any. I needed to keep displays of my sweet tooth down to a minimum.

That was an identifying factor too.

The preserved meals I'd brought covered the purchase of a solar battery recharger. That worked out. Being warm in the winter trumped chocolate right now, at least in the smart portion of my brain.

I also bought fruit and nut energy bars to help cover the calorie deficit from teleporting. From the very beginning, I left no tracks that led to my home, using the teleport working when I was barely a quarter mile from Old Ginger's home and under cover.

Nowadays I traded dried berries and other fruits from around my cave, since I didn't hunt and I wasn't the only person who had a sweet tooth. The stream near me had gold in it too and I used the nuggets I gathered. Old Ginger tried to figure out where I lived, and my stealth and woodcraft had become legendary in the area. They all assumed I was leaving no tracks because I'd somehow concealed them.

Shaking off memory, the void in my belly filled, I reinforced the 'look away from this' working I kept on the portion of the valley near the cave. Subtle and magic hungry, it turned creature's eyes and attention away from my home and the small garden near the cave mouth. It was the only thing that saved my beans and sunflowers from the deer and drying berries from the birds.

No one had come for me in the four years since I ran. That only meant they didn't want to work to find me yet.

The quiet deep within the stone of my cave seeped into me, a contrast to the rising wind outside the windbreak. The light was gone, pitch black from the storm clouds. The only light in the cave came from the stove, which was plenty for my needs.

Moments of peace were worth all the work. Now I could take the time to talk to squirrels. After the first year here I didn't cry with stress or guilt every night. The animals and spirits didn't fake being friends.

I opened my mind to the light of life and death around me again. If I thought about the past too much the nightmares would start up again.

The ghost waited outside the cave, a flickering humanoid outline. I toasted my tea in the direction of the entrance.

"Cheers to you, ghost. Here's to another day of freedom."

The steam from the tea spiraled up in the amber light. Since the windbreak fully blocked the cave mouth right now, I couldn't see outside with my eyes. The view would have been trees, snow, and more trees, with a few bushes for variety. I traced a finger through the steam, drawing an abstract shape before the swirl drifted back to formlessness.

The wind slapped at the windbreak, howling like a teenage V-pop singer outside the cave. The wood and canvas rattled and a draft swirled in above and below it. I'd forgotten to push the roll of rag braided carpet back in front of it when I came in. I rose from my wooden chair and shifted the carpet roll, blocking the draft.

"Got plenty of full batteries and wood though, if this turns into a blizzard. Still not a popsicle."

My voice was soft enough the wind all but drowned it out. This time, though, it echoed—like someone had whispered my own words back. I straightened, stepping back. A shadow stood in front of me, barely more solid than the smoke from the fire.

The ghost had slipped in, through my wards. To pass the wards, it would have no ill intent, but it was still a situation to assess carefully.

"Who are you?" Smooth and calm, my voice fell in a trained cadence. The sound of it made me sick, as did my reflexive readying of a working to bind and control him. I didn't let the working lapse, though. Some ghosts were hungry for life, even if they didn't *intend* harm.

Memories tried to choke me as I stared at him. I pushed them back.

Not the time, Elena.

His form gained clarity as I waited for his answer. In a few minutes, a pale watercolor of a living man stood before me, middle aged, with dark hair and eyes. He wore a jacket and flannel shirt and jeans with knee high hiking boots, all of them years out of date.

His eyes, probably some shade of dark brown in life, were guarded but lively and curious as he stared at me. Good and bad; he retained enough of himself he could be communicated with and potentially bad if he didn't realize he was dead.

"My name's Sean. Why are you calling me here?"

I could barely hear his voice over the sound of the storm. His words made me stare at him in surprise. As they got older, ghosts lost a lot of what made them feel and act human, fading to endlessly repeating memories.

Anger and malice were the last to fade. Hence haunted houses.

Keeping the control working ready just in case, I tilted my head.

"I'm not sure what you mean. If I've called you, it wasn't on purpose. Do you know you're a ghost?"

"Yeah, I figured that out when I walked through the wall," he said drily. "Before, I think I was sleeping, but this...call...I'd wake up, and it was spring, then I'd roll over and it would be fall. And you were always nearby. Are you a spirit?" He moved closer to me, pausing to examine my pantry.

"No."

"Huh. I was hoping you were 'cause I've never heard of a spirit liking ramen."

I laughed, as he'd intended. It was nice to have company. Even if he was a potential threat, he was much more personable than Old Ginger.

But I had to ask him.

"Are you looking for help to move on? I'm afraid I'll have to research, but I'm willing to try." The method I learned in school magically ripped the ghost- the soul- to shreds so small there was no unity of memory or personality. Probably so nobody else could get information from them besides preventing the ghost from retaliating.

Another terrible thing I'd done when I worked for MOD, another guilt I carried. Reading Magical Instruction over the past winters, I'd puzzled out the basics of another working that I could try if he wanted to leave this world.

Sean pondered a moment, turning his attention to the stove. He poked at it, his finger sliding into its side. "I don't think so, not yet."

"Do you know what happened to you?" I settled into my chair, watching him drift around the cave.

"I don't remember. I was a ranger working for the state, it was summer, I was checking the area out. Then I blinked and it was spring and you were swearing and hauling wood to the side of the cave mouth. Then more blinks, usually with you nearby. This is the first time I've stayed awake long enough to say hi."

Odd. I took a sip of tea. "If you'd like to socialize, I have no objection. Do you like to play board games? I have a couple. No music or vid, I'm afraid, but I do have some books on my tablet too."

"Not sure if I can turn the pages on a tablet," he said ruefully, turning his hands palm up.

"Could you hold cards?"

He nodded.

I pulled a deck of cards and a cribbage board from on top of the pantry. Normally I played solitaire, but I knew how to play cribbage and a two person game would be more interesting.

"Do you know how to play cribbage?"

"No."

"Then I'll explain the rules. It'll pass the time, this sounds like it's going to be a long storm."

Sean learned fast and wasn't a bad player. His endless flow of talk about the forest, animals, and scientific detail about both was interesting. He also had an interesting perspective on forty year old news, which matched the style of clothing he wore.

Days passed as we played games and I learned about the forest in which I lived.

For example, I had never known grizzly bears hibernated much more deeply than brown bears, and the bear den nearby was a brown bear's. And that I probably needed to be careful so I didn't acquire a short term involuntary roommate.

Like many ghosts, he could move light objects. On consideration, I thought he'd been in some kind of stasis after he died, which was unusual. I couldn't research, but my only guess was that he'd been killed by a spirit who'd put him in the stasis. I didn't want to ask the spirits in the area though.

My aura would have attracted him because it strengthened his connection to the world, breaking the stasis. If he remained around me he'd keep getting stronger, since he would unknowingly tap into my magic as long as I permitted it. He couldn't take what I didn't choose to give, so I had no issue with it.

And having someone I could talk with was sweet after such a long time alone. Even better, he was funny and curious, and laughed at my jokes. The days passed much faster after he came to live with me.

EVEN IN THE SHADE IT WAS BROILING HOT. MY SHIRT stuck to me, soaked in sweat from the sultry heat as I examined young trees near the cave. I needed to fell some to make sure I had firewood. I'd learned that wood took time to season, so I harvested in the spring. That first year had been a bear, though.

"Need a hand with that?"

I jumped. "Sean! Don't sneak up on me like that! Especially when I have an ax in hand!"

"Sorry, being silent kinda comes with the territory." He grinned at me, the pale sunlight shining through him. A squirrel shook its tail and threw a twig at him.

It passed through him and landed at my feet. The squirrel chittered and threw another.

"You seem to have made an impression," I said.

Sean pointed at a grove of trees downslope. "If you're looking for trees to cut down, go for these."

It was a stand of youngish trees. I'd harvested them the year I got here, actually. They grew back fast but chopping them down and dealing with the spines to get smaller logs had been a chore.

"Why them in particular?" I asked.

"They're black locust trees. They're an invasive species in Montana. For your needs, they're hardwood and they burn well. If you harvest them young, they spit out coals less. You'll help diversify the biome in this area if you cut them back."

Alrighty then. I'd had no idea, but if the thought of me chopping them down made Sean happy, I'd roll with it. A long day later they were felled. The next morning I got to work cutting them into logs I could carry up to the concealed platform where I seasoned the firewood.

"Here, let me." Sean guided a log into position, holding it steady as I brought the ax down. The pull on my magic felt good, exercising it even when I didn't use it

The satisfying crack of splitting wood made me feel like I was accomplishing a lot.

"Grab more magic and put them into the frame," I said.

He grinned at me. "Sure!"

The logs floated up and I strolled next to them. The energy exerted was close to the same as hauling them physically, but now I'd be less sore in the morning.

The logs stacked, Sean gazed down the hill. "If you want, I can show you where the good berry patches were around here. Before the birds get to all of them."

I liked berries, though I was pretty sure I'd found all the nearby patches of them. "Let's check that out. It's been a while since I've had jam. And good company."

He gave me a sideways look. "For as long as you want company."

I grinned at him, my heart squeezing in painful pleasure. "I'm very bribable with sweets. And I had an idea. I'm going to talk to Old Ginger about getting canning lids. I saved the old jars and bands when I got jam last year, but I don't have any tops. This way I can make some jam and have a sweet other than dried berries."

He smiled. "Follow me."

To my surprise, Sean knew the location of a couple stands of berries that I hadn't found. I needed to go to Old Ginger and get the lids. This would be a two trip year, but I could risk it. After filling a basket with fresh berries, I teleported to my memorized spot nearby Old Ginger's cabin. I'd snared the energy pattern that was Sean and took him along.

On the other side his eyes were huge. If he could have paled he would have. "Warn me next time!"

"Sorry..." I whispered.

He shook his head. "It's ok, just warn me."

I nodded, then turned in the direction of the trading cabin and shouted, "Ginger! I have berries to trade!"

"Bring them in," he yelled back.

I picked my way down the path. I'd been here often enough I knew the path in that didn't trigger any traps. Sean floated next to me, rubbernecking.

Old Ginger didn't react when we came in beyond granting me a dour stare. "What do you need, Berry-lady?"

"Canning lids," I said, setting the brimming basket on the wooden board that served as his counter.

He snorted, then reached behind him, producing a box of exactly what I wanted. "Had them on order for someone else, but you got here first."

Old Ginger had connections, and he could get you almost anything. The downside was that he charged a premium for it, since most of the people living around here had reasons they wanted to avoid town.

Sean made a face at him.

Old Ginger's brow creased, and he gazed around the dim room alertly. "Do you feel that?"

"Feel what?" I asked. When he turned to put the berries behind him, I frowned at Sean. This did verify that Sean wasn't visible to regular people, but the magically sensitive could feel his presence.

"You coming back again this year, or do you want your whole order? The basket of berries won't cover it," Old Ginger said flatly.

"No, I'll be back in the fall. Do I have any extra credit from this visit?"

He gave a number and I smiled. "I'll take the chess set then."

"You're in a good mood today." He passed the box to me.

"Happens to the best of us," I said with a smile as I walked out.

That evening I found out Sean was a very good chess player. A shark, in fact.

A few weeks later I had a variety of jams to trade with people in the fall. It was a good summer, happy, and the winter seemed shorter once it started. I'd started creating basic workings again, searching for a way to give Sean more strength when he needed to move something. Perhaps even grant him a physical form for a short while, like a golem, to help him connect to the world better.

It was kind of weird feeling happy and busy. I kept waiting for the other shoe to drop.

February brought a warm snap and Sean and I were outside. The temperature was only a few degrees below freezing, nice and warm. Snowball fights against a ghost were unfair, but I'd fashioned a working that used a tiny trickle of magic to make him feel the impact if it hit him. A risk using magic, yes, but fun.

Sean froze and the snowball arced gracefully through his head. My back tingled, like I'd suddenly gotten a huge sunburn.

"Elena. Look south." Sean pointed, his eyebrows climbing toward his hairline.

I squinted southward, my heart skipping a beat in reaction. The horizon was ablaze with magic, an eerie light pluming into the sky, like a vid special effect. But this was real and happening here and now. "That's a lot of magic. Bomb levels of 'a lot'. People gossiped about the magic bombs project when I was still with MOD, but if we can see an aura this far away a lot of people are dead. This isn't good. 'A war's been declared' levels of bad, honestly."

"Should we check it out? I'm not sure how far I can travel from here." Sean took a step forward, protective instincts plain to be read on his face.

I shook my head, adrenaline flooding my veins and my insides clenching. "It's far away. And I'm here for a reason, my friend. Government types are going to be all over that. I don't know if I can do anything and if I go there, I'll be snatched back into the Bureau."

"Yes, but...." Sean gestured at the terrifying stream of magic touching the sky.

"I know. It bothers me too." I had to force the words out. Picking up the bucket of chopped ice I'd put down for the snowball fight, I headed for the cave.

The unnatural aurora to the south disturbed me, frightened me, and the unpleasant tingling at the base of my skull made it worse. I hurried for my shelter. Sean paced me, though he left no tracks.

Once we were in the cave, I set the bucket down and paced. I couldn't settle, I could see and feel the power even through the stone. Someone had set off so much magic. What was happening there?

"Berry lady! Come out! We need to talk!" Old Ginger shouted. "There's been an accident, we need medical help."

What on earth? How was he here?

I pulled my crystal out of my pocket and focused on it, casting my magic to see what was going on outside. Old Ginger stood a distance away, bundled in a thick coat colored with winter camouflage, near the trail that led into the valley, a light snowmobile parked beside him.

As I watched, he scanned the area, focusing on the churned up snow where Sean and I had been playing.

It was possible he didn't know exactly where the cave was. I'd gone to a lot of trouble to keep it concealed. But my tracks were everywhere around here, and Old Ginger wasn't a slouch at finding prey.

Finding out what he wanted was first priority. Then I'd decide if I needed to kill him to protect my home. I hoped I didn't have to. Risking a 'port seemed best, in case he had a weapon and planned to take me out as I emerged.

I really wanted to know how he'd found this place.

Pulling the working around me, I pocketed the crystal and spent the power. The winter-chilled wind swept around me, even in my thick coat as I dropped into the snow perhaps ten feet from Ginger.

"What are you doing here?"

His mouth clamped harder than usual, Old Ginger glared at me. "Getting shut of the trouble you've brought here."

A dark silhouette detached from the trees near Ginger. Howard Graves, my ex-supervisor, wearing tactical gear, with a stunner clamped in his large fist. My nightmare realized.

He'd gained weight, fleshy but still strong, dark hair now streaked with white, and the meanest smile I'd ever encountered on his face.

MOD had found me.

Sean floated out of the cave and my heart twisted. Howard's petty cruelties inflicted on the dead were a bad memory.

His eyes didn't track to Sean, though. Perhaps he hadn't noticed the ghost drifting behind him.

"Huh, Tubbygirl got skinny, put on some muscle. Hope you keep the weight off back at the office. Please tell me you're going to be unreasonable and I get to do this the hard way?" His thin smile curved his lips as he walked toward me, his presence violating my home.

His eyes on me brought my cringe reflex to the fore, and I had to fight to stand straight. His stunner was flashing the red green pattern that meant it was set to lethal protocols, which didn't make sense if he planned to stun me.

Old Ginger cleared his throat. "Um, the reward?"

In a lightning move Howard shot him, letting him fall face first in the snow, the stunner on me again before I had a chance to take more than one step. My throat burned. Once again, betrayed. Just business, Old Ginger would say, except he was face first in the snow and needed to be flipped over to avoid suffocating if the shot hadn't killed him. He had a twenty percent chance of surviving with some neurological issues.

My old nightmare wore a grade ten ward to fend off magical attacks, the blur of its magic plain as day. His own magic hung around him as well. Even if he was a grade one practitioner, how was he missing the inferno to the south?

"Not funny, Howard." My head throbbed. "If you have a functional brain, how are you not looking at the lightshow? And did you find me, or just wait for a tip to be called in?"

He paused, the stunner pointed at my midsection. His hand flexed, and the red faded, replaced by a steady pulse of green. "You got careless and lazy. As for the fireworks, so what if they're doing a defense test? You've got a nice big reward on you, and I plan to collect. And I'll keep collecting from you for the inconvenience these past couple years, where I had to cover for your lazy whiny ass."

"Last time I checked the thirteenth amendment was still on the books. I quit." I'd had this conversation in nightmares, so I at least had witty responses already figured out. Weird how I'd known exactly what he'd say.

"Funny, Tubbygirl. You didn't finish your contract, and I'm just the enforcement mechanism. Who are you going to complain to anyway?"

"Anyone with ears."

Harold snorted. "You can discuss that in MOD HQ. If you don't want me to shred your ghost friend, turn around and let me cuff you." The stunner flashed brighter green as he primed it. I could either be conscious and cuffed, or wake up cuffed with a screaming headache, probably tied to the snowmobile as we left.

With Sean still in this valley, his soul ripped into tiny pieces.

"Run, Sean," I said softly as I turned around.

Sean regarded me with a frown and I shook my head. Howard could destroy him.

Click. The cold rune engraved metal of the mage cuffs bit into my wrists, a stark reminder of the hellhole I'd return to. These really were enough to contain me. I inhaled sharply as the burn started, traveling down my arms, my hands spasming.

As long as it kept Sean safe...

"Move, Tubby."

"What about Old Ginger?"

"I had the stun ramped up to full. He's dead." Graves grinned at me. "He was an idiot."

"He might be alive. High stun doesn't kill all the time, but suffocation does."

Graves laughed again, but walked over and hooked a boot under Old Ginger's side. "You want him to die slow of exposure if he survived the stun? Didn't know you had it in you, Tubbygirl."

He kept me covered as he flipped Old Ginger. As soon as I saw his face I winced. He hadn't survived the stun.

Movement caught my eye and I looked up. Thousands of floating creatures filled the sky above us, glowing even to normal eyes, flying and swooping everywhere. I took a quick step backward and landed on my butt.

"Do you see them," I squeaked. The sight, beautiful and terrifying, made me want to reach out with my magic. Spasms in my arms reminded me I couldn't.

Howard grabbed my arm and yanked me up, wrenching my shoulder. "Snowmobile. Stay with me."

The nearest road was miles away.

Before we made it more than a step toward the vehicle, the creatures were on us. One of the creatures swooped into Old Ginger.

His body twitched, eyes opening as he sat up.

Graves, eyes bulging, called fire from his hands, turning the body into ash where it stood. He dropped his personal ward to do so.

One of the creatures dove for him as another smacked into me, hitting me square in the breastbone and continuing into my body. The edges of my mind tingled, the sensation growing more painful with each second. I dropped to my knees, aware of Sean's frantic presence next to me.

"Elena! Stay with me, Elena."

"Where else would I go?" I gasped.

If it was the last thing I said to anyone, I didn't want it to be pathetic.

Pain bubbled from my chest up into my head and down into my feet and fingers, gushing like a river in the spring, swirling and carrying another presence, cold and alien. The sound of wings fluttered in my head.

Let me in

"No," I half sobbed, hardening my shields. I focused on my will, what made me Elena, as the presence hammered at me. The pain it was inflicting drowned out the pain the cuffs forced on me.

The next jolt of pain, like talons slashing inside me, yanked a stifled scream from my throat. I'd endured abuse in my training for MOD, and the memory gave me the strength to hold onto my concentration.

Howard gurgled and screamed, snow flying as he thrashed on the ground nearby.

Sean floated next to me, expression frantic.

I used my magic, pressing back against the jellyfish melded into my body, mentally shoving against the invasion, my inner and outer voice a scream. "Get out!"

The next wave of agony almost whited me out. Panting and moaning, I held onto consciousness by my fingernails, and when my eyes focused again Sean's face was next to mine, his face set with grim determination. Our eyes met, and then he plunged forward, his body passing into mine as well.

I whimpered. Sean's presence wrapped around my mind, interfering with the spasms of torment from the creature and the cuff, allowing me to fully concentrate on the alien presence.

The jellyfish form was a soul, armored with magic, but souls were what my magic excelled at. In just a few moments, the entity had woven itself into my life force- I wasn't sure I could root it out of myself without dying.

But with Sean shielding me from the pain, I could contain it and retain control of my body.

I felt rather than heard Sean grunt. He was feeling the pain in my place.

The realization hurried me in building the cage, sparing what magic I could to sustain Sean.

Inside a cage of pure magic, its consciousness screeched at me, sounding like an enraged bird.

Let me out!

"Make up your mind," I mumbled.

At least the cage took away its ability to cause me pain, leaving only the cuff.

I felt Sean's presence inside me, like a cool breeze sweeping off a stand of pine.

"Can you leave?"

I paused for him to answer, and he took over my vocal cords to do so.

"I'm trying, but while I was fighting it, I seem to have gotten... stuck...in you."

I stifled an inappropriate snicker, brought on by exhaustion and fear. Humor warmed me from Sean. He'd caught it too.

Opening my eyes, the scene in front of me made me stagger to my feet. Howard wavered on his hands and knees. His hands curved into the snow, and when he raised one I saw bloody bone claws had erupted from his fingertips. His broad face had elongated and his eyes were now larger and slightly tilted upward.

His mouth was full of teeth that would make a jaguar proud. Ripping and tearing teeth.

His brown eyes, wide and bulging, held nothing of thought or humanity.

I wanted to help, but instinct told me to kill or run. Lacking any offensive ability at the moment, I opted to run.

Graves ran after me, his hands outstretched, those bony claws far too close. But it wasn't the grace of a man used to his body; this was the desperate flailing of a puppet with its strings tangled.

Dodge. Weave. I moved on instinct, my body remembering the evasion tactics I'd honed over years of running, hiding, surviving. But with my hands restrained and this... thing wearing Howard's face relentless in its pursuit, options were running thin.

"Elena, kill him, do it fast!" Sean said, again using my mouth.

"I can't with the cuff on."

"Then run faster."

Helpful, Sean.

I gasped and swore as the breeze of air moved by Howard's lunge brushed my arm, barely missing me.

Howard's stunner would be locked to his aura. He still had his government issued ward, which meant any magic would slide off him unless I hit him hard.

Difficult, with my hands cuffed behind my back.

Graves howled. I risked a glance behind me. He'd tripped in a dip in the ground hidden by snow. I bolted toward the cave mouth.

"We need a weapon."

"Any suggestions welcome," I puffed. My chest and belly hurt as I burst past the windbreaker, my eyes darted around the room, heart pounding in my ears. My gardening tools hung from the wall.

I crouched, putting my wrists behind my knees, then crouched further. One step...I grunted at the strain in my shoulders. Graves had cuffed me pretty tight, but I was also flexible.

Movement beyond the windbreaker. I took the second step, then with my hands in front of me I darted for the tools as Howard limped into the cave. One of his ankles was badly swollen; nobody normal could have walked on it.

Zombie, remember?

The hoe. I grabbed it, gripping the cold metal and swinging it with more hope than skill. I had to stay out of reach while I did this.

"Back up, buy yourself some time!" Sean said using my lips.

I retreated, narrowly avoiding another strike. I wished I'd been trained in this kind of fight, rather than only magic.

"Keep moving!"

A plate rocked, then flew off the shelf and hit Graves, followed by silverware. Distracted, he flailed at them as a tin cup hit him square in the face, breaking his nose.

Sean could throw much harder than he'd ever shown me.

"Hit him now!"

I didn't pause to think. I couldn't. With a scream that tore at my throat, I swung the hoe with both hands. It hit Graves, square on the neck. My stomach spasmed as the head sank into his throat, blood spraying everywhere. He staggered, and I swang again for his head. Then another hit, and another.

Howard's body convulsed, the alien presence shrieking within him. I swung again, my actions mechanical, detached from the horror of what I was doing. And then, silence. Howard stopped moving.

And then the jellyfish thing poured out of him and floated for a moment, then zipped away.

I stumbled back a step, then ran outside before I vomited.

Crouched in the snow, after the spasms stopped, I found myself still holding the hoe.

"Elena, we have to—"

"Get out of here. I know." I glanced toward the hill, my hands shaking.

I couldn't bring myself to say sorry to Howard's corpse. Old Ginger's hurt to see, though I hadn't killed him.

"Come on, Elena. We need to move."

"Right. Survival first." But even as I stood, there was a weight on my soul.

I'd murdered Graves. But whatever that was had taken him over completely. Were those creatures doing this everywhere?

Sweat trickled down my back as I crouched, methodically cleaning the hoe in the snow. Thoughts tumbled through my head like pebbles in my stream.

"Are you going to be okay?"

"Define 'okay,' Sean," I muttered, looking up. The jellyfish creatures streamed above our heads, a river of terror. "We're talking about an invasion."

"You can help because of what you can do." I could picture his face saying that, even though he was inside me now.

"Right. Because I can bind souls." I closed my eyes. "And now, because I don't want our world turned into...whatever those things want it to be."

"Good thing we have a snowmobile then, right?"

"Yeah." The word hung between us, more loaded than a baked potato at a steakhouse. "Do you think you can get loose of my body?"

"Not sure. I've been trying with no luck. Till I do get out, I've got your back."

Warmth spread through my chest. I wasn't alone. He was still a friend.

"Can you use your power to open the cuff? It won't respond to my magic, but if you keep your power clear of mine it should be enough."

A moment later, the cuff clicked up. I pulled it off my wrist and threw it as far away as I could.

I headed back to what had been my home. I'd started shivering hard. I needed to warm up and eat. "First we need to figure out a way to talk without using my voice to avoid future problems."

"We can work on that."

The cave felt smaller, and I tried to ignore the body. Maybe it was just the enormity of the decision pressing in on me. Leaving my shelter and home to try to protect humanity. As if I could tuck everyone under my wing like a broody hen.

"Protect humanity," I rolled the words around my mouth like bitter candy. "No pressure."

"Nobody's better suited for it than you, Elena."

I let out a small laugh. Small, but real. "Because of my charming personality?"

"Because you're one of the strongest people I know. And hey, charm helps."

"Charm..." My lips twitched. "Is that why you stuck around?"

"Your magnetic personality was irresistible. I'm stuck to you now."

I snorted a laugh out. It helped. The fact he was trying so hard to make me laugh helped more. I heated water while I packed, avoiding looking at the body. Then I sighed and went through his pockets, pulling out the fob for the vehicle.

"Okay then." I stood, feeling the resolve harden within me. "Let's do this."

"If this is happening everywhere, people are going to be busy."

"Yeah." I went back outside with my pack, headed for the snowmobile, each step crunching in snow. "We'll need to go to one of the research centers, like El Paso or MIT."

I paused, looking back at the cave..

"Sean?"

"Yeah?"

"Thanks."

"Anytime."

The rapidly cooling evening air nipped at my cheeks as I fiddled with the vehicle. It purred to life when I pressed the button, its fob snug in my pocket. The mountain and trees were the same as they'd been this morning, unmoved, a testament to the world's indifference to changes on the human scale.

"Ready?" Sean asked.

"Yep." My lips curled into a firm smile, but my heart drummed a staccato rhythm against my ribs. I headed slowly for the trail, learning how to operate the vehicle. Leaving behind the cave that had been my sanctuary for years.

"Remember, pace yourself. It's not a sprint; it's a marathon."

"Sean, since when did you try to teach me my business?"

"Since you decided to take on extraterrestrials and save humanity. Plus, I've got nothing better to do."

"Point."

The terrain shifted, the gentle slope becoming a rugged descent. I slowed further, not wanting to risk toppling over. We reached a ridge that offered a panoramic view, the grandeur a stark contrast to the chaos that I knew brewed beyond my line of sight.

Smoke smudged the evening sky. Buildings were on fire.

I would do this. "Let's keep moving. We've got a long road ahead."

"Lead the way, Elena."

I trudged onward, three souls in one body.

I would find a way.

About Daphne Moore

Meet Daphne Moore, a USA Today bestselling author who has been spinning tales since before she could even read. Her love for storytelling has only grown stronger since then, and now she spends her days searching for the perfect story idea and furiously typing away at her keyboard, hoping to catch all those fleeing plot bunnies.

When she's not lost in the world of her imagination, you can find her in her small Ohio suburb, playing with her son's pup. She's also the proud aunt to a several humans and two adorable dogs. The dogs all insist they're the true muses behind her writing.

As a writer of speculative fiction, Daphne adds just the right amount of romance to make your heart skip a beat.

So if you're looking for a good laugh, a thrilling adventure, or a heartwarming romance, Daphne Moore is the author for you. Just don't distract her from her writing process or you might become a character in her next book!

She's even got a free short story waiting for you on her website, so you can get another taste of her writing before diving headfirst into one of her amazing books.

https://www.daphnekmoore.com

THE WINCHESTER HOUSE

MAYA BLACK

The Winchester House

Maya Black

PROLOGUE

May, 2014

"Welcome to your new home, Mr. and Mrs. Yoshida," the agent said.

"Thank you," they both said, their faces beaming.

"I will quickly take my leave now," the agent said as he cleared his throat and literally ran away.

The couple looked at each other and shrugged confusedly by the agent's actions.

The movers finished taking in all their belongings and then stared at the Japanese couple.

"You do know that this house is haunted right?" the owner of the moving truck said as he was about to leave.

The couple looked at each other and laughed.

"Do you really believe in that? It is just an old Victorian home with secrets, that is why they call it haunted. My wife and I have checked the house and we believe that the Winchester house is perfect for us," Mr. Yoshida shared with the mover who still thought that it was a bad idea to move into this house.

"You know, we hear screams from this house every night and it doesn't sound human at all," the mover spoke again.

"It was just some broken pipes and it has been fixed," Mrs. Yoshida said before laughing as she turned around, walking in with her husband while the mover left.

"I just think saying a house is haunted is stupid. If it is truly haunted, do they really think it would be on the market for people to buy it?"

Mr. Yoshida shook his head while his wife laughed.

"It's probably a folklore that parents told their kids around the area so they wouldn't stay out too late," Mrs. Yoshida said as she twirled around the house. "This house is beautiful. I can't wait to decorate our new home," she squealed.

"Yes honey, I will check if all the taps are working and we can try to arrange some of our things today and then we can continue tomorrow, okay?"

He looked at her as she nodded.

"HONEY, I THINK THE PIPE IS FAULTY, CAN YOU PASS ME the flash light?" Mr. Yoshida asked as he heard footsteps but he got no reply.

"Honey?" he said again with his hand stretched out, then he was handed a flashlight and he continued looking at the pipes.

When he was done, he went back to the living room to explain what he found.

"Babe, I noticed that the pillows were floating when I came into the living room. That is such a wonderful trick!" Mrs. Yoshida clapped her hands.

"Really? I would have loved to see that, but if you were in the living room, who would have handed me the flashlight?" He asked.

"Handed you the flashlight?"

"You didn't come to the basement to check on me?"

He remembered he could feel someone's breath on his neck and he just assumed it was his wife until she walked went away.

"No," Mrs. Yoshida said, looking at her husband like he had grown a head.

"I felt you standing over me," Mr. Yoshida continued but when she repeatedly asked how that could be, he dropped it.

"Ok, well let's have dinner at that fancy restaurant we saw on our way to our new home!" Mrs. Yoshida smiled at her husband.

"Yes, I think it is the best fit. Our gas is not installed anyway, it will be installed tomorrow," he informed his wife as they walked outside the house.

"Cheers to our new beginning and our new home," they chorused as they clinked their glasses together for one last drink before leaving the restaurant.

"That meal was wonderful," Mrs. Yoshida smiled, a little tipsy from the wine they just had.

"Yeah." Her husband nodded as he walked her to the car.

"Hey, dude, are you the one that moved in recently to the Winchester house?" the valet asked him.

"Yes," he replied.

"The house is so beautiful." Mrs. Yoshida hiccupped as she smiled.

"Yeah, well I'd advise you both to sleep somewhere else tonight. That place is haunted and no one has ever lasted more than a night in that house," the valet told them.

They looked at each other, then at the valet.

"Thank you for that information, but it is not really needed. My wife and I are already settled in," Mr. Yoshida said in a tone that stated they were done with this conversation and then he walked away with his wife.

They got into the car and Mr. Yoshida began to drive toward home carefully. "I can't understand what everyone's problem is, first the mover, now that valet. It is just...." His sentence was interrupted as a crow smashed into their windshield. He swerved from surprise, veering too far to the right and hit somebody's mailbox.

"Fuck," he cursed as he got out to check the damage done to his car, the mailbox, and the bird.

His wife followed him and gasped as they looked down at the dead bird.

"Looks like the mailbox is okay," she informed him after getting over her shock.

"Let's get going then," he said angrily. They settled back in and as he drove away saying, "Could this night get any worse?"

The rest of the drive home was quiet as both were lost in their own thoughts. Once they got home, they got out, glanced at each other and walked to the front door. Mr. Yoshida had the house key in his hand and reached toward the knob but the door suddenly creaked open.

"What? I locked the door," he said.

"You probably just didn't lock it properly, or the lock is broken. We will have someone check it in the morning," she said as they walked into the house.

"Oh my god! It is freezing!" Mrs. Yoshida said as she ran to turn on the heater. "It's the beginning of summer, why is it so cold in here?" she whined as goosebumps erupted over her arms.

"Maybe the air conditioning was left on." Mr. Yoshida shrugged.

"No, I turned it off," she replied.

He continued walking further into the house when he tripped on something. "What the hell? Who put that there?" He crouched down to pick up a doll.

"We don't even have dolls," Mrs. Yoshida commented as she felt uneasy. "Babe, I think we should sleep in a hotel tonight as the valet suggested," she said.

He angrily dismissed her concerns. "No, we will stay here. This is our home and don't tell me you are letting those people get into your head."

"N—no," she said quickly.

"Good." He walked upstairs and she followed him quickly.

They both got ready to go to bed but she had to do her skincare routine first. She applied her facial cleanser and opened the tap to wash it off as she squeezed her eyes closed.

After rinsing off the cleaners, she opened her eyes to see her face was red. Behind her, she saw a little girl holding a doll behind her. Blood flowed out of the tap.

"Hahn!" she screamed.

"What is the problem?!"

He rushed into the bathroom.

"T—th –the girl, blood.." she stammered out as she pointed into the mirror with shaky hands.

"What? There is no girl and where is the blood?" he asked her.

She looked down at her hands and then at the mirror and then the sink. "I –the tap..." She quickly turned on the tap but only water rushed out.

"I think you are still tipsy from the wine and you are letting these people get into your head."

"B-but I..." She looked back into the mirror at her face.

"It's okay, honey, let's go to bed," he said as he led her to bed.

"AH!" MRS. YOSHIDA SCREAMED AS SHE OPENED HER EYES to see the silhouette of a person looming over her.

"What happened?" her husband said as he was startled by her scream.

"There is someone there," she pointed in front of their bed as she started crying.

"No, there is no one. I think you are just terrified. You probably had a dream. We will talk about this in the morning," he cuddled her as they tried to fall asleep again.

"Ahh!" he screamed as he felt someone holding his ankle.

"Babe! What is ..... AHH!" Mrs. Yoshida screamed and jumped from the bed as she saw the silhouette fling her husband from the bed to the other side of the room.

She immediately got up and started running and her husband joined her while they heard a banshee scream and a woman with a white flowing gown stained with blood started pursuing them.

"Ahh!" she screamed as she tripped on the rug and fell down.

"Harriet!" Mr. Yoshida called out to his wife but ran away

immediately after he saw the woman was already on the heels of his wife.

"AHH," he let out a deep breath as he bent down to steady his breathing when he reached the outside of the house.

He looked up to see a young man with gold teeth smiling at him and crows flying around the house, then he heard the screams of his wife and he started to run again making his way down the driveway, not seeing the truck until it was too late.

"GOOD MORNING, EVERYONE, IT IS REALLY SAD AS WE record another death in San Jose. Mr. Yoshida, aged 34 years, and his wife, aged 32 years, were found dead this morning. Mr. Yoshida was said to be running when he got hit by a truck, while his wife was found hanged to death on a tree close to their home. May their souls rest in peace," the news reporter said.

LUCIA

"Welcome to your new home, Mr. and Mrs. Martini," the agent said to them.

"The house is beautiful," Mrs. Martini gushed as she stared at the Winchester house.

"Yeah, it is," Mr. Martini smiled at his wife.

"I think it needs to be repainted," I said as I studied the house through my thick rimmed glasses.

"It's yours, you may do as you wish. I will quickly take my leave now," the agent said as he cleared his throat and literally ran away.

"I would advise you to run and leave this place immediately. This house is haunted, nobody lasts for more than a day here. You need to leave or you might be recorded as the next dead person in San Jose," the mover warned as he drove off.

"What does he mean by that?" I said, looking amused. "And I thought my stay here would be boring!"

I smirked at my parents who just ignored me, as usual, and walked into the house.

AS I WALKED INTO THE HOUSE I SAW THEM AS THEY
stared back at me. They seemed to be glued to the wall.

"Hi guys," I waved at them but they didn't respond to me.

They appeared to be studying me.

"Who are you saying hi to?" mother asked me as she looked at the
wall and back at me.

"I am talking to those people, they are weirdly dressed."

I chuckled.

"Who?" My mother said, looking at me weirdly.

"You can't see them?"

I was confused.

"See who?" she replied again.

"Them!" I pointed at them feeling frustrated that my mother was
looking at me like I had lost my mind.

My parents looked at each other and then back at me again.

"Have you stopped taking your meds?" my father asked.

"I do not need my meds. I am not depressed!" I said to my parents.

"Dear child, I am not saying you are depressed but you need to
take your meds," my mother softened her voice as she lightly touched
my cheeks.

"Okay, Mom," I replied as I wondered how my life would have
been if I wasn't out with my friends that night.

I waited until my parents walked out and then I walked towards
them.

"You do know that I can see you, right?" I asked them, laughing.

Then the little girl moved towards me with her creepy doll and her
tangled hair that seemed to be covered in blood.

"What happened to you?" I asked her as I took a deep breath
assessing the injuries at the back of her head.

"You are rude. You didn't even ask me what my name is," she said
in a little voice and looked away like she was hurt.

I knew she was just playing mind games but I decided to play
along with her as I crouched down and smiled at her.

"I am sorry. What is your name?" I asked her.

"My name is Madeline and I was killed in the backyard. My step
mother had enough of me and my sister and she pushed us from the

balcony. My sister found peace and went to the afterlife but I decided to stay back and torment my step mother. I enjoyed every piece of it and I killed her but I think I enjoyed it a little too much," she said looking at me with doe eyes that I didn't fall for.

I looked at her for longer and she thought I didn't notice when she moved closer to me so she could hold my hand.

I stood still and continued to watch her as she held my hand and smiled at me.

It wasn't a cute smile, it looked like I had seen the true face of evil and she suddenly started to chant something.

I quickly removed my hands from her and she lost concentration, staring at me like I had done something bad to her.

"Not today, sweetheart."

I laughed and walked away.

ANTHONY

I woke up this morning feeling anything but happy. I was very tired and very irritated. Partly because of the annoying ghost I had to deal with last night and because she appeared in my dreams again.

"Hello, dear."

Mother smiled at me but I didn't feel like returning the smile, so I walked towards her and hugged her instead.

"Good morning, Mom," I said walking to the kitchen island.

"Morning, baby, why that sulky face? You saw her again?" she asked me.

"No, well, yes. She appeared but she isn't the main cause of my annoyance, just my irritation."

I sat down and took a sip of my coffee.

"The ghost from yesterday, that is," I continued.

"I thought as much. She was really loud and asked a lot of questions," Mother said, mentioning all the things I disliked and I just grunted in reply.

"Ha, I just knew he'd be mad this morning," Lucien said as he took his laptop from the coffee table and headed to the door.

"See y'all later today."

He saluted us and left.

I sighed.

Sometimes I wished my life was as simple as his, since he really didn't have many responsibilities, unlike me. I have to head the Ghost Inc and still worry about our hotels and resorts.

"Hey, sweetheart," my father kissed my mother's forehead and moved into the kitchen. "He is still mad from yesterday's ghost?" he asked my mom.

"Yeah, she was pretty annoying, taunting him with all his painful memories and then he dreamed of her," my mother filled my father in.

"Hmm. I think he needs a break," Father shrugged.

"And he is here, and leaving."

I stood up and left.

I loved my family but sometimes they can be extremely annoying.

I looked at my mail, then I showered and put on my new Armani suit and walked out of the house.

You might be wondering why a thirty-year-old man is still living with his parents. Well, let's just say I have my own penthouse in New York close to our company's headquarters, but I still love spending time with my family anytime I can.

I walked into the Veritas Resorts and Real Estate headquarters and I noticed all the staff rushing to get busy so I didn't shout at them or get them fired.

It's funny how they gave me a nickname, Mr. Grumpy. I promise I am not grumpy. I am just not in the mood to smile stupidly half of the time.

"Good morning, Mr. Veritas, we got a new intel on the land you sorted out last week. It is available and up for sale," my secretary informed me.

"What is the price that it was listed at?" I asked as I continued to walk to my office with him behind me.

"It is two hundred thousand dollars for three plots," he responded.

"I will take it at only one fifty. I know they are selling because they need the money and the land has lost its value. Tell them one fifty or nothing," I told him as I walked away.

"Okay, I will do that," he nodded.

"Mother! Why did you book a vacation without my notice? I am attending a fundraiser that week," I complained.

"You need to unwind, you have been extra grumpy lately." Mother ignored everything I said.

"I do not need to unwind. I will not be following you all on the vacation," I threatened.

"Anthony Sebastien Veritas! You will do no such thing!" she raised her voice.

"We will see, Mother," I held my laughter knowing I would follow them on the vacation but I just wanted to add extra spice and make her agitated.

"Anthony!" she screamed.

"Okay, Mother, I was joking."

I laughed.

"I have idiots for sons," I heard her complaining to my father before she hung up the phone.

I quickly called my brother.

"Damien, what are you doing in Spain? I need you at the headquarters tomorrow. We are going on vacation at the end of the week. I need to close certain deals this week and I need you to help me coax one very annoying ghost to the afterlife," I explained to him.

"I am having the time of my life and no, I cannot come back anytime soon. I am busy with ...."

"Damien," I heard a lady moan.

"Just don't get anyone pregnant and I want you here by Thursday," I said to my playboy brother before ending the call.

"Anthony," Lyra walked into my office.

"Hi, boo," she said sitting on my desk.

"Lyra, this is not the time, I am busy," I said to my girlfriend.

"I just found out that you are going on a vacation without me," she whined.

"It is a family vacation, Lyra," I said tiredly.

"So, you mean I am not family?" she asked.

Why am I even with her? How did I start dating her?

Honestly, I could have never seen myself with a woman like Lyra five years ago and after the incident with the woman that haunts my dreams, I am very sure that I have no feelings for Lyra but I can't just break her heart like that.

I really need to tell her that I don't have feelings for her.

LUCIA

"AHH!" I HEARD MY MOTHER SCREAM A FEW NIGHTS LATER as she ran out of the bedroom.

Father and I were in the sitting room. "What happened?" he asked as he stood up.

I watched as the ghosts laughed and I saw Berry coming down the stairs. I had found out that the only person I could talk to, or that would talk to me, was Madeline and she was still trying to kill me even though I could tell that she enjoyed talking to me.

"I saw a woman in a wedding dress in the mirror when I entered the bathroom," she said looking very scared.

"I know we have been experiencing abnormal activities. I mean, last night when I came down to drink some milk because I couldn't sleep, I saw the pillows moving around in the air and one floated towards me," he informed us.

"Yes, there are ghosts in the house," I said to my parents who turned to me with wide eyes.

"Ghosts?" she asked.

"Yes, ghosts. There are five of them to be precise, that I've seen so far. They are the people I saw when I first came into the house. I can't talk to all of them, only Madeline. She told me that she died in the nineteen hundreds and she wanted revenge and she has been living here ever since," I explained to my parents.

"Th –that's impossible," she stuttered.

"What do you mean there are five ghosts living with us?" he asked, looking at me like he was finally understanding what I was saying.

"I can see them," I said.

"Are you not taking your medication again, honey?" she asked me as she took a step towards me.

I took a step back.

"I am taking my medication and I am not just making up things. I have a feeling you don't believe me."

I looked towards Madeline.

"Show them that you guys are here," I told her.

She had a mischievous glint in her eyes as she ran towards my mother and bit her before kicking my father's legs.

"Ouch!" they both screamed at the same time and ran behind me.

"There is a ghost!" she screamed dramatically as my father tried to calm her down.

Finally, my parents calmed down and my father asked me, "Is there any way they can leave?"

I looked at Madeline and back at him.

"No, they can't, or won't," I said to my parents.

"Alright, can we share and will they agree to not torment us?" she asked.

"They want us to leave and the only reason they haven't killed us yet is because I can see them," I said exactly what Madeline said and chills ran through my body but at the same time I was thrilled.

My mother gasped and threw her hands up in the air and shouted as she had become angry. "There is no way I am going to leave this house for them. I love the house and I am staying!"

They all stared at her and at that moment I felt fear flow through me as I noticed the murderous glint in their eyes.

They will try to kill my mother, I know it.

ANTHONY

"I CAN'T BELIEVE YOU GUYS DECIDED WE NEEDED VACATION in Australia!" Lucien complained for the hundredth time.

"Lucien, please, I am jet lagged. Stop being a baby and suck it up." Christian walked past Lucien into the bedroom.

"How are you people not complaining? This country is dangerous. It is filled with poisonous animals and kangaroos. What is there to love here?" Lucien shouted in frustration.

"Please, stop, you are making my ears bleed." Christian walked into the living room again.

"I cannot believe..."

"Hey!" Lucien shouted as Christian slapped the back of his head.

"Shut up, man," he responded.

"Boys! I will not have you guys fight in my living room," Mother said sternly as Lucien stood up to hit Christian back.

"I don't understand why you are fighting. This place is beautiful and we are close to the beach. Our house is literally on the beach," Damien said.

"More reason to be scared. There could be sharks or sirens in that water," Lucien commented.

Christian shook his head.

I stood up and walked into the room. I have had enough of their drama and now I want to get back to work and vanish my disturbing thoughts.

"ANTHONY, PLEASE DON'T LEAVE ME, I LOVE YOU," she cried as I walked towards my car parked on the other side of the road.

"Anthony, please," she cried as she ran after me, not seeing the truck moving towards her until it was too late.

"Ahhh!" she screamed.

I turned back in horror to see her lying lifelessly on the ground.

Almost immediately, I saw her spirit staring at me with tears flowing from her eyes.

My heart hurt and my head felt too heavy.

I had just watched the love of my life die.

"Isabel," I called out.

I opened my eyes.

"It was just a dream," I breathed out but it was more than that. It was a daily reminder of how I had lost the one woman I would have done anything for.

I let out a deep breath and stood up from the bed as I walked into the bathroom.

I have to get out of here.

I rushed out of my room, towards the door.

"What some cinnamon toast?" my mother asked.

"No, I am not hungry," I said as I walked out of the house.

I felt choked.

I needed to breathe.

I walked along the beach as I allowed myself to think of everything that happened that day.

My breath hitched as I saw a silhouette floating on the water.

"Fuck no, I am not doing ghost duty on vacation," I cursed as I walked back to the house.

"Hey, boys, do you all want to go on a boat cruise?" Mother asked with all smiles.

"Hell yeah, I need that," Damien said while Lucien looked at Mother suspiciously.

"Why do you want us to go on a boat cruise?" he squinted his eyes at her.

"Nothing serious, I just want to spend more time with my family," she shrugged nonchalantly and I knew something was up.

"If you don't give me the real reason, I will not go along with you." Lucien stared at mother.

"Okay fine, I found out someone drowned here last week and the spirit has been disturbing the fishermen. We are actually here to send her to the afterlife," Mother confessed.

"Hell no, I am not doing that on vacation," Damien said as he turned away.

"You all are coming along with me. This ghost is really mischievous and it's on water. Anything can happen, plus I need your wits and we haven't gone on an operation like this in forever. It is also very dangerous for me and your father to go alone," Mother said, looking at us with doe eyes.

"Fuck!"

"Damn!"

"We are trapped!" my brothers exclaimed and I turned to look at our mother.

"I guess we are all going then." I shook my head and Mother showed us her perfect pearly white teeth.

Mother can be overbearing sometimes.

I had a lot of work to do and she has known for a while that I am not interested in any kind of ghost hunting because I am always reminded of Isabel and the ghosts have been more annoying lately.

"Mother! I cannot believe that you booked a cruise boat just because you wanted to track down a ghost!" Lucien exclaimed.

"It is a vacation, we have to enjoy ourselves obviously." Mother rolled her eyes like Lucien had asked a stupid question.

Damien and I made eye contact and shook our heads. We decided to enjoy ourselves since we are on vacation and had been out here for hours.

"I see her!" Christian said, alerting all of us.

"Okay, looking at her, can you tell us any backstory?" Mother asked him.

"She wasn't drowned as people believe. I think that is why her spirit didn't go to the afterlife. She was strangled to death by her abusive boyfriend," Christian said.

You'd be surprised by the number of ghosts that are killed by their partners because of some argument.

"Okay, so this is the plan. Lucien, you will try to track her trail. I know it is harder because we are on water but you will have to find a way. While, Christian, continue to get more information on the events that led to her death. Anthony, you will talk to her to find out why she is still here and who hurt her and promise her to make the person pay for it. Finally, Damien, you will coax her and lead her to the afterlife," Mother informed us.

"What will you be doing, Mother?" Lucien asked.

We all rolled our eyes even though what he said was right. Mother is the best ghost hunter amongst all of us and she has special abilities, but since she retired, she left everything to us. She prefers to sit and watch.

"And what about Father?" Damien asked.

"He is in the cabin resting," she smiled at us and walked away towards the cabin.

"I can't believe this, they brought us to work but they are on vacation," Damien shook his head.

LUCIA

IT'S BEEN THREE MONTHS NOW AND THE GHOSTS ARE getting more violent. Berry has tried multiple times to kill Mother. The last time, she possessed Mother and took her to the rooftop so she could jump down and kill herself.

I pleaded with Madeline, who made me appease her by buying a lot of candy, not that she could eat it.

"I am tired of all this already!" Mother screamed.

Dominique kicked her leg and she crouched down, moaning in pain with pure rage on her face. "What the fuck!" she stared at me and my father like we were the cause of her pain.

"Honey, stop annoying them and they will stop bothering you," my father suggested to my mother who looked at him like he had just said the most stupid thing she had ever heard.

"Can you hear yourself? I should stop annoying them? They are the ones annoying me! We literally bought this house and it was very expensive and you expect me to leave? Never! I will make sure they leave! Even when I didn't do anything to provoke them, what did they do? They went into my kitchen and scattered all the contents in my fridge and mind you, they were all perishable goods! I will make them pay," she said and stormed away.

I walked upstairs and went to research more on ghosts and reasons why they can remain in the house. I knew something for sure, they wouldn't tell anyone their story and I am very sure they didn't know each other's story either. I was determined to find out what happened to each and every one of them.

My mind screamed that it was a bad idea but I think they are good people overall and that they only started possessing and killing people as a defense mechanism and for revenge as Madeline said.

That night I decided to buy a Ouija board.

"I am telling you, Cat; it is a whole lot. Sometimes I wake up to them watching me sleep and I can tell you that it is creepy as hell," I spoke to my best friend, Catherina, who was currently exploring Italy about the psychotic ghosts I live with.

"I am so glad you don't feel I am running mad. My parents felt I was seeing things at first because I told them about the ghosts. They started believing me when they started getting disturbed by the ghosts. Now my mother annoys them and they are determined to end her life," I said to Cat.

"I believe you because I can see them too," she whispered to me.

"For real?" I gasped.

"Yes, I went to one lady here in Italy for a spiritual cleansing and the opening of my third eye and what I have experienced since the cleansing, I cannot explain it," she confided in me.

"Woah, that's really crazy. Is it weird that I am fascinated by the fact that I can see them? I just bought a Ouija board," I said to Cat.

"Girl! Are you for real? One thing my mama told me is that I should not fuck with anything that is spiritual and I take that seriously. The spiritual cleansing I went for that has gotten me into trouble was a drunken dare. I had to go with Rina because I was forced to, not because I wanted to," she explained.

"I am just curious," I replied.

"Alright, sweety, whatever you do, please be careful, we will continue our discussion later, I've got to go," she said and we said our goodbyes and ended the call.

ANTHONY

"MOTHER, I THINK WE NEED TO GO TO THE SHORE NOW. It's already too late. I think the water gets more dangerous at night and don't forget the sirens will be watching too and they would want to see what we are up to and the ones that are not so nice will try to enchant us all," I said to my mother as the ghost mysteriously disappeared and we didn't see her again.

My brothers and I have been trying to get hold of our little ghost friend. I think she noticed we were following her sometime in the mid-afternoon and she decided to disappear or hide.

"I think I can see her," Damien said instantly.

"Where?" Lucien asked as he tried to track her trail.

"Behind that rock," Damien pointed to some weirdly shaped rock just standing at the left side of the beach.

"Hell no! I cannot and will not be following you people towards that rock," Christian spoke firmly.

"Why?" Lucien countered.

"Because, it has a lot of sharks around it and that is the siren's rock. There is no way I will be going towards that rock and that is final. You guys can drop me at the shore and come back over here," Christian repeated.

"But we need more information about the ghost," Damien argued.

"Her name is Grace," Mother interrupted and we all turned to face her.

"How long have you known?" I asked her, getting slightly annoyed.

"Since we set our eyes on her," she shrugged.

"And you didn't think to tell us, Mom?" Christian looked at her like she hurt his feelings.

"I'm sorry, loves."

She blew air kisses at us.

We all shook our heads and continued our ride back to the shore.

This is something Mother usually does, I guess that is why I am not so surprised. She loves seeing us struggle to get the job done, even when she knows that we are clueless on what to do and she knows ways she can give us a head start.

"Come on, my babies, you all shouldn't be angry at me. You know I just really love seeing you guys work together and that it's to make you stronger." She looked at us like we were bullying her.

"Mother, we would have still worked together and the case would probably be solved by now if you had given us all the information you knew." Lucien shook his head and we all looked at mother in agreement with what he said.

"IT'S BEEN TWO DAYS AND THE GHOST HASN'T BEEN ON these waters, do you think she has migrated somewhere else? You know, because she thinks we are looking for her?" Christian asked.

"No, she's probably still around. Do you remember ten years ago when we went on that dangerous case in London that the ghost was very angry and displeased and us showing up made her angrier? I think the situation is similar," Damien said.

"Come on boys, don't be discouraged. I have an idea on how we will catch her but first we need to spend some family time together. What do you think of going downtown for a nice dinner tonight?"

Mother smiled at us.

"Finally, we get to do something I like," Lucien cheered and we all agreed.

"I am so happy that I can spend this amount of time together with my babies!" Mother started crying.

"What is going on, Mom?" I held my mother's hand, feeling worried.

"I just.. you all were drifting apart and I couldn't bear it. I just love seeing you boys together and working together. It makes me happy. I could have solved this case alone with your father but I wanted you all to bond and solve this case together. My dear boys, I want you to understand the importance of family and working together is the best way." She smiled at all of us.

"Ughh! You just really know how to pull on our heart strings and make us do your bidding. We had no choice anyways." Lucien rolled his eyes while Mother laughed.

"Yeah, that's true. We are actually enjoying this. I don't remember the last time I was with you all together in the same room or when we were eating dinner together," I said looking at my brothers.

"I HAVE FOUND INFORMATION ON THE GHOST!" CHRISTIAN said excitedly the next morning as we all sat on the breakfast table.

"Really? What did you find?" Damien asked while we all looked at him expectantly.

"Okay, so I researched all the women with the name Grace that came here for vacation within the last month, which I suspect was the time frame in which Grace was killed and I was right. Because I found a woman with exactly the same frame and hair as the ghost, we found walking on the sea. Her name is Grace Donovan." He stood up and ran upstairs. He came down with his laptop.

"Look, she came here with her boyfriend and went missing about two weeks ago. He reported her missing and they found her body in the sea."

He showed us her details.

"Okay, how can this help with our hunt?" Lucien asked, still not getting Christian's point.

"We know she was strangled and thrown into the water, but her autopsy suggests she was also raped," Christian continued.

"Well, now we fully understand why her spirit would still be roaming looking for vengeance," Damien added.

"I have an idea," I spoke up instantly.

"Let's go to the sea now and Christian can check the hotel she was staying at with her boyfriend before she went missing," I said as I added air quotes to missing.

"She was at the Seaside Hotel. It is on the other side of the beach," Christian responded to me after checking for the hotel.

"Just as I guessed, now it all makes sense why she would be roaming around the sea and I can tell you just where she would be," I looked at all of them and they understood instantly.

"Okay, but we need a plan this time or she will disappear again," Damien said, reminding us of what happened when she saw us the last time.

"Okay, we will work like this. We need to find out when her boyfriend left and what caused him to kill her. Then we need to find her and talk to her. We need to know her actual intention on the reason why she chose to remain here, we need to understand her line of thought. Then we will find a way to convince her to go to the afterlife and we will find evidence to make sure her boyfriend ends up behind bars," I said to my brothers.

"I will hack into the airport's database to check who she came with and her boyfriend's name, although from what I am seeing here, I think they came from Argentina." Lucien stared at Christian's laptop.

"Okay, I've gotten into the airport's database," Lucien rejoiced after typing furiously for about fifteen minutes.

We all rolled our eyes because this was normal, we were used to seeing him showing off his hacking skills.

"His name is Roberto Fernandez, he is from Italy but he lives in Argentina." He then searched up information about Roberto.

"Guys, you need to see this," he spoke up but his eyes were still glued to the screen.

We all gathered at his back as we looked at the laptop.

"Grace is not his first victim, she is just the first lady he has killed," Christian repeated all we had just read out loud.

"So, we are dealing with a rapist and an abuser who has been to jail four times in the past three years," Damien said.

"How does he keep getting out of jail? We need more information on him to find out what is actually going on." I looked at Lucien who went back to digging out more information.

"His brother is a lawyer," he responded to my question in five minutes.

"The hell?! Now I know why he has the audacity to continue abusing women," Damien spat out angrily.

"The last woman before Grace was abused so badly, she ended up in the psychiatric ward," Lucien continued.

"What do we do? He will get out of jail again if we provide evidence against him and we may not even be taken seriously. I mean his brother is a lawyer and all of this happened in a different country from where they live," Lucien asked.

"We will find a way to lure him out and we have to catch him in the act so he will be sanctioned in a country where his brother has no right to act and he will definitely be sent to jail," I spoke with finality in my tone.

People like him infuriated me.

"Okay, good, now that is sorted, we need to call Amelia to meet him in Argentina," Damien said and we all nodded in agreement.

"Now we have a ghost to catch," I smiled at my brother who got ready and we walked down to the boat.

"Oh my God! Grace, no!" Lucien shouted as we reached the other side of the beach to see Grace trying to drown a kid.

She stopped and turned to look at us. She started fading away when we stopped the boat.

"Don't you dare, Grace," I spoke in a tone full of authority.

"Fine! What do you want from me and why can you see me?" she said in a whiny voice, like we were about to steal a candy from her.

"We want to make a bargain with you and we hope you can stop disturbing this body of water," I spoke to her.

"And why will I stop? Do you even know why I am here?" she asked as her eyes flashed in rage and I almost groaned out loud. Dealing with angry ghosts was like dealing with toddlers.

"Obviously, we know why you are here. If not, we wouldn't be speaking to you. You need to listen," I said in the calmest voice I could muster.

"We have to speak to you on some matters. Will you be kind enough to give us an audience?" Damien threw her his most charming smile.

"Hmph!" she huffed as she floated towards us.

When she got close enough, she stared at us and asked, "What do you want to say?"

"Why are you here? Why didn't you go to the afterlife like other spirits?" Lucien asked this time.

"I want to meet somebody; I have tried going home several times but I cannot because I am stuck here. My body was buried here and I really just want to go home," she shrugged and started fading away but I quickly threw our spring towards her and it wrapped around her arm making her bound to me.

"Let me go," she started making rough movements to remove the spring from her but it wasn't going to work.

"Tell us the truth, why are you here?" I asked her more sternly now.

"Okay, fine, I am here because I want to take revenge on someone. He will be here by this time next month with another woman and I will be able to kill him and gain eternal peace," she said, her eyes turning from blank to red to indicate her rage.

"Can you tell us details on the last events before your death?" Damien asked.

"Roberto and I came here for a vacation, or so I thought. I noticed some weird things about him and I found out he was cheating on me with another woman who was back home in Argentina. I confronted him and things got heated. He used his tie to strangle me and then he raped me and threw me in the water. I was already out of breath and I was bleeding from various injuries. I couldn't swim. He watched me drown," she explained to us.

I knew it was a watered-down version of the story she gave us because I could see her last memories from being bound to her by the spring. Chills filled my body with a murderous intent.

I will make sure that fucker ends up in jail, or better still, dead. The world didn't need people like him.

"We can promise you that we have made arrangements to make sure he ends up in jail and we just want you to be at peace. You being here is disrupting the balance of this world and every day that you are angry, you tend to have a lot of energy and you release it on to anything on your path. You are causing harm to everyone around here. Please will you go to the afterlife and we promise to handle this for you," Damien said gently.

"No! My life was cut short! Everyone deserves to suffer like I did. I am not going anywhere!" she screamed in a shrill voice.

No, not again. I cannot be faced with another peaceful soul being turned into a monster.

One thing my family and I have realized is that when these ghosts stay in our world too long with a murderous intent, even the most gentle one amongst them could become very dangerous and cause havoc that will affect innocent lives.

"We do not want to force you, please leave," my mother said sternly now as she came down from the boat and walked towards us.

My mother walked with a certain kind of authority that brought a chill down our spines, like it always does when ghost hunting.

"You don't want me making you leave this world."

My mother smiled at her in the most unhinged way.

"I... you... no! I need to take my revenge!" Grace screamed desperately as she felt my mother moving closely towards her.

We could all feel it, my mother had opened the portal to the afterlife.

"We will take care of Roberto, he won't hurt anyone again, and if he tries to get out of charges because of his brother, he will meet you in the afterlife and you can spend eternity hating on him and trying to kill him out there. Now, I will say it one last time. You better go into this whirlpool now while you can or I will make you, and trust me, it will be very painful. Your soul would be scarred," Mother spoke in a very spooky voice.

I had goosebumps.

"I will go, but you have given me your word that Roberto will pay!" She stared into Mother's eyes and Mother stared back at her and nodded.

"Of course, he will pay dearly." Mother smiled at her.

She nodded and walked into the portal that Mother had made between our world and the afterlife.

"Good bye, Grace," Mother called and the portal closed.

We all turned and stared at our mother.

"You know we could have done that, yeah? You didn't need to show up or show off." Damien faced Mother with a scowl.

"I know, but I got bored of watching you guys and this was already taking up most of our vacation that I very much still intend to have." She turned and walked away, leaving us staring at each other with similar thoughts.

"I am still slightly mad that Mother didn't let us end the case and something tells me she just wanted to watch us struggle to see if we still had it in us to handle the case," Lucien confirmed all that we knew.

"Yeah, but let's look at the bright side, we get to spend the rest of the vacation in peace."

Christian smiled and then Mother walked back in with a scary grin on her face.

"I knew it was too good to be true. There is no way we were going to have a good vacation that was full of relaxation," Lucien said angrily.

"What makes you think we cannot continue our vacation in a haunted house?" Mother looked very excited, like a child with their favorite candy.

"Mom, can you hear yourself? Vacation in a haunted house? And I am being told you aren't a psychopath." Damien shook his head.

"Damien Alejandro Veritas! I will not allow you to speak to your mother like that," Father defended Mother as he came around the corner.

"Okay, I am sorry!" Damien raised his hand to show that he was not trying to offend my mother.

LUCIA

I SAT ON THE FLOOR WITH THE CANDLES THAT I HAD purchased along with the Ouija board. I had researched how to communicate with the dead. They claim you have to be partly psychic and you have to make sure you don't summon some other spirits that are not meant to be there.

I lit the candles and noticed that Berry stood in front of me. After I moved the sage around, I began asking my questions.

Normally the way a Ouija board works is that the letters on the board are supposed to spell something for me but instead, Berry was actually responding. I could hear her voice; it was raspy and kind of soft.

I felt scared but at the same time I was very excited, her voice left goose bumps on my hands.

"Why are you still here?" I asked her.

"Because I want to take my revenge on the man that murdered me. Look at me, I am still in my wedding dress. I had a wonderful life and he robbed me of it. Now I will make sure to kill everyone that steps in this house." Her eyes turned red and my candle lights began to flicker off, one after the other.

I suddenly felt chills down my spine as I became scared.

Why the fuck did I decide this was a good idea?

Berry picked my legs up and started to drag me out of the room.

"Help!"

Madeline appeared in front of Berry.

I couldn't hear their conversation because they weren't moving their mouths, just their eyes.

"Why did you try to talk to her?" Madeline asked me.

"I... I just wanted to know her story," I stuttered.

"You made her angry. Part of me wants to teach you a lesson for not listening to me!"

At that moment, I realized it was very easy to annoy spirits. These ghosts were now mad at me, so it was no longer thrilling, just downright scary.

"Please, I am sorry," I begged as tears started to fall from my eyes.

They ignored me as Berry dragged me to the basement.

There was no one else at home.

I should have listened to Cat, now nobody can save me.

I am going to die.

As we got to the basement door, I already had a few injuries from being dragged from upstairs down to this point.

"Lucia?" Mother called out.

"Mom!" I screamed as the tears continued to flow freely from my eyes.

"Lucia!" she called again; this time I could hear panic in her voice.

"Mom, I'm in front of the basement!" I cried.

I heard her running through the hallway towards me.

"Oh my God, my baby," she gasped as she sat beside me.

"What happened?" she asked as she took in my wounds, my disheveled hair, and the tears streaking on my face.

I held my mother and I started sobbing.

"I.... I ... t–tried. I wanted to speak," I choked on my words and couldn't speak anymore. I just continued sobbing but I am sure Mother understood because she became angry.

"This is it, I have had enough. You all can do anything you like but trying to harm my daughter is where you have crossed the line," Mother shouted angrily at the air not knowing where they stood.

I saw them all look at me and smile and I knew that this was the beginning of my problems.

"Mom, let's just leave. They will try to kill us," I said in fear.

"No, this is my home and I am not leaving. Instead, they will be the ones that will be leaving," Mother spat out in anger.

I did not go back to my room. I spoke with my mother in the living room until my father got back. She narrated the entire thing to him.

"Oh, Lucy, you should not have tried to talk to them. Now they are angry and we don't know the lengths they are willing to take." My father hugged me, bringing me some comfort.

"We will sleep in a hotel tonight," he said and I nodded.

"No, we are not going anywhere, those ghosts will have to leave my house tonight. They have no idea what an angry mother can do," Mother responded.

"Honey, we cannot stay here. They tried to kill Lucia. What makes you think they won't try to kill us all while we sleep?" my father asked.

"I'd love to see them try," Mother replied as I saw them file into the room with psychotic smiles.

My mother had challenged them.

Mother did everything to make me feel comfortable and that night after dinner, I refused to be in my room alone.

"Mom, Dad, can I stay in your room tonight?" I asked in a small voice.

"Of course, darling, there is no way I will allow you to stay by yourself after all you have experienced," my father said and I sat on their bed.

It didn't help that I could see them and their reactions. It made everything scary, and I just wanted to run away from the house.

I should not have tried to talk to Berry.

My family has never been religious but that night I wished we could say a little prayer before going to bed.

At exactly midnight, I heard giggles. I opened my eyes and looked at my parents to make sure they heard it, but they were asleep.

I must have imagined it.

I closed my eyes to go back to sleep.

I heard giggles again but this time a melody followed. I opened my eyes again and this time I could see a little silhouette standing at the foot of the bed.

I was sure it was Madeline but I was so scared because I already had made her angry.

"M..m..mom.." I lightly tapped my mother as the melodies grew louder.

"Hmm?" she answered sleepily.

"Can you hear that?" I whispered.

"Hear what?" she answered.

This time the melody continued but it sounded far away like it wasn't from our room.

She heard it, I felt her body stiffen.

Just when we thought things couldn't get worse, Berry appeared and this time my mother could see her, too.

"Ahhh!" Mother screamed and I shook in fear.

"What is going.... Jesus Christ!" my father exclaimed as he saw Berry stepping towards our bed with her neck positioned in a very weird manner.

"I will give you only five minutes, leave this house now or I'll kill all of you and your bodies won't be found," a very low chilly voice said but Berry's mouth did not move, making me feel a greater fear envelop me.

"We are not leaving. Be ready to put up a fight with me because you are not touching my family," Mother spoke defiantly.

"Your wish," the voice said, then laughed.

"Mom!?" I called out to my mother as I started crying.

I didn't want to die now and even if death was to come, certainly not like this.

Blood started to trickle from the ceiling and when I looked up, I saw a dead woman's body pinned up there.

I screamed and jumped off the bed alongside my parents.

Mother opened the drawer close to her bed quickly and took out some leaves that were tied together and a lighter.

She lit it up and instantly the room was filled with a scented smoke and Berry started to scream. She disappeared and everything stopped, the dead woman on the ceiling was no longer there and everywhere was suddenly calm.

"What is that and where did you get that from?" my father asked my mother.

"I went to meet my new Haitian friend today and she gave it to me. She told me it was sage and I should put it in whatever room I am in. When burned, it will cleanse the air, and the ghosts won't be able to stay wherever it is," Mother explained.

"Okay, but wouldn't that make them even more angry and make them try other means?" I asked.

"Yes, that is why we will call the best ghost hunters in the world to help us get rid of them." Mother smiled and took out her phone.

ANTHONY

Ever since Mother had told us that we were going to a haunted house, Damien had been smiling in the most unhinged way.

"What is wrong with you, bro? Why are you so excited?" I asked for the hundredth time as we flew back to America in our private jet.

"I don't know anything about being in a haunted house and dealing with more than one ghost excites me!" He laughed.

I shook my head. "No, this is not real. You are so weird."

My other brothers laughed at us.

"Mom, where exactly are we going?" Christian asked our mother.

"We are going to the Winchester House," Mother stated with a smile.

"What?!" we all said in unison.

"Multiple people have died in that house," Lucien said.

"Yes," Mother responded.

"Mother, seriously, that place houses the most dangerous ghosts!" Damien said.

"Not ghosts we can't handle." Mother shrugged.

"Plus, it will be fun," Father added as we just stared at each other.

Fun?

I don't think so.
A shitload of work?
Yes definitely!

"This is crazy," Lucien said as the chauffeur picked us up and drove us toward the Winchester House.

"Do people even live in this house?" Christian asked.

"Of course! What do you think? That we will go to an empty haunted house?" Mother jokes.

"Not putting you both past it, we can actually do that," Lucien said to my parents and they just chuckled.

"Wow, the house is big and scary as hell. I don't know how this family has been living here for three months but based on what I have read, no one has been able to stay in the house before for more than a night," Christian told us as he continued with his research.

"The lady that employed us told me that her daughter can see them, that is why they didn't disturb them at first but then she..."

"Annoyed them by trying to communicate with them," I finished for my mother who just nodded.

"Except, she could already communicate to one of the ghosts. She just wanted to talk to all of them," Mother continued.

"No, that family must be crazy because there is no way I am walking into a haunted house and deciding to live there after I have seen ghosts."

Damien laughed.

"We will understand their line of thought when we get there," father said.

We all sat in comfortable silence until we got to the house.

"Woah, it's actually beautiful," Christian said as he got out of the car.

"Yes, it is," Mother said, then we all spotted something.

A little girl with a creepy doll that waved at us.

"That is a ghost," Lucien said.

"Is she here to welcome us? Because now that is creepy, even for me," Damien added.

"Hopefully not," Christian said and we laughed.

"Hello? Mrs. Martini, we are here and we are standing outside your door," Mother said over the phone to whom I assumed to be the owner of the house.

A lady walked out of the front door to meet us.

"Hello," she greeted us before she smiled.

"Hi, we are the Veritas ghost hunters, owners of the Veritas Ghost Hunting Inc.," Mother introduced us.

"Oh…" the woman seemed speechless at the fact that the entire family was present.

"We were on a vacation when you called so we decided to continue our vacation here," Mother explained further.

"Oh, that's wonderful."

"Mom?" I heard a voice call out and I looked towards the door to see the most beautiful girl I have ever seen in my life.

Damien hit my back in a subtle manner and whispered in my ears but I am sure my other brother caught it because they snickered.

"Stop staring at her like you want to eat her," Damien whispered.

I almost slapped him back but I realized we were outside and Mother would not approve.

"Shut up!" I whispered harshly.

"Lucy, this is the ghost hunters I told you about earlier today. They will handle the issues we are facing," Mrs. Martini said to her daughter, who nodded while looking at us.

"Hi, um, my name is Lucia." She waved awkwardly at us like she just realized she was supposed to say some type of greeting to us.

"Hi," we responded in unison, making Mother and Mrs. Martini laugh.

"You all should come in." Mrs. Martini opened up the door.

"Hell, no," Lucien said as we entered the house and saw the ghosts standing on the staircase railing as if welcoming us.

"You can see them too, right?" Lucia asked and we all nodded.

"That's about seven ghosts. I see why this place is known to be haunted," Damien jokes.

"There is something wrong. I mean I cannot get through to them. It's like there is a blockage."

Christian groaned because he knew this means it will take longer.

"They have been ghosts here for a very long time. They feel like they own the house and they see us as a disturbance. They don't want us here. I can feel their energy," Mother said.

We walked into the sitting room and we took our seats while Mother asked them some questions to know the full extent of what has been going on.

"How have you stayed here for three months without considering you could have called us before?" Mother was intrigued by the fact that they lived so long with such violent ghosts.

"They liked me, at least Madeline did, but she got angry when I tried to speak with Berry," Lucia explained.

"What do you mean by they liked you?" Christian asked, shocked.

"When we got here, I saw them all and I tried to say hi to them but they didn't respond. Only Madeline did and we have been talking for a while and I asked her why I couldn't speak with the others. She told me it was because they weren't in the mood to speak," Lucia replied.

"So, you went against her and tried to speak with one of them?" Damien questioned.

"Yeah."

"Wow, you are really brave. It is a shock you are not dead yet. Normally ghosts don't like being disobeyed, especially territorial ghosts like the ones you have here," Mother explained to them, although I could tell they already learned that the hard way.

"Mom, the ghosts have disappeared." Lucien looked spooked.

"No, they only dematerialized. I can still feel them, they are here," Mother explained.

"This is not normal, nothing about this is normal." Lucien looked around and I knew from his look that he couldn't see their trails.

This will be one very tough ghost hunting.

I am sure Mother is loving it because she is smiling ear to ear.

"Let's get you all settled in and then we can find a way to proceed with this ghost issue."

Mrs. Martini smiled warmly as she showed us to our rooms.

I really don't know how the Martinis have been staying here for so long, the place had the air of death and was really cold. I felt uneasy and it wasn't something I could brush off.

That evening we all had dinner in the dining room with the Martini's. Lucia wasn't very conversational and only spoke when she was questioned or someone spoke to her.

"Stop ogling her!" Christian whispered harshly into my ears but Damien by my other side heard it because he snickered.

I stomped both of their feet and Mother looked at me with stern eyes. I am very sure she heard everything and she knew what was going on, even under the table.

After dinner, we all tried to make a small conversation and Lucia was the first to stand up.

"Good night, everyone." She smiled at us and we all said it back and she left.

I wanted to go with her, to talk to her at least. She is so quiet.

"ANTHONY, DON'T LEAVE ME," SHE CRIED.

"Please stop crying, I could never leave you," I begged and when she looked up at me, she was faceless.

I gasped as I opened my eyes. I saw a silhouette standing at the foot of my bed. Most people would have been scared but I have been through worse.

"What do you want?" I questioned the figure.

"Take your family and leave. This is no place for you," she said trying to sound intimidating but she only made me laugh.

"What is your name?" I asked her.

"Berry," she answered.

"Who killed you?" I asked another question.

"My father-in-law wanted his son to get married to his rich friend's daughter. We were in love and he couldn't handle it. On my wedding night, he pushed me from the third floor and when I landed, I was still alive but he proceeded to smash my head with a statue. I can still remember the pain I felt. I promised myself that I would get my revenge," Berry said to me.

"Have you gotten your revenge?" I asked.

"No, the fucker died in a car crash and his son refused to live in this house. My soul has been lonely since then and no matter how many lives I torment, I am not satisfied," she spoke truthfully.

"I understand why you are angry now, you never got the revenge you deserve because the man you'd swore to haunt died prematurely and you hate it. You hate it that he got peace and you didn't," I spoke to her and for the third time in my life, I saw ghost tears.

"But do you realize you are in so much pain because you refuse to let go? If you are willing to let go, I can lead you to peace," I comforted her. "I can lead you to the afterlife," I said calmly.

She looked convinced for a moment but the next second, her eyes turned red and I knew she was about to let all hell loose.

"No!" she screamed in a shrill voice and ran towards me and leaped on to me but I was quicker and moved out of the way.

I took out my cuff from my bed and pinned her hands to my bed post.

"Ahhh!" she screamed and now I was sure everyone was awake because they all ran into my room to see Berry pinned to the bed.

"What's going on?" my mother asked with fear in her voice as she moved to check that I hadn't sustained any wound from how violent Berry is.

"We need to calm her," Father said as we all looked back to Berry, who was thrashing against the bed trying to go out.

"She is really hurt, I can feel her emotions. It is full of rage," Lucia said, surprising all of us.

"You can make her calm," Mother said quickly, voicing out all of our thoughts.

"How?" she asked, confused.

"Make yourself calm," I answered.

"Okay," she nodded and took a deep breath.

LUCIA

I TRIED TO FOCUS ON MY BREATHING TO CALM DOWN BUT it was becoming harder and harder. I started to choke. It felt like someone was holding on to my throat.

Black spots began to fill my vision as I felt myself sway back and forth.

"She's choking," I heard someone say and the person held on to me and I started to feel better.

I opened my eyes and it felt like I would lose my breath again. The person that was holding on to me was Anthony, he was very handsome with jet black hair and gray eyes.

"Are you okay?" he asked me.

I nodded as I pulled out of his arms and stood properly.

Berry smiled at us and then she stared at me for a while. There was something hypnotic about her eyes because it felt like I could get lost in it.

"Stop, Lucia, don't look at her. She is trying to bond herself with you," someone shouted as Anthony walked in front of me.

I snapped back to reality as I looked at everyone around me.

"What was that?" I asked, suddenly feeling confused.

"I don't think it worked," Anthony said to everyone.

"I have opened the portal to the afterlife, Berry. You have to get in now," Mrs. Veritas said.

"I will not go, you cannot chase me from my home," Berry responded angrily.

I didn't understand why but I suddenly became angry that they were trying to send Berry to the afterlife.

This is what I want right?

So, why am I mad that they are about to send her to the afterlife?

"Ahhh!" Berry screamed in pain and soon I too started to feel an intense pain.

"Ahh! Stop that!" I screamed at the top of my voice.

"Hell no!" Lucien shouted as he kicked the bed while Berry smiled.

"She bound me?" I asked in a scared small voice and they all looked at me with pity, but they nodded.

"She doesn't want to go, so she bound to you because whatever she feels you will feel it too and if she gets pulled into the afterlife, you will follow," Christian explained to me.

"You mean death?" my mother asked and they nodded.

Nope, there is no way I am dying young.

I shook my head.

ANTHONY

Mother suspected that Lucia would be able to help us find whatever Berry was looking for since she was now emotionally connected to her.

We decided to start our search from the basement because it made more sense as we found out that Berry spends most of her time in the basement.

After three days of searching and not finding anything that was worth anything, we decided to search somewhere else.

"Let's look through the attic," Lucia said and we all looked at each other.

"That place is way more creepy, and I don't think I want to be involved in looking for a ghost's item in the attic," Lucien said.

We all nodded in agreement.

But we have to find the item.

We tried entering the attic but we found that it was sealed off. It was sealed off with a material that was so solid, we could not break it down. We needed a device that would be used to blow up the door.

We were still discussing different ways in which we could enter the attic when the little girl appeared.

"I think you all should blow it up, we really want to see inside," she said.

"You all can't go inside either?" Christian asked and she nodded.

"Well now we know this door was intentionally built to hide something from the living and dead," Damien said and we all grunted in agreement.

I moved forward and I checked what the door was made from and I had a few guesses but I had to call Michael to know if it was truly what I thought.

"Do you know what it is?" Mother asked.

"I can take a guess, I'll be back," I walked downstairs.

"Michael," I called out to him as soon as he picked the call.

"Yes?" he responded.

"Your last assignment, the door that guarded the house and trapped in the ghosts, can you send me a description? I think I have found something like it," I said.

"I'll email it to you now," he responded.

I opened up the email and I compared the details to the door in the attic, it was eerily similar.

"This is surely a Teflon door. To break it down we will need to use the same device that Michael and his team used," I informed my mother.

"Okay, I will make a call to have the device shipped now," Mother said.

Over dinner, we were all discussing about the turn of events and then it occurred to me that Berry is likely the oldest ghost here and she is the one keeping the other ghosts together.

"I think we can send all the other ghosts away, if we send Berry away first," I said to everyone seated on the dining table.

"Yes, that has been my theory too," Damien agreed with me.

"Thank goodness, the package is here already," Mother exclaimed in joy as she opened up the delivery box.

We took the blaster and immediately fixed it to the Teflon doors and took cover while Lucien excitedly pressed the explode button.

The door burst open and we walked inside. The attic looked like some kind of shrine and we all looked at each other.

Lucia launched forward and went directly to the back of what looked like an altar and took out some kind of Ruby stone.

"This is what Berry is looking for, this is her lost item," she said calmly but her eyes had some kind of shine in them.

"What is that?" Christian asked as he collected the stone from her and stared at it in amazement.

"It is a birthstone," Mother responded and we walked towards the room where Berry was bound.

Berry was no longer thrashing against the bed and she looked relieved to see us.

"Why were you looking for this birthstone?" Mother asked.

"Because it is mine," Berry said.

"Okay, good. Now you can go peacefully into the afterlife right?" Lucia asked.

"I need to be buried with it," Berry responded.

"Where is your grave?" Mother asked calmly.

"I don't have one. I was thrown into the ocean to rot," Berry replied and I felt pity for her.

"We can have a bargain. We will host a funeral for you and you will move to the afterlife?" Damien suggested.

"Yes, I am okay with that," Berry agreed and I released a breath of relief. Some part of me thought she would reject it.

We arranged for Berry's funeral that night and the following day we had her buried properly with her birthstone and she agreed to go to the afterlife.

The other ghosts were easier to persuade to go and soon we had sent them all to the afterlife.

"Ha, another job well done," Christian sighed as we planned how we were going back to our jobs and everyday lives, when we sensed a sudden chill that flowed through the house.

"What was that?" Lucien asked.

"I don't know but I felt it, did you feel it too?" I asked my brothers.

"Yes," they all responded and our mother came running downstairs with every other person in the house.

The look on their face said they experienced it too and this wasn't like anything we had experienced.

It had the chill of pure evil.

"AHHH!" WE HEARD THE CHILLING SCREAM COMING FROM upstairs as we were setting the dinner table and we all ran to see what it was.

Mrs. Martini was the only person upstairs, she was in the bathroom.

We walked into the room she was in and we saw a message written in blood and a crushed skull kept on the bed.

"THIS IS JUST THE BEGINNING," It read.

"What the hell is this about?" Lucien said.

"I think something more evil and powerful was locked up in that attic that we opened up," Mother said as we tried to explain the weird occurrence that had been going on in the house. Even though we had been hunting ghosts all our lives, we were moved to a point of fear.

"I DON'T UNDERSTAND, WHY WOULDN'T YOU LIKE THAT restaurant. I think it is...

What I was saying was cut short as we walked into the house. We met five people sitting on the chairs with their heads twisted in an odd angle.

The living room suddenly felt very cold and we all felt shivers go down our spines.

"We have been dropping warnings but you people do not listen," the big guy sitting in the middle said as he stared at us with his blood red eyes.

We all stood at the door scared to fully come inside or stay outside.

"Who are you?" Mother asked.

"We are the legion and we are the souls of the altar that you disturbed," another one answered.

"Disturbed?" Lucia answered.

"You broke into our home in the attic," they responded together and that made me want to walk back outside.

"You don't belong here, your home is the afterlife," Father said.

"Hahahahaha," they all laughed together.

"We are not like the others, we are different."

The man stood and suddenly everything in my body screamed I should run but before I could make any moves, we were all drawn inside and the door shut.

I was back in that penthouse, it looked too small and she walked towards me.

"Hi baby, welcome back home," she smiled at me and hugged me.

"You are not meant to be here, you are dead. I led you to the afterlife myself," I said and she looked at me like I sounded deranged.

"Babe, what are you talking about?" she asked.

"You are dead, Isabel, this is not real!" I shouted and she started to cry.

"You want me dead? I thought we were in love?" she asked me.

"I love you, Isabel. I still do, but you are dead," I said suddenly, not understanding what was going on.

"You killed me! You killed me, Anthony!" she cried as she walked towards me, blood flowing out of her eyes appearing like tears.

"No, Isabel no," I repeated moving backwards until I was trapped by a wall. "Isabel, I didn't try to kill you. I never wanted you dead, you know that. It was an accident," I tried explaining to her.

"No, Anthony. You wanted me dead and now, I will kill you too!" Her eyes became bloodshot red and her teeth elongated, her nails became sharp and she moved towards me.

I couldn't move. I saw a hand hold me from the wall and I tried to struggle but the hands were so strong.

"Ah.." I tried to scream but another hand clasped my mouth silencing me while another held my throat.

Isabel was already so close to me and smiled in a very cold animal like manner.

She dug her fingers deep into my chest and I screamed as I felt pain like I have never felt before.

I opened my eyes quickly and I saw faces of people I have never seen before all staring at me curiously.

Their faces were shaped weirdly. I wanted to say something but I found myself drifting back to sleep.

"Ahhh," I screamed, opening my eyes to see myself surrounded by my family members.

I took in their stares and it looked like one of concern but I was trying to remember something.

Why did I scream before I opened my eyes?

"What happened?" I tried to stand up but pain instantly gripped my entire body.

"Ahh!" I shouted again.

"Mother, look, he is bleeding." Lucien pointed to my chest and I looked down to see a pool of blood.

"What the fuck?" I removed my shirt and I found fresh claw marks on my chest and my mind instantly went to her.

"Anthony! What happened to you?" Mother asked, looking alarmed.

"Isabella, Isabella attacked me. Mother, something is wrong. There are people in the .... Ahh!" I screamed as something with a very large head appeared before my mother and tried to eat her head.

"Mother, watch out!" I screamed but they all looked at me like I was going crazy.

"I have brought the..... Ahhhh!" Lucia screamed, pointing to my mother's head.

"Mrs. Veritas, your head!" she shouted at the human-like creature that was salivating at my mother's head.

"What are you both talking about?" Mother turned around and so did everyone but they didn't see anything.

The creature smiled at us and disappeared.

"You saw it, didn't you?" I asked and she nodded while everyone looked at the both of us like we had gone crazy.

Something was definitely wrong.

LUCIA

"What creature are you both fussing about?" Mrs. Veritas asked us.

"I cannot explain what it looked like, it was kind of human but at the same time it had animalistic features," I explained.

"First, we need to clean up Anthony's wounds. Something weird is going on," Mother said as she brought out the first aid kit.

"What do you mean Isabela did this to you, Anthony? She is dead," Damien said.

"She came to my dream. She blamed me for her death, then she turned feral and I tried to run but I was held back. She clawed at me and when I opened my eyes, I saw faces that were shaped weirdly and my eyes were heavy and I closed them and I woke up shouting to see myself surrounded by everyone," Anthony explained.

"This is really strange and you both said you saw a creature standing over me?" Mrs. Veritas referred to both of us.

"Yes," we said in unison as we both nodded.

"I think it has something to do with the attic," Anthony said.

"Yes, that's true. I felt I was being watched last night and when I opened my eyes, I saw a shadow but it was gone immediately like I imagined it," I said to them.

"Yes, I have been having a strange feeling of unease," Christian added.

"This is strange. I think there is more to this house than we know and we need to get to the root of this problem," Mr. Veritas said.

"Yes, I am very sure that there is something creepy going on. Remember the warning we received? We have mistakenly unleashed something. They are called the Legion."

Anthony shook his head.

"I remember something," I said and everyone turned to me.

"I usually heard some cries at night when we first moved to the house and I thought it was the ghosts, but Madeline told me something that made me change my mind. She said it was the locked ones," I explained.

"What did she mean by that?" Lucien asked.

"I don't know, but there must be a connection between them and this room because how is it that only Anthony is affected? And how can only the both of them see creatures that no one else can see?" Damien questioned.

Everyone remained silent because no one knew the answer.

It was like we were left in the dark about what was truly in this house because every day weirder incidents occurred and there was no explanation for it.

Anthony got crankier because of the disturbing dreams he was having of Isabela, who happened to be his ex-girlfriend.

I got up one morning and I had the dying urge to search my room. I felt like something was hidden in my room. I didn't know why but the urge was maddening and I even had to call my mother to join me.

After hours of searching for God knows what with no new leads, Mother tried to get me to stop searching but I couldn't stop. It was like I was being possessed by something and I was led to find something. I went through my closet many times, tapping every hard inch of the wall until I found it.

I tapped one part of the wall and my hands bounced back. I ran towards my cabinet and I came out with a small blade that I used to cut open that part of the wall.

"Found it!" I smiled triumphantly as I pulled out what looked like a journal and Mother stared at me like I had gone mad.

"How did you know that would be there?" she asked me.

I just shrugged.

"I don't know. I just had the insane urge to go through my room for something. Although, last night I felt like I saw a lady hiding something in my room."

Mother's eyes widened.

"I hope we have not bagged more trouble that is worth it by getting this house because why are we just experiencing all of this," Mother said, then she looked at me again.

"Why do you have a blade in your cabinet, Lucia?" She looked at me accusingly and I felt she would burst into tears.

"Mother, it is not what you think. I was not planning on harming myself. I have had this blade for a very long time," I reassured her.

"Please don't repeat what happened. I don't think I will be able to go through seeing you lying lifeless again. If you don't feel too well, please tell me," she pleaded as tears filled her eyes and I felt sick in my stomach.

"Mom, don't worry, I know better than to try and end my life," I smiled at her.

Are you sure?

Do you really know better?

A small voice in my head asked me but I ignored it and decided to change the topic.

"Let's check out what this journal is all about," I said to my mother.

"Why don't we call the Veritas first and tell them what we have found," she suggested but I talked her out of it.

"It doesn't matter, Mom, it is a journal," I tried to persuade her to let me look at it first before informing Veritas.

The journal belonged to a woman named Maria, she built this house with her husband. The first few chapters I read are about how she and her husband decided to build the house and how their lives were going. I thought it was just a story of a woman's life and how lovely her life was until it wasn't.

Her husband was in a voodoo cult and that was his altar in the attic, but that wasn't all. I had just read the first few pages of her journal and now I always see people I have never seen in my dream, telling me things.

Most times, it is either a warning or they are saying things that are strange to me.

"WHY DIDN'T YOU TELL US YOU FOUND A JOURNAL?!" Anthony shouted at me.

"I thought it was a harmless book! How did I know that it was going to intertwine our dreams?!" I shouted back.

"You really don't see what you did wrong? Why are we dreaming of the same thing and why are those people warning us?!" he asked as he used his fingers to comb through his hair, his face mirroring frustration.

"I don't know," I replied in a quiet voice.

"Okay, enough of this shouting. We need to understand what is going on to find a solution to this issue," Mrs. Veritas spoke calmly.

"This would not have happened if some people were intelligent enough to know that there are some things you have to show the ghost hunters that you hired first." Anthony eyed me.

"First of all, this is my home, and secondly, you are spitting trash because you could have told me.. that you found another journal but you kept it to yourself and I did the same but somehow you are blaming me because things are now going south," I retorted.

"You have no fucking right to talk to me like that! You and your family dragged us into this mess. I am the one that is getting dreams of the woman I loved torturing me while you sleep soundly at night. You are the one that caused a problem with Berry the last time and you are doing it again all because you are stupid and you don't think!" he shouted.

The room suddenly felt too small. It felt like the room was packed with people and they were all staring at me to find out my reaction. At one point, it looked like they were all laughing at me.

I did the next thing that felt right to me, I turned around and I ran away. I ran out the front door and I didn't stop until I was far away from the house.

ANTHONY

I DON'T KNOW WHY BUT SOMETHING ABOUT LUCIA started to annoy me, seeing her recently in my dreams was a lot for me because I was still dealing with the loss of Isabel, even though I didn't want to admit it and being attracted to our employer's daughter was not part of the plan.

A small part of my brain told me that I had that reaction to Lucia because she kind of reminded me of how I felt when I first met Isabel, but that is not true.

Normally, my dream would always be horrible and I dreaded going to sleep but last night it wasn't bad at all. In fact, it was the most pleasant dream I have had in a while but that was what iced me. I was extremely disturbed that she was in my dreams.

I felt bad when I saw the look on her face before she ran out. I should not have said what I did. Everyone was staring at me like I was the villain and Mother shook her head because she could not fathom why I acted like that to Lucia.

"How dare you talk to her like that?" Mrs. Martini spat angrily.

"I... "

"No, I don't want to hear it. Just make sure my daughter comes back to me whole. You weren't here last year when she was so uninterested in life and I found my child's lifeless body in her room. You weren't there to feel what I felt and you weren't there when I cried every night that she was in rehab or when I had to plead with her to take her medication every night. Now she is finally doing well and she is interested in something and you talk to her like that. What gives you the right to think you can talk to her like that?!" Mrs. Martini shouted.

I took in her words and it felt like I was pouring a bucket of cold water over myself. If I wasn't feeling any remorse before, I was definitely feeling it now and not just that, I felt like an asshole.

"Calm down, honey, we need to go after her," Mr. Martini said to his wife and she stopped throwing daggers at me with her eyes and ran outside with her husband.

"Why did you talk to her like that?" Damien asked me.

"I don't know," I sighed as I rubbed my temple.

"That is weird, normally you keep your cool during situations like this. Was the dream that bad that you had to lash out?" Lucien asked.

"No, it wasn't bad. I just didn't appreciate the idea of Lucia in my dream," I replied frustratedly.

"This discussion can be continued later. We need to find Lucia," Mother said and we all walked out of the house.

After hours of searching, we finally found her in the park sitting by herself. Her mother started walking towards her but I stopped her and begged her to let me go by myself.

I was the one who caused this mess, so I will solve it myself.

I walked towards Lucia.

"Hey," I said as I sat beside her.

"Hi," she said in a small voice.

"I'm sorry for the way I spoke. I haven't really been in a good mood but that doesn't make up for it and it is not a good enough reason for me to act like an asshole," I apologize to her.

"I'm sorry, too. I mean I should have told you guys about the book. I really don't know what I was trying to prove by keeping the book to myself," she said quietly.

"It was not your fault. You were only trying to be involved and understand things. I should have said something about the journal I found also," I said too.

"Hmm, yeah."

She shrugged and I stared at her for a while, then I chuckled.

"What's funny?" she asked.

"It's just funny with all of the weird things that are going on that you still find a way to be dramatic as hell. It is funny and kind of pleasing," I said and she laughed too while nodding.

"Are you ready to go back now? Our families are kind of waiting for us," I told her after a while.

She stood up and we walked back to our families together.

LUCIA

"Maria is talking about something that is hidden in the floorboards. We have to take a look," I said to everyone as I walked into the sitting room.

We realize that there were multiple journals from Maria and Dominique. They are not related to each other as their journals date to different times, but it is giving us some kind of insight as to what is going on.

"What do you think is hidden in the floorboards?" Lucien asked me.

"I don't know but if there is anything I am learning from this book is that her husband was an evil practitioner and whatever we are experiencing now is an aftermath of his poor choices," I responded.

"Okay, where exactly are we to look?" Damien asked me.

"I think it is here in the sitting room," I said and we started moving around the tiles checking if there was any loose one.

"I think I have found it!" Lucien declared excitedly as he tried to remove the tile while we gathered around him.

He finally removed the tile and we found a sack hidden in the little hole.

He brought out the sack and opened it. Inside we found a

necklace. It was Marie's protection necklace according to what I have read in the book.

"How does this help us or improve our search?" Lucien asked as he set the necklace on the table.

"I don't know," I said after studying the necklace for a while.

"What did the necklace protect Maria from?" Father asked.

"It protected her from whatever her husband was conjuring up in the attic," I responded and suddenly it clicked.

When Maria died, she wasn't with her necklace. Whatever killed her could have come up from what her husband conjured.

"In Maria's tenth journal, she wrote that she had misplaced her protection necklace and she had been having a lot of lucid dreams in which she would wake up with marks on her body," I said remembering all I read.

"It is possible that whatever killed her must have come from the attic," Anthony finished up.

"Could it be that somebody wanted Maria dead? But then how did you know about the floorboards. Maria was the one that wrote about it. Doesn't that mean she was the one that hid her necklace on the floorboard?" Damien questioned.

And we all became confused again.

"I think it was Dominique that hid the necklace in the floorboards and from what I am reading, I don't think he lived in the house at the same time as Maria. He got here after Maria and her husband had died. He even mentioned seeing Maria's ghost once," Anthony said.

"It all doesn't make sense. I mean, there is a possibility that Maria's ghost is locked up somewhere in this house," I responded.

"What are we to do now? All of this is getting messy," my father said.

"I think we need to start from the attic," Mrs. Veritas said and I shook my head.

There is no way I will be entering that attic after all the dreams I have had and the funniest part of it all was that I and Anthony had the same dreams and saw each other in our dreams most times.

"I don't think I will like to venture into the attic," I spoke up immediately.

"Same here," Anthony agreed with me and we just stared at each other and laughed while every other person looked at us like we had run mad.

"What is going on? Is there some kind of sick humor that we know nothing of, but you both know about?" Christian asked and everyone slightly nodded like they agreed with him.

"We won't be going to the attic because we have both seen the horrors the attic holds," Anthony said.

"What do you mean by the horrors the attic holds?" my mother asked.

"Okay, how do I explain this? Do you remember when we said we saw a creature by mother's head?" Anthony said and everyone nodded.

"What does that have to do with the attic?" Mr. Veritas asked.

"We are getting there," I responded.

"Do you remember the feeling of unease we all felt that night?" I asked and they all nodded.

"Good. Now there are a group of spirits called the legion that believe their territory is the attic, thanks to Maria's husband who used that place as their altar," I explained.

"Berry's birthstone wasn't meant to be there and I can't help but think that we made a mistake by opening the attic," Anthony continued.

"Why?" Damien asked.

"Because these spirits are pure evil. There is something about them that brings chills to my body. I and Anthony have felt their presence many times in our dreams and when we wake up, it looks like we were being watched in our sleep," I replied.

"How is this happening to only the two of you?" Lucien asked another question.

"That is a question we can't answer," Anthony said.

"It's crazy how you both were at each other's throats before and now you are completing sentences for each other," Christian laughed.

"Yeah, they are acting like the odd twins," my mother chipped in and I threw a glare her way.

"What? I am just saying," she raised her hands and shrugged.

I just shook my head, not saying anything.

"Somebody has to go to the attic," Mrs. Veritas said and we all nodded.

My father and Mr. Veritas volunteered to go and Lucien opted to go at the last minute.

ANTHONY

Today was the third day that we were attempting to go to the attic. For some fucked up reason, no one was able to enter the attic without running back out.

"It is becoming concerning. What are they seeing in the attic? What is making them run out?" Lucia asked me.

"I really don't know. they all refused to talk. Things are getting creepier." I shook my head.

"I think we should go together. It looks like whatever is in there breaks them and makes them very scared. Haven't you noticed all their weird behaviors after coming out of the attic? We have to talk to them about this," Lucia said.

"Yes, but are we going into the attic right now?" I questioned.

"Yes," she held my hand and we walked into the attic.

We both gasped when we looked into the attic. It looked exactly like our dream, except the faceless people had faces and they were staring at us.

"We were waiting for the both of you," they all smiled at us.

"Why?" I asked them.

"Only you both can fully understand our ways," they responded, but their mouths didn't move.

I looked at Lucia and her face told me she heard too.

"Who are you people?" Lucia asked.

"We are the legion," they replied.

"No, who are you? Truly, who are you?" she asked.

"We are spirits that refuse to leave your world," they answered.

"Why are you here?" I asked them again.

"We are here because Maria summoned us," they responded.

"Where is Maria?" Lucia looked curious.

"We are getting to that," they explained.

I and Lucia looked at each other and we knew something was missing.

How did Maria relate to Dominique and why were they waiting for us? It didn't make sense.

"I know you have questions and they will all be answered but you have to follow us," they said and I looked at Lucia who looked at me and nodded and we walked together still holding each other's hands.

We followed the legion to a beach. It looked like some bonfire party.

We looked around and then we noticed the woman singing on the stage. It was Maria.

"Maria was a musician?" Lucia whispered.

"Yes, one of the best," they answered and we moved to another scene. This time it was a hospital. Maria gave birth to a baby boy.

"But her journals said her husband sacrificed....

"Wait, you'll see," the legion interrupted Lucia.

They took us back to the attic where Maria uttered some foreign words and she began to move in circles and slit her baby's throat.

Lucia moved back in horror.

The legion showed us the truth regarding Maria. In her own sick universe. she was a good person and it was her husband that committed all the crimes, but she had no husband.

Her journals were a lie and it made me wonder if Dominique's journals were a lie too, but it turns out he came here after Maria was killed and he wasn't a ghost hunter. But he knew a few tricks and he locked Maria's ghosts somewhere in the house.

"Now we need to talk," Lucia told everyone as we ate dinner.

"What do we need to talk about?" her mother asked curiously.

"What did you see in the attic? I have a feeling you all saw different things. We need to know that. This runs deeper than we know. From what the legion told me and Anthony, Maria's journal could be a lie and we need to work together to find out this mystery," Lucia addressed everyone.

"Okay, I will go first," Mother said.

"I was looking up in a room with different ghosts. They tormented me. I could not send them to the afterlife and that frightened me," Mother spoke and I understood what she meant. That was every ghost hunter's worst fear.

"We were trapped in the middle of the sea, we didn't know our bearing and that wasn't the worst of it. We kept on seeing strange faces and we still couldn't make out what they looked like. We were tormented by pure evil," Lucien spoke for himself, my father and Mr. Martini.

"I found Lucia drowned," Mrs. Martini said and I realized something.

"The attic was showing you all your fear and you were living in it," I said to all of them and they nodded.

"I think if we want to get anything done, we need to go in together," Lucia stood up from the table.

The lights flickered off.

"What is going on?" I heard Damien whisper.

The room became very cold, it felt like we were outside during a snowstorm.

Then we heard footsteps.

"Who is there?" Mother called out but received no response.

Lucia came close to me and whispered in my ears. "Maria."

The lights suddenly came on and they were way too bright. My eyes hurt and I had to close my eyes.

Then the light dimmed.

"Whatever you are, you've got to stop playing with the lights," Mrs. Martini shouted and the lights came back to normal and it looked like nothing happened and we just imagined it.

"What the hell just happened?" Christian asked.

"Look," Lucien pointed to the staircase.

"The trails, they lead upstairs," he looked at us.

We all stood up and walked behind Lucien as he traced the trails. They led to the attic.

We all walked in together and we saw her.

"Maria," I called out.

"Oh, hello. I didn't mean to scare you guys," she said in a nice tone and I instantly knew something was up.

She moved closer to us and I spoke up, "Stay back, Maria, why have you awakened?"

"My shrine," she giggled.

"You practice voodoo? Your journals said your..."

"What about my husband? Come on, I just wrote that so nobody would find me out and I can cover up my tracks well." She shrugged.

I suddenly felt a chill and a feeling of unease settled in my gut. Something was not right about her.

I knew she was violent and she was putting up a sweet girl act but there was something else that made me want to recoil and run from her. Her feelings, it was different.

She was no ordinary ghost.

"Welcome to my home," she smiled at us and I felt a shiver run down my spine as goose pimples appeared in my arms.

We left quickly before deciding to go to dinner to talk away from ghostly ears.

"THERE IS SOMETHING OFF ABOUT HER. I DON'T KNOW what but I can feel it and it is making me uneasy," I told them in the restaurant and Lucia agreed with me.

"She has an evil essence around her," Lucia said.

"I think she is just a normal ghost that was locked away and she wants to go to the afterlife," Christian shrugged.

"No, she wants to stay here. She already claimed the house as her home," Lucia responded to Christian and a look of understanding spread across their faces.

"I think we should stay away from the house for now. It is dangerous to go in," Mother said as everything dawned on her.

"What? But that is my home," Mrs. Martini said.

"We know, Mom," Lucia replied.

"We are not saying we should abandon the house. I just want to see Maria's true intentions, we need to leave for at least a week," my mother explained to the Martini's.

"She has a glint of evil in her eyes. If we stay the night, trust me, she will try to kill us. She wants to raise a legion army," I spoke, realizing what Lucia's trip to the attic meant.

"She has been angry and trapped for years. She has grown stronger and she is waiting to release her wrath on whomever she can, and if we let her, we will all be dead before we know it," I added.

"Where is Dominique's journal?" Lucia asked me and I brought it out.

She turned to the last page and she looked at it then turned it around. She stared at it for a while and said to us, "The last page is missing,"

"We will get the last page later but definitely not now," I replied.

That night we stayed in one of our resorts in the state. In the morning, we got back to the house and we found the house arranged in a different way.

Maria was nowhere to be seen and we took the things we needed quickly and left the house.

LUCIA

"I AM TIRED OF THIS. I NEED TO GO HOME!" MY MOTHER complained for the hundredth time today.

"We will go home soon, Mother. We need to get more information on Maria. Christian is on it," I tried to calm her down.

"Honey, you have to be calm. We don't know how violent Maria can get and from what we have heard, she could just be pretending," my father said to my mom.

"I just want our home back," she spoke quietly.

I knew how attached my mother was to the house because she had been wanting to have her own house for as long as I can remember. And just when things were finally going good, we just had to choose a ghost house.

MARIA

It feels good to be back again. That stupid Dominique locked me up but not before I made him write my journals. I wanted them to be my biography one day.

I am finally free because some people came meddling in my attic, but that is no issue. I just need to make a few adjustments and I will have my home again.

I know they gave me space because they want to find out more about me but I already took care of that years ago. They wouldn't find anything about me except surface things that I created myself.

They will be back and I will be ready.

I smiled.

ANTHONY

Almost two weeks have passed and we still haven't found anything about Maria. Something tells me that she knew that we would find nothing about her and we would have to go back to the house.

Lucia walked into our apartment at the resort and her eyes instantly met mine.

I smiled automatically and walked towards her. "Hey, found anything new?"

"No, but my mother is very restless. She has been saying that she wants to go back to the house. I feel scared," she whispered to me.

Since our argument and the dreams we have been having together, we have gotten closer and we can easily confide in each other. What amazes me is how I easily want to comfort her whenever I see her stressed. I don't know if it was her presence in my dreams but Isabel decided to rest and she has stopped disturbing me.

I held her hand and squeezed lightly, "Everything will be alright. We will find a way to cleanse your house and your mother will have her home back," I reassured her.

"I think I have found something!" Christian shouted.

We all ran to the room where Christian sat. We hunched over him as he typed rapidly on his laptop.

He turned to us as he said, "Maria strategically put everything about her out here in the world. If we are going to ever find out anything real about her, we will have to go back to that house regardless of the precautions we may want to take. But luckily, she wasn't so secure about others... because I found a file about Dominique. It is not open to the public and it took me a very long time to find it. I think Dominique was possessed by Maria. I don't think Maria was the one that wrote her journal, I think Dominique did. The reports say he killed himself and although there is a really high chance that he is already in the afterlife, I really doubt it. I think Maria had something to do with his ghosts. That is how they are intertwined. All my research says that Dominique was the next person to stay in the haunted house after its owner, Maria DeLaurenti, passed away."

I nodded a lot. It felt like I was taking in information I already knew but I didn't care to think about it or admit it to myself. I looked at Lucia and the look on her face told me she already knew, too.

She turned back to my brother. "That means we are going back to the house," she stated.

"The sooner the better." My brother nodded.

"Okay, let me inform my mother." She turned and quickly left.

"I think someone has gotten over Isabela and is now into Lucia," Damien teased.

"Shut up," I said coldly but a grin broke out on my feigned stoic face.

"Are you in love with her? Or you are still figuring out what you feel?" Lucien asked me as they all sat around me trying to pry information out of me.

"I don't know. I will say I am still figuring out what I feel for her but I know she makes me very calm," I answered honestly.

"I thought she used to irritate you? How did you suddenly start tolerating her? And having feelings?" Christian asked.

"I honestly don't know. All I know is that her happiness matters to me and I don't want her feeling sad. I like when she is talking to me but at the same time I don't want it to look like I like it. I don't know. It is something I will figure out with time, I hope."

All my brothers looked at me like I was deceiving myself and they could see right through me.

"You are whipped, bro," Damien said.

They all laughed but I knew what he was talking about. I felt fear grip me as I thought about what loving Isabel did to her.

That night I could not really sleep even though I knew we had a long day tomorrow. I was tossing and turning and thinking about this thing I feel for Lucia.

Does she even feel the same way?

Will getting closer to her cause her more harm than good?

I kept questioned myself because I knew she had already been through so much. I couldn't just let her fall in love with me without knowing what it could cause her. If she even felt the same way.

I finally got some sleep at dawn before my alarm woke me up. In just under two hours, we were driving back to the house. Lucia sat beside me and held my hand tightly.

What if she saw me as emotional support only?

We got back to the house and Mrs. Martini was very eager to go inside. I saw the change in her features when she realized the house had been rearranged.

"Welcome home," Maria appeared with a very wide smile that looked creepy.

"Why are you still here? You had the opportunity to go to the afterlife. Why didn't you go?" Mother asked her.

"Something about the afterlife seems boring, don't you think? I didn't want to die. I was brutally murdered but that is fine. I was already researching how I would get another body for myself. The world must know who Maria is!" She sat down on one of the chairs.

Suddenly, I realized something. "You sacrificed your son to the legion because you wanted to remain here after your passing. You knew you were going to die and you sacrificed your child because he was a bastard baby. That is why there is nothing about you getting pregnant in your journal," I said.

She looked at me for a while in surprise before she started clapping and laughing.

"You are so smart," she said like a proud mother. "You know many people wouldn't have been able to guess that?"

She rested her back on the chair.

"You created the legion. You went to the afterlife before. You found them and bound them to you!" Lucia gasped when she finished.

We all turned to Lucia because what she said sounded impossible but real at the same time. We looked back to Maria.

She laughed and responded, "Why do you all look shocked? What if I did? I knew I never belonged to the afterlife and my journey there proved it. That place is so damn boring and there is no way I will spend eternity there." She rolled her eyes.

While we were talking, I realized there was a new presence among us. It was the legion, they had taken shape and they looked like her army. But something in their faces didn't look right.

They didn't want to be here.

"Maria, you need to release the legion and send them back. You are messing with the world's balance and you have been messing with it for centuries," Mother spoke seriously.

"So?" Maria asked nonchalantly as she checked her nails.

We walked upstairs, away from Maria. We decided to adjust the two largest rooms so we could all stay together. We didn't think staying in separate rooms would be best this time. We took off the door separating the two rooms so Maria wouldn't be able to control it.

"We need to get some protection and something that will make her not be able to come in here. This room should be only for us. This is where we should be able to discuss matters freely without being worried that some ghost or her army can hear us. We can do that, right?" Lucia's mother said.

"We can, and will. I will send for some materials. We will need to line our walls with Teflon. That is the one thing ghosts or spirits can't go through and we will add a reformer. They won't be able to listen to us," Mother explained to us.

I sat down close to Lucia. I could see the exhaustion etched on her face. I wrapped one of her hands in mine as she laid her head on my shoulders and took a deep breath.

I was sure we were thinking the same thing. That we just wanted this nightmare over with.

LUCIA

THE LAST FEW DAYS IN THIS PLACE THAT WAS MEANT TO BE my home has been very depressing. Starting from the fact that Maria was everywhere except our room and we couldn't stay in the room all the time because of the Teflon made the room stuffy. We couldn't open windows either, or they'd be able to hear us and enter the room. It made us all on edge.

I started taking my medications again. I noticed Anthony was putting in extra effort to cheer me up lately but it was barely working because of everything. I was worried constantly because something in Maria's eyes tells me she has a plan, I just don't know what it is.

I feel like I am constantly living in fear.

"I found another tile that's off kilter," Mr. Veritas told us that evening in the room.

"Where?" I asked.

"In the place that would have been Dominique's room. I am reading his journal and Maria's side by side. His journal tells me he was very disturbed and he was being bullied by someone or something. I think it is Maria," he said quietly.

"We will take a look at it and try to get whatever is inside out," Christian replied.

Everyday Maria became more of her true self, she was no longer pretending to be a good ghost anymore. We started searching desperately for more clues, with or without her watchful eyes.

The legion watched me carefully and was always around me. Something made me feel like they wanted to talk to me but they were scared of Maria.

I took them into our room and closed the door, so it was just me and them.

"The others won't like this," they said to me.

"You all want to speak to me, I can tell," I responded, ignoring what they said at first. If that offended them, they didn't show it.

"Maria has gotten access to some kind of power that she was not supposed to have. She summoned us and bound us with her blood when she was alive. We should have been able to leave when she died but she somehow bound us to the house. When Dominique came, she possessed him, and then bound us to him. Now that she has been released from her prison, she is looking for Dominique. You will need to find him first. If she finds him before you do, she will yield full power over us and that would be very destructive. Thank you for your audience." They bowed to me and moved toward the door, showing me that they were done.

I left them out of the room and stayed inside, locking the door.

I brought out all the journals that Dominique had written in. He obviously wanted someone to find him, leaving clues so we could. I just had to decipher his hidden messages to find him.

I laid each journal out according to the year he wrote them. He journaled every year for six years and I arranged them in that order.

There was a knock on the door.

"Who is it?" I asked, knowing that Maria could pretend to knock.

"It's us," Anthony responded.

I open the door, letting them in quickly.

"What are you doing?" Christian asked.

"The legion had an audience with me. They told me something interesting about Maria." I proceed to fill them in on everything.

"So I have all of Dominique's journals laid out in order. About ten pages are missing from the end of each journal, except the first journal is complete," I explained to everyone.

"That explains the confusion. What kind of power does Dominique have over the legion that Maria wants? She pretty much controls them now as it is," Damien said.

"Maria is power hungry. She has some kind of sick ambition to take a human body and make herself popular. She wants to rule the world. I got information on her death and it was not pretty. Yes, she was brutally killed but it was her boyfriend's wife that killed her. She was dating a politician who was married. His wife put an end to his life when she found out that Maria was been pregnant. I think she is now full of vengeance because she felt like she didn't yield enough power to protect her life and she wants to avenge that. She knew she was going to be killed, that is why she put all of this in place. She is very dangerous," Mrs. Veritas said.

She had traveled back to their HQ to get more information on Maria.

We prepared a plan on how to find Dominique and his hidden pages.

MARIA

They have been trying to outsmart me and I am now losing my grip on the legion but it won't be for long, I will get Dominique soon. I can feel it.

"What are they planning?" I asked the legion.

"We cannot hear them, remember?" they responded.

"You all are useless. Get out of my sight!" I shouted and walked away.

I paced around the house and then I saw her. I could feel her desperation and I could see a lot of me in her. She could be my ticket to accomplishing my goals.

She loved the house as much as I loved it and that made me happy.

She will be perfect for me.

At least for now.

I smiled.

To be continued in my solo release on October 25, 2025 at https://books2read.com/winchesterhouse

ABOUT MAYA BLACK

Maya Black lives in the Rocky Mountains with her husband and animals and loves being out in nature. She loves all things coffee and books!

She's a new author but has been an avid reader her whole life with stories brewing in her mind. She's finally putting pen to paper to write in a mix of genres but all will include an element of romance.

If you'd like to join my newsletter you can do so at https://www.subscribepage.com/p3j3r1

What do you get? Inside peeks at covers, help choosing characters, what I'm working on next, and so many more fun items!

See you there!

ALSO BY MAYA BLACK

ANTHOLOGIES

- No Place Like Home
- Cracked Fairy Tales
- Practical Potions
- Twisted Fairy Tales
- Echoes of the Dead
- Rose of Disgrace - Coming December 2024
- Evil Hearts - Coming February 2025

STANDALONES

- What Might Have Been
- Yule Spice
- Unchained Melody
- Alice's Illusions
- Wishful Witch - Coming September 2024
- Snowed in with the Mafia - Coming December 2024
- Snowed in with the Billionaire - Coming January 2025
- Snowed in with the Brother's Best Friend - Coming February 2025
- Bet on Love - Coming April 2025
- The Winchester House - Coming October 2025

Thank you for reading!

The Indie Author's Advocate thanks you for supporting the authors in this anthology! They all have worked hard with deadlines and writing an amazing piece for you each to read. Please make sure to follow each and every one of them (if they fit in your genre preferences of course!) and show them your support.

Thank you to the amazing authors who joined me in this endeavor and trusted me to bring their visions to life! You are all amazing and I am glad to have gotten to know each of you and count you as friends.

Please keep an eye out for more anthologies from The Indie Author's Advocate in the next few years!

2024
Rose of Disgrace

2025 and Beyond
Love & Books
The Cozy Canine Conspiracy
The Haunted Meow

More coming soon!

Are you an author interested in joining anthologies?

Email me here for more details: laura.martinez@theindieauthorsadvocate.com

Milton Keynes UK
Ingram Content Group UK Ltd.
UKHW030959231024
450026UK00011B/725